HELL TO PAY

A Korean Conflict Novel: a Navy Pilot's Life-changing Adventure

2nd Edition, 2017

Peter J. Azzole

ISBN-13: 978-0692914465
ISBN-10: 0692914463

DEDICATION

To my Mother
It was my good fortune that her love of aviation was passed on to me.

To Naval Aviators, past, present and future.

ACKNOWLEDGMENTS

There are many people who have been helpful in the development of **HELL TO PAY (First Edition)**. Foremost is my wife, Nancy, whose patience, contributions and criticisms were invaluable. My very special thanks also go to those individuals who made research material available and provided critiques of drafts.

For their editorial assistance in the production of the **Second Edition**, I would like to express my appreciation to Sharon Friedheim and Jim Green.

Front cover photo credit: Map of Korea; U.S. Library of Congress

Back cover photo credit: AD Skyraider Aircraft aboard USS Valley Forge (CV-45); U.S. Naval History and Heritage Command

PREFACE

"We've got to stop those sons of bitches, no matter what!"
President Harry S. Truman

The 38th parallel of latitude in Korea was officially established when General of the Army Douglas MacArthur, Supreme Commander for the Allied Powers, issued General Order Number One on September 2, 1945. The essence of this order was that Japanese forces north of the Korean 38th parallel would surrender to the Soviet Commander, and those south of the line would surrender to the American Commander. There was no suspicion or intention that the 38th parallel would become a line in the sand between two sovereigns. However, the Soviets took advantage of the instrument of surrender and set upon a strategy and series of actions to seize the Korean peninsula for themselves, beginning with the North.

International discussions on the return of an all-Korean democratic, self-determined rule were foiled by the Soviets and North Korean politicians at every turn. On September 9, 1948, the Democratic Peoples Republic of Korea was proclaimed by a North Korean puppet government of the Soviet Union.. The Soviets designated Kim Il-sung as the DPRK Premier, elevating him from the Soviet-designated post, some three years prior, as Chairman of the North Korean Communist Party. By 1949, Kim was asserting himself prominently and assumed the title "Great Leader."

The North Korean government, headquartered in Pyongyang, became increasingly aggressive and nationalistic. Soviet control slowly eroded. The Soviet hunger for the industrial and agricultural resources of both North and South Korea was not abated. Thus the Soviets remained aligned with and supportive of the emerging North Korean political leaders and attempted to exercise influence and control wherever possible.

Soviet and DPRK leaders interpreted the U.S. policy concerning Korea to be progressively more weak and noncommittal. Perhaps confirming this was Secretary of State Dean Acheson, when he gave a speech to the National Press Club on January 12, 1950. In that speech, he delineated the U.S. defensive perimeter in the Far East. Korea was conspicuously absent.

Intelligence analysts began warning that the North Korean People's Army (NKPA) was actively planning an invasion of the Republic of Korea (ROK). Estimates on the timing of an invasion ranged from spring to fall. Evidence consisted of continued troop buildups at many locations along the 38th parallel. Differing intelligence conclusions, resulting from differing U.S. political influences, detracted from the credibility of all estimates. This was reflected in the opinions formed by high level U.S. officials. For example, Secretary of State Dean Acheson was open about his opinion that there would be no civil war. He was convinced that the Communists would engage only in guerilla activities and psychological warfare against the South Koreans. Intelligence analysts became cautious of reporting North Korean intentions due to the widely differing opinions of high political leaders and intelligence organs.

Despite the heightening tensions between North and South Korea and the continued buildup of Communist forces along the 38th parallel, the U.S. government portrayed no interest or sympathy with the plight of the Republic of Korea. The sting of WW2, only five years past, still existed in the U.S. population. There was clearly no appetite for war or military actions of any scale on foreign soil. The North Korean and Soviet governments concluded that the U.S. would not intervene in the defense of South Korea.

At 4 am, Saturday, June 25, 1950, the North Korean People's Army commenced an artillery bombardment across the 38th parallel. This was a brief prelude for the incursion of a massive force of about 100,000 men in infantry and armored divisions, equipped with Soviet weapons, including tanks. ROK forces were not even marginally prepared to defend against such an onslaught and were driven rapidly south in retreat. Secretary Acheson, shocked into reality, made an abrupt change in his opinions and policy relative to Korea. He implored upon President Truman and the United Nations to commit military forces in defense of South Korea.

To the surprise and dismay of the Soviet Union, the United Nations Security Council reacted within twenty-four hours. A resolution was passed deploring the action taken by North Korea, calling for an immediate cease fire and the return of all NKPA forces above the 38th parallel.

President Truman, on the eve of June 25, authorized General MacArthur, then Commander in Chief Far East, to take action to evacuate certain U.S. personnel from South Korea. Truman further authorized MacArthur to protect the cities of Seoul, Inchon and Kimpo, and to provide military supplies to the ROK forces.

During the following day, it became obvious that the UN resolution was being ignored by North Korea and another emergency session was convened at the United Nations. Within two days of the invasion, the UN Security Council passed a second resolution which essentially requested all member nations to come to the unrestricted aid of the Republic of Korea. President Truman promptly authorized extensive military action against the North Korean invasion forces. The UN Security Council approved the establishment of a unified UN command in the Far East on July 7, 1950; it also assigned the U.S. as the executive agent for those forces. President Truman promptly appointed General MacArthur as the Commander in Chief, United Nations Command. These UN resolutions would not have been possible except that the Soviet Union had been boycotting the UN since January 1950. They were demonstrating against the refusal of the members of the Security Council to admit Communist China to that body.

In only three days, the North Koreans had captured the South Korean capitol city of Seoul. By July 30, just five days into the invasion, the ROK forces had been pushed into the southeast corner of the Korean peninsula. A roughly fifty-mile wide strip between the ports of P'ohang and Pusan bound the only remaining area of South Korea not under Communist control. It was a grim situation. The "peace dividend" claimed by the U.S. following WW II had drawn the U.S. armed forces down to skeletal levels. At the outbreak of the conflict, the USS Valley Forge was the only U.S. Navy aircraft carrier in Far Eastern waters; the British Navy made a carrier force available to the U.S. quickly after the outbreak. Appropriate numbers of U.S. and ROK ground forces to defend against the invasion were not available. It took until July 7th to transport the seven hundred men of General Dean's 24th Division from Japan to South Korea. General Dean and the badly mauled ROK Army, despite being shockingly outnumbered and without tanks, miraculously maintained a toe-hold until other regular ground forces in the Far East and other theaters could be mobilized and delivered. The telling difference was Naval air power, which immediately established air superiority, pounded enemy troops at the front and relentlessly attacked NKPA logistic support systems. Nonetheless, U.S. and ROK forces sustained an outrageous battering. General Dean and many others were taken prisoner.

Massive activation of U.S military reserve forces and drafts by the U.S. Armed Services were necessary to assemble the resources to dispatch the invading forces.

An absolute turning point in the conflict was the successful execution of General MacArthur's brilliant gamble—a massive amphibious landing at Inchon, just west of Seoul, on September 15, 1950. This single military action snatched the Republic of Korea from the rapidly closing jaws of the North Korean invasion forces. In the ten days beginning with the landing at Inchon, the NKPA was rendered ineffective as an offensive threat in the south and Seoul was reclaimed. The North Korean Army had been rapidly reduced to a splintered, disorganized and retreating army. The communists were pushed north to the Yalu River, the natural border between North Korea and China. However, the "mopping up operations" were extremely difficult and costly, beyond anyone's worst dream. North Koreans, supported and motivated by the Soviet Union and particularly Communist China, were not disposed to surrender. They realized that the U.S. Forces were not authorized to pursue beyond the Korean border. Chinese Mig fighter aircraft operated freely and effectively from bases adjacent to the Yalu River. Thousands of Chinese Communist troops began flowing into North Korea, at first bolstering the NKPA forces and eventually taking over the war. Massive amounts of arms and supplies were sent to North Korea from China and the Soviet Union. The Communists believed that the patience and commitment of the United States would deteriorate under the strong and continued opposition they could mount from their safe havens across the border. The strength of the communist forces built so rapidly that UN forces were forced into full retreat and were driven back below the 38th Parallel. For a time, Seoul was retaken by the NKPA. North Korea and the UN entered into prolonged negotiations, both realizing that neither could win.

The central characteristics which were chiefly responsible for General MacArthur's successful career brought him down—confidence and defiance. He had tremendous intellect and superior intuition for strategy, of which he was keenly aware. This often motivated him to seize authority and pay little attention to guidance. Reflecting his great frustration with national leaders, he defied Washington and made negative public comments. His unabashed statements concerning national policy, often contrary, became widely known to congress and the press. Truman felt compelled to relieve General MacArthur of command and replaced him with General Matthew B. Ridgway, U.S. Army, on April 11, 1951. The national policy then became one of holding the real estate below the 38th parallel and for the negotiation of a truce.

The "United Nations police action" in Korea lasted for three years, one month and two days—until July 27, 1953. On that date an armistice, essentially a cease-fire, was negotiated and implemented. The 38th parallel was reaffirmed as the demarcation line between North and South Korea, with a Demilitarized Zone (DMZ) on either side of that line. There was no declaration of war, no winner, no surrender. Both sides paid a heavy price. This delicate armistice remains in effect to this day.

It is estimated that there were 1,500,000 communist casualties. There were 142,091 U.S. casualties. It is difficult to determine the dollar cost of the U.S. involvement in Korea. A conservative estimate was made shortly after the conflict which assessed it to be in excess of $20 billion. In 2017 dollars, that would be in excess of $188 billion.

Peter J. Azzole

Liberties have been taken with certain events, personalities and activities, but within the framework of history. Factual and fictional information and events have been blended. This facilitated the setting and the telling of a part of the Navy's role in the Korean Conflict in an exciting and suspenseful manner.

Names, biographies, descriptions, personalities and activities of the main characters are fictitious and any resemblance to those of actual persons is purely accidental.

PHOTOS AND MAPS

The following photographs, maps and information are pertinent to the story and are provided for reference and background information.

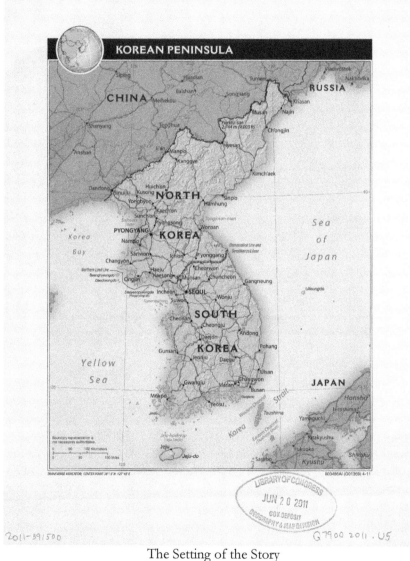

The Setting of the Story

The illustration below shows the Operation Chromite plan for the immense movement of about 75,000 troops, 261 naval vessels and other resources from multiple locations. This was a time-coordinated rendezvous of forces at "Point California" just prior to the invasion on the port of Inchon, South Korea.

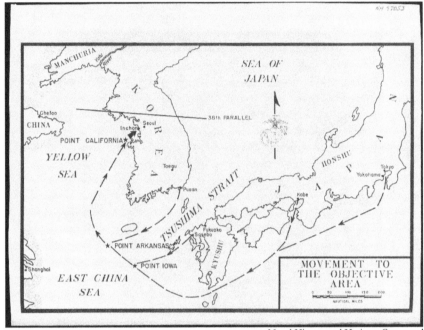

Naval History and Heritage Command

Chromite achieved a massive, surprise amphibious landing that took place on September 15, 1950. Inchon was taken so completely and swiftly that General MacArthur and his senior staff openly inspected the Port on foot the following day.

Chromite was the brilliant strategic brainchild of General MacArthur, initially rejected by Washington at the highest levels due to its difficulties and complexity. The surprise was achieved by a successful deception and disinformation plan for an assault on the Port of Kunsan, about 85 miles south of Inchon.

Operation Chromite was the turning point in the Korean Conflict.

"Occupied Tokyo," Published by Gekkan-Okinawa Sha
General MacArthur's Headquarters
Dai-ichi building, Tokyo
(photo circa 1950)
Japanese Emperor's Imperial Gardens moat in the foreground

General of the Army Douglas MacArthur, appointed by President Truman as the Supreme Commander of the Allied Powers, selected the office building of the Dai-ichi insurance company as his headquarters for the supervision of the occupancy of Japan. His office was in the middle of the sixth floor (top), with windows facing the Imperial palace, moat and gardens.

Today, this building is the offices of Dai-ichi Mutual Life Insurance. General MacArthur's office suite and original furnishings have been preserved and can be toured by appointment.

Naval History and Heritage Command

USS Valley Forge (CV-45) (photo circa 1947-49)

Essex Class Aircraft Carrier
Length: 888 feet, Beam 93 feet
Complement: about 3,500 officers and enlisted men
Aircraft capacity: 90-100

The protagonist, Captain Hal Kirby, U.S. Navy, is the Air Group Commander aboard the USS Valley Forge.

Naval History and Heritage Command

F9F Panther
Tail-hook down, lining up for landing (aircraft carrier in right background)

Single jet engine, single pilot fighter-bomber
Length: 37 feet, 5 inches, Wingspan 38 feet
Maximum speed: 500 knots (575 mph)
Maximum Range: 1,353 miles
Service ceiling: 44,600 feet
Guns: four 20mm AN/M3 cannons
Rockets: up to six 5 inch rockets
Bombs: up to 2,000 pounds of bombs

The Panther was the first jet aircraft for the U.S. Navy. A squadron of them was assigned to the USS Valley Forge when the Korean Conflict began. Panthers provided close air support to ground troops, as well as tactical bombing and air superiority missions.

Naval History and Heritage Command

AD (Able Dog) Skyraider (aboard USS Valley Forge)

Single piston engine, single pilot, fighter bomber
Length: 38 feet, 10 inches, Wingspan 50 feet, 9 inches
Maximum speed: 278 knots (320 mph)
Maximum Range: 900 miles
Service ceiling: 25,400 feet
Guns: four 20mm AN/M3 cannons
15 external hardpoints with a capacity of 8,000 pounds of
    combinations of bombs, torpedoes, mine dispensers,
    unguided rockets, and gun pods

The versatile Skyraider, was capable of carrying a large amount of
weaponry. A squadron of them was assigned to the USS Valley Forge when
the Korean Conflict began. They played a major role in the provision of
close air support to ground troops and also flew tactical bombing missions.

U.S. Air Force

B-29 Superfortress

Four piston engines, strategic bomber
Length: 99 feet, Wingspan 141 feet, 3 inches
Maximum speed: 310 knots (357 mph)
Maximum Range: 3,250 miles
Service ceiling: 31,850 feet

The story employs B29 aircraft in a special, albeit fictional, role and configuration, codenamed AQUABOX. They were part of the fictional overall project codenamed AQUAMARINE. The special configuration provided an on-scene high technology laboratory to process high-altitude photoreconnaissance films to facilitate rapid photo analysis and intelligence reporting.

U.S. Air Force Historical Research Agency
TR1 (aka U-2) Dragon Lady

Single jet engine, single pilot, ultra-high altitude reconnaissance aircraft
Length: 63 feet, Wingspan 103 feet
Maximum speed: 434 knots (500 mph)
Maximum Range: 5,566 miles
Service ceiling: 70,000+ feet

The Dragon Lady's first flight took place on August 1st, 1955. The story employs a fictional early research and development model of this aircraft codenamed AQUABALL. The "BALL" aircraft were part of the fictional overall project codenamed AQUAMARINE. The aircraft's role in the story is ultra-high altitude photo and electronic reconnaissance.

U.S. Navy/U.S. National Archives

Port of Inchon, "Red Beach," September 16, 1950

This photo was taken the day after the Operation Chromite amphibious landing in the Port of Inchon. Troops, equipment and resources are being staged. The enemy was quickly dispatched and the thrust toward Seoul and the southeast was already well underway at this point.

Wolmi-do Island (background) was heavily armed with tanks and artillery to provide port attack protection. It was pounded heavily prior to the invasion by U.S. Marine aircraft sorties. The night before the attack, U.S. Marine forces landed, seized and secured the island.

Note the clear illustration of the low tide status of the 20-plus foot rise and fall of the tide which complicated the invasion planning.

U.S. Navy/U.S. National Archives

General MacArthur Inspecting "Red Beach," September 16, 1950

General MacArthur and his senior commanders tour the Port of Inchon the day after the incredibly successful Operation Chromite amphibious landing.

Those present (front row, left to right) are: Vice Admiral Arthur D. Struble, USN, Commander, Joint Task Force Seven; General of the Army Douglas MacArthur, Commander in Chief, Far East Command and Major General Oliver P. Smith, USMC, Commanding General, First Marine Division.

CHAPTER 1

1055, Wednesday, July 20, 1950
Tokyo

Abrupt braking, a jolt from the right front tire and the sound of rubber scuffing against the curb signaled the end of a wild ride for Captain Hal Kirby, USN. The trip from Haneda Airport to the Dai–ichi Building in Tokyo was unnerving even for a Navy combat pilot. The driver, an Army Corporal, fearlessly weaved through cars, trucks, bicycles and pedestrians. To drive in Tokyo, one had to assume that using the horn was sufficient warning and that your way would be cleared even if it was at the very last possible moment. The Corporal hurriedly set the hand brake and rammed his shoulder into the door he knew would be stubborn. It opened with a sound that a graveyard gate would be proud to claim. He hurried to the passenger side and pulled the right-side door open. Hal Kirby was a tall lanky man and had to pry himself out of the old two–door coupe's cramped back seat. He drank in the scene around him while the driver got his bags out of the trunk. It was a beautiful sunny day with a warm refreshing breeze. Across the street was the shimmering outer moat of the Imperial Palace, home of the Emperor of Japan. Two stately snow-white swans were giving their chicks swimming lessons among large milk-colored water lilies on the far side. The water's edge was near to ground level and abutted a narrow strip of grass and trees that ran along the sidewalk for many blocks. It was hard for Hal to imagine that just five years ago he was waging a fierce war against Japanese naval forces. Hiroshima had not been bombed at that point, but Tokyo and most large cities in Japan had been reduced to ashes by General LeMay's incendiary bombing campaign. Kirby flashed back to a horrifying twenty–minute slice of a mission flown from the USS Hancock, near Okinawa. The mission had produced no excitement for an hour. Then

1

suddenly, Japanese fighters swarmed down out of the sun. One of their new Kawasaki KI–100s managed to outmaneuver him, riddled his engine compartment and left a diagonal trail of holes across his starboard wing. The canopy was immediately bathed in thick black oil and the engine quit. Up to that time it had been an impersonal war, his machine against their machines. Hanging from the parachute shrouds that day, praying like hell that they wouldn't come around and strafe him, Hal's hatred for Japan became intense. A Japanese pilot had taken him within an inch of his life. Today he stood on the very soil of the land of the rising sun—at the doorstep of the Emperor no less. Japanese citizens were walking dispassionately by him. A chill ran down his spine.

"Your bags are just inside the doorway Colonel," said the Corporal, interrupting Hal's daydreaming.

He returned the Corporal's perfunctory salute but responded in kind for being called a Colonel. "Thank you, Seaman," he said and walked down the sidewalk to take a tourist's look at the side of the impressive Dai–ichi Building. General of the Army Douglas MacArthur chose this building as his headquarters. The noble Dai–ichi could well have been one of the gray granite government buildings in Washington, DC. It had the same kind of presence and authority. Each side of the building had insets in the facade that rose from the ground to the fifth floor of seven, creating the effect of majestic columns. He lifted his hat and smoothed his hand over the prickly stubble of a fresh crew cut. Enough sight-seeing Kirby. It's time to go to work.

He returned the salutes of the sentries on either side of the two massive entrance doors to the Dai–ichi as he passed between them. An Army Sergeant was sitting slumped half-onto a wooden stool at the 'Officer Reception Desk' in the grand lobby. He had a huge potbelly, a deeply wrinkled face and a bored, distant expression. Hal studied him as he approached the desk. Geez, he must be the oldest Sergeant on active duty. Looks miserable. Hal presented the manila envelope that carried his orders and service record. Without a word, the Sergeant checked Hal's ID card, imprinted several copies of the orders with a black rubber stamp and filled in blank lines with the date and time.

"Sir, have a seat while I contact your organization," said the Sergeant in coarse monotone Brooklynese while motioning generally toward several varnished unstained oak wood benches on the wall of the lobby. The ancient warrior grabbed a telephone and studied a phone list taped to the top of the desk. Anticipating a long wait for the Army's administrative wheels to turn, Hal went to his bag and pulled out a novel. A bench that was bathed by sunlight from a large side window caught his eye. He sat next to a young WAC Corporal who was talking the ear off an American civilian wearing a press tag on his suit pocket.

She glanced at Hal's book cover, "Oh, For Whom the Bell Tolls. You'll love that book sir. Hemingway is my favorite author and that's a wonderful story."

Hal smiled at her politely, "I like him too." While she thought about what she might say next, she demonstrated a pair of cute dimples in her cheeks that elaborated when she smiled. She promptly went back to work on the press reporter. Somewhere on page 11 a sound captured Hal's attention. It was the clacking sound of high heels coming down a wide staircase at the rear of the lobby. He began to conjure up a vision of the person wearing those shoes. He didn't look up. Rather, he stared blankly at the open book, putting together the image stimulated by the sounds. The sounds changed to clicks as they left the stairs and moved across the highly-polished marble floor. He mentally followed them to the reception desk counter and then after a short pause, through a squeaky swinging door into the waiting area. They seemed to be approaching his side of the lobby. When he realized that the sounds were perhaps only twenty feet away he was unable to wait any longer to compare the imaginary with the real. He looked up; his eyes went straight to the sound his ears were tracking. He scanned up slowly from her brown and black two–toned strapped high heels. A natty milk chocolate linen suit fit her statuesque five–foot–ten frame perfectly. Below the skirt hem were insurable, gorgeous legs like those on his Betty Grable calendar. Geez, look at that. That's not a walk, that's a parade. With each step her ample but firm breasts jounced slightly under a tan silk blouse. Natural honey-blonde hair, with abundant, fine, straight strands, flowed loosely past her shoulders and appeared to reach completely down her back. Large emerald eyes were set in a cheery cover-girl face with a lustrous complexion and shapely red lips. Glamourlovely! Thirtyish – dynamite! Could pass for Rita Hayworth's younger sister. Solid confidence. His eyes panned down again, then returned to her face; he suddenly realized that she had been looking straight at him with a Hollywood smile since he first set eyes on her. Hal blushed, caught in the act of ogling.

"Captain Kirby?" she inquired with a sweet medium toned southern drawl.

"Yes ma'am, the very one," he said, springing to his feet.

She held out her hand, "I'm Marmette Clements, Admiral Joy's Admin Division Head. Very nice to meet you. Don't you have any bags?"

"Pleased to meet you. Yes, I do," he said, pointing toward the doorway. "Sorry for the stare - I've been at sea too long and you're a very pretty lady." He was surprised at the firmness of the grip delivered by such warm soft hands.

A mild blush filled her cheeks, "Uh, thank you for the compliment. I'll have someone take your bags to your quarters. I understand you and

Admiral Joy have not met," she said, as they walked briskly toward the inner lobby.

"That's right ma'am, I've never had the pleasure." They navigated through the half-door at the reception counter and headed for the staircase. He caught a whiff of her perfume. It smelled like the Plumeria blossoms he had in his yard when he lived in Hawaii—a unique bouquet that was pleasant and captivating. Her hair flowed down below her belt in perfectly straight strands. The ends were trimmed precisely even.

"You look very fit," she said, "Do you mind taking the stairs? It's faster."

"Not at all ma'am, it'll be good exercise."

"Please call me Marmette. What do your friends call you?"

"Lots of things, but I prefer Hal." She giggled. "Where you from Marmette?"

"New Orleans. You're from Texas, right?" she asked.

"Affirmative, Mineral Wells. How'd you know?"

"A little bird told me," she said with a teasing smile. "I know where that is. My father used to go to Dallas a lot on business and took us out in that direction often."

"What was in Mineral Wells?" he asked.

"My father's brother was a banker in Dallas and he had a small ranch near Mineral Wells."

Hal thought for a minute, "The name doesn't ring a bell."

"Oh, his name isn't Clements, it's LaFayette. Clements was my late husband's name."

"I'm sorry, I didn't mean to—"

She interrupted him, "It's not a sensitive subject, really. It's been a little over three years. Ever been to New Orleans?"

"Oh yes," he said, "New Orleans is one of my favorite cities. I used to rent light planes and fly over there on weekends from Pensacola with Alice, my wife. The jazz was terrific and the Café du Monde in the French Quarter was great fun. We used to spend hours sitting by the river, drinking cafe au lait."

"I miss it very much," she said. "But there's so much of this exciting world I haven't seen yet. Where are the wife and kids living? Oh, sorry, that little bird has a big mouth."

"Marmette, you haven't opened those records up yet, just who is this little bird?" asked Hal.

"In due time Hal," she said, smiling. "Where did you say, they are?"

Hal laughed, "Alice and the kids stayed in Great Falls, Virginia. When I got orders to the USS Valley Forge, Alice was looking forward to moving back to Hawaii, but Susan and Joe didn't want to change high schools."

They seemed to run out of small talk and the silence bothered him.

"This is a handsome building Marmette, very impressive," he said.

"It was built in 1938; they say that it was the fourth largest building in Japan at the time. Interestingly, it was designed to be bombproof—it worked."

"I counted seven stories," he said.

"You're very observant," she said, "and there's also four floors below ground. General MacArthur's suite is on the top floor and his senior staff officers are on the sixth and seventh. We're headed for the sixth." As they climbed the stairs, his mind wandered. No engagement or wedding ring? I can't believe she could last three years with a face, body and personality like hers. Those eyes are lethal.

She motioned for him to turn right at the sixth-floor landing. The first door on the left was marked "Commander, Naval Forces, Far East (COMNAVFE)." Marmette took him directly to the Admiral's inner office; the door was open.

"Admiral, this is Captain Hal Kirby—Captain, please meet Admiral Joy."

"I'm very happy to meet you Captain Kirby," he said, coming from behind an antique cherry wood desk to shake hands. "Would you like coffee?"

"I haven't had any since 0600. Yes sir, I sure would, thank you."

"I'll get the steward, Admiral," said Marmette." She gave Hal a bright smile as she closed the door behind her. The breeze from the closing door wafted another sample of her fascinating fragrance past his nose.

They sat in dark green leather chairs opposite a beautiful colonial cherry butler's table with brightly shined brass fittings.

"That's a fine piece of furniture," said Hal, "must be yours personally."

"Thank you; yes, it was a gift from my wife when I was selected for Rear Admiral. Welcome to Japan. Glad to have you aboard. I sorely need your experience. You're doing a great job on the Valley Forge despite the challenges you're facing. By the way, congratulations on your early selection to Captain. What's BUPERS going to do with you?"

"Thank you, sir. Well, I hope they let me stay in the Air Group Commander's slot on the Valley Forge for a normal length tour. I've only been in it for three months."

"Good luck," the Admiral said with a tinge of sarcasm and a grin, "the Bureau of Personnel doesn't always seem to be logic driven."

Hal laughed, "I can't think of an assignment BUPERS gave me that I had on my dream sheet."

The Admiral handed Hal a message he brought from his desk, "About twenty minutes ago I received the post-mission report from your ship's second mission today. Here, take a minute and read it."

As Hal read, a smile appeared on his face and grew wider with each paragraph. When he finished reading he looked up, "Looks like the Top Secret special intelligence message you sent us paid off, Admiral. The detail on their order of battle and logistic supply system was surprising."

"We have covert sources in Inchon and Seoul. It's a Navy Eyes Only source Hal, so please don't let this slip to anyone else. Especially the egotist who is MacArthur's G–2, Major General Willoughby. Only a few other people here at HQ know about this source beside you and me. I feel you need to be aware of that source and his information in order to have a complete picture, for planning purposes. Enough said on that. I have a meeting to attend shortly. I have extended my appreciation to Admiral Hawkins for sending you here this week. Let me give you a quick summary on what you're here to do. My Chief of Staff, Rear Admiral Al Morehouse, will expand on this later this afternoon when he returns from a meeting in Yokosuka."

Marmette knocked on the door and brought in the Admiral's steward. The young Filipino sailor quietly set a silver service on the butler table, poured two cups of delicious smelling coffee, set out sugar, cream, napkins and spoons, and departed.

Admiral Joy resumed, "OK. Now, Operation Chromite is classified Top Secret. It is the plan to land the X Corps at Inchon as the primary landing force and will consist of the 1st Marine Division and the Army's 7th Division. The Joint Chiefs of Staff are making us designate three alternative landing sites. The General hates the thought of them running the war from the Pentagon, but he's playing along with JCS so they don't kill it before he's had a chance to make the Inchon landing site a fait accompli."

"Is there a problem with Inchon?" asked Hal.

The admiral laughed, "When you take a look at Inchon, you'll see. It's not just one problem, it's many. It may well be the worst place to attempt an amphibious landing in all of Korea. But, if you know anything about General MacArthur, you know that we'll land at Inchon and for damn good reasons. At any rate, we have, through the efforts of an airdale on Vice Admiral Struble's 7th Fleet staff and my own people, put together a straw man for the air support section of the operation plan. It got us this far, but it's time we take it from the conceptual level to a higher level of detail and merge it with the rest of the operation."

A gleaming brass ship's clock on the wall by the Admiral's desk began sounding bells. "1130—I have fifteen minutes," said the Admiral, "You are personally responsible for the air section of the op-plan. Nothing is sacred in the existing version. I understand you pulled a tour with Plans and Programs in the Pentagon. Struble and Hawkins tell me you're the man for this job. So, I have every confidence that you can give me a thorough, sailor-proof first draft of your plan for Inchon by Friday night. Do as much as you can on the other three options, but NOT at any expense of the

Inchon plan. You'll brief General MacArthur Saturday morning at 1030. I realize that you can't develop a smooth plan in this short period of time, but you've got to come as close as you can within this time frame. When it is time to go to the next level, we'll pull you off the USS Valley Forge again, no matter where it is or what it is doing. Operation Chromite is that important. Any questions?"

"No sir." He lied. There were hundreds of questions, but this was not the time.

"Good. Starting tomorrow, brief me on your progress at least once a day. Al Morehouse and I are available to you any time. I told Marmette that you have direct access to us."

"Aye, aye sir, thank you."

"Plan to be in my office at 1115 tomorrow, we're going topside to see the 'old man.' I'm glad to have you aboard. Please excuse me, but I must run."

Marmette intercepted Hal as he came out of the Admiral's office. "Captain, I have a few things for you to do, then I'll take you down and introduce you to the rest of the Navy staff. By the way, there's a man down there who says he's anxious to get his hands on you."

Hal thought for a minute. Well, it's not Luther Garr—I left that slimy son of a bitch back on the ship. "I don't think I know anyone here—any hints?" he asked.

She smiled and playfully explained, "No, he wants you to stew for a while. Have a seat, I have some security papers for you to read and sign."

When he placed his autograph on the last of the documents she shoved under his nose, she said, "OK, Captain, let's go visit the pit." She noted his expression, smiled and said, "Don't ask how it got its name; it just happened."

As they walked down the hallway to the staircase, exchanging small talk, his sense of smell was treated to more of the mesmerizing perfume. She led him down one flight of stairs and along the hallway to the door marked COMNAVFE OPS. It was a large austere room with no windows, filled with a couple dozen desks and some file safes. One wall was covered with maps, some of which bristled with color headed pins. A small conference area and table occupied one end of the room, where some officers were huddled, busily pursuing something.

"I'd like you all to meet THE Captain Hal Kirby," she announced loudly.

"Ring knocking whale shit from the bottom of the sea," growled someone from the end of the room opposite the conference area.

Marmette chuckled, "Time for me to go, the party's getting rough."

Hal's eyes immediately spotted the source of the slur—a large green Marine uniform. "Dusty!"

"Sir, Lieutenant Colonel Dusty Rhodes, USMC, sir, at your service, Captain sir," he bellowed irreverently as he rushed toward Hal. Dusty was one year behind Hal at the Naval Academy. They were on the rowing team and became close friends during their academy years. They had not seen each other since Hal's wedding after graduation, but wrote intermittently during the ensuing years. "I've been reading your mission reports from the bird farm, wondering if we'd run into each other. Damn those eagles look mighty fine on you. Congratulations!" he said, giving Hal a bear hug. It was obvious that Dusty had maintained his weight training program since Annapolis. He was huge and rock solid. A little gray hair streaked what little black there was in his crew cut with white sidewalls. His handsome face belied his age.

"As I recall, last Christmas you were at Twenty–Nine Palms," said Hal.

"Yeah and as I recall, your ass was wallowing in the luxuries of the Pentagon. It's so strange that after all these years we would meet in Tokyo. It's good to see you. You look great. Speaking of things that look great, what do you think of Miss Iron Pants?"

"You mean Marmette?" asked Hal rhetorically, "Four point oh. Why do you call her that?"

Dusty laughed, "It's her nickname around here. Nobody's ever had a second date—plenty tried. Only a few have gotten the first one. One of the Navy guys in this office got his ass in a jam because he wouldn't stop asking her out. Weird duck, name's Tullis, Tyler Tullis. He's the Lieutenant Commander standing by the map over there. She complained about him following her around and caught him sneaking a picture once—he's a photography nut. He just wouldn't let her alone; he was obsessed. Admiral Joy personally ordered me to counsel and reprimand him. No wonder Seventh Fleet loaned him to us – a real asshole, that guy."

"That would make two assholes that Seventh Fleet pawned off. Remember that yellow-bellied bastard I had all the trouble with six years ago? Luther Garr? Well guess who just reported aboard the ship from the Seventh Fleet flagship as our new Flag Intelligence Officer? Dusty, the entire Navy's not big enough for him and me, let alone us both being on the same aircraft carrier."

"Is that the guy who threatened you?" asked Dusty.

Hal nodded, "Several times. The jackass doesn't realize that he's no match for me. I'm going to have his ass – once and for all. Anyway, as you were saying, what's Miss Iron Pants' problem?" asked Hal.

"No problem. Actually, she's a really good friend of LouAnn and me. So, I can tell you that she is a fine person and quite normal."

"So why hasn't she remarried?"

"She doesn't like the idea of going out with coworkers. But, I think it goes beyond that. Maybe she's still not over it. Don't know. She's a looker though. Nice scenery and a good sport. We tease her a lot."

"Ran my engine up to red-line," said Hal.

"Damn horny-ass fleet sailor." They laughed heartily. "Let me introduce you to the staff," said Dusty, motioning toward the other end of the room where the others were huddled. Dusty provided personal introductions to everyone. None of them wore wings, which explained Admiral Joy's problem with the air support planning. Hal noted that Tullis had a distant manner and a cold fish handshake.

Dusty slammed Hal's shoulder, "Let's get you squared away—these guys need to get back to figuring out how we're going to steal some of the Atlantic Fleet ships and get some mothballed ships overhauled and sent over here."

"Are you top dog here?" asked Hal.

"Damn tootin'. Our operations boss, a senior Captain, transferred to Seventh Fleet a few weeks ago without replacement. He was a friend of Admiral Ewen. Don't get any ideas of pushing me off the hill. You're just on TAD here," Dusty said kidding.

Hal plowed a clenched fist into Dusty's dense shoulder. "So, boss, where's my office?" asked Hal.

"See that clean desk next to mine? That was the Captain's—now it's your home sweet home."

Hal went to his desk and sat down; he immediately listed thirty degrees to the right—one wheel was missing from the three-wheeled chair. Dusty broke into a hearty laugh.

"Is this the way you treat all your guests?" asked Hal.

"Hell no! We don't offer our guests chairs," Dusty said, still chuckling as he left the office. A few minutes later he returned holding a chair above his head. "Now stop your pissing and moaning and get to work. Where do you want to start?"

"Give me a copy of the entire op-plan as it stands now and let me spend the rest of the afternoon reading."

"I had a yeoman put one together for you this morning. It's in the bottom drawer of file safe number three over there. That whole bottom drawer is yours."

After lunch Hal acclimated to the distractions of his new environment and concentrated deeply on the draft Operation Chromite plan. He lost track of time passage.

Dusty tapped his shoulder, "It's 1830. We have a rule here; everyone quits at 1900 unless there's an emergency. Why don't you go check out your quarters? I'll stop by about 1915 and introduce you to my main squeeze. We're taking you to supper tonight."

"Oh damn, I just realized that I don't know where I'm staying. Marmette said she'd have someone take my bags there but didn't say where. I hope she's still topside."

Dusty laughed, "Details, details. You'll learn that she never does anything half-assed. Since you're a high muckety-muck O–6 now, she got you a bunk in the senior visiting officer quarters in the building. Don't get your hopes up, it's more of a convenience than a palace." Dusty opened his middle desk drawer and pulled out a key attached to a large oval brass tag with 'VOQ-6' crudely imprinted by repeated hammering with a nail punch. "You're down below on the G2 level."

Hal looked at the monstrosity Dusty handed him and said, "For God's sake, I'll need a seaman just to carry this damn thing around for me. I'll find it. Where's your tent?"

"The Army commandeered, I should say leased, the Imperial Hotel a couple blocks from here. It's a beautiful place—designed by Frank Lloyd Wright, believe it or not. Somehow it managed to escape the bombing. They made a few interior modifications and combined some rooms into BOQ suites for senior officers. It's small but real comfortable and the Japanese staff is terrific. See you in a little while."

Office of Congressman "HL" Bradbury (D–VA)
Washington, DC

"Tim this is Bradbury. It's official—I'm the new Chairman of the Defense Appropriations Subcommittee." Bradbury pushed his short chubby body deep into his brown leather judge's chair, stretching the telephone cord to its limit. A slippery grin formed on his round puffy face.

"Congratulations," said Colonel Tim Yardley, USAF, "Say, I have someone in the office, can I call you back?"

Bradbury leaned forward and planted his elbows onto the desk, "That won't be necessary Tim. I just wanted to give you the news and tell you that we can now move forward with our plan. Get in touch with Will Crandall and tell him we'll meet at his house Thursday evening at 9. Oh, one more thing quickly, I received a letter from Logan Bennett yesterday. He definitely wants in on the deal."

CHAPTER 2

Dai–ichi Building
Tokyo

Hal found the door with a large black Bakelite plate embossed with white letters 'VOQ-6'. After some skillful jiggling of the key, the door opened. There were no windows and it was pitch black. He felt around the wall and found the light switch. Dusty was right, it was small and plain but comfortable. There was a tiny sitting room, a private bath and a bedroom. His bags sat snugly between the foot of his bed and a small plain chest of drawers against the wall. The furniture was vintage GI issue, probably out of some base warehouse in California or Hawaii. The pieces were plain, uncoordinated in style and color, a little banged up here and there, but clean and functional. There was a phone on the side table in the sitting room.

A fast shower and shave restored Hal's vitality. As he was slipping on his trousers, the heavy hand of a Marine banged on his door. Hal tucked in his dress shirt, pulled up his zipper and opened the door.

"I'd like to you to meet Captain LouAnn Woodyard," said Dusty, squeezing the shoulder of a pretty young lady. Uniquely bright blue eyes dominated her facial features. Her trim figure topped out at Dusty's shoulder. Regulation length light brown hair was partially covered by her uniform hat. Hal motioned for them to step inside. He shook LouAnn's hand and said, "A very pretty lady, pleased to meet you, come on in. I'll be ready in five minutes."

LouAnn blushed a little, "Thank you. I've heard so much about you, I'm glad to meet you, sir."

Hal was pleased to find that she too had a drawl. "Dusty has a big mouth—don't believe his lies, and please call me Hal. Another southern belle! Where from?"

"Born and raised in Fort Worth," she said proudly.

"Dusty told me you're from Mineral Wells. We're a long way from the Lone Star State."

Hal nodded, "A very long way LouAnn." Dusty disappeared for a pit stop. Hal finished dressing in front of the full-length mirror mounted on the back of the door. He slipped his tie around his neck, buttoned his collar and tied a quick four-in-hand knot. "Are you on General MacArthur's staff LouAnn?" he asked.

"Yes, G-2, Intelligence," LouAnn said.

"Ah, you work for the infamous Count!" said Hal.

"How did you learn about that so quickly?" she asked, making herself comfortable on the faded brown stuffed chair in the sitting room.

"I keep my ear to the ground. Is he really such a bastard?"

She smiled, "Now you know I can't talk about a superior officer. By the way, we hope you don't mind Hal, but we invited Marmette to come along with us. She's a hell of a lot of fun—the three of us pal around a lot."

"I don't mind a bit. It's been a long time since I've been in the company of two pretty rebels. I take it we're going to eat Japanese food tonight."

She laughed and exaggerated her accent, "Sho nuff, it's so hod ta fand biskits and sawsage grayvuh round heah."

Hal laughed, "I'll just bet!"

"We've found a wonderful little place we go to regularly," she said with great enthusiasm.

"I've only been on Japanese soil twice—Sasebo and Yokosuka—and never made it off the base. Closest to Japanese food I've had is sukiyaki at the O-Club. I'm looking forward to strapping on a genuine Japanese feed bag."

Someone tapped a "shave and a haircut" sequence on the door. When Hal opened it, he noted Marmette had changed into a dark blue summer weight suit trimmed in white lace, with an off-white sheer silk blouse. Two strands of fresh water pearls and matching pearl-diamond earrings finished the outfit. The number of times in Hal's life that he was totally lost for words could be counted on one hand—this was one of them. He felt awkward standing there staring into her eyes; his ears began to get hot.

"Ready?" she asked gleefully.

"Forwarrrrd, march," commanded Dusty.

Their leisurely stroll north on Hibaya-dori Avenue included chatter about the pros and cons of television, the wonderful music of Les Paul and Mary Ford and other stuff. It was a welcome break from their intense preoccupation with the war during the day. A few blocks past the Dai–ichi Building, they turned into a small alley. They stopped at what appeared to Hal to be someone's apartment. LouAnn slid a fragile wood frame doorway aside and was greeted by a young Japanese girl in a beautiful red and white kimono. It suddenly dawned upon Hal that LouAnn was conversing in Japanese. Hal motioned for Marmette to precede him. As she passed by him he noted that she had rejuvenated her perfume.

Dusty warned about the low door clearance. Hal was distracted by Marmette taking off her shoes and bumped his head lightly. They put their shoes in little pigeonholes at the entrance and followed the hostess. Semi-private dining areas were created by arranging beautiful folding screens made of four hinged panels. The panels were decorated with stunning silkscreen artwork. Each dining area had its own low table and cushions. Subdued lighting throughout the restaurant emanated from delicate wood and paper lanterns in which candlelight flickered and danced. The hostess motioned for them to enter a dining area bounded by screens showing lake scenes with large white egrets in the foreground. They got themselves situated on plump floor cushions around the low table. The owners came to visit them, bowed deeply and said things that sounded pleasant to Hal, as did the things LouAnn said in return. LouAnn introduced 'Hal-san' to Takeshi and his wife Setsuko, whose smiles beamed broadly and whose aprons carried fresh stains of varying colors from the evening's delights.

"Are they going to bring us menus?" asked Hal.

LouAnn looked at him devilishly, "Just leave everything to us."

"I wouldn't be worried if Dusty wasn't here," he said.

"What are you worried about?" teased Dusty, "They wouldn't serve us anything they wouldn't eat themselves."

"That's no consolation. There's probably a lot of things they eat that I wouldn't even try."

LouAnn motioned at him, "Whatever you can't eat, we'll give to Dusty!" Everyone laughed. "Seriously, there is no menu. They prepare something different each night. But there will be plenty variation among the courses—you'll get plenty to eat."

Their Japanese hostesses fawned over them. There was never a time when one of them was not present, anticipating every need. Light conversation flowed like water; it settled onto memorable slices of their school years. Dusty told stories about Hal at the Academy. Hal countered with stories about Dusty at the Academy. Marmette recounted her freshman and sophomore years as an art major in Paris, then two years at Notre Dame. LouAnn described her tribulations at Iowa State University as an agriculture major.

Hal saw little change in Dusty since their days in Annapolis. He was still tremendous fun. However, despite his avowing to remain single forever, it appeared that Dusty had fallen head over heels for LouAnn. The infamous arrow had likewise struck her and it was clear that maidens across the globe would no doubt soon be saddened.

Marmette was simply intriguing. Every bit as bright as Dusty had suggested, she was delightful company, exuded energy and shared a pleasant personality. She was not the expected spoiled brat of a doting mother and father of great means. During the course of supper, there were several instances when their eyes met. Neither gave quarter and looked away before smiles were exchanged.

As for Japanese cuisine, Hal learned several lessons: tuna sushi was tasty; the 'green stuff' was hotter than anything he had ever experienced; baby octopus simmered in soy sauce was rubbery; and tempura vegetables and fish were delicious. He also discovered that there was no way of telling how much hot sake you had drunk at any point in the evening. Sake cups were refilled every sip or two, bless the little Japanese hostess' hearts. After a simply marvelous and entertaining two and a half hour meal, they reclaimed their shoes. They then ceremoniously bid their sayonaras to the Japanese girls.

Hal, being a quick-minded fighter pilot, stooped low enough this time to exit painlessly, without prompting. Marmette slipped her arm under Hal's as they turned the corner of the little alley.

Their return to the Dai–ichi Building was slow and indirect. At Hal's urging, they crossed the street at the alley and paused along the sidewalk bordering the palace moat. Light from a nearly full moon gave the bridge across the moat and the glassy water an interesting glow. LouAnn held school, for Hal's benefit, on the relationship between General MacArthur and the Emperor, and the military-political events following the war. It was difficult to be serious; they were mellow from the hot sake that made them all just a little silly.

Hal was fascinated with Marmette's perfume, "I just have to ask you about the perfume you're wearing."

"It's one of my favorites," she said, "it's from France—called Le Jardin Botanique. Do you like it?"

Dusty broke in, "I told her that she's not allowed in the pit when she's wearing that stuff. I just can't be responsible for her safety."

"I know what you mean," Hal said.

"I take it that's a yes?" she asked, tugging on Hal's arm.

Hal laughed and said, "That's a rajah dajah."

LouAnn muttered, "I've got to get a bottle of that stuff!"

Loose tongued from sake, Hal asked, "Marmette, how is it that someone like you isn't married?"

Dusty piped up, "It sure isn't lack of possibilities." LouAnn jammed her elbow in his ribs.

Marmette hesitated, "I haven't found the right man. I'm in no hurry."

"You must have loved your husband very much," said Hal.

"Oh, I'm not still mourning, if that's what you think. Actually, I've come to realize that we were more friends than lovers. He was very kind to me, very intelligent—a good companion. Being married to a diplomat was very comfortable and enjoyable. But, I see life differently now than I did when I married him. There are exciting people, places and things out there," she said, leaving the thought unfinished.

Dusty asked, "So what does prince charming have to be like?"

"I'm not sure," Marmette said slowly, hunting through her inner feelings. "I'll know him when I see him. He'll excite me and adore me. And I'll excite and adore him."

"Not to change the subject," LouAnn said, rescuing Marmette from additional probes, "but what do you guys think about the new solid black and white fashions for the ladies?"

The next morning, Hal's desk phone rang at 1105, "This is Captain Kirby."

"Hal, it's Marmette. Admiral Joy is taking you up topside for a meeting right now, pronto cowboy."

"I'm on my horse," he said and hurried up the stairs. Admiral Joy was waiting in the hallway. "Good morning Admiral."

"Good morning Hal, the General has just arrived and wants to see us now."

"Which General, sir?"

"General MacArthur!" Hal's heart skipped a beat. "He's very low key," assured the Admiral, "but be very formal."

When they entered the outer office, Admiral Joy introduced Hal to MacArthur's aide, Brigadier General Courtney Whitney, who escorted Hal and the Admiral into the inner sanctum and closed the door, leaving them alone with General MacArthur. The General was sitting behind a large mahogany table-desk, in a very worn green leather chair, concentrating on a document. Hal's mouth was getting dry. Hal looked around the surprisingly modest sized wood-paneled office. Directly behind the General were two side by side windows, facing the Japanese imperial gardens moat, gardens and Emperor's palace. This enchanting landscape was visible through semi-transparent white sculpted curtains which flooded the room with sunlight. General MacArthur didn't look up as they approached. He continued reading a message that had SECRET stamped in large red ink letters, top and bottom. They walked quietly across the cadet-gray rug and stopped a few feet away from the General's desk. There were several paintings on the walls. He wanted more than anything to walk over to admire them more closely and note the signatures. On the left side of the General's desk a folded copy of the Stars & Stripes newspaper laid perfectly aligned with the side edge. To the left of the paper there was a pair of aviator style sun glasses, a humidor two–thirds filled with a very dark tobacco and a pipe rack which held a dozen or so pipes of varied colors and shapes. He noted that there wasn't just one corncob pipe—there were five. As the General read, he took notes on a yellow-lined pad, preceding each note with a circled numeral. There were several documents overlaid carefully on the left side of the desk. In the front center of the desk were a marble-based double pen set and a stand of miniature Allied flags with the American flag standing tall in the center. Off the left end of the desk, against the wall, was a dark hardwood bookcase with glass doors. A majestic onyx clock stood proudly on top of the case. One thing was missing and puzzled Hal; there was no telephone.

General MacArthur looked up after a few moments. Admiral Joy opened, "Good morning General, may I present Captain Hal Kirby, Commander of Air Group Five aboard the USS Valley Forge." General MacArthur rose, came around his desk and offered his hand.

Hal had not been in the presence of a five–star officer before. Flag and General rank officers normally sparkle and glitter with stars, ribbons, badges and whatnot. But, here stood the legendary General of the Army, in open collar informal khakis, without ribbons and sporting only those fascinating circles of stars on his collars. General MacArthur's dark, flashing eyes focused with intensity on Hal, "Captain, it is my pleasure to meet officers who lead men through example, who look the enemy squarely in the face, who take calculated risks and have innate instincts for winning battles." The dramatic greeting astonished Hal; he felt his face flush. "Please sit for a few moments," said the General, motioning toward the stuffed chairs in front of his desk. Admiral Joy and Hal took their seats. The General sat back into his chair.

"Your feats and abilities are known to me Captain. The opening air attack of this war, at Pyongyang Airfield, was brilliantly executed. Your airmen established and maintained air superiority over the battlefield from the outset. I am also indebted to you and your men for keeping the North Koreans from overrunning General Dean's troops. Admiral Joy advised me that your raid on Wonsan foiled the Russian resupply plan and severely impacted North Korean logistic support of the war effort. It was a masterstroke. Of course, you owe Admiral Joy a great debt regarding the Air Force in that matter. I had to remind General Stratemeyer of the ultimate objective of your Wonsan raid, but I suspect he and his staff would still like to discuss it with you," MacArthur said with a trace of a smile. He continued, "I asked Admiral Joy to bring you by so that I could personally state the importance of your duties this week. Captain, you will develop a plan for the air support of perhaps one of the most difficult amphibious landings attempted in modern times. We must land at Inchon because it is the single effective option for crippling the backbone of the enemy's southern structure. If we do not land the X Corps at Inchon—and quickly—we will lose Korea. Your plan must be thorough, convincing and without flaw. I make no exaggeration when I say that only sweeping, overpowering air support will allow this invasion to succeed. Any questions Captain?"

"No sir." He lied. There were hundreds of questions.

"Thank you. I'm counting on you," MacArthur said emphatically. The General got up from his chair, "Admiral, thank you very much for coming by, I enjoyed talking with you both."

As they stepped into the hallway, Hal asked, "Why do I feel like I had a conversation, when all I did was listen?"

Joy laughed, "That, Captain, was classic General MacArthur. You'll find that people either love him or hate him. I personally love him. He's amazing. He knows how to cultivate relationships and how to convince people of his views. And make no mistake about something, he is depending on you—it's the sole reason you got this audience. There are O6s on his staff that have never set foot in his office. But, he knows that your plan will make or break this operation and he made it his business to know you inside and out."

"I'm certainly impressed," said Hal.

"The politics on Inchon are daunting, Hal. Washington is opposed in principle to an Inchon landing. Most of MacArthur's far eastern commanders don't like the idea. The Pacific Fleet Commander is very skeptical. Hell, even the amphibious task force commander is hedging. The fact is, his only chance of not having a disaster at Inchon is for Naval air power to eliminate the threat to the landing forces before our ships come up the channel."

Hal nodded, "Guess that puts me in a tight spot Admiral. Oh, what exactly did you do with the Air Force that I owe you this great debt?"

"The General exaggerated a little," said Admiral Joy smiling. "But, one of General Stratemeyer's senior operations staff officers, a Colonel Logan Bennett—you'll meet him eventually—tried to get your Wonsan attack disapproved. His position was that it was on the Air Force list of targets. When MacArthur's staff asked him if the Air Force could execute a bombing raid on Wonsan before the Russian ships arrived, he admitted they couldn't. That was, of course, a great embarrassment and he tried to redirect the attention by going back to his office and fired off a message to CINCPAC chastising the Navy for the uncoordinated strike on Wonsan. I guess he hoped to burn us all with it. His mistake was that he didn't get his bosses chop on it before it went out and that too backfired. The entire incident came to the attention of General Stratemeyer who didn't like getting a black eye and Bennett got reassigned to the logistics staff. Stratemeyer was angry with me for not personally discussing the Wonsan raid with him or his staff in advance and I had to go over there and make peace.

Hal smiled, "Well then, I owe you sir. Speaking of the Air Force, what's their role in Chromite? I didn't see anything in the Operations Plan."

"That's another sore point with Colonel Bennett. As it stands now, the Air Force is not involved in the Seoul or Inchon areas on D–Day," said the Admiral, "but that's now up to you. You may certainly use them. There is a separate plan for them to perform strategic bombing raids on Pyongyang and other locations, leading up to and during the amphibious landing at Inchon. My recommendation is to give the Air Force as much of an opportunity to play a supporting role as you can. Luckily, you won't have to coordinate with Bennett. Colonel Johnson was moved into Bennett's job.

CHAPTER 3

Residence of Will Crandall
Falls Church, VA

"Good to see you, HL," said Will Crandall as he ushered Horace Bradbury into the den and motioned toward the poker table.

"Evenin' gents," said Bradbury, "Nice place you have here Will. I love red cedar paneling, it smells great." He took off his suit jacket and threw it over the arm of a chair in the sitting area.

"Evening, HL," said Tim Yardley, holding a glass of wine in a salute.

"Help yourself HL," said Will, "That's port in the crystal decanter on the tiffany lamp table and there's a box of Havanas too."

"And both are excellent too," said Tim, swirling port in his glass, savoring deep inhales of the delightful aroma.

Bradbury sank heavily into the black leather covered seat of a straight-back chair, poured a full glass of wine and lit up a cigar. "OK gents, let's get down to brass tacks here. Will, what do you have for us?"

Will opened one of the files stacked in front of him, "It's going well. The owners have agreed to a cash buyout of all their stock at the price we offered."

"Of course they agreed! Hell fire, they were damn near bankrupt," blared Bradbury, "We were probably too damn generous."

Tim grinned, "I heard through the grapevine that they think they screwed us. They don't have any idea why they stopped getting contracts."

"Good, let's keep it that way," said Bradbury. "When can we close the deal?"

"The lawyers will have the papers ready Monday," said Will, "and the corporate officers will clear their offices out Monday also. Oh, and by the way, I checked this morning and the cash was transferred into the

19

investment account from each of your banks, including Logan's bank."

Tim shook his head, "I hope those damn lawyers don't screw up somehow. I still don't understand how they are going to do this so that it's impossible to track back to us as the owners. I think we should be careful what we say on the telephone from now on."

"Relax Tim," assured Will, "These guys do a lot of work for the CIA and CIA contractors. They know what they are doing. I agree about the telephones though."

Bradbury nodded, reluctantly, then grabbed the decanter, filled their glasses and stood, "Toast! To Will, the new President of Electronic Surveillance Technologies and to the new owners!"

The Pit, Dai–ichi Building
Tokyo

"Hal, that was LouAnn," said Dusty as he hung up his phone. "They just got a flash message topside—General Dean is missing in action. His HQ appears to have been overrun."

"Damn, I'm glad I'm not the CAG on the Philippine Sea! Geez! The ground forces had to retreat from Taejon yesterday, now this."

Dusty nodded, "That would be bad news for a carrier air group commander alright. The enemy is making another desperate surge. They've probably put two and two together, the news about the draft calls, reserve activations and the massing of amphibious forces here in Japan."

"They're going to need the Valley Forge back on station ASAP," said Hal.

Dusty nodded, "Admirals Joy and Struble have already exchanged messages about that. They're in that folder there—they came in while you were up with Admiral Morehouse. Listen, we need to finish up here and get some chow before it gets too late. You have all your ducks in line for tomorrow's presentation?"

Hal took a deep breath and said, "Geez Dusty, General Dean has been captured, the shit's hitting the royal fan on the front and you're worried about getting out of here to go eat?"

"Hal, relax. You're not on the Valley Forge right now, and you couldn't do anything about the ground situation if you stayed here until breakfast. I learned a long time ago, when someone offers you steak, take it—tomorrow it could be C–rations or worse." Hal flopped down into his chair, leaned back and closed his eyes.

Dusty dropped a clenched fist on Hal's shoulder, "Since Valley Forge is probably going to sea in the morning, it's probably your last night. We have a special night lined up for you. Marmette got her hands on four tickets, thanks to Admiral Joy, to the Kabuki-za. The three of us are taking off now for the hotel to freshen up and we'll come by to get you. We'll eat something quick down in the Ginza."

"What is this place we're going to?"

Dusty thought for a moment, "Close as I can come for an explanation is an opera house, Japanese style."

Hal shrugged his shoulders, "I can't break loose from here so soon, Dusty! I should go through tomorrow's briefing at least one more time."

"The briefing isn't 'til noon, you've got plenty of time in the morning to rehearse it. The dry run was terrific today and Admiral Morehouse said so. You can hack it, loosen up. See you in forty–five minutes, swab jockey," Dusty said and thumped Hal's shoulder firmly again.

"Jarheads," Hal complained half-heartedly.

Hal waited outside the Dai–ichi Building, admiring the view of the moat. It was very pleasing to watch the graceful swans against the backdrop of the massive gray granite palace wall. Japanese people passed by without a concern or curiosity for his presence. It still felt surreal to Hal, as though Pearl Harbor, Hiroshima and Nagasaki never happened. The three musketeers were walking toward him a half block away. As they crossed the street, he couldn't help but admire Marmette. A light breeze wafted through her long hair. She had changed into a stunning beige suit and a lacy, powder blue silk blouse. Several long strands of alternating black and white pearls swayed rhythmically with her steps. He repositioned his hat. My god she's a smashing dresser. I don't think I've seen her in anything twice.

They walked the half-mile jaunt to the Kabuki-za—his first visit to the Ginza area of Tokyo. The lack of evidence of the severe damage inflicted by the wartime bombing was astonishing to Hal. Near the theater, a little hole-in-the-wall take-out food shop buzzed with activity. It served only chicken yakitori, unique tasting soy-soaked chicken shish kabobs and bowls of soba noodles. Hal figured he'd slurp broth all over the front of him if he tried to eat soup standing up, so he settled on several sticks of yakitori.

They stood on the sidewalk, people watching, while sliding chunks of chicken off the bamboo sticks with their teeth. Hal noticed a toddler staring at Dusty and him. The boy stood transfixed, waving a stick of yakitori indiscriminately. His mother and father were facing the opposite way, speaking to another couple. Hal reached into his pocket for a pack of gum, which he had begun carrying for opportunities like this. When Hal offered it to the boy, the youngster's face took on a curious gaze. Hal stooped down to get at eye level with the youngster. The boy turned and looked at his mother and father and said something. His father turned and scowled at Hal and Dusty. He began a tirade with very animated gestures, grabbed his son's hand and hauled him down the block.

"What was that all about?" asked Hal.

LouAnn, showing obvious embarrassment, explained, "He called you murderers, said you were responsible for the loss of many relatives and offered a few other unsavory things."

Hal's face turned red, "His view of history is just a little biased and incomplete!" The little boy repeatedly looked back as he was pulled along.

Marmette, trying to move the conversation to more pleasant thoughts, said to Hal, "It's going to be a wonderful night. We wore flats so we could walk back to the BOQ."

"Sounds great," said Hal. He looked up at the face of the ornate three–story white and gold trimmed 'Kabuki-za'. "This building looks very old, but I thought this area was destroyed."

"It was, but the brick and concrete buildings were only gutted," said LouAnn. "Some were torn down and rebuilt, but this is the original Kabuki-za structure, refurbished inside and out." Two colorful vertical silk banners of Japanese characters, about twenty feet long and three feet wide, hung from both sides of the alcove-like entrance area. They undulated with gentle gusts of wind.

Inside, the decor reflected the sanctity of a nation's culture and the dignity befitting an ancient art form. Hal looked around, absorbing its style and detail; it invoked a good feeling. All of the Japanese women were dressed in their finest kimonos. Most of the men wore western style business suits, others were in kimonos. It was interesting that many people brought food into the theater in little wooden boxes, which LouAnn instructed were called obento. They found their seats, on the right side, halfway back. Hal sat between Marmette and LouAnn.

LouAnn scanned the program sheet and summarized, "This play was written originally as a puppet theater piece in 1752. That is common with kabuki. This show is about events that took place about 1350 AD. In a nutshell, a samurai has betrayed his lord by falling in love with and seducing his lord's wife. The samurai and the woman have decided to commit seppuku, take their own lives, to preserve the honor of their lord." There are apparently quite a few samisens, which are stringed instruments. There is no other music. Some lines will be sung, but most will be spoken." Just then, samisens began playing behind the curtain—show time. It was a unique but beautiful stringed instrument sound. As the house lights dimmed, the curtain rose revealing a beautiful and elaborate set. The opening scenery portrayed a Japanese garden with Mount Fuji in the background. A dozen young ladies were seated among fallen cherry blossom petals. Costuming was exquisite, with a wonderful array of blues, grays, reds, golds, purples and black. Movement of the players was sometimes akin to ballet and at other times exaggerated.

When they departed the Kabuki-za, they were greeted by a delightful summer evening—perfect for a walk. Dusty suggested that they stop at his quarters for a drink. It sounded like a great idea to everyone. Using their imaginations during their walk, they searched for constellations in the star-studded heavens and debated the chance of life on other planets.

Dusty's quarters reflected LouAnn's influence and labor. The rooms were very small and included a mini-living room, bedroom, bathroom and a very small room that didn't quite qualify for even the term, kitchenette. The little galley had a small sink and a counter that held a toaster and a double hot plate. There was an insulated box in one corner of the living room where perishables were at the mercy of a block of ice. It was not a luxury arrangement, but it worked. Inside an armoire in the living room was the liquor cache. They toasted Hal's promotion, his departure and several other things.

"Good grief, it's midnight," Hal exclaimed and pried himself out of a soft, comfortable chair.

Dusty got up and gave Hal a bear hug and slapped his back energetically, "Hal, I'm sorry we haven't had a chance to visit all these years, we've missed a lot. This has been a great week. You'll just have to come back and spend more time with us."

"It's been a damn good time. I'll miss all of you, but I will be back again for the grand finale," said Hal, "as much as I am going to hate the luxury." They laughed.

Marmette interjected, "Admiral Joy is very impressed with you, Hal. He just got the word from DC that an O6 aviation officer billet was approved for his staff structure and I'm sure he'd be happy to have you fill it."

Hal responded immediately, "If you think I'd be excited about leaving the perfect slot for a pilot to be in during this war you're crazy. This may be the last war I'll see in my career and I'm smack in the middle of it, where I belong. Geez, don't put any ideas into his head."

Dusty laughed, "Marmette, pilots think shore duty is hell."

LouAnn gave Hal a heartfelt hug, "If I don't see you before you leave tomorrow, best of luck. We're all going to start reading the Valley Forge mission reports again to check on you. Take care of yourself." Her eyes filled up.

"See you in the mornin' sailor," Dusty said.

It dawned on Hal that LouAnn wasn't leaving. He looked at Marmette and said, "C'mon, let's leave these love birds."

"Rajah, dajah," she mimicked. She hooked his arm and squeezed it against her side as they walked quietly down the hallway to the stairwell. He sensed her take a long look at him and heard a deep sigh. He had words on the tip of his tongue, but kept them to himself. Damn, I didn't want this to happen. I just wanted to be casual friends and enjoy her company. He held the door to the stairwell for her and their eyes connected. "My, my Miss Iron Pants, look at that sad face. How are you going to maintain your reputation acting like this?"

"That's not funny, damn you. I have had so much fun. I just hate to see it end." He couldn't find the words he needed. They went down one level and paused in front of the door bearing the sign—Senior Bachelor Women's Quarters. She said, "My place is just a few doors down the hall. I'm sure I'll see you before you go tomorrow." She stalled a moment, "We must have met in another life." She put the side of her head on his chest and gave him a long hug. Her hair was soft and weightless under his hands as he held her. Marmette looked up with a mysterious look. It had been a long time since he experienced the special warmth of a woman's body held close or the feeling of a pair of breasts against his chest. His self-control was stretched to the breaking point. "Please send us a note now and then and let us know what's going on in your life," she said.

Hal kissed her forehead, "I will." Their eyes met and searched. "You're a dear friend and an exceptional lady," said Hal, "I won't be forgetting you any time soon."

She stood on the tips of her toes, gave him a brief kiss and said, "Please be careful up there in the wild blue yonder." She turned and walked quickly through the doorway and down the hall. He watched her through the small chicken-wire sandwiched pane of glass in the door until she entered her quarters. She didn't look back. He shook his head. Why did I let this happen? Why couldn't I control this situation? The walk back to the Dai–ichi Building was lonely, despite the commotion of Tokyo's busy nightlife.

General MacArthur's Conference Room

Admirals Joy and Morehouse entered and walked to the front of the conference room where Hal was checking the order of his maps and illustrations on the easel.

Admiral Joy said in a low voice, "It has not been officially announced, but General MacArthur has notified the Pentagon of his selection of General Almond as Commanding General of the invasion force, the X Corps."

"Thanks for the heads up, sir. That will certainly change his viewpoint."

Admiral Morehouse shook Hal's hand briefly, "Good luck."

A sentry ducked his head in the door and hollered, "Ten hut!" Everyone promptly came to their feet. General MacArthur came through the door with his characteristic gusto and filled the room with a powerful presence.

General Almond followed just behind him.

"Good Morning gentlemen, please be seated," said General Macarthur as he pulled his chair from the head of the conference table. He had the fabled corncob pipe in his hand; it was empty. No one sat until MacArthur settled into the large brown leather high-back judge's chair. He began to pack tobacco into his pipe with his forefinger. "Please continue Captain," he said, while striking a match and lighting the pipe.

Hal plunged into it, "Good morning, gentlemen. In front of you is a copy of the draft naval air operations section of the Chromite plan. Please turn to page..."

Hal spent nearly two hours going through the draft plan, supplemented by enlarged charts, air reconnaissance photos and drawings on the easel. There were lively, sometimes provoking, sometimes confrontational discussions. General MacArthur merely listened intently and took notes on his yellow pad.

When Hal had completed his briefing, and discussion appeared complete, MacArthur looked at General Almond, "General?"

Without the slightest hesitation, Almond replied, "It's an excellent plan, but too detailed. Detail stifles ingenuity." Hal's ears got hot. Too detailed! When his X Corps goes ashore unopposed he'll frigging well be glad there was detail.

MacArthur seemed to dismiss Almond's comment and turned to Admiral Joy, "Admiral, can you provide the resources that Captain Kirby requires?"

"Absolutely, General."

The General tapped the pipe bowl in the center of a dark brown glass ashtray, discharging smoldering ashes. "Captain, do you have any other observations or comments concerning the Chromite plan you wish to make?"

"No sir," replied Hal, breathing a hidden sigh of relief.

MacArthur drew two parallel lines under the last line of notes on his pad and sat back. "Gentlemen, at the great risk of preaching to the choir, I reiterate, Chromite, at Inchon, during the mid–September tidal window, is the only chance we have to save South Korea. No other location and timing will snatch victory from the Communists. We must make this work or there will be heavy U.S. casualties and unspeakable political embarrassment to the United States." MacArthur then stood and everyone promptly rose. "Admiral Joy, Captain Kirby, please remain for just one minute."

As the room emptied, Hal's pucker factor rose. MacArthur looked intently at Hal, then turned to Admiral Joy, "Admiral, it is critical to this operation that Captain Kirby return in sufficient time to prepare for and participate in next month's VIP briefing. God knows we need him on the Valley Forge too."

"I'll arrange for that, General."

"Thank you very much Admiral. Captain Kirby, I appreciate your efforts. Godspeed. Thank you, gentlemen." The General collected his notes, pipe and tobacco pouch and departed.

Dusty was waiting for Admiral Joy and Hal when they returned to the office. "The shit is hitting the fan, Admiral. We just received a Flash message from Eighth Army. The North Korean People's Army appears to be preparing for a major thrust along several fronts and General Walker is screaming for intensified air support. Valley Forge is en route now and will be on the southwest station in about two hours. They are already launching ADs and F4Us though. The Philippine Sea already has everything with wings airborne. There are several messages on your desk you need to read. It looks like the U.S. and ROK troops are getting trapped simultaneously at several locations."

"Thanks, Dusty," said the Admiral. "Well Hal, you need to go join the foray!"

"Aye, aye, sir!"

"You did one hell of a fine job. Take care of yourself. I'll send a message to Admiral Hawkins just as soon as I know when we need you back here for the big show." They shook hands vigorously.

CHAPTER 4

20,000 feet above the Yellow Sea

Sparsely scattered white clouds and excellent visibility made a breathtaking view of the southeastern tip of Korea. Hal was returning to the USS Valley Forge from Japan. He repositioned his oxygen mask to relieve a slight pinch and peered down at the spectacular topography. The natural beauty of the terrain from this altitude belied the strife and carnage taking place.

"COATHANGER this is 202," Hal transmitted to the Valley Forge.

"202, this is COATHANGER, say position and altitude," replied the air coordinator in the ship's Combat Information Center.

"Approaching southern tip of Korea, angels two zero."

"Roger 202, squawk three two zero two, altimeter two niner niner seven. Fly heading two eight zero—bring 'er home."

Hal took a deep breath; he was happy to be back in the real world of gray paint, sea and airplanes. It was a bright, clear day; life was a charm. He dropped onto the flight deck of the Valley Forge in a textbook landing. As he taxied to the forward deck elevator, Lieutenant Commander Ted Spence, his Executive Officer, trotted across the flight deck to meet him.

"Welcome back CAG," Ted hollered up to Hal after the jet engine was shut down.

///Hal gave a thumbs-up, "Did you get your battery charged in Yokosuka Ted?"

Ted grinned, "Is a pig's ass pork?"

"Here, catch," said Hal as he tossed a package down to Ted.

"What's this?" Ted asked as Hal climbed down the side of the Panther.

"It's the draft plan for Operation Chromite. That needs to go directly to Admiral Hawkins."

"Rog. How was Tokyo?"

"Fine as frog's hair. What's happening on the beach?" asked Hal as they quick-paced toward the ship's island. "I hear it's pretty damn grim."

"That's an understatement," Ted replied with a serious tone, "I've got eighteen prop sorties airborne now. He looked at his watch, "In fact, they should be over the target now." He pointed to the after deck, now a beehive of activity, "They're bringing up the Corsairs now. We're getting everyone airborne as fast as we can. The squadron COs are putting together a list of pilot and plane availability to support a max effort for the next few days. I have all of today's message traffic on your desk."

"Sounds like you got it under control Ted. Anything else new?"

"Nope, same old routine panic CAG. The Admiral gave Luther Garr the responsibility of gleaning gems from the Top Secret intelligence supplements in order to suggest search areas and targets. I'm not too thrilled about that at all."

Hal shook his head, "After all, it is his job, not ours. We've been doing those functions because we didn't have a Flag Intelligence Officer. Now we do, and he's it."

"I gotta tell ya boss, I'm beginning to really dislike that guy. I thought you just had an old axe to grind, but there's just something about him that smells bad. Anyway, the old man has an evening meeting set up for us to hear Garr's situation estimate and recommendations for tomorrow's missions."

"That's going to be interesting," said Hal, "Who's invited?"

"Just you, me and Garr."

"Now ain't that cozy," said Hal. "Garr and I toe to toe for the first time in six years. That's going to be real fun."

At 1955, Hal and Ted entered the Admiral Hawkins' office. The Admiral was sitting at a table with maps and messages sprawled in front of him. The Operation Chromite plan was on the end of the table. Garr was sitting across from the Admiral, scribbling on a pad while referring to a Top Secret message.

"Good evening Admiral," said Hal.

Hawkins pushed himself away from the table slightly and reached up to shake Hal's hand. "Welcome back aboard. Help yourself," he said, pointing at a side table where a coffee pot and a tray of mixed sandwich halves awaited their fate. Hal and Ted piled some food on plates, filled cups with coffee and took their seats at the table. The Admiral took a bite of a sandwich and continued, "I've skimmed through the Chromite plan, but we'll talk a little about that later. First I want to discuss tomorrow's missions."

"Aye, aye sir," said Hal.

"We received a second Top Secret intell message from Tokyo on the way back to Sasebo," continued the Admiral, "and a third one arrived an hour ago. I assume you're aware of these messages and their contents."

"Affirmative," replied Hal, "In fact, I saw the draft of the third just before I left Tokyo. "

"Mr. Garr is just finishing up with the latest message." Garr still hadn't looked up or otherwise acknowledged the presence of Hal or Ted. He continued his hurried scribbling.

After a few moments, Garr looked at the Admiral, "I'm ready sir."

"Very well," said the Admiral and nodded for Garr to proceed.

Garr began his briefing of the intelligence picture along the segment of the front that the Admiral had assigned to the Valley Forge. He looked only at the Admiral while speaking from his notes. Garr identified areas he suggested that armed reconnaissance be conducted, where he estimated enemy troop concentrations would be heavy. It was as though Garr was alone in the room with the Admiral. Hal fidgeted with the cup handle. I can't believe he's behaving like this in front of the old man.

When Garr finished, the Admiral looked at Hal, "Any questions?"

"Yes sir. I have a question for Ted. If this area along here," Hal ran his finger along the chart, "is the area of highest concentration and greatest threat to friendly forces, why did you direct only six sorties to that area today?" Ted's face flushed; Garr shifted in his chair and ran his eyes around the map.

"Garr didn't brief that area as a zone of high threat concentration, CAG. The six planes I sent in there on armed reconnaissance went purely on a hunch I had."

Admiral Hawkins' eyes darted between Hal and Garr. Hal glared at Garr and bit his tongue. Looking alternately between Garr and Ted, Hal could hold back no longer. "I'd say we accomplished zip point shit on interdiction today because we failed to send our planes to the obvious areas of high payoff. Hell, the armed recon missions based on Ted's hunch bagged nearly as much game as the remainder of the missions combined." His blood was boiling. He turned to Garr, "What the hell is going on here Garr?" He glared into Garr's blank face where nervous muscles were twitching. Hal had a flashback of six years. The last time Hal saw a look like that on Garr's face was after a court martial took Luther's wings away from him.

Admiral Hawkins was forcefully tapping the eraser of his pencil on the tabletop. Garr stared fiercely at Hal for a moment. "Look, Captain, intelligence information and ground situations are dynamic. When I briefed those missions, I gave them the best information I had." Hal and Garr locked eyes without blinking for seemingly an eon, like two gladiators fighting to the death merely through their eyes.

Hal rose from his chair and without breaking his stare at Garr said,

"Admiral, would you excuse Mr. Garr and me for a moment?" Hal nodded at Garr to follow him, left the table and walked to the hatch. Garr reluctantly followed Hal out to the catwalk surrounding the Flag Plot. Hal rested his arms on the vertical steel armor plate that ran along the outer edge of the catwalk. Looking out into humid darkness gave him a chance to gather his thoughts. He took a deep breath and turned to Garr, "Mister, if I catch you screwing around with my pilot's lives so that you can serve some twisted personal goal, I'll see that your asshole gets stretched across a fifty–gallon drum." The forceful intonation Hal used left nothing to the imagination.

Garr's face showed fury, "Are you threatening me, Captain?"

Hal stood tall and crossed his arms, "That's not a threat, Lieutenant Commander Garr, it's a promise!"

"Well, I meant what I said to you the last time we faced off, Kirby. You're going to pay for taking my wings. I've prayed for the day that I'd be in a position to see you get what's coming to you. My prayers have been answered." Garr's eyes were wide and seemed glazed. Sweat beads sparkled on Garr's forehead, lit by the glow from a porthole. His trembling hand reached up slowly and wiped his brow.

"Mr. Garr, you didn't get anything you didn't earn. You let that yellow stripe down your back get the best of you and you deserted me in the face of enemy fighters. I'm telling you, get your stuff together and watch your six. I can either maintain a professional relationship with you or shoot your ass down—your choice! Don't even think of crossing me. You'll lose—again."

Garr's eyes threw fire tipped daggers; his jaw chattered. In a quiet voice, he said slowly but emphatically, "Kirby, I'm gonna get you! Someday, some way. You won't even know what hit you." He turned quickly and walked along the catwalk to a ladder and disappeared to a lower level.

Hal rapped his fist into his hand. That's one sick son of a bitch! Should I unload this on the Admiral? Hal went back into the Admiral's cabin.

Ted asked, "Whatcha do, throw him overboard?"

Admiral Hawkins' forehead veins were blue and bulging with anger, "I have no patience for this kind of horse shit Kirby. We have enough problems with the North Koreans on the beach. I can't tolerate fighting among my officers."

"Yes sir, I just told him to get squared away." Hawkins' face indicated disbelief then transformed into a grim, stern look. He sat back in his chair, chewed and puffed on a cigar that went out some time ago and began massaging his leg stub while he thought. Hal heard rumors of how tough the 'old man' was before he met him for the first time on this cruise. The rumors were wrong – they were understatements at best. The 'old man' was tough as nails and totally intolerant of incompetence. Hawkins fired his

Chief of Staff in his first week aboard the Valley Forge and told the Bureau of Personnel he didn't need a replacement. He was a living legend in stoic determination and self-discipline. The Admiral lost a leg during the war but that didn't slow him down. He vowed to return to the cockpit and put himself on a brutal physical therapy regimen. Navy policy dictated his release from active duty on disability, but Hawkins battled with the Bureaus of Aviation and Medicine. He won a chance to prove his competency in the air and was reinstated to flight status. Hal wanted to like him; he certainly respected him. Hal realized his career was really on the line. The Admiral relit his cigar and puffed a blue smoke ring that expanded as it traveled up toward the lamp hanging above the table. "Hal, you know damn well how to deal with shitbird officers. With cunning, not a fist fight." The furrowed brows under that blue V on his forehead said a thousand words.

"Admiral, if I may, he had it coming. Acting like I don't exist is bad enough, but the thought that he sabotaged the success of a mission behind my back was too much. I wanted him to know where he stood with me. I'm not going to stand by and watch while he plays games to make the Air Group look bad."

Hawkins clenched his jaw, "Number one, he works for me. It's up to me to have his ass and if he doesn't shape up, I'll have it. Number two, we don't know if he purposely withheld information. Number three, politics and personality conflicts are not going to get easier; those new eagles you're wearing have put you into another league. You can't think and act like a stick and rudder pilot anymore! Not if you ever hope to wear stars. It's obvious something's going on here that I don't know anything about. Talk!"

Hal took in a deep breath, "Our quarrel goes back to 1944; I was instrumental in getting him court martialed—he lost his wings. That was the last time we were assigned together. He vowed to get even with me. Based on his behavior, it doesn't look like he's over it, but the ball is in his court. I'll never have any respect for him, but I'm prepared to maintain a professional relationship. I won't take any crap from him though. He's trouble sir."

The Admiral's frown was intense. Looking into his eyes seemed painful. Vibrations from the ship's engines and deck elevators came to the foreground until the Admiral spoke forcefully through his teeth, "Keep it professional Kirby."

Aye, aye, sir," said Hal.

Garr knocked on the hatch, entered quietly and sat down at the table like nothing had happened. "Mr. Garr," said the Admiral in his deep gravel-modulated voice, "I'll give you the benefit of the doubt on this occasion only. You must, from this moment on, demonstrate that you are capable of performing effectively under the tempo of carrier warfare operations or you're going back where you came from. Do you stand by the situation brief you just gave for tomorrow morning or would you like a half–hour to study it more?"

Without hesitation, Garr replied, "It is the best estimate that can be made at this time Admiral."

Hawkins got up, refilled his cup and returned to his chair. There was an eerie silence. The Admiral savored a sip of coffee, then turned to Hal, "Any questions concerning the estimate Mr. Garr has provided?"

"No sir." Actually, Hal questioned every word of it and would confirm it all himself with the intelligence reports.

Hawkins nodded at Garr, "That being the case, you are excused." Luther promptly gathered his things and departed. The Admiral's demeanor changed completely, "Gentlemen, I am curious about your inference that he knowingly provided a false or incomplete intelligence briefing. I'd like you to investigate what information he had when he made those recommendations. I want to know if he made them orally or in writing? Recreate the information on hand in the four–hour timeline prior to the briefing."

"Aye, aye sir, we'll go back through the files, check the times of receipt of the intelligence messages from the beach and lay out the entire situation."

"You two keep this little argument and the investigation to yourselves. I won't tolerate open dissension. I have no problem whatsoever with professional disagreements, but I absolutely won't stand for any more bullshit like I've seen."

CHAPTER 5

Aboard USS Valley Forge

Admiral Hawkins began morning battle staff meetings promptly. Today was no exception and he had a full head of steam going. "Gentlemen, just in case you haven't noticed, the volleying of flash messages that has continued since last evening isn't just paranoia. General Walker's Eighth Army is in a critical ground situation." Hawkins stood up and leaned on the back of his chair, scanning around the table, carefully making positive contact with each pair of eyes glued on him. They all knew the foreboding blue veins in his forehead meant that they were going to catch hell. "This situation is momentous. The perimeter around Pusan is getting smaller by the hour. Attrition is taking its toll. I'll get right to the point. You people and the Philippine Sea haven't been able to keep the enemy contained. You haven't taken out enough ground troops. You haven't taken out enough tanks and artillery pieces. And you haven't cut off their logistic support. General Walker believes the ground situation is so bad that he urged CINCFE to develop a contingency plan ASAP that would get what's left of his forces out of Korea with minimal notice. If they execute that plan, we will have failed our mission." The Admiral's eyes burned everyone they fell upon. He began pacing to collect his thoughts.

Hal broke the silence, "Admiral, our results have consistently been better than the Philippine Sea," he didn't get a chance to finish his thought.

"Kirby, I don't give a damn about comparisons of arbitrary quantities. I'm telling you, as clear as I can, that the airplanes of this entire task force are not doing the job. And don't think I haven't torn the asshole out of the Philippine Sea, because I've already done that. Look gentlemen, NKPA forces are getting so thick that we may not be able to hold them back for many more days. We'll have the Princeton in range to start launching missions tomorrow morning, which is none too soon. I put them on notice too. From this moment on, we need to destroy large quantities of NKPA troops," he pounded the table, "mechanized iron," another fist slammed onto the table, "and supplies. Today and every other flaming day through the Chromite landing too." His eyes were now ablaze. He scanned around a silent table and continued, "Sure, you're working hard, and you're tired. Most of you remember what it was like after Pearl Harbor. You remember that tired was when your hands were raw, every muscle in your body burned, your mind was numb and you couldn't sleep. Pushing the limit is how we won that war; putting absolutely everything, everything you have into every aspect of the battle. You, the Princeton and the Philippine Sea are going to give everything you have. You are going to keep General Walker and his army alive." Hawkins pulled a big black cigar from his breast pocket and sat down. It was so quiet that the snap of his lighter cover, the rasping of the flint and his first puffs filled their ears. They waited.

The Admiral looked down the far end of the table at Luther, "Mr. Garr, in case you haven't guessed, this puts the onus on you to tell us where to send planes to get the job done." Luther's best response was to mutter an obligatory two–word acknowledgment and look down into his plate. Hawkins' eyebrows bounced then he shifted his gaze to Kirby, "And you've got to keep every damn plane you've got in the air, kicking ass from first light to dark."

Hal nodded and replied with steeped energy, "Aye, aye sir. We have developed a withering flight schedule and the pilots have been told to expect to be able to do three things, and three things only, for the foreseeable future: fly constantly during daylight, sleep and eat, in that priority."

The Admiral's attention instantly returned to Luther, "What's the latest poop, Garr? I need insight into what's happening with the NKPA at this very moment."

Garr's stunned look was that of a deer in headlights. "Yes sir, well, uh, the enemy appears to be in major logistic reinforcement and is mounting front line penetration operations in a last-ditch effort to secure the remainder of Korea before the landing can be executed."

"No shit, Dick Tracy," someone whispered. Several snickers escaped. Hawkins shot a chilling look around the table.

Garr tweaked the sides of his lips in disgust and continued, "USAF photo recon shows they are beefing up defenses at the ports of Inchon and Kunsan."

"Mr. Garr," the Admiral interrupted, "We all know the frigging general situation. What I need from you are specifics, where in hell their troops, tanks, lines of communications and depots are located."

Garr's face was crimson, "The problem is this, Admiral, the intell we get from Tokyo and Hawaii is too old by the time we get it. The NKPA are moving fast on the ground. I don't see any evidence that they are stockpiling large quantities anywhere. Men and equipment are being routed and distributed directly to the forces at the front. They know that if they bunch anything up, we'll hit it." Garr looked down into his plate of pastry crumbs, unable to endure the Admiral's visual ire.

Hawkins shrugged his shoulders and displayed a look of dismay. He puffed a rich blue smoke ring toward Garr. "So, what's that mean in terms of where to send airplanes?" he asked, fidgeting with his cigar. After a scant moment of silence, the Admiral repeated himself, "Mr. Garr! What's your best estimate on where the hell we should send our airplanes?" Garr was visibly upset and couldn't find words. Hawkins bellowed, "I hope the intell briefs you have for Kirby's squadrons and the Philippine Sea this morning are better than this. I want to know, right now, where you think we should send them today?"

Garr shuffled through papers in a folder, "My suggestion, is to fly, uh close air support, uh," he gave up trying to find a document, and continued without benefit of his notes, "uh, fly CAS along the active fronts and to fly recon beyond the front lines to locate and track enemy reinforcements, patrols and end-arounds." Hal shook his head. Look at his smug face. He really believes he has just been brilliant. If he pays attention to Hawkins' face, he'd figure out that the old man isn't the slightest bit impressed.

Hal dropped his coffee cup onto the saucer a bit heavy and exclaimed, "Mr. Garr, that means nothing to me! Give me a chart with locations noted and labeled with what's there and in what numbers. That's what I need."

The Admiral slammed his hand on the table, "Dammit Mr. Garr, the front runs along a sixty by one-hundred-mile semi-oval around Pusan. Three bird farms full of airplanes can't cover that much territory. Do you think you can be just a little more specific?" The Admiral took a short drag on his cigar, angrily jerked it from his mouth and smashed the lit end into his ashtray.

Luther's face was flushed, "Admiral, I am doing the best I can with the intelligence I am getting from the beach."

Hawkins leaned back in his chair, which let out a loud squeal that seemed to be amplified in the silence. "Lewis, get this damn thing a grease job," the Admiral growled at his aide. Lewis disappeared promptly on a mission to find an oilcan. Hawkins glared at Luther, "Mr. Garr, I want you to provide a written intell briefing to these gentlemen prior to every morning meeting. The brief will provide the coordinates of friendly units at the front, with indications of the severity of threat to those units, the boundaries of suggested areas for CAS, and recommended recon tracks, in priority order. Have that information on this table by 0545 daily."

"Aye, aye sir," replied Garr. He looked away from the Admiral and concentrated again on his coffee cup. Hal sipped the last of his coffee, smiling inside. Brilliant Admiral, brilliant—you just hung his incompetent butt on a wall hook.

Admiral Hawkins tapped his fingers firmly on the table with a rolling motion for a few moments, then continued, "Mr. Garr, directly following this meeting, I want you to compose a memo containing this morning's intell situation, including the information I prescribed, and draft a message version for the Philippine Sea. Deliver them to Captain Kirby and me by 0730 this morning to facilitate planning the late morning missions. Add the Princeton to the addressee list too."

"Aye, aye sir," Garr acknowledged. "By your leave sir, I'll get started." He departed the meeting.

Admiral Hawkins crossed his arms, leaned his elbows on the table and looked at each of his staff officers, "I don't have to tell you gentlemen that when things start turning sour, fingers start pointing. I received a heads-up from Admiral Joy that General Stratemeyer has been making noise at meetings with General MacArthur's staff that he feels the Navy air assets are not effective. His motive, of course, is he wants more Air Force fighter and bomber assets transferred into his command. He also told MacArthur that the Navy has ignored CINCFE policy of coordinating ground support missions through the Air Force Joint Operations Center at Taegu."

Hal wasted no time responding, "When that policy came out, we attempted to work with JOC. We experienced crippling incompatibility problems trying to work with them. When we did fly missions under their control, they were usually wild goose chases. We just stopped trying."

"Incompatibilities—like what?" asked Hawkins.

"Their inbound contact frequency is saturated with long winded jet jocks out of Japan. When we do get through, they hand us off to airborne forward air controllers flying mosquitoes at the front that use Air Force maps with grids we've never heard of." Hal suddenly realized that this was not what the old man wanted to hear. "Sir, I'm sorry, that's water over the dam. I'll order every ground support flight leader to coordinate through JOC from now on."

"Kirby, frankly, I don't give a rat's ass what the problems are. Just fix 'em! Today!" ordered the Admiral. "I don't want to hear any more bullshit from those damn blue-suits." He took a gulp of coffee and bellowed, "Dismissed! Kirby, remain behind." The room emptied in record time. "Kirby, what have you learned in your investigation?"

"Sir, we recreated the information base that existed at the time of the briefing. There is no question, he had better information available. And we believe this has been true all along. An Ensign fresh out of OCS could do better. He is either grossly incompetent or, more likely, he is purposely seeing to it that the missions don't accomplish much. Either way, I recommend that he be relieved immediately."

The Admiral shrugged, "Well, based on his performance thus far, I don't think his future on my staff is very long lived," Hawkins added, "Same goes for you CAG if your Air Group doesn't start hurting the enemy. And that's no shit." A chill ran through Hal's body.

VA–55 Ready Room
Aboard USS Valley Forge

Hal entered the ready room where a group of Skyraider pilots were gathering for a debriefing after a mission. They were grumbling and surly. Someone called, "Attention on deck," when Hal came through the hatch.

When Hal had taken his reserved front row seat and nodded to the mission leader, Lieutenant Magee launched into his mission's debrief, "CAG, no medals on this one. We just spent three hours in holding patterns then scoured a vast amount of empty countryside. Those JOC people are assholes. They send the Air Force F–80s to the hot spots and use us for search and cleanup." Magee continued with an animated and colorful debrief. He finished up, ". . .We were unable to find a single enemy target in the search areas assigned to us by JOC. After two and a half hours, I checked out of the JOC system and flew the roads and valleys that lead generally toward the ship. Then and only then, did we find some targets. We destroyed three trucks, a tank, two artillery pieces and strafed a troop concentration. Big frigging deal. That's about it."

Hal rose from his chair and said, "Magee, please meet me in my office after you're cleaned up."

Magee came bounding through the hatch of the Air Group Office. A shower, clean flight suit and time to wind down changed his temperament.

"Geez Magee," said Hal, "you've got enough Old Spice on you to gag a maggot. Listen, on the JOC business, I'm frustrated too, but we've got to look at this from their point of view. The Joint Operations Center is run by the Air Force but it's a joint operation and so we are part of it by definition. However, they don't know anything about naval air that we don't teach them. They're just men—like you and me."

"CAG, they aren't like you and me, they've had frontal lobotomies. I think my golden retriever has a higher IQ than those guys."

"Well Magee, you're going to get a chance to find out."

Mouth agape and his expression frozen for a moment, Magee asked, "What do you mean, CAG?"

"You, my red-headed friend, are going to pick a buddy and fly into the Taegu JOC within the hour. You are going to teach the animals in that zoo what they need to know to make our life pleasant and productive."

"Shit CAG!"

"No shit Magee!"

"I'm sorry CAG, I wasn't expecting—"

Hal cut Magee off, "There's just no other way to solve this problem in the time that we have. The grunts are getting chewed up and there's no future in hand wringing and whining. So, you are going to provide JOC with our WAC charts and data sheets on air ordnance and aircraft."

"Aye, aye sir. I'd like to take Bruce with me, OK? And, how long do we have to stay there?"

"I don't care who you take, as long as your CO agrees; I've already talked with "Bridge" Danley about sending you. Taking Bruce would be a good idea; that will give JOC a look at an Able Dog and a Panther. Tomorrow I'll find a hog pilot to drop in and add a Corsair to the show and tell. Get twenty sets of data sheets and charts together and get your butts in there ASAP. Maybe we can salvage some of this day. Spend some time in their O–Club tonight and do a little public relations work. I want you to fly back in three days. Shove off."

"Aye, aye sir," Magee said enthusiastically.

"And Magee, I'm flying the dawn CAS mission tomorrow. If I have a bad day, it's going to be your ass," Hal said with a mix of jest and seriousness. Magee flashed a thumbs-up signal as he ducked out of the office hatch.

CHAPTER 6

12,000 feet over Pusan

"JACKHAMMER this is BLUEBERRY–1 over," Hal repeated, trying to squeeze between the others. He continued calling.

"Good Morning BLUEBERRY–1 this is JACKHAMMER. Standby please. We are working some F–80s which only have fuel for ten minutes over the target."

"BLUEBERRY–1 Roger," Hal replied. Geez. Here I am with twelve Able Dogs, thirty-six bombs, a half-gross of rockets and I'm waiting for fighter pilots with 10 minutes of gas!

Hal's turn finally came, "BLUEBERRY–1 this is JACKHAMMER, contact mosquito WILDWEST–7 on frequency one point niner."

"BLUEBERRY–1 roger out," said Hal and selected the mosquito's radio channel. "WILDWEST–7 this is BLUEBERRY–1, twelve Able Dogs, two–hundred–fifty pounders and rockets."

"Roger BLUEBERRY, assignment is grid JIG GEORGE two fiver one fiver, a reported enemy concentration, including mechanized armor, one zero miles west of the Naktong river. Air Force pilots reported them in bivouac at dusk last night. My location three zero miles west of that location."

"BLUEBERRY–1 roger."

"BLUEBERRY–7 from 1, did you copy WILDWEST–7?"

"A–firm CAG"

"OK 7, detach with 9 and 11 and proceed to coordinates HOW GEORGE one five five zero. Search the valley eastbound toward us," ordered Hal.

"7 roger."

Hal watched the three section leaders and their wingmen peel off to the left. "BLUEBERRY–3 and 5 from 1, we'll search westbound from the Naktong."

"3 roger." "5 roger."

From 20,000 feet, the scenery was captivating. Wildly ranging topography reflected its violent volcanic origin. Altitudes noted on the map showed peaks of 5,000 feet. Their steep angles, shadows and conformations created fascinating illusions. Looking down at the terrain around Taegu, it appeared that the city had been established in the basin of a huge caldera. Flying a northwesterly heading, he intercepted the Naktong River and led his Skyraiders north along the snaking muddy water. A valley came into view that corresponded to the valley identified in the mosquito's grid reference.

"3 and 5 from 1, here we go," he said, giving notice of a heading and altitude change. He rolled left, began a descent to 5,000 feet and headed west into the valley. Mountain ranges on either side had crests of 2,000 to 3,000 feet. The valley center appeared sandy with patches of sagebrush-like vegetation. Flat areas at the bases of the ranges were heavily bushed with pine trees running part way up the gentle slopes. Hal's mind went into overdrive. OK. It's been a while since they've been seen. Could be anywhere. Anything moving in the valley will be kicking up a dust cloud though. They could have moved into the trees, which would leave tracks into their hiding places. No evidence of tank or tire tracks so far. They haven't been through here. Better spread out.

"3 from 1, run down the middle. 5 take the northern edge. I've got the south side."

Ten miles into the valley, Hal spotted tracks; as did one of his flight leaders.

"CAG from 3, tracks up ahead; they're angling off from the center of the valley toward your side."

"Roger 3, I have 'em. Anything your side 5?"

"Negative CAG."

"OK. 3 and 5 keep going down the valley, I'm going to beat the bushes over here. I'll call you if anything is there," said Hal.

The vehicle and tank tracks intersected with heavy natural cover. When he passed by the intersection, he spotted NKPA tanks, trucks, towed howitzers and tents scattered under the trees along the valley edge. He turned to look at his wingman and saw a beaming face and a bouncing thumb. "BLUEBERRY flight from 1, TALLY HO, ten west of the river, south side. Make your strafing runs from east to west. 7, 9 and 11 if you are negative out there, bring 'em over here."

All flight leaders acknowledged his orders with the peaked enthusiasm of a school of sharks that had picked up a taste of blood. Hal jerked the stick to the right and grunted hard against the strain of a nearly six–G turn.

As he leveled onto a southeast heading along the edge of the heavy brush, he noted how well his young wingman was able to follow—like glue.

Hal changed his radio to the frequency for the mosquito, "WILDWEST–7 this is BLUEBERRY–1 over."

"Hey BLUEBERRY, how you making out?"

"BLUEBERRY–1 has located enemy mechanized units ten west of Naktong. Will recontact after we've finished up, over."

"Roger BLUEBERRY–1, I'll be here, out."

Hal shifted back to the frequency for his flight. "OK BLUEBERRIES, concentrate on the tanks, towed artillery and trucks. Pull out at 2.5, there's going to be a lot of small arms fire down there."

As the enemy's hiding place passed by his starboard wing, he tried to discern where the various elements of the force were located. Hal set up the armament panel switches to drop the 250–pound bombs in singles. "Here we go Sammy," he advised his wingman. He began a dive onto the target. The altimeter unwound like a runaway clock. He noticed some cannon barrels poking out of camouflaged Russian T–34 tanks parked near Russian 122mm howitzers and jeeps. Two–ton canvas-covered trucks were parked willy-nilly under the trees. Tiny flashes of light from small arms fire were visible along the tree line, where they contrasted against dark foliage. He smiled. Dumb-asses, they're clumped up into nice groups. My two–fifty's will like that! He lined up on an area where there were several tank barrels close together. Coming through 3,500 feet, his thumb squeezed the bomb release switch twice in short succession. He pulled up slightly and lined up on a group of towed howitzers, dropped another bomb and pulled back hard on the stick. Hal climbed back to 7,000 feet and circled to set up for the next pass. BLUEBERRY–3 and his wingman were releasing their bombs on the target and BLUEBERRY–5 was in front of him, just rolling into their first dive.

"BLUEBERRY–1 from 7, have you in sight, save some fun for us!"

"Plenty to go around," said Hal.

Pulling out from the third pass on the target, he spotted two T–34s that decided to escape to the northwest at full speed. It was an interesting sight—one was dragging a camouflage tent and netting across the valley floor. "Sammy, Take the guy with the tent." He set the armament switches for rockets. Near the pullout altitude of the dive, with airstream noise at a scream, Hal's finger closed on the firing switch. A pair of rockets struck the right side of the tank, resulting in a track belt failure. The tank veered sharply, turned brutally hard onto its side and slid a short distance in the sand. Sammy's rockets hit their target and caused a secondary explosion of stored cannon rounds.

Headed back to the tree line after the T–34 chase, Hal smiled at what he saw when he leveled off at 12,000 feet. The target area was full of planes climbing, diving, attacking, pulling out—it was a frenzy. Scattered throughout the trees and heavy foliage there were multiple fires from burning tanks, trucks and jeeps. Vehicles were only now beginning to disperse. Hal headed for a group of T–34 tanks headed northwest—toward him. He and Sammy took out the tanks easily with rockets.

"T–34s zero, rockets six," said Sammy.

"Rajah dajah," Hal replied. Geez, it must be over 100 on the deck if it's this hot at 3,000 feet. Hal climbed back to 7,000 feet and continued toward the enemy main body. Air was notably cooler at 7,000 feet and felt wonderful on his soaked flight suit. He spotted dust plumes—vehicles moving out at high speed across the valley floor toward the Naktong River. As Hal approached directly from the rear, he identified three two–ton trucks towing artillery pieces. When he was two miles behind them, he eased the nose over and lined up the rearmost artillery piece in the gunsight. Passing through 3,500 feet, he squeezed the cannon trigger switch and pulled up slowly, walking the tracers up through the line of howitzers and trucks. Muzzle flashes from small arms became visible in the shadows of the canvas-covered trucks—they were full of soldiers. "Geez! Break right Sammy, break right!" he hollered when he spotted the telltale rapid and bright flashes and tracers of a machine gun chattering away at him. A loud metallic bang made his heart skip a beat. Oil began slithering in branches over the canopy. Son of a bitch! The engine oil pressure gauge was sinking slowly toward the zero peg. Severe queasiness filled his entire chest cavity; his ears began ringing; his heart was beating in rapid, powerful thuds. Well Kirby, you've got yourself in deep horse hockey this time—real deep. He leveled off and set the power and propeller pitch for minimum strain on his sick engine. Hal looked over at Sammy.

"I see it CAG, I'll get some help." said Sammy.

Hal pointed toward the river, "I'm going as far as I can before she seizes up. Strafe those trucks from the front and take them out. I don't want them chasing me down. Be careful of those damn machine guns."

"Got you covered CAG. Take care of yourself. I'll stick with you."

"Rajah, dajah," Hal replied. His hands and knees were vibrating from a massive adrenaline dump into his bloodstream. He angled toward the north side of the valley. Sammy was busy advising the others of the situation. I don't like the looks of this situation one damn bit. Hal kept his eye on the thick line of trees and brush running along the slopes. He estimated it would be about three miles to the river from where he'd probably go down. Silence added to his anxiety; the prop abruptly stopped spinning. Drained of oil, the engine had locked up tight.

Sammy radioed, "CAG, if you're listening, the trucks are immobilized. We're headed for you now. Zeke is talking with Taegu to get more cover and an angel. Danley is calling for RESCAP. Good luck CAG. We're overhead." Hal was too busy to talk—he had little altitude left. He was flying parallel to the tree line, over flat land. He dropped full flaps and tightened the shoulder straps and seat belt. Hal pulled the canopy lever. As the canopy came back, air flushed through the cockpit. He toggled the red master electrical switch to 'OFF'. It became relatively quiet—nothing but slipstream noise. The airframe slammed onto the ground. After some scraping and jerking, the plane came to a stop. He threw off his helmet, released himself from the belts, straps, hoses and wires and climbed down from the broken bird. Geez, it has to be at least 115 degrees. He saw a dust cloud kicking up a couple miles away. "Keep those bastards off me guys," he mumbled, and began running full bore for cover. I wonder how much ammo my guys have left? Can't be much. I wonder how many trucks and jeeps are left? How long will it be before RESCAP and the angel get here? He ran inward into the brush until the density and height of it made it difficult to run hard, then headed east for the river. Plowing through brush and scrub that was between thigh and waist height was exhausting. Running stooped over to reduce detection added to the challenge. After a mile of very labored sprinting, severe pain in the pit of his stomach and burning, rubbery leg muscles signaled the onset of oxygen debt. I'm going to have to spend more time in the gym—I'm out of gas already. He slowed to a trot to catch his breath. The sound of an AD approaching was comforting. Sammy passed overhead, wings wagging. Hal raised a thumb high as he trotted. Use the signal mirror Kirby. Geez, don't let him lose sight. Sweat was flushing out of every pore in his body. His heart was banging in his ears and he was gasping for air.

The BLUEBERRIES remained on the scene as long as they could, making strafing runs with widely spaced short gun bursts to minimize the round expenditures. They were buying him time. He kept plowing ahead through the thick brush. Even at a trot, he was unable to catch his breath. The ADs, ordnance and fuel now expended, were being ignored by the ground troops. The Blueberries flew by him on their way out of the valley, wagged good-bye, and turned south toward the ship. Departure of the air cover meant that the enemy grunts were free to come out of hiding to find him. He looked over his shoulder. There must be fifty grunts coming this way. Damn! Soldier's voices were becoming audible now that the aircraft were gone. At some point, I'm going to have to hide. Already exhausted, outrunning them was out of the question. There was a dense area of brush and pine trees about twenty yards ahead; he headed for it. Trying to keep from leaving a trail they could follow, he carefully moved into the dense brush, crawled deep into a thicket and froze. His heart was pounding as though it wanted to be free of his chest. Burning, heaving lungs begged for cool air. Nausea was building. Closing his eyes didn't make the dancing spots of light go away. He recalled the advice he got from a crusty old

Commander he met in the Pacific: "When all you have is chicken shit, think of some way to turn it into chicken salad." I have to come up with something or these bastards are going to have another scalp on their belt. I can't let 'em find me. Geez, what's it feel like to take one between the eyes. Just yesterday, Hal read a situation report from General Walker that included information about a common grave that was found filled with U.S. and ROK soldiers with bullet holes in their heads. It was not the first incident that showed the enemy's disdain for taking prisoners. Enemy voices became progressively louder until it was obvious that they were very close. Several soldiers passed within 50 feet, searching in the direction of the river. He restrained the biological demands for heavy breathing to remain quiet. Dizziness and nausea harassed his senses. God, I can't puke now, there's no way to do that quietly.

Lying quietly for a half–hour kept him from being detected and rejuvenated his body. Even so, a racing mind kept the hysteria level high. A near continuous procession of soldiers on the hunt precluded any movement. He swiped sweat from his forehead and eyes. Sooner or later, one of those commie bastards is going to decide to come over this way and find me. Sounds of an approaching jeep aroused his curiosity. It stopped at the edge of the tree line. Someone in the jeep was hollering. Soldiers were leaving the bushes and appeared to be gathering around the jeep. Hal could hear discussion among the men mixed in with the roughly idling jeep engine. The unmistakable sound of Panthers in the distance became music to his ears. The jeep hastily departed to the west. Soldiers were running wildly into the bushes. Geez, they're heading my way—this is it. I have to get the attention of the Panthers so they'll keep the grunts away from me. As the F–9s came screaming around the valley entrance, he cautiously stuck his mirror up just far enough out of the cover to signal to them. None of the Panthers seemed to acknowledge his signaling, but they immediately spotted the enemy. Aircraft cannon fire and rocket explosions put a smile on his face. Soldiers scampered through the brush east and west of him. Beautiful, now I'm sandwiched. Can't stay here! Hell, if I'm running through the brush while they're running and confused, they probably won't know the sound is not from one of them. He moved with caution into shoulder-high brush and started running head-down toward the river. He took his pearl handled stainless steel .357 Smith & Wesson out of its shoulder holster. When dad gave me this thing for Christmas, I was disappointed: too extravagant; too big; too heavy. But, oh baby, if I have to use this mother today, I'll be damn glad I don't have that piss ant .32 caliber standard issue. Brush progressively became thinner and more intermittent. Coming out of a clump he found himself headed straight for two soldiers hunkered down, not thirty feet away. Their faces showed utter shock. Hal's senses went into slow motion. He fired at them as he sprinted. They rolled away from him in fright. He fired three rounds and dashed past them. This is probably it. I think I hit one of them. Will they knock me off or take me prisoner? No! I can't let that happen. A loud bang accompanied a blow to the left side of his head. Uh oh, they've come to their senses—I'm still alive. Keep running! Increase the range—keep your head down. Still experiencing the phenomenon of slow motion, he heard another bang, then another. Something slammed into his stomach and knocked him down. Turning his body toward the shooter evoked sharp pains in his left side; the soldier was a mere fifteen feet away, frantically fiddling with his rifle. Two rounds Kirby—make 'em count. Maybe that'll give me time to reload before another guy comes over. Nobody else seems to be moving—the F9s have them lying low. This is pure chicken shit. Hal blanked out the pain and reached around with his left hand to steady his aim. The soldier saw Hal's gun come up and rushed him with the rifle butt cocked back in both hands for a skull crushing downward thrust. Hal fired two rounds in rapid succession; the first struck just above the rim of soldier's helmet, snapping his head back and knocked off his helmet. The second round entered under the soldier's raised chin and threw him to the ground like a bag of rice. A series of powerful stomach contractions caused Hal to vomit. He wanted to sit, but was so drained of energy that he couldn't even roll off his stomach. Even baking in the hellish sun felt good. Aimless daydreaming consumed him.

As his senses returned, he looked at the motionless soldier. Geez, did that ever drop him—hollow-point bullets may not be in accord with the Geneva Convention, but I've got no complaints. I must've bagged the other bastard too. There was a large ragged hole in the top of the soldier's head that gushed blood mixed with gray matter. Looks like spaghetti sauce with mushrooms. Ugh. Some strength returned and he succeeded in rolling over on his back. He ejected the spent rounds from his revolver and refilled the chambers with the extra rounds he carried in a patch pocket. Sitting up was terribly painful but there was an inner voice yelling at him to get up. His fingers explored the side of his head. Blood was seeping out of a small wound and was running down his neck, soaking his skivvy shirt. He could feel it was a scalp wound about a quarter–inch deep by two inches long that penetrated to the skull but glanced off the bone. Something didn't feel right—the top third of his ear was gone. His fingers found a piece was dangling behind the remaining portion of his ear, hanging by a small strand of skin. A quick jerk pulled it off. He looked at it for a moment then angrily tossed it into the sand. His left side was burning intensely; he finally worked up the courage to look at it carefully. There was a large bloodstain on the left lower side of his flight suit and a large circle of clotting blood on the sand. A bullet hole in the flight suit stared back at him. Unzipping the flight suit revealed a jagged exit wound on his lower left side below the last rib.

The bastard shot me in the back! This ain't good, Kirby. The wound was oozing at a good rate and demanded attention. I've lost too much already. I must get this stopped. He pulled a handkerchief from his pocket and applied pressure on the wound with his left hand. I just have to get up, no matter what, or I'll never make any chicken salad. "God, please give me the strength and wisdom to get out of this. I'm not ready to die," he whispered.

Panthers were still working on the ground troops with their rockets and guns, so he decided to try and continue moving toward the river. Running, even trotting, was out of the question. Pain on his left side had progressed from a burn to an intense ache throughout his trunk, accompanied by erratic cramping. Just standing and keeping balance was a task. He trudged along in a slow, awkward gait. Attempting to remain undetected, he stayed close to the lower slope of the mountain where most of the bushes and trees were at least as tall as he was.

Six Panthers were approaching, running along the northern edge of the brush line, five hundred feet off the deck. He began signaling to them with his mirror. They wagged as they passed. Damn, their cannon ammo and fuel is depleted and they are returning to the ship. With the jets gone, it became terribly quiet again. He stood still and listened. There was no sound or sight of the enemy. Hal continued his slow trek toward the river. A familiar drone became audible. Corsairs! We had no Corsair missions up here this morning! Panthers either for that matter. Geez, there are no flyable planes left on the ship at this hour. Admiral Hawkins, God bless him, is robbing the missions. Four Corsairs rounded the valley corner and headed westward. He signaled to them with his mirror. There was no reaction. Anger came over him from desperation. It will be fatal if they lose track of me and can't tell the angel where I'm at. When the Corsairs were about three miles past him, they started strafing. The enemy retreated to the other end of the valley. He felt exhausted and fought hard against the temptation to rest. There was only about a mile to go to the river area, but he knew he couldn't make it that far. I need to head away from the brush line, into open terrain where they can see me if I lose consciousness. Two of the Corsairs were flying toward him low and slow, obviously searching. He could see the sun glints from his mirror on their blue airframes as they got near. A canopy slid back and a hand waved at him. They throttled back and circled. Hal felt safe now. It was the kind of feeling you got when you were a kid and your mother came into your room and tucked you in after a bad dream. I'll just keep walking slowly toward the river. Chopper probably ain't too far behind these guys. He was sweating profusely and was losing his breath. Exposed to the rising sun, he felt as though he was in an oven. Gripping his wrist to check his pulse, he found a beat so rapid that it alarmed him. Ringing in his ears became louder. Shock is setting in—maybe I should kneel down. No, then I'll want to lie down. If I lie down, I'll die.

His fear was intense. The muscles in his left arm were beginning to cramp from holding the makeshift compress on his wound. He put his pistol into his shoulder holster and relieved his left hand. His legs were beginning to feel like logs and screamed for mercy. Soaking wet from perspiration and blood, his flight suit felt like it weighed a hundred pounds. Pain was now extreme through his entire upper body. He was losing peripheral vision and more nausea caused him profound concern. Damn, I've got to kneel or I'm going to lose it. When they see me do that, they'll know I'm in trouble. Before he could do it consciously, his legs gave out involuntarily and he dropped to his knees. "Please God, not now. Not here. Not like this. Fight it off Kirby." Dizziness set in, his vision slowly faded. There was only gray now and total silence. He felt his fingers digging into sand.

Unintelligible voices began to fade in and out. They were very distant and sounded hollow, as though they were at the far end of a tunnel. It was dark and he could not feel or see anything. One voice was becoming nearly understandable, but was still a long way off. Hal tried to make sense out of a mysterious cloudy scene fading into view. He was looking down from a hundred feet or so, maybe from a helicopter, he wasn't sure. This was confusing. There was a pilot lying on the ground being worked on by two hospital corpsmen. As he seemed to drift closer to the scene, the voices became more audible. He tried to blink but couldn't feel his eyelids. He tried to talk—but couldn't. He had no feeling in his arms and legs.

"Hang on sir, if you can hear me, squeeze your right hand?"

"God damn it, hang on!" said a corpsman as he inserted an airway tube into the pilot's mouth.

"Pulse is weak and tachy," the other said.

"OK, let's get him on the litter and get the hell out of here."

Hal watched them lift the pilot onto the metal basket-like stretcher and load him into the chopper. The scene faded to solid gray as the chopper lifted from the ground. He could still hear the voices.

"Get the Ringer's lactate going stat. We've got trouble here—gunshot trauma, blood loss, shock, maybe sunstroke. I'll cut this poopy suit away from the wound."

"OK. Turn on the O2."

"Anterior entry wound, this is the exit here. No sucking. Looks close enough to the side to miss organs. Let's get some sulfa and occlusive dressings on these."

"Except for the scalp graze, I don't see any other wounds."

"Good. Don't go sour on me dammit, hang on!"

Hal felt a cool wet towel on his forehead. Then he felt the sensation of water being poured all over his body. Geez, this is no time to dream. Damn, what is happening? Oh my God, is this what it feels like to die? Is that what's happening?

Noise woke him—a helicopter engine. Even with his eyes open, everything was gray. Two men were hollering above the noise.

"Vitals coming up."

"Captain Kirby, can you hear me? Captain Kirby, can you hear me? Squeeze my hand if you hear me."

Geez, it's me they're working on. No, can't be, the guy was down below. This whole thing better be a bad dream.

"Captain Kirby, can you hear me?"

Hal managed to grunt, sort of. His whole body tingled. He opened his eyes and saw two corpsmen hovering over him.

"Terrific! You're doing fine Captain, we're on the way back to the Happy Valley, just relax."

Unable to muster the strength to raise a thumb, Hal attempted a smile. A corpsman gently patted his shoulder. "Close call on the side of the head Captain," he remarked as he cleaned the wound and the ear tip with cotton balls soaked with hydrogen peroxide. Hal could hear the bubbling of the peroxide that trickled into his ear canal; he could smell its distinctive odor.

"Doc will have you back in the air tomorrow, don't worry," the other corpsman yelled. "We dressed the gut wound while you were taking a nap. Don't look like there's any organ penetration. You're a lucky man."

Hal smiled. Lucky! He thinks I'm lucky. Things are damn sure relative.

CHAPTER 7

Aboard USS Valley Forge

The Valley Forge and her surrounding ships were contrasted against a glistening blue sea. Foamy white streaks trailed behind each of the ships in the Task Force. Hal flew the approach to and landing on the Valley Forge – grudgingly – from the back seat of the carrier's onboard delivery aircraft, affectionately known as the COD. Getting out of the Navy Hospital in Sasebo and getting back aboard the Valley Forge was worth the humility of a back-seat ride, however. Hal's gut ached, but he ignored that; he was beginning to feel tired, but he ignored that too. When the engine coughed to a stop Hal climbed down onto the flight deck. That hurt, but he didn't let it show.

Ted trotted out to the COD's parking spot and saluted Hal, "Welcome back CAG." They exchanged a spirited handshake. "Did you get your battery charged in Sasebo boss?"

Hal laughed, "Hell no – that would've torn my stitches. I damn sure didn't want to do anything to delay my departure. I think they would like to have kept me a while longer, but they were happy just to get rid of me." They walked toward the island.

"No special back or groin rubs or anything?" Ted asked with a chuckle.

"Oh, I did enjoy those back rubs. But man, let me tell you, I haven't changed my opinion of hospitals. They are no place for either patients or visitors. Geez Ted, that was like being incarcerated. I spent a lot of time trying to cheer up ground pounders that got banged up in Korea. They're sending the wounded everywhere there's beds for them. I haven't had that much spare time since God knows when. Played more poker than I've played in years."

"Did you win?"

"Damn tootin' Ted! They were Army guys, remember?" They laughed.

"CAG, you're just in time for the matinee. As a baseball fan, you'll love it. The flick is last month's all-star game. I'll take the National League, even. Want a piece of the action?"

"You're a jackass Ted."

"Glad you're back CAG, the Admiral wouldn't let me fly the whole time you were gone."

"So that's why you're glad," he slammed Ted's shoulder, "You're a sorry son of a bitch. Say, did the old man relieve Garr of duty yet?"

"No CAG, we can talk about that later," said Ted.

Hal shrugged his shoulders in frustration, "Look, I'm going to pass on the matinee. I'm going to my room for an hour, then I'll go topside to the office." They navigated through the island hatch.

"How about going to the wardroom first for a cup of coffee so I can bring you up to speed? I'm buying."

"No, thanks, it'll wait. Have Slater get my bag out of the COD."

"Dammit Hal, the reason no one else is out here is the guys put together a little welcoming party. My mission is to bring you to the wardroom, so don't give me any more damn trouble."

Hal laughed, "OK, OK, but I've got to see a man about a horse first."

When Kirby stepped into the wardroom, he stopped short to behold a strange scene. There was toilet paper draped around the room light fixtures, pipes and conduits. Admiral Hawkins was sitting by himself at a table in one end of the room. It seemed like there was three times as many people in the room than chairs. A bluish cloud of pungent smoke from cigars and cigarettes hovered over the crowd. The din of catcalls and mischief was deafening. Someone blew a boatswain's pipe, obviously without prior practice or aptitude. Silence settled over the mischievous throng.

Admiral Hawkins pounded a claw hammer on a hardwood block and grumbled, "Bailiff, bring the accused forward."

"Y'all should be flying!" Hal yelled. Ted took Hal by the arm and brought him front and center to the Admiral. Hal played along and came to attention.

The Admiral maintained his standard poker face, "Captain Kirby, you committed crimes against the Navy and must be tried. Wipe that smile off your face. You won't be so damn happy when we're through with you. Let me make the rules of this court clear. You have no rights. You may speak only when ordered to do so. You may not seek a defense attorney and you cannot make any calls. Prosecutor, come forward and read the first charge."

Lieutenant Commander "Bridge" Danley came to the end of the Admiral's table, "Your honor, specification one, that Captain Kirby did, on or about 26 July, leave his wingman during combat."

"All those who believe Captain Kirby is guilty say aye," hollered the Admiral. There was an earsplitting response.

"Recorder, let the transcript show him guilty by acclamation. Next charge."

Danley regained control over his laughter and resumed, "Charge two, that on or about 26 July, Captain Kirby did execute an unauthorized landing."

"Guilty," bellowed the Admiral and another outbreak of slurs and laughter delayed the proceedings.

Hal hollered, "Objection!"

"Overruled! Next charge, prosecutor," growled the Admiral.

"Charge three, that Captain Kirby, on or about 26 July, did willfully destroy a VA–55 Able Dog and other related government property and delivered that property, cost free, to the enemy!"

"Very serious indeed," said Hawkins, "have you brought back any pieces or parts of the aircraft whatsoever?"

"No sir," Hal replied, grinning.

"Surely, you didn't lose your helmet? How about the piece from your ear?"

"Sorry sir, lost 'em both."

"Grossly negligent. Guilty as charged." The room filled with vulgarity and boos. And so it went. Several more charges were levied and adjudicated. Hal was getting tired of standing and laughing was increasingly painful. But he wasn't going to give any hint of that.

Admiral Hawkins rose. "It is time for your sentencing, Captain Kirby. All rise."

"Hang the guilty bastard," a voice called out. Everyone broke into rowdy laughter.

"Silence in the court room," the Admiral admonished. "Captain Kirby, with the authority vested in me, I sentence you to the maximum possible punishment—continuation in the position of Carrier Air Group Commander."

The crowd's hue and cry contained a vast assortment of crude and profane comments. A shrill and ridiculously blown boatswain's pipe brought decorum back to the room.

"Attention on deck," yelled the Admiral's aide.

Admiral Hawkins got up, walked around the table to Hal and pinned a Purple Heart on Hal's breast pocket flap. They exchanged a strong handshake.

Later that evening, Hal searched through a box of 78–rpm record albums and pulled out one of his favorites—Best of Glenn Miller. This album contained recordings of selected Glenn Miller concerts in Europe. Hal carefully placed the needle on the outer edge of the platter; the needle settled into the groove that spiraled from the edge into the first cut. The record opened with applause from an enthusiastic crowd of GIs. A master of ceremonies with a deep radio voice followed the warm welcome of the audience with an announcement, "It's medley time; saluting the mothers, wives, sweethearts and sisters of the boys in the A–A–F. Something old, something new, something borrowed, something blue. Now, the old song, 'Long, Long, Ago'."

He sat on the edge of his bunk, took off his shoes and stretched out with a doubled pillow under his head. The music transported him backward in time to the 40s. In many ways, it seemed that it was just yesterday, but it also seemed like ages had passed. Amid all that war's anguish, ferocity and carnage, Glenn Miller's music served to remind him then that there were nooks in the world where one could find softness, gentility and normality. Nearly ten years later, Glenn's music had the same effect. His bunk felt incredibly good. His mind wandered aimlessly while the music soaked into his senses.

There was a pause between cuts and then the MC's smooth deep timbre introduced the next song in the medley, "Something new—Johnny Desmond sings, 'The Music Stops'."

Hal reread a letter from Alice. It arrived today, via the hospital in Sasebo. She was responding to his first letter telling of his episode with the North Koreans at the Naktong River. I don't understand what's happening to Alice. She's become paranoid. She can't take stress any more. I'm a Captain now and should leave the flying to the young kids. I should request a transfer back to the Pentagon before I kill myself. She and the kids need me. Geez! She's being so selfish. No honey, you're wrong. The grunts on the front, Operation Chromite, they need me too. She just has no confidence in me anymore. No appreciation. I better not answer this letter until I've cooled down. Dammit, she knows what it takes to succeed as a Naval Aviator. It sure as hell ain't counting beans or making pipe dreams in the Pentagon!

The band's announcer sounded off again, dampening Hal's mental tirade, "We borrow Lieutenant Larry Clinton's theme, 'Dipsey Doodle'." He forced his mind to drop his ever-deepening feud with Alice. As he stared at the overhead, concentrating on the music, his feet swaying side to side with the music, he thought about how good it felt to be back aboard the Valley Forge. He looked down into the gaping 'care package' he received from Alice. A paperback novel was hiding under a box of salt water taffy; he pulled it out, "Point of No Return." There was a folded piece of fragrant lavender notepaper tucked into it. He opened the note:

"Hal, I know you'll like this. Come home soon. Love, Alice."

"Now something blue – 'Wabash Blues'," crooned the MC. Hal's feet picked up the rhythm of the beat; the rack springs squeaked in cadence. He smiled from the unexpected flashback the spring noises created. Visions of Lucy mingled through his thoughts. She was an old flame from school— emphasis on flame. They were 'steadies' from seventh grade until he went to the Naval Academy. He often thought of her. Something normally insignificant could cue those memories, like the springs. Hal covered his eyes with his hand while he daydreamed. We didn't wake her little brother anymore after I oiled her bedsprings. He laughed aloud. Lucy, Lucy. Where are you today? Best girl next door a boy ever had. Geez, flushing all those damn rubbers down her toilet was sure stupid. One clog and her dad would have drawn and quartered me. We didn't just lose our virginity to each other—we lost our minds too. Geez, half the kids in seventh grade hadn't even been kissed yet and here we were, like rabbits. Like Siamese twins all those years; never fought, never tired of each other. No wonder the specter of four years of Annapolis and sea duty separation was too much for her. I could have survived it just by knowing what was in store when I returned. God, she broke my heart. We were so daring, too. Like reading about the rhythm method. Boy, were we excited the first time we tried that. That was the night we made love in the rocking chair on my front porch, while Mom and Dad were reading the papers and listening to the radio just inside. Ah, those camping trips to the mountain lake with her parents in the summers. We did it in the lake, on the lake—it's a wonder the canoe didn't roll over. Geez, why she didn't get knocked up is a miracle. I've never known anything like her. Man oh man, did I miss her at Annapolis. I wonder what would happen if we ran into each other tomorrow.

"Here is Captain Glenn Miller," the MC declared, shattering the sweet memories. Hal's ears perked up to hear Glenn's voice every time he played this record. I wonder what great music he would have written. Damn shame we lost him.

"Thank you, Lieutenant Donald Briggs, and hello everybody," Miller greeted his audience, "First off in the music department, an old favorite we thought you might like – 'In the Mood'." Hal opened 'Point of No Return' and read the first page. He set the alarm clock for 0430 in case he dozed off. He was several pages into the first chapter when the telephone rang and startled him. He raised the heavy gray hand set to his ear, "Captain Kirby."

The gravel-voice was unmistakable, "How are you feeling? Can you come up to my cabin for dessert and coffee, I have a few things I want to chat about."

"I'm doing fine sir. I'll be right up." I wonder what's on the old man's mind? He returned the needle arm of the phonograph back onto its pedestal and dressed quickly. Hal dialed the Flag Admin Office and looked at his watch. The line was busy.

Lieutenant Junior Grade Ripley Lewis, the Admiral's aide, was still on the phone when Hal got to the Flag Admin Office. Lewis jumped to his feet, "Can I help you sir?"

"Rip, the old man just called me to an impromptu private meeting—got any idea what the subject might be?"

"No sir, nothing unusual is happening! The Commander's selection list and a personal message from Admiral Joy came in; I took them to him about an hour ago."

"Thanks Lewis, I think you hit the nail on the head." He hurried to the Admiral's cabin. If that jackass Garr managed to get selected for Commander, I'm going to vomit. He's already been passed over once though. Can't be any chance, even with the war. Geez, maybe this manpower buildup opened the system.

"Good evening, Admiral!" Hal picked up the scent of apple pie the moment he cracked the hatch of Hawkins' sea cabin. "That smells terrific," he said, watching the Steward cut the pie into four quarters.

Hawkins motioned for Hal to sit in the chair across from him. The Steward served their coffee and pie then excused himself.

"No cheese?" asked Hal.

"Being grounded doesn't give you license to be insulting or demanding. Anyway, by the time Doc thinks you'll be ready for full duty, you'll be gone."

That tidbit caught Hal mid-swallow of his first sip of coffee—he coughed on it. "Excuse me—down the wrong pipe. What do you mean sir?"

Expressionless, the Admiral cut the tip from his quarter pie with the side of his fork, slid the tines under the crust and delivered the morsel to his mouth ceremoniously, purposefully prolonging Hal's agony. "We have some business to discuss Hal, two items in fact. I received a personal message from Admiral Joy a little while ago. They've nailed down the date for the big powwow in Tokyo—the twenty–third."

"When does he want me there?"

"ASAP. I already sent Turner a reply that we had a COD departing at 0600 tomorrow which will drop you off at Haneda."

"This is going to be one hell of a meeting," said Hal, "According to a Marine pal on staff over there, the big guns from DC are coming in with every intent of scuttling General MacArthur's plans for landing at Inchon."

Hawkins nodded affirmatively, "Admiral Struble invited me to a supper meeting with Admiral Joy on the flagship when we were in port last time— while you were in Tokyo. He gave me a good briefing on the political undertow and we discussed the problems with Inchon." He put another piece of pie in his mouth. Hal did the same.

Hal shook his head, "It's become an even hotter bed of coals than it was when I left Tokyo. The more stubborn MacArthur is to suggestions from Washington and CINCPAC to dump the Inchon option, the larger and more tangled the web of opposition becomes."

"And more dangerous," added the Admiral, "Look, I'm not going to belabor this. I should keep my mouth shut. But I think I should warn you that I think your ass is hanging out—you could be expendable. Watch your six. You're between a rock and a hard place. Those heavy hitting major leaguers will eat your butt for breakfast if they get the chance. I see the look on your face. Why? Because effective air support makes this landing feasible, therefore the air plan—your air plan---could make it very difficult for them to pronounce the operation unsound."

Hal shook his head, "But the people at this meeting will all be Flag and General officers. If there are any civilians, there won't be more than one or two. Surely flag officers wouldn't jeopardize a well-planned, critically required operation for some nonmilitary agenda. Especially when there is no reasonable option."

Admiral Hawkins studied Hal while he carefully picked his words. He took a deep breath, "Hal, there are civilians in our government whose passion for bouncing MacArthur is damn near greater than for saving South Korea. There are Admirals and generals who don't give a rat's ass about Korean real estate. And then there are those who wouldn't buck their bosses over Inchon, no matter what their personal opinion or better judgement might be."

Hal took a deep breath, "It's hard for me to relate to such thinking Admiral, but I know it's probably out there."

The Admiral nodded agreement, "But presidential appointees hold powerful positions. That makes them power brokers, which in turn, gives rise to alliances with military leaders and vice versa. One of those distinguished military men could turn out to be a torpedo with your name on it. Enough said!"

"I appreciate your concern Admiral, and your frankness. I'll handle it. Geez, here on the ship it's me against Garr; in Japan, it's me against my senior chain of command. I had no idea this job would be so much fun."

Hawkins produced a rare smile that wiped itself off as quickly as it had appeared. "That brings up the second subject—Garr. The Commander selection list is in—he's not on it. That's his second pass over so he'll get the boot."

"Can't say I'm sorry to hear it."

The Admiral continued, "Rip checked for me, he doesn't qualify for continuation to retirement under normal policy. BUPERS will probably let him stay on active duty until the war is over though, because of the freeze on retirements and resignations."

"That's both good and bad news Admiral. Bad because he'll be more bitter than ever. I'm going to watch him like a hawk."

"Keep it professional," Hawkins warned.

Hal nodded, "Aye, aye sir. I can't help thinking that at this point, he'll be after the both of us. You will be in this now because you represent the Navy to him. Does he know about getting passed over yet?"

"No. I told Captain Rice not to release the information to the ship until 0700 tomorrow, after the morning meeting; I'll tell Garr immediately after the meeting. You'll be off the ship by then."

"Admiral, you don't know how much I'd like to be the one to tell that bilge rat the news."

Residence of Will Crandall
Falls Church, VA

Bradbury boomed into the den and apologized for his late arrival and traded pleasantries with Will and Tim. He opened the wooden cigar box on the side table, grabbed one of the Cuban masterpieces and sank into a leather stuffed chair. "I think we've got the last of the pieces of this puzzle put together. Yesterday I met with Chadbrook and I just came from a meeting with Kingston." He lit the cigar and took a long appreciative drag, "The bottom line is this, Friday is your last day at the Pentagon, Tim. You will have orders to report to CIA the following Monday. The CIA military personnel office will immediately process your retirement from active duty. You will then be hired as a civilian employee and will be appointed as the CIA Project Officer for Project AQUAMARINE."

"Terrific," said Tim. "How about Bennett?"

Bradbury shook his head, "Oh, this couldn't have come at a better time. Logan somehow managed to get his ass in a jam with General Stratemeyer, so getting him released was easy. He will leave Japan in two or three weeks with orders to the Joint Chiefs of Staff and will fill your vacant spot as the JCS Liaison Officer for Project AQUAMARINE."

Will made a circle with his thumbs and forefingers, "Fantastic HL, that closes the loop between JCS and CIA. Now we've got total control." Bradbury had a possum-eating grin plastered on his face.

CHAPTER 8

Dai–ichi Building, Tokyo

"Here comes a military motorcade, clearing the street," said the driver, looking in his rear-view mirror. Hal turned around and saw motorcycle MPs leading a large black sedan. As the motorcycles neared, they motioned to Hal's driver to pull over.

"Five stars—General MacArthur. He's getting a late start today," said the driver as the motorcade passed.

"Don't kid yourself, he's right on schedule," Hal said, checking his watch.

General MacArthur's black '41 Cadillac, sporting five–star fender flags and a license plate of "1" was led and followed by motorcycle MPs with shiny white helmets. An olive drab Army sedan packed with armed soldiers trailed the Cadillac.

Hal continued, "The General's up with the roosters every mornin'. He works at home 'til ten or eleven every day, then comes to the headquarters—seven days a week."

"I'll be damned," said the driver. "I don't get up here often, it's the first time I've seen this. Look at all those Japanese people down there by HQ."

"They're out there four times a day; they know his schedule. They just want to see him." The driver shrugged his shoulders, puzzled.

"To them, he's not a General, or even the General. More like a national hero, I think."

An MP stood rigid curbside, waiting for the General's car to come to a halt. The moment the door handle came within reach, he opened the rear door and came to attention with a crisp salute. General MacArthur's tall frame climbed out wearing his usual open collar khaki's and floppy hat. A folded newspaper was clutched under his left arm. He was also carrying a brown leather attaché pouch with his left hand. As if by command, the several hundred Japanese well-wishers of all ages began a series of deep bows. Every square foot of space that was not cordoned off—a considerable area—was packed. Ropes provided a narrow path to the building entrance, putting the onlookers just out of reach. The General waved his hat to the crowd, looking from side to side as he walked to the building, recognizing their bows. When he passed through the doors, the crowd quietly dispersed.

When the General's car and escorts pulled away, Hal's driver moved up to the front of the building and opened the door for Hal. MPs were already removing the ropes. "I'll put your bags inside the doorway Colonel."

Hal grimaced. Damn, you'd think the Army would teach its drivers the uniforms and rank insignia of the other services. Three different drivers—all called me Colonel. I've been called worse I guess.

Marmette looked up with a surprised face when Hal opened the door to Admiral Joy's outer office. She jumped up, beaming. Before she could get out a word, her eyes locked onto what remained of his left ear and her smile shattered. She quickly recovered, turned on her natural Southern charm and gave him a platonic hug. The wonderful scent of her French perfume welcomed him. She grabbed his arm and hustled him into Admiral Joy's office. "Admiral, look what they scraped off the Naktong river bank."

"You had us worried for a while," said Admiral Joy. "General MacArthur was as anxious as the rest of us. He asked me to convey his best wishes. Please have a seat."

Hal watched Marmette walk to the door as Admiral Joy fussed with something on his desk. Marmette turned as she was closing the door and said, "By the way Captain, I couldn't get you a room in this building, too many flag rank officers coming in. You're over with us in the Imperial Hotel. Are your bags at the front door?"

"That's a rajah dajah!"

"I'll get them delivered to the hotel for you," she said and closed the door.

"Did you hear about Admiral Struble's orders before you left the ship?" asked Joy.

"No sir."

"It was announced early this morning that, effective tomorrow, he's in command of Joint Task Force Seven, with overall responsibility for Operation Chromite. Admiral Ewen will succeed him as Commander, Seventh Fleet."

Hal gave that a moment to sink in, "As I recall, he's not too thrilled with the Inchon option and I know he's not an easy man to sway."

"100% correct. I know firsthand that he was impressed with the draft air support plan though and it seemed to dampen his objections to going into Inchon. Don't worry about him. General MacArthur will bring him around. They go back a long time. They worked closely during WW II and are very good friends."

Joy's steward brought in a coffee service with a plate of cookies, poured two cups and departed. While Hal sampled shortbread cookies, Joy went to his desk. He returned with a large manila envelope marked 'TOP SECRET ADMIRAL JOY EYES ONLY' and handed it to Hal.

Hal pulled out a stack of 8"x10" Air Force recon photos of Wolmi-do Island, which lies adjacent to the port of Inchon. "Hot damn!" exclaimed Hal, recognizing the island.

Admiral Joy pointed at features on the top photo, "Look at this Hal. There was no previous hint about some of this stuff. We knew about the tanks and these large sandbag bunkers," he said running his finger around the map, "but look at all these holes. They scare the hell out of me because the intell guys think they are probably for artillery and mortar batteries. Their sheer numbers would mean punishment for our ships when they steam up Flying Fish Channel to Inchon. "

Hal studied the photos, "Yeah, well, they don't bother me. Our Marine pilots will convert anything in those positions to carbon with napalm. Sir, I need to study these photos thoroughly."

Joy nodded, "I'll tell Marmette that you are authorized to see them whenever you wish. They must stay in this office, however. You can work on them in here when I'm not here, or Marmette can scrounge up some desk space out there."

"Aye, aye sir, thank you."

"Let me know when you think you will have the Chromite air section smoothed up and ready for presentation to our staff. Then I'll set up the dry run with all the HQ players."

"I can tell you that now. You can arrange for the briefing on Thursday morning sir, I'll have it finished and coordinated by then."

Later that afternoon, Marmette heard the hallway door open; LouAnn stepped in and whispered to Marmette, "Dusty and Hal just got back; I saw them racing each other up the staircase. Find out what they'd like to do tonight. I have a meeting with General Willoughby. See you in twenty minutes."

Marmette stopped at the pit on the way to the powder room. Dusty was just about to dial his telephone. "Hi Dusty, I heard you just got back. Where's Hal, did he leave already?"

"Nope, he'll be back; he's giving his lizard a drink."

"You guys are tooooo much," she said, chuckling from the impact of Dusty's line.

"To what do we owe the pleasure of your company young lady? And how many times do I have to tell you about coming in here with that perfume?" asked Dusty when she walked to his desk.

"I came to suggest a sukiyaki dinner at my place tonight, uh, sorry, that's supper in Navy and Marine talk."

"Great! You and LouAnn take care of the food, I'll bring the booze and drag Hal."

Hal and Dusty knocked on the door to Marmette's quarters, hands full with bags of wine and other goodies. LouAnn opened the door and gave Hal a big welcome hug. Marmette peeked around the corner of the little galley, waved a wooden spoon and gave Hal a warm smile.

"We could smell this stuff down the hall. I'm ravenous," said Hal.

"I'm so hungry I could eat the ass out of a teddy bear," Dusty advised in typical infantry form.

"Just fifteen more minutes or so—hold your horses," Marmette hollered from the kitchen.

The delicious smell of vegetables, beef, noodles and bean curd simmering in a soy and sake sauce filled the suite.

"This place looks great Marmette," said Hal, looking around for the first time. LouAnn gave Hal the nickel tour. He could, of course, see the kitchen from the living room, leaving only the head and bedroom unaccounted for. The little apartment was furnished completely and exquisitely in Japanese decor, mostly black lacquered woods. When he looked into the bedroom, he imagined how sore he'd be if he slept all night on a futon.

Finally, after suffering great harassment from the men, the ladies served supper. The four musketeers sat on large pillows around an ornately carved low table of dark hardwood. Marmette dished out sukiyaki from a large skillet atop a monkey pod trivet. Hal still had not mastered chopsticks, but he wouldn't starve. Dusty kept everyone's hot sake cup full. The ladies had gone to special efforts, in food and dress. They wore long blue and white Japanese cotton robes; each had a unique print.

"You gals look great in those dresses," said Hal.

LouAnn replied, "We haven't gotten you fully indoctrinated yet Hal. These are called yukata—informal kimono."

Hal's mind wandered. How bizarre this is. A few weeks ago, I was lying in that God forsaken valley. Now here I am, back in this other world.

"Hello, hello," said Marmette, waving her hand in front of Hal's face. "Where were you, sailor? Mind your helm, you drifted off course."

"Just day dreaming. Say, you're getting really good with salty talk there mate."

"Hal, want to put some money on the fight? I'm taking Ezzard Charles," said Dusty.

"I wouldn't bet against Ezzard. I think he'll have Fred Beshore on the mat in less than ten rounds."

"Who'd you pick last week?" asked Dusty.

"Sugar Ray, of course," Hal said.

LouAnn interrupted, "Don't forget the rules: no cigars, no sports and no shop talk!"

They dined and chatted with an album of Strauss waltzes for background. Marmette sat across the table from Hal. It seemed that every time he looked up at her, she already had her eyes fixed on him. When their eyes met, they tended to linger. They were involuntarily picking up where they left off the last trip, playing little private flirt games when Dusty and LouAnn weren't looking.

After clearing the table, the ladies served coffee. Hal stretched out on the floor and rested his head on a pillow. "My legs went asleep from sitting cross-legged so long," he said. His left side, still early into the healing process, was stiff and sore.

"You'll get used to it," said Dusty.

Hal waved his finger, "I won't be here long enough for that. This land of milk and honey would spoil me."

"Hal, tell us about the Naktong," said LouAnn.

Hal looked at her with surprise, "You can't be serious. Isn't one of the rules that we can't talk shop?"

Dusty gave LouAnn a stern look, "Gals, he doesn't want to talk about it—it's been a real pleasant evening so far."

"But, we only know what was in the message summaries," said Marmette. "LouAnn and I were talking about this yesterday; Hal's our link to the real war, Dusty. We have no idea what it's like, sitting here in Tokyo with the bureaucrats. I'm curious. I want to know what it was really like. Do you mind Hal?" asked Marmette with liquid New Orleans charm.

"That was a masterful job of priming the pump," said Hal. They all chuckled. "You brought up an interesting point. When I was flying back to the Valley Forge from my last TAD here—it seems like yesterday—I thought about the eerie double life I was living. They're so dissimilar. It hit me again this evening. There's the real world, at least for me, on the Valley Forge and there's the Land of Oz here in Tokyo. I can appreciate what you are saying, Marmette. So, for you folks in Oz, here goes. I think I can cure you with just this one story."

Hal stared aimlessly at the light fixture on the ceiling while he spoke, reliving the events of his last mission. He began with his first sighting of the tracks on the valley floor and concluded with the ride back to the ship in the rescue chopper. The ladies listened intently, like little kids glued to their radios, listening to 'Big John and Sparky' on Saturday morning. They asked several questions. Dusty remained quiet, having had a big dose of reality in the South Pacific during WW II; he had earned two purple hearts and several personal decorations for bravery in action. Hal came to the end of his episode, "So, there you have it." He looked away from the ceiling for the first time since he started his tale. Marmette and LouAnn were wiping the corners of their eyes. "Hey, cut that out! Let's not put a damper on the evening," said Hal.

Marmette shook her head slowly, "What a powerful storyteller—so graphic. That's more reality than I bargained for. I didn't realize that you had been so close to, well—"

"I didn't either," said Dusty.

"Oh, come on, I probably over-dramatized it. Wasn't as bad as it sounded."

"Welcome back to the land of Oz," said LouAnn. "New rule, no war stories!"

Somewhere during their intellectual discussion of the pros and cons of granting U.S. citizenship to the Guamanians and the stateside developments of the day, the sandman visited Hal. He'd been up since 0430 and his tired healing body decided that it was time to shut down. When he awoke, the living room was empty. He could hear Marmette humming along with the sound track of 'South Pacific' while she was washing the supper dishes. He looked at his watch—2350. "Why didn't you wake me?" he called out, stretching some very stiff muscles.

"We knew you had a long day," she said, coming into the living room. "I was going to wake you when I finished the dishes."

Marmette leaned over and offered her hands to help him from the floor. The two crossing panels of her yukata fell forward. His eyes were filled with full breasts muffled in a light blue brassiere of very thin material. She made no attempt to cover up and retained an innocent expression. Her long blonde hair swung around to the side as she tilted her head. He flashed back to the day they met, watching her walk toward him in the lobby. Now he was fully awake. They continued to hold hands after he was back on his feet, gazing into each other's eyes.

"Hal, I want you to know that I'm very glad that you made it back safely from the Naktong; and I'm happy you're TAD here again," she said in a sexy whisper. She pulled on his hands so softly he nearly didn't detect her subtle signal for him to bring her close to him. Her big green eyes were wet and deep. "Do you really have to go?" she asked.

"Marmette, damn it, I need to tell you—please, don't misunderstand my intentions. I enjoy your company but—"

Before he could continue, she interrupted, "I don't misunderstand, not even a little bit. I know you haven't flirted with me. Well, maybe I can't say that, but you're a normal red-blooded male. I've had a little fun flirting with you too. A lot of fun, to be honest. You're an exceptional man and I'm very attracted to you—you've become very special to me."

Hal shook her shoulders gently, "We can't let anything happen. I can feel it too, Geez. I'm fighting it, cause there is no future in it for us."

"I realize that Hal." She rested her forehead on his chest, "I intended to keep this to myself, but I'm very vocal about my feelings."

"Marmette, I think we better not see each other socially anymore. Hell's fire, I can't be your Prince Charming." He began pacing.

"Don't over react Hal. On the twenty–fourth you'll be back in your real world, we'll both get over it and our lives will go on." Her mascara was running. "There's no reason to terminate our friendship though. My philosophy is that life is for the living—the here and now. You, of all people know how short life could be." Marmette smiled and grabbed his arms, "Hold still, you're making me terribly nervous. Look, it was a mistake for me to bring this up. Now I've got you upset."

"Marmette, you're such an exciting woman. I know you realize what you do to me. Under different circumstances, I'd give you my heart and soul. But, it's just not right to let ourselves go any further down this path. Let's keep it at the level it's at."

She squeezed his hands, "Alice is a very, very lucky woman. I'm so envious."" She tenderly put her hands on his cheeks. "OK, we both understand each other." Their eyes coupled, silently trading deep emotion.

He whispered, "We're playing with matches, Marmette." She poured a glass of sake and offered him some. "No thanks, my brain is fuzzy enough right now," said Hal. "This is very hard to rationalize. Let's call it a night. I don't think either one of us is thinking straight. The sake has horns growing on both of us." She smiled generously. "Supper was wonderful. Thank you," he said as he picked up his hat and jacket.

"You're quite welcome. Please don't be angry with me. It was a relief just to get my feelings off my chest."

"I'm not angry. I just don't want to see us get pulled into something more powerful than we can control," said Hal.

"We'll be just fine, Hal. Good night, see you at breakfast." She gave him a quick hug as he opened the door and pushed him playfully into the hallway. Hal thought he heard the sound of a camera shutter, but the hallway was clear in both directions.

His tired body dragged to the staircase and up to his quarters on the next floor. He daydreamed as he walked. How in the hell did I get into such a mess? Damn, bombing the enemy's brains out and dogfighting are easy, by comparison. This really is a fantasy land. His mind shifted gears to another nagging trouble. I wonder what happened when the Admiral told

Garr he was passed over.

Completely drained, he crashed and burned on the cot with his trousers and shoes on.

CHAPTER 9

Imperial Hotel, Tokyo

Captain Kirby hung his trousers in a tall metal locker in the corner of the bedroom, stuffed his shirt and socks in the laundry bag and dropped onto the cot in his skivvies. He rubbed his belly. What a meal, I'm stuffed. I'm glad I only have two more days here. My trousers are beginning to feel a little tight. If the real briefing goes as well as today's dress rehearsal, I'll be in tall cotton. He lit the bedside table lamp and stretched long and hard. It felt good to lie down and relax, but getting to sleep would be a task, as usual. Aboard ship, the routine was physically rigorous. Falling asleep was nearly instantaneous after the head hits the pillow. Here in the Land of Oz, things were different. There were full meals every night with hot sake flowing like water. There was anxiety over Operation Chromite that was building by the hour. There was also the powerful gravitational pull toward Marmette that kept his mind racing.

Tonight, the four musketeers dined at their favorite hole in the wall down the street from the Dai–ichi. Sake had his mind meandering through vast fields of thoughts. He put his hands between his head and the pillow. Garr—what's he up to these days? No damn good, that's for sure. What'll he cook up for me when I get back? Son of a bitch is the only man I've ever hated. Hal glanced over at the side table where a letter he received from his kids Susan and Joe caught his eye. He thought about what he read in that letter earlier. Geez, are the kids exaggerating? Alice hitting the bottle? I can't picture it. But it would answer some questions about her letters though. I've got to figure a way to handle that. Wish I could just go home for a week or two. Hey, the agents at Inchon—maybe on D–Day they could knock out the commander's HQ and his communications networks—got to work on that tomorrow. Marmette—Geez—I can't go ten minutes without thinking

65

about her. She looked absolutely gorgeous tonight. What is it about her? About me? I've been around pretty women before. It's not the things we do or say. That's been innocent enough, particularly since our little discussion. There's something that still makes me want to plunge. It's when our eyes meet. Without saying a word, we say things to each other—subconsciously. Lucy and I could sit at the supper table and make love, just with our eyes. Whoa Kirby, this Garden of Eden will dissolve on the twenty–third. Don't eat the apple! He grabbed the 'Kon Tiki' paperback from the table. Maybe this will make me sleepy and keep my mind occupied. Hal chuckled at several beer can sweat rings on the cover. Dusty isn't particular about his choice of coasters. What a character. I can't believe he read this horse choker in four nights.

After reading two pages, Hal realized that his restless mind was not even minutely interested in the book. He put the place marker back where he started. He went to the bathroom, took his jock strap and Navy regulation bathing suit off the makeshift drying rack—shower spigots—and put them on. "Steam bath will do it," he whispered. He slid into shower shoes, threw a bath towel over his shoulder and left his quarters for the stairs to the basement.

Hal opened the door to the steam bath facility. The only sound was the intermittent hiss of steam. It was usually empty after 10 PM because the Japanese staff of masseuses went home at 9. He was also a little uncomfortable taking coed steam baths, particularly with Marmette and LouAnn. Dusty and the ladies introduced him to the facility last Tuesday night after supper. Regardless the ladies' judicious use of towels and bathing suits, it was still difficult—embarrassing—for Hal, that is. Perhaps the term stimulating is more to the point.

He put his towel in a locker, showered and went to the steam room. The thermostat by the door was set on HIGH; he turned it down to MEDIUM and went in. Hal got comfortable, face down on the second tier of three wide steps of chalk white ceramic tiles on the left side of the room. Hot tiles smarted deliciously against his skin. He quickly learned to inhale slowly; the air was so hot that it hurt his nose and throat otherwise. Stinging hot condensation droplets fell randomly onto his body from the ceiling. He tried to keep his mind from drifting to the Operation Chromite plan or to visions of Marmette.

Hal heard a shower run briefly on the lady's side of the facility. The pipes banged when the shower shut off. A squeak emitted from the hinge spring on the door of the steam room and then the door banged shut. Someone came in and sat on the opposite side of the room. He fought the temptation to turn his head to the other cheek to see who it was. Almost immediately, the person got up and moved near him on the lower tier.

"Captain Kirby I presume," said a poorly disguised feminine voice.

"You can't hide that New Orleans drawl," he replied.

Marmette laughed, "You sneaky devil. You told us you were tired and wanted to go to bed."

"That's right," said Hal, "but I couldn't get to sleep. I thought coming down here for a while would help me relax."

"Me too. I like coming down here this time of the night. I like having the place to myself. Present company excepted," she quickly added.

Hal took a deep breath—the hot air burned his throat and nostrils. "I meant to ask before we left work, did Pam finish typing the memo on my meeting with General Smith today?"

"Yes, don't worry, it's already in Admiral Joy's reading folder," she replied. "I didn't have time to read it. What was the problem?"

"Well, he's got a big burr under his saddle about Chromite. Actually, it's just with the Inchon option. Dusty and I had to meet him at Haneda during his plane's refueling stop and try and take care of it. Number one, he doesn't think he'll have enough Marines on D–Day and number two, he wants to land at Pusong-myon instead of Inchon. Son of a bitch even managed to get a team of UDTs to check out the Pusong beach and general area. We have our hands full with that guy. I wanted to tell him he didn't have a snowball's chance in hell. But Admiral Joy said I was there to listen and explain—only."

"Where's Pusong? And are UDTs known as frogmen?"

"About fifty miles south of Inchon and yep, UDTs are frogmen—underwater demolition teams."

She thought for a minute, "What's so great about Pusong?"

"It's the closest location to Inchon that's suitable as a landing area, but doesn't have the tidal rise and fall problems that Inchon does. But, Dusty checked it out and the road system won't support the volume of vehicles and the logistic support system the operation demands." Hal, still facing away, heard her changing position. A pair of soft hands with firm fingers began kneading his shoulder muscles.

"Mind?" she asked.

"Not if you can behave yourself."

"Little ole me?" she cooed. As she worked each muscle, she softly spoke its technical name. "Deltoid . . . trapezius . . . latissimus dorsi . . . triceps."

"I thought you were an art major. Where did you pick that stuff up?"

"Anatomic Art—Sorbonne."

"I'm impressed," he said.

She began rapidly chopping his neck and back muscles with the sides of her hands, like the Japanese masseuses. "Good?" she asked.

"G–o–o–o–o–o–d," he said in staccato, sounding like a helicopter pilot on a radio.

She left the upper body and began massaging his calves and upper leg muscles.

"Good?" she asked. He couldn't grasp the words he needed.

"Cat got your tongue?" Without pausing for an answer, knowing none was forthcoming, she continued, "You aren't doing enough stretching, your hamstrings are very taught. You're in really good shape though."

"Yes nurse. Geez, nothing worse than a nag for a therapist."

"Do they have a gym on the ship?" she asked.

"Yep. I try to get to the weights three times a week, I exercise every morning and play basketball with the squadrons."

"It shows."

"Yeah, but you folks are working on it. I never ate so much and did so little. All I've done is sit, write, eat and sleep."

She laughed, "Roll over, this side is done," she said.

"I can't," he said after a slight hesitation.

She giggled and returned her kneading hands to his shoulders and neck. After a few minutes, she exerted a gentle rolling tug to his shoulder.

"I'm telling you, I can't—and I won't!" said Hal. He took a slow, deep breath while his mind scrambled.

"Rajah dajah, skipper," she said softly. He detected pressure from her finger tenderly running over the top edge of his ear scar and along the healed wound on the side of his head. "Hurt?"

"Nope, actually it's numb there. They told me feeling would gradually return over the next few months."

Her fingers ran back and forth lightly over the rear extension of the little zipper Sasebo put in the left side of his torso. "Same here?"

"Yep." He was doing all he could to keep authority over his mind and body. It wasn't working and probably wouldn't as long as she was touching him.

"I've been in here too long," said Hal, "I need to cool down—skedaddle!"

"OK! Cool shower will feel good," she said.

When he heard her go through the door to the ladies dressing room, he got up and headed for the men's shower. He slowly changed the shower water mixture down from hot until only invigorating chilly water flowed onto his head and shoulders. Refreshed and ready for another broiling, he returned to the steam room.

She was lying on her stomach in a pink one–piece swimsuit with white floral designs. She flaunted a cute grin when he came through the door, "My turn."

"Turn your head the other way," he said, "Close your eyes and keep them closed."

She snickered, "Aye, aye, Captain!"

Seeing her sensationally molded, half bare body was an overwhelming sight.

Hal knelt on the lower step next to her and went to work on her shoulders. Examining her body and touching her flesh had instantaneous physiological effects on him. Geez, I hope nobody else comes in here. God, look at those legs—unh, unh, unh.

"Easy does it, feels like you've got iron bolts for fingers," she said. "Ah, much better. That's good. Very good."

Both had a lot of sake circulating through their blood and their inhibitions were suppressed. "How'd you get such athletic shape to your legs?" he asked.

"Volley ball team in high school, soccer in France and gymnastics at Notre Dame, and I exercise a lot. Gives me a release. They too muscular?"

"Uh, no. They look pretty damn perfect to me." He paused a moment, sorting through several things he wanted to say. "Listen, I want to tell you," said Hal, "I was sure our situation was going to be unworkable—miserable—but this has been a pleasant week. I've really enjoyed spending suppers with you three characters. And you've been a very good girl," said Hal.

"Well, I haven't turned over yet!"

He smacked her bottom, "You are hopeless. A shameless hussy."

"Actually, I have a great deal of hope. And I'm no hussy," she crooned.

Hal sighed, "Here I am trying to be serious and all you can do is tease and flirt. I'd smack your butt again, but I suspect you'd enjoy it. I'll tell you this, if you begin to roll, the next noise you'll hear will be my flip-flops hauling ass out of here," he half-joked.

"Aha! Don't trust yourself huh?" she replied.

"Frankly, no!"

She giggled, "There's hope after all!"

"Time out. New subject."

"My brain is boiling, I've had enough," she said.

"Me too, I need to hit the rack."

"It's not terribly late," she paused, "I have some beer and wine if you'd like to have something before you turn in. I've got a new album we can christen, Mozart piano concertos. I know you love Mozart."

"No thanks, I appreciate the offer though. Tempting, but I need my beauty rest," he said. "See you at breakfast."

He showered quickly and left the facility before she was finished showering. By the time he reached his quarters he was sweating profusely. A cool shower in his room did the trick. He dried off, slipped on his shorts, turned out the light and settled onto the bunk. After twenty minutes of tossing and turning in the pitch black, he cursed the energizing cold shower. Recurring thoughts about Marmette commandeered his senses. He turned on the bed lamp, got up, retrieved the July issue of 'Life Magazine' from the table by the sitting room chair and returned to bed. Visions of Marmette crept into his mind as he perused the pages of the magazine. That bathing suit looked terrific—fit her like a glove. Her skin felt so warm and soft. And those legs. If I would have rolled her over, hell, I don't even want to think about it. Making love to her would be—whoa hoss – remember, don't eat the apple. The last page of 'Life' came before sleepiness. Apparitions of Marmette mingled with every conscious thought of every page. Putting out the light seemed only to intensify his longing for her. Geez Marmette, you make me crazy. I'm as horny as a goat with six peckers. An overpowering gravitational force had total control of his logic and senses. The restless tiger arose and paced. Words she had spoken sung in his ears, 'You, of all people, know how short life is, or could be.' He looked at the carefully folded white terry cloth hotel robe sitting atop the dresser. He put it on and slid his feet into shower shoes. I don't know—or care right now—how this is going to work out.

Hal listened at Marmette's door. Light rays extended out from under the door bottom; water was running—a dish clanked. He knocked lightly on the door—no response. Again, he knocked, but a little louder. The running water stopped and shadows broke the light under the door.

"Yes, who is it?" she asked.

"Hal," he whispered, "I can't sleep."

"Just a minute, I'm not presentable." Shortly she returned and began fussing with the lock.

When the door opened, Marmette, a towel piled high on her head, flooded his eyes with a stunning full-length blue-on-blue silk brocade robe. Wow! Even without makeup and wearing a turban she's dynamite.

"Well, don't just stand there," she said, grinning.

"Geez, that's a beautiful robe," he said, jolted back to consciousness. "I couldn't get to sleep. Maybe I do need a nightcap. I didn't knock until I heard you were still up. Do you mind?"

"No, no," she whispered quietly, "I invited you, remember?" She closed and locked the door and turned to say something. The words halted on the tip of her tongue. They looked at each other with giddy smiles and soft gazes. Their eyes exchanged something subconsciously. "Kick off your flip flops, pull the table back from the record player and set the big cushions up in front of it. The album is on the table, so's a bottle of Chardonnay. There's a six–pack on the kitchen floor on the right if you prefer that. I'll be right out." She went into the bedroom and closed the door.

Hal pried the top off a bottle of beer and took a swig; it dazzled his tongue and throat. Getting used to drinking room temperature beer had not been easy, but he had extensive training in that specialty during WW II.

Besides, he never met a beer he didn't like, unless it had ice cubes in it. The cellophane around the album was still intact. A fingernail got a rip started in the crackly wrapping. He carefully removed platter one from its brown paper sheath and placed it A–side up on the turntable.

"I'm back," she announced, "I just had to finish towel-drying and combing out my hair. This is the best I could do." Hal could see that she also put on some makeup. What couldn't be missed was that she traded her long robe for stunning red silk pajamas with a golden oriental dragon print. Her breasts moved freely as she walked; the silk clung to them just enough to hint at the details of their natural shape. The top three buttons were unfastened revealing a delicate pattern of tiny freckles. It was impossible for his eyes to resist drinking in every square inch of her. Marmette enjoyed his flirtatious perusal, smiled winsomely and cast him a saucy wink. She lit a candle in a Japanese ceramic lantern on a black lacquer and gold trimmed table and turned out the lights. "Smells like ginger," he said inhaling a sample of her perfume as she passed by him. "I'm surprised you didn't splash yourself with that French stuff."

"Variety and surprise!" she said hauntingly. "Do you like it? I just bought it—it's from Hong Kong."

"It's intoxicating. I poured you a glass of chardonnay," he said, trying to find a comfortable position for his legs and adjusted his position on the large sitting pillow.

"Magnifique, monsieur," she murmured and continued with a long sentence in French with dramatized low husky tones.

"What did you say? Or shouldn't I ask?"

She evaded his question and turned slowly in front of him on her tiptoes, "New jammies, aren't they pretty?" The silk bottoms fit her snugly enough to explicitly outline comely cheeks.

"Gluteus maximi," he quipped.

She broke into a hearty giggle, "I love your sense of humor."

He took a sip of the beer sitting beside him. If she keeps speaking French and showing off her stuff, her ass will be grass and I'm going to be the lawn mower—before the record even gets started.

"OK. Let's get comfortable," she said cheerfully and lowered the needle onto the record. She adjusted her cushion and sat on it cross-legged beside him.

Listening to the music in flickering subdued light was very hypnotic, but sitting on the floor was something he couldn't get used to. His legs were beginning to tingle; he rolled off the pillow, pulled it under his head, stretched out and closed his eyes to concentrate on the music. He felt her flattened palm running lightly over the bristly ends of his fresh GI haircut. "You're not concentrating on the music," he said.

"Yes, I am," she whispered. She stretched out and pulled the pillow under her head. A warm hand slipped under his arm and her head settled against the side of his shoulder. Concentrating on the music was a difficult task for both. They knew where this road was going. The only question was just how and when the first real move would be made—and who would make it. They listened quietly, sensing each other's movements, breathing and touch. When side A of the record ended, the needle arm moved to its perch and begged for attention. "I'm too comfortable to get up," she said.

He thought about the craziness of the thoughts bouncing around in his head. "I need to go," he said, "I've got to get some sleep. Let's save the flip side for tomorrow, after supper." In exaggerated motions, she came up on one knee, put one palm on the table, the other on her hip and tilted her head. Her long hair, no longer damp, spilled to the side, scintillating candlelight through the delicate fibers. Twinkling eyes pleaded with him while her lips formed a fetching pout. He couldn't help but break up. "I don't know where you get your energy. Or your magic."

"I just delight in being with you. You bring it out of me." She paused, her eyes darting back and forth between his eyes, "I don't want it to end," she said and promptly jumped up. "Stay put, I'll get you another beer; pour me some wine."

As he topped off her wine glass, he couldn't help but wonder about this Land of Oz. Where's my self-control? I'm sliding deep down into sheep dip here.

She returned with his beer and cued up side B. He sat cross-legged until half the beer was gone, then laid back onto the pillow. He clasped his hands behind his head and closed his eyes. Marmette set her pillow against his and placed her head gently onto his shoulder. Her forehead just touched his jaw; her hair tickled his ear. One breast gently rested on his arm, the other touched his ribs. His mind developed a picture of him at the top of a steep ski slope. He raised one knee to conceal the effect she was having on him. They listened to the music, each becoming aware of their own heartbeats.

When the first cut of side–B finished, Marmette leaned up and looked deep into his eyes, "I'm glad you're sharing such wonderful moments with me—suppers, walks in the park, steam room, music. They mean a lot to me. We shouldn't waste such wonderful feelings by keeping them inside." Her eyes glistened; she waited patiently for a response.

Hal reached up and pinched her chin, "You are terrific. Knowing you has been," he fell silent, tongue-tied. Their eyes roamed each other's faces. He could hear her breathing pattern becoming more rapid; as was his. Heat was rushing to his face. She slipped her hand under his robe lapel and combed the hair on his chest with her fingernails. As their eyes exchanged unspoken cravings, he reached for the back of her neck and pulled her gently to him. Their incessant teasing and flirting had finally fanned the embers of their friendship to an uncontrollable blaze.

Their lips met, parted and met, again and again. They kissed vigorously and with deep emotion. His hands ran through her lush fine hair and caressed her back and sides firmly through the cool, thin, smooth silk. His fingers found the hem of her pajama top and slid under it to explore the soft warm skin of her back; the dip at the base of her spine was damp. His hands moved eagerly from her back and found a hot, firm breast, evoking an ecstatic sigh from her. She rolled onto her back; he unbuttoned her top. His palm circled gently from one hard nipple to the other.

"Oh, my god, that feels so wonderful," she whispered. Her fingers impatiently found the sash of his robe, untied it and slipped her warm hand into his boxer shorts. A short low monotone escaped involuntarily from his throat. His heart hammered as their tongues chased between their lips. She knelt alongside him. Her sparkling eyes remained fixed on his while she removed her top. He explored her beauty unabashedly.

"Damn honey, I've wanted to see you like this since I met you in the lobby."

"I know it," she whispered, grinning saucily, "I saw it in those brilliant blue eyes." She took his hand and kissed it tenderly. "You were looking at me in a wonderful, exciting way—I can't explain it. I get lots of leering, lusting looks. But this was different. My heart just melted at that very moment." She brought his hand to her breast, leaned over, cupped his face with her hands and gave him a long passionate kiss. His hands caressed her breasts gingerly. He ached with arousal. She slowly withdrew her lips, moving her hands sensuously down from his face, palmed his stomach and chewed lightly on his nipples. He shivered from the rapture she built. Hal tried to roll toward her. She leaned down to stop his roll and nuzzled his neck. Her hand smoothed down over his torso and slid under the band of his shorts; her magic fingers sent another shiver through him.

Hal opened his eyes when she knelt astride his thighs. She reached back and brought her hair forward equally on each side of her neck. Partially concealed breasts rose and fell with her heavy breathing; the golden strands reached nearly to the floor. The movement of her shoulders, breasts and hair was fiercely arousing. He leaned up and wrapped his arms around her in an intense embrace. His hands smoothed their way into her pajama bottoms and caressed her cheeks. As she stood up he slid the red silk down past her thighs revealing the remainder of her natural beauty. She stepped out of the silk at her ankles and kicked it aside. He stood up, shrugged out of his robe and pulled her to him firmly and kissed her with unrestrained emotion. A wave of desire surged through his body. He hugged her with such force they soon found themselves craving air. With a smooth motion, he swooped her up with the conviction of an eagle capturing its prey and carried her to the futon in the bedroom, knelt at the edge and let her down carefully. A small candle lantern on a bench near the futon broadcast a flickering golden light on her smiling face and body. He lost himself in her outstretched arms. Fingernails clawed his back gingerly while his lips caressed their way around her torso.

She moaned softly as his hand searched down past her stomach. She writhed with delight as his fingers teased her. He kissed her breasts hungrily. She found the strength to force him over and rolled on top of him. Their glistening bodies were afire. They kissed and hugged each other frantically. Now free to consume each other rather than to flirt and tease, their intensely aroused souls exploded into convulsion. They cried out together as the fireworks erupted.

As they lay in quiet embrace in the afterglow, she kissed him tenderly as he stroked her gleaming body. They hugged and caressed each other for an endless time without saying a word. Hal took a deep breath and rolled onto his back, "Who'd ever thought, that first day in the lobby, that it would turn out like this?"

She rolled to cuddle into the side of his chest, "When they called from the lobby and said you had arrived, I came down the steps anxious about what you'd be like. It was silly of me, and I knew it. I finally got to see the Navy pilot whom I'd come to know so much about from Dusty. I found a handsome man devouring me before my very eyes. It was exciting. This was inevitable."

He hugged her tightly; his mind reeled. I wish I could understand what's happened. It's wonderful, perplexing and treacherous, all at the same time. Has to be a dream. Perhaps I died at the Naktong River."

She looked into his eyes, "Sweetheart, you are very much alive. It was meant to be. The paths of our lives were meant to merge for a moment, for some reason. It's not necessary for us to understand why right now—we may never understand."

"Life sure takes strange twists and turns," he said. His eyes closed and his mind wandered. How do I deal with this? Can a person just walk away and return to another world, like taking a trip to the park one sunny Saturday? He thought about what she said. Her words echoed through his consciousness, "We shouldn't waste such wonderful feelings by keeping them inside." They seemed to make sense—he wanted them to make sense.

CHAPTER 10

0555, Tuesday, August 23, 1950
Morning of the High-Level Operation Chromite Conference
Imperial Hotel, Tokyo

Marmette was just getting seated as Hal came through the doorway into the dining room. Dusty and LouAnn were sipping their second cup of coffee. Marmette smiled affectionately at Hal as he approached the table. Watching carefully out of the corner of her eye, she snatched a moment when Dusty and LouAnn weren't paying attention, formed her lips into a kiss and winked at him. He blushed and tried to remain nonchalant. Hal sat in the chair opposite Marmette, "Good morning folks, did you all sleep well?"

Dusty looked at him, "Yep, sure did. You look refreshed for a change. The stress has really shown on you Hal, your eyes have looked like two piss holes in the snow the last couple mornings, uh, sorry ladies, little field humor. Dusty flinched from LouAnn's under-table kick.

Hal blushed and turned to LouAnn, "Honey, you better teach this goon some couth." They all laughed.

"Ready for the big show this afternoon, Hal?" asked Dusty, quickly changing the subject.

"You're damn right I am. It's going to be exciting in there today." Marmette's smooth nylon stocking covered foot began running slowly up and down his leg. She had the cutest, most innocent smile on her face.

"That's one of the few benefits of high level staff duty," said Dusty, "Exhilarating at times, always frustrating and sometimes plain-ass boring."

"Roger that, but it hasn't been boring for me, that's for damn sure," Hal said, looking at Marmette over his coffee cup. She looked at him with a silly grin and crossed her eyes. He laughed into his coffee, nearly choking.

"What the hell's so funny?" asked Dusty.

"Nothing, just thought of something silly." Dusty looked at Hal and Marmette suspiciously for a moment and shook his head.

After they had ordered their breakfast, Hal asked Dusty, "Are you sure you don't have any idea about the purpose of the early meeting with General MacArthur this morning?"

He shrugged his shoulders, "Nope. Admiral Joy didn't say much to me about it except to tell you that it was scheduled for 1100."

Hal shook his head, "General MacArthur never had 'just a meeting' in his life. It has my curiosity up. How about you, Marmette? Any idea?"

"No, Hal, I told you I know less than Dusty about it," she replied.

"Relax, you're as tight as a hornet's ass," said Dusty, dismissing the subject.

Hal shook his head, "I just want to be prepared. I'm not anxious to get caught with my skivvies down."

Later that morning, a noise resembling a mixture of ring, buzz and rattle emanated from Hal's rickety desk phone. The phone needed help, but everyone figured it was better off in the office than languishing for weeks in the bowels of the Army Signal Corps.

"Captain Kirby," he answered.

"Hi Kirby! Clements here," Marmette said in a staged official tone. Then she whispered, "Hello darling." His face turned red. Regaining her normal tone, she said, "Admiral Joy is bogged down topside and can't see you before the meeting. He said to stay by the phone until they need you in about an hour."

"Damn, did he shed any light on what's going on?"

"No, he didn't," she said.

"Rajah dajah! I'll be standing by."

At 1055, Hal's phone sounded off again, "Captain this is Sergeant Walters. Admiral Joy requests that you come to General MacArthur's conference room sir."

"On my way," he said. He grabbed his pad and pencil, paused to check himself out in the full-length mirror on the back of the hallway door and hustled to the stairwell. The armed MPs on the top floor now recognized him on sight and no longer checked his I.D. card. He hurried down the hall to the conference room. The door to the conference room was open; two Corporals in crisp uniforms with shiny rifles stood on each side of the doorway. When he stepped inside, Admiral Joy rose from his chair at the conference table and came around to greet him. General MacArthur was sitting at the head of the long, brilliantly shined mahogany table. Also at the table were: Admiral Sherman, Chief of Naval Operations; Admiral Struble, Commander, Joint Task Force Seven; Admiral Doyle, Commander

Amphibious Group One; General Shephard, Commanding General, Fleet Marine Force, Pacific; General Almond, MacArthur's Chief of Staff and Admiral Morehouse. There was one person in the room that stunned him. It was Marmette, sitting on a chair at the side of the room, near the lectern, with a lap full of documents. Next to her was a photographer. She kept her eyes fixed on him, wearing a mischievous grin. Admiral Joy introduced Hal to those at the table.

When the introductions were completed, General MacArthur rose from his chair and walked behind the lectern. "Captain Kirby, front and center," he said. Hal came to attention in front of the General. "Captain, I hoped that Admiral Radford, Commander in Chief, U.S. Pacific Fleet, could be present, but, his aircraft was delayed in Guam and won't arrive for another two hours." MacArthur opened a folder on the lectern and studied the document momentarily, then looked up, "Gentlemen, Captain Kirby has distinguished himself and has brought great credit upon the Navy. He is a superior officer and leader. He has not only been of tremendous value to this staff in Naval air support planning, but he has made valuable contributions across the wide spectrum of Operation Chromite. I sincerely appreciate that the Navy made him available to perform these important tasks. Now, it is my pleasure and honor to present the following awards." He paused and carefully read from the document in front of him, " . . . the Silver Star for uncommon gallantry, leadership and professionalism of the highest order in planning and leading attacks on Pyongyang Airfield, and the port of Wonsan, North Korea . . ." General MacArthur read with great expression. Marmette opened a navy-blue case and handed the Silver Star medal to the General. The photographer began taking a series of blinding shots from different angles. MacArthur came around the lectern, pinned the medal on Hal's left breast pocket flap, looked squarely into Hal's eyes and shook hands with an iron grip. "Captain, you're a valiant warrior and I'm proud to know you."

Hal saluted, overexcited and moved, "Thank you very much, general."

MacArthur gave a rare smile and said, "Please excuse us now Captain. We look forward to your briefing later this afternoon."

Hal could not muster up the elegant words he sought. He saluted again, did an about face and departed. Admiral Joy led the group in a round of applause as Hal left the room. Marmette was right behind Hal with the citation and medal box.

When they were on the stairs, out of earshot of the MPs, Hal said, "Damn your hide Marmette, you not only knew about this, but you were up to your eyeballs in it."

"That's correct!" she said proudly.

In the early afternoon, Hal was studying his briefing outlines when his telephone rang; "Captain Kirby!"

"Hi sweetheart," whispered Marmette, "still angry with me?"

"You're damn right I am. You should be roped and branded."

"Oooh, just say when and where," she teased quietly.

Hal laughed, "Your nickel."

"Admiral Joy just told me Admiral Radford has arrived and is going directly into a private meeting with General MacArthur. Following that, they'll get the show on the road. We'll call you. Could be real soon, but there's no telling."

"Rajah dajah," said Hal, "I'm standing by." He looked at the revised listing of out-of-town dignitaries attending the briefing. There would be a dozen or so Flag and General officers attending, including those from MacArthur's staff. As he went down the list, he mentally reviewed the objections and politics in each instance. Judging from the message traffic concerning Chromite, particularly over the past week, it promised to be an intense meeting. Support for the Inchon option was yet to be enthusiastically received from anyone and not at all from several commanders, even at this late date. Worst of all, the Joint Chiefs of Staff seemed near to making a formal rejection of the Inchon option. The Pentagon and the Pacific commanders were consumed with the complexity and difficulty of executing a landing at Inchon, not to mention doing it on the accelerated timetable that MacArthur was driving down their throats. The consensus favored a landing, but at the port of Kunsan, located about eighty–five miles south of Inchon. It was evident that Admirals Struble and Doyle were less than fully supportive of the Inchon option and their concurrence was critical. However, their respect for General MacArthur and his wisdom had bridled their misgivings so far. He recalled the words of his peg-legged sage, Admiral Hawkins, "Watch your six!"

Eventually, the word came. Hal gave himself a quick uniform inspection and hurried to the conference room with his viewgraphs and pad. There was a hardwood straight-back chair reserved for him in the peanut gallery at the rear of the room. He set his materials down under his chair and stood at attention in front of it. Dignitaries were beginning to assemble. Admirals Joy and Morehouse entered and came over to Hal.

Admiral Joy spoke to Hal softly, "When the questions start coming at you, keep your answers short and to the point. You understand what's going on here. The nay-sayers will be looking for a soft underbelly."

"Aye, aye sir."

"Good luck," said Admiral Joy, echoed by Admiral Morehouse. Joy took his place at the conference table with Morehouse sitting directly behind him in a straight-back chair against the wall.

Stars soon filled the long table and spilled over to fill the side chairs against both walls. There was only a handful of men below Flag or General officer rank in the room. The only enlisted man was the transparency projector operator, a Master Sergeant from General Almond's office. General MacArthur entered with a quick paced swagger, bringing everyone out of their chairs. In one fell swoop, ten more stars were added to the constellation in the room, five on each of MacArthur's open collars.

Hal could barely believe his eyes. What self-confidence. A day like this and no dress canvas; no tie—no ribbons. He owns this place and he knows it. Hal was in awe of being part of this assembly; it was at once humbling and exciting.

General MacArthur rested his large freckled hands on top of the chair back. He glanced quickly around the table, making eye contact with each of his visitors. He puffed on his corncob pipe. "Gentlemen, please be seated," he said and nodded to General Wright, standing with pointer in hand at an easel full of flip charts and maps.

Wright was MacArthur's G–3/Assistant Chief of Staff for Operations. General Wright proceeded directly into the overview portion of the briefing, "The objective of Operation Chromite is to isolate the North Korean attacking forces below the 38th Parallel. As you recall, there are three options for landing sites," General Wright pointed to each of the locations on a map, "Chinnamp'o—the beach west of Pyongyang—and the western coast ports of Inchon, and Kunsan."

USAF General Edwards interrupted, "Is this a restatement of priority order for those options?"

Hal grinned. Wishful thinking general.

"No sir," answered Wright, "The position of the staff is now and always has been that Inchon is the only operationally effective landing site. You have all been provided a copy of the complete Chromite Operation Plan, including all options. Today, we will formally brief only the Inchon option." Wright completed the overview without further interruption. "If there are no preliminary questions or comments, I'll relinquish the floor to Admiral Struble, Commander of Joint Task Force Seven, the operational commander of Chromite."

Hal was watching MacArthur and the faces and hands of those at the conference table carefully. All were showing their emotions—except one of course. Poker face MacArthur merely puffed rhythmically on his pipe and cagily surveyed the room. There was silence. No one was brave enough, or foolish enough, to open any cans of worms at this point.

"Admiral Struble, it's all yours," said General Wright.

"Gentlemen," began Admiral Struble, "I defer my comments until the completion of the Navy portion of the briefing. Officers from the staffs of Admiral Joy and the Seventh Fleet will provide thorough coverage of the air operations, surface operations, amphibious operations, intelligence, navigation, communications, hydrographic and weather sections of the plan, in that order. Air operations will be first because that is the linchpin of this plan. Carrier-based air support, both prior and during the landing phases, is crucial to the success of the operation. If we do not have concurrence on this portion, then all other sections are nullified. We believe that you will find that it is a strong and comprehensive plan for overwhelming employment of airborne assets which will destroy the enemy's ability to resist the landing."

Hal felt his face get hot. They had changed the order of the topics. He had been moved up from third to first. The room was warm and the ventilation was inadequate; there were no windows to open. Perspiration was forming on his upper lip. Admiral Struble's pointed remark about that concurrence of his section of the plan carrying the remainder of the operation also took him by surprise. There had obviously been some brainstorming going on this morning. The impact of the advice he had received from Admirals Hawkins and Joy slammed home. Hal's self-control, confidence and determination reclaimed his composure. He wiped his upper lip. I've been in tougher spots than this!

Admiral Struble continued, "We are prepared to field questions during these presentations. Captain Kirby, the Air Group Commander on the Valley Forge and chief planner for Chromite air operations will now brief you."

Hal handed his transparencies to the Master Sergeant at the projector and went to the lectern at the side of the projection screen. The Master Sergeant turned on the projector and dimmed the lights. Hal took a 45–minute chunk of the scheduled one and a half hour briefing. He fielded many questions and concerns, many of which were quite pointed. MacArthur and many others took notes on their pads throughout. Having completed his briefing, Hal asked, "Are there any further questions?" Although just about everyone had asked questions, blatantly sniped or stated some concern with one specific point or another, General MacArthur had remained quiet, but alert. Hal sensed MacArthur was on the verge of breaking radio silence. Many in the room were fidgeting; the moment of reckoning was near. USAF Colonel Logan Bennett, III whispered something in USAF General Stratemeyer's ear. Hal studied Bennett carefully. So that is the infamous Colonel Bennett. I can't wait for this question.

"Captain Kirby," said General Stratemeyer, "Do I understand that you guarantee effective air support even at marginal ceilings in that terrain?"

Hal took a deep breath. Geez, after the umpteenth attempt to skewer me today, you'd think Bennett would quit! Stratemeyer seemed to be getting progressively more agitated. "Yes sir, we've been operating at even worse conditions along the front routinely since the start of the war," explained

Hal in a professional manner and congenial tone, "My aviators have become accustomed to it. We were faced with the choice of learning to operate under those conditions or to watch our ground troops become North Korean door mats when the weather was bad." Hal detected the slightest movement at the sides of MacArthur's lips. He glanced at Admirals Joy and Morehouse – Joy was watching Stratemeyer; Morehouse was rolling his thumbs.

Admiral Struble was anxious to terminate the discussion, "Thank you Captain, well done. Gentlemen, are there any other remarks or concerns concerning air support?" He waited a scant moment, and then said, "Hearing none, I assume your concurrence in the adequacy of the air support plan for the Inchon invasion." The silence was deafening. Hal quickly collected his transparencies from the Master Sergeant and took his seat.

Hal wiped his brow with his handkerchief. That was clever. Struble snookered them into accepting Inchon by not finding fault with the air plan. I thought Struble was lukewarm on Inchon; the old man has gotten to him. And my credibility was established with the senior Navy officers with the awards ceremony. Clever!

When the last Navy briefer finished, Admiral Doyle stood up and provided a summary of concerns from his perspective as Commander of Amphibious Group One. When it appeared that he had completed his summary, he paused, struggling with something. Then he said, "Nothing I've heard today makes me comfortable with taking a landing force up Flying Fish Channel to Inchon. It's narrow, shallow, has a treacherous tidal flow, and we must operate within effective range of enemy artillery. In the event of air attack, we have no opportunity for evasive tactics. If a ship is sunk by mines or other hazards, ships up-channel will be trapped. "

Hal studied General MacArthur and Admiral Sherman while Admiral Doyle finished his remarks. Sherman's face began getting red; he threw his pencil down on his pad. MacArthur calmly looked down the table, slowly rolling a box of matches on the table while puffing on his pipe.

Sherman responded to Doyle's comments, "I would not hesitate to sail a force up Flying Fish, given the information presented."

MacArthur showed reaction for the first time; he abruptly sat up in his chair and said, "Spoken like Admiral Farragut! Waging war requires high spirit and confidence!"

Hal's eyebrows popped up. I can't believe these guys are duking it out like this. This is great!

Doyle recovered somewhat gracefully from that broadside and thought intently for a moment. He looked directly at General MacArthur and said, "General, I have not been asked nor have I volunteered my opinion about this landing. If I were asked however, the best I could say is that Inchon is not impossible." With that, Doyle tilted back in his chair.

MacArthur paused, showing no emotion, in deep thought. He relit his pipe and rhythmically shook the matchbox in his right hand, creating a maraca-like noise. It was a compelling sound in a dead silent room. Hal was trying not to grin, thoroughly enjoying his introduction to high stakes military poker. MacArthur's reputation for well-executed dramatics was confirmed. Without commenting on Doyle's finale, MacArthur began polling the table. He nodded to General Collins, who then voiced his opinion against Inchon and recommended the Kunsan option. Admiral Sherman signed up for Inchon and General Shephard voiced his preference for Kunsan. And so it went, with some being noncommittal, making circumspect comments that stopped well short of concurring with a landing at Inchon. There was no clear consensus for Inchon. MacArthur sat back in silence for a few moments. All present watched anxiously as he tapped spent tobacco from his pipe into the glass ashtray, making bone chilling clinking noises. Traces of smoke spiraled upward from the dregs in the ashtray. He repacked the pipe with tobacco from a small brown leather pouch and drew a match from the box. A swipe across the abrasive strip flared the tip; he held it upright while the igniting compound burned off, and then touched the tobacco with the orange flame. MacArthur rose and paced in deep concentration, puffing clouds of smoke, further delaying the satisfaction of their curiosity. All eyes watched in heightened anticipation. They all knew MacArthur well enough to know something was coming. When he decided on his words, or more likely, decided the silence had gone exactly as long as he wanted, he returned to his chair. MacArthur put his pipe into the glass ashtray with a distinct clink. He looked around the table and took a deep breath. MacArthur then treated the gathering to the most inspiring speech that they probably had ever and would ever hear in their lives.

"I must admit," MacArthur began, "that, based on sterile logic, the odds of successfully executing the Inchon landing could be perceived to be 5,000 to one. But, I am accustomed to making decisions of this nature and magnitude. You must carefully consider, as I have, the many pertinent factors that demand the selection of Inchon. I'm aware that there is discussion to the effect that a September 15th D–Day is unattainable. I do not believe that and have not received a convincing argument to the contrary. As you heard, the next acceptable tidal window at Inchon is nearly a month from that date—October 11th. We cannot wait that long! I want all of South Korea back in our hands before the rice harvest. I don't want North Koreans to get that crop." Hal noticed that there were many in the room who hadn't heard that little tidbit before. This was a completely human consideration, but one of immense importance to the South Koreans and to MacArthur. He went on to summarize the pertinent aspects of the current intelligence on enemy preparations and inclinations. He suggested that the enemy's assessment of near impossibility of a successful landing at Inchon confirmed the utter surprise that would be achieved. The relevance of historical incidents of victory gained through surprise was explained. "Particularly parallel to Inchon, recall how, in 1759, the Marquis de Montcalm lost Quebec to General James Wolfe. The walls of the city adjacent the sheer and hazardous riverbanks were very lightly defended. Montcalm had decided that it would be militarily foolish for the enemy to attempt an attack up those banks. Of course, that is precisely what Wolfe did. Quebec fell and the French and Indian War was essentially won." He described how the Japanese successfully landed large seaborne forces at Inchon—under opposition—not once, but twice, in 1894 and 1904. "I have total faith in the Navy's ability to conduct effective, daring amphibious landings. I do not forget their performance in the Pacific campaigns. It appears however that my confidence in the Navy exceeds that which the Navy has in itself!"

Hal was on the edge of his chair. Damn, the old man really torpedoed 'em with that. He's not holding anything back.

MacArthur paused to allow those words to settle in, then continued, "History of war proves, nine times out of ten, an army will be destroyed when its supply lines have been severed. You are all aware of the difficulty we've had in doing that so far. A landing at Kunsan will not accomplish that—Inchon will. Deep envelopment, combined with surprise, which severs the enemy's supply lines, is and always has been the most decisive maneuver of war. A short envelopment that fails and leaves the enemy's supply system intact, merely divides your own forces and can lead to heavy losses and even jeopardy. I just cannot overemphasize the fact that a landing at Kunsan will have no direct or immediate impact on North Korean Army logistics. It will, therefore likely result in a high cost of U.S. casualties." MacArthur looked around the room, allowing them to ponder that thought. Then, in an ever-increasing tone and volume he continued, "Are you content to let our troops stay in that bloody perimeter like beef cattle in the slaughterhouse? Who will take the responsibility for such a tragedy? Certainly, I will not! The prestige of the Western world hangs in the balance. The Orient has their eyes on this conflict. Communism has chosen Asia as its target for commencing world domination. To fail in blocking Communist expansion in Asia could conceivably jeopardize Europe. Make the wrong decision here today—the fatal decision of inertia—and we will be done. I can almost hear the ticking of the second hand of destiny. We must act now or we will die. Inchon will not fail! It will succeed. And it will save 100,000 lives," he said, closing his dramatic and emotional address.

A chill ran from the base of Hal's spine to the tip of his short graying hair. He felt ten feet tall; he wanted to jump to his feet and applaud. Geez, if Admiral Hawkins delivered that speech on the Valley Forge, my pilots would be up on the tables hollering at the top of their lungs. Those around the conference table sat motionless—mesmerized. General MacArthur settled calmly into his chair and tapped tobacco from his pipe into a new pile in the ashtray. A thought struck Hal like a ton of bricks. Damn, MacArthur just taught a bunch of brass, and me, that it is possible to get caught up in statistics and probabilities and forget leadership, strategy and tactics. That's the stuff that won WW II and hundreds of other battles.

Admiral Joy greeted Hal with a warm handshake, "Well done, Hal, well done. Ned Almond just passed MacArthur's compliments. Now, have you seen the message traffic since you came back from the meeting?"

"No sir, I was briefing the staff on the meeting."

Admiral Joy motioned for Hal to join him in the sitting area, "Hal, you need to know that Admiral Ewen ordered the Valley Forge to sea ASAP. They'll probably sail tomorrow at daybreak. Admiral Hawkins has arranged for a COD to stop at Haneda tomorrow at 1000 to pick you up. Marmette is lining up your transportation to the airport. But check your messages for anything that might have changed."

"Aye, aye sir."

"The North Koreans are hastily reallocating their northern reserves of supplies, armor and troops to the southeast. They are mounting another desperate push to overrun our real estate before the invasion can be executed."

Hal shook his head, "At least we've got some help this trip out. Philippine Sea is on the southeast station and we'll soon have the two jeep carriers on the west coast with us. We'll kick their asses boss."

"I'm sure you will," said Admiral Joy, smiling. "I have another subject to discuss with you. Would you consider a permanent transfer to my staff?"

"Admiral, uh, with all due respect sir, I like being on the leading edge of the war."

Joy nodded, "I can appreciate that. Suppose BUPERS decides to pull you out of the CAG slot early?"

Hal faltered. Geez, would he do that to me? He asked with a smile to soften the directness, "Do you think that might happen?"

"Rest assured," said the Admiral, "I know that it's not in the Navy's best interest to take you off the Valley Forge against your will." Joy studied Hal for a moment, then said, "Think about it. If you change your mind, get in touch with me."

Hal nodded, "I'll do that. I'll need some time to think it through sir."

The Admiral rose, "It's been a real pleasure, sincerely." Hal got up and shook Joy's hand. "Best of luck Hal, and stay out of trouble. Remember the story about the old, bold pilots. I mean that. Please take the rest of the day and go sightseeing or something. You've earned a little free time before you get back into the breach."

"I will sir, thanks for everything. It's been a great experience for me."

As he left the Admiral's office, Marmette handed him a folded sheet of paper and said in a very professional manner, "Here's the details on your transportation to Haneda tomorrow morning. And, if I don't see you again, have a safe trip. It's been a pleasure working with you."

Hal shook her hand, continuing the public charade for the benefit of the clerks in the office. "Likewise. Keep the pit in line," he said and waved to the others as he left.

While walking to the stairs, he unfolded the note she had given him:

'Supper, my place, 7pm, alone – don't plan on getting any sleep tonight. Love, Me'

He returned to the pit to say goodbye to Dusty. "I'm sure sorry to see you go pal," said Dusty

"I have mixed emotions too," said Hal.

"Must have been some speech. Was there a recorder or stenographer there?"

"No clerks or secretaries were in the room and I didn't see any machines or microphones either."

"Dammit," Dusty said, "I think someone screwed up royally. That meeting should have been recorded for historical purposes. Besides, I'd like to be able to hear that speech, verbatim. When you leaving Hal?"

"Tomorrow morning bright and early. I'm going to clean out the desk and safe drawer, then take off for the rest of the afternoon."

"Good idea. What are you going to do?"

"I haven't had a chance to see Yokohama yet."

"It's like Tokyo, but worth the taxi fare. In the meantime, I'll talk to LouAnn and get our ducks in line for supper."

"Uh, Dusty, I'd rather just relax tonight."

"Well, we don't have to go out, we'll do something at my place, or Marmette's."

"No, what I mean is, I'd like to be alone tonight."

Dusty sat down, put his feet up on the desk, and studied Hal's pale blue eyes.

Hal knew him all too well, "What's on your mind Dusty?"

Dusty took a deep breath and whispered, "Something going on between you and Marmette?"

"Geez Dusty-"

Dusty broke in, "It's none of our business, of course, but LouAnn and I have noticed the way you two look at each other. Hell, you guys hit it off the first night we went to supper. She was a wreck when the message came in saying you were shot down. LouAnn called a little while ago and said she tried to arrange something with Marmette for tonight and got the same bullshit about wanting to be alone."

"Listen," Hal said in a forceful whisper, "We don't want a bunch of rumors going around. The situation defies logic. Don't try and understand it. I'm not sure I do."

"Don't worry about LouAnn and me, we think the world of both you. On the one hand, we've enjoyed watching you guys. On the other, we're upset that we unwittingly started something. It wasn't our intention to play cupid. Christ, we don't want either of you to get hurt."

"That never crossed my mind Dusty. We have no one to blame but ourselves, but it ends tonight. We tried to keep it secret. I suppose it was impossible to hide from you and LouAnn. Anyway, Marmette and I have spent a lot of time talking about this. We'll be OK. Remember what you said about how to act if you were offered steak? Well, we're just eating steak this week. Tomorrow it's back to C–rations."

Dusty laughed, "She's getting C–rations now, but you're getting prime rib and lobster." Hal chuckled. Dusty's smiling face turned serious, "We really hope this works out OK for you both. Listen, LouAnn and I are going to miss you. We want to see you tonight. How about you guys dropping by at 2200 for a sayonara toast."

"For a jarhead, you're a good man. Uh, how about 1930, and just for one drink, OK?" Dusty laughed heartily.

CHAPTER 11

Flag Mess
Aboard the USS Valley Forge

The Valley Forge was slicing through blue water at 30 knots—Japan in its wake—hell-bent to bring her might into attack range of the enemy. Admiral Hawkins washed down the last bite of apple brown betty with a slug of black coffee. He announced in his unique, hearty voice, "Gentlemen, I'd like to press on. Would the Battle Staff Officers please remain," Those who were not part of the Battle Staff, politely excused themselves.

Admiral Hawkins sat forward and leaned cross-armed on the table, "I convened this meeting so that Captain Kirby could brief us on the latest and greatest concerning Operation Chromite." He gave a nod.

Hal provided a general summary of the operation and gave a more detailed treatment of the air portion of the plan. He finished, ". . . so, although the Inchon option has been tentative up until now, it appears to have finally been put to bed and formal approval by JCS is expected shortly." Hal noted that during the entire briefing, Garr sat as still as a statue, staring into a distant place. Hal watched him carefully. Garr was a different man today than when Hal last saw him and that was worrisome.

"Thank you, Captain," said Hawkins. He trained his eyes around the table, "I want you all to know the Air Section of Chromite inside out, and any other section that may be pertinent to your function. There is no room for mistakes in this operation. You will make none, and you will train and inform your people so that they will make none. Thank you, gentlemen." He gave Hal a subtle look that meant 'I want to talk to you.' Hal followed him to his sea cabin.

Hawkins motioned to Hal to have a seat, "How was it?"

"Treacherous seas, Admiral, but no damage to the bulkheads. And I want to thank you for initiating the decoration."

"Congratulations. Well deserved. Admiral Joy sent me a note saying he was able to get General MacArthur to do the honors."

"Damn near my whole chain of command was there. More attention than I needed, but it served a purpose for the General."

"Getting enough of that kind of exposure is hard to do. But it is critically important. Many deserving souls are never in the right place at the right time. By the way, Admiral Joy also thanked me, both for him and General MacArthur, for making you available to work on Chromite. He said you did one hell of a job."

"It was a great experience."

The Admiral brought Hal up to speed on the ground situation and his thoughts about the more immediate employment of Valley Forge and the other carrier's air assets. When they finished those discussions, Hawkins paused. "Did you notice Garr?" asked the Admiral.

"Yes sir. If it were anyone else, I'd say he had been reduced to a sluggish, humiliated mass. But, I don't know, there's not a pinch of remorse or humility in his entire body. How did he react when you told him about getting passed over?"

"He glared at me in a rage, turned a dense red, then his expression became colder than a witch's tit. He put his morning briefing notes at every chair and disappeared until noon."

"He's a bizarre man, Admiral. We need to pay special attention to him."

"I must tell you though, his intell briefings have been, so far as I can tell, correct and effective. That's Ted's assessment too."

Hal shook his head, "He's smart enough to know he's going to another court-martial if he pulls anything in black and white."

Hawkins nodded in agreement, "But, there's a new wrinkle. The day after I told him he was passed over, he came up with the idea of regular one–day visits to the intelligence center in Yokosuka. In the interest of better intelligence support, quote, unquote. What do you make of that?"

"I'll have to think about this," said Hal. "It strikes me as odd. How often?" asked Hal.

"Every few days while we were in the operating area."

"I'll go back through the records and message traffic to find out what I can about this. I have a friend, an ex-neighbor, who's the XO of the center. I don't think we should risk sending a message to him, but the next time I'm in Japan, I'll give him a call."

Hawkins' face and silence indicated Hal's suggestion wasn't what the Admiral was looking for. "Garr is planning to ride the 0600 COD tomorrow," said Hawkins. "I need to decide whether to let him take this or any more of these damn trips." Hawkins looked at his watch. "I have a meeting with Captain Rice now. Come to my cabin at 2130 and we'll continue this conversation."

During the course of the day, despite launch and recovery operations and the hectic routine of an Air Group Commander, Hal researched the records of the COD flights that Garr had taken.

Hal's alter ego, Ted Spence, came into the Air Group Office. "I feel like a new man CAG. Anything I can help you with?"

"Pull up a chair. Nice job on the Kunsan Harbor attack."

"Thanks CAG. Went as smooth as a new baby's ass."

Hal turned to his Yeoman, "Slater, I need ten minutes in private with Mr. Spence."

"Aye, aye sir," Slater replied, tapped his seaman on the shoulder and the two left the office.

"Ted, do you have any inkling why Garr finds it necessary to make these trips to Yokosuka? And can you think of a specific incident where they paid off?"

"I can't think of anything on either count," Ted replied. "I'm pretty sure that everything he told us was in the data we already got from the beach; I've been watching that closely. But, his behavior has changed. He's in another world. Oh, yeah, it seems odd to me that he takes a gym bag with him on those flights."

Hal thought for a minute, "Oh, I don't know Ted, could just be an overnight kit in case he gets stranded on the beach. Why do you think that's strange?"

Ted mulled that over, "I don't know. Where's he been going?"

Hal replied, "Haneda, then to Yokosuka. Ship's Personnel Officer says he gets a set of TAD orders each time and claims expenses against them, including round trip taxi fares between Haneda and the Yokosuka gate."

Ted cracked his knuckles, "Well, he hasn't tried to pull any tricks with intell briefings since the Admiral nailed him to the tree. Perhaps he's giving the people at the center some insight which allows them to better report the data we need to get."

"Sure, Ted, and the big bad wolf don't want to eat Little Red Riding Hood."

"CAG, no disrespect sir, but are you sure you aren't over reacting on this?"

"Bullshit," Hal replied. "I'm telling you Ted, he's up to something. Be careful with that son of a bitch."

Ted stared at the deck a few moments. "What in hell happened between you and Garr?" he asked cautiously.

Hal trudged to his quarters after a long day's work. There was 45 minutes before his evening meeting with the Admiral. It was the first opportunity to relax since he returned to the ship from Japan. There were three letters from home that had arrived today. He picked them up, arranged them in postmark order and stretched out on the bunk. His body ached; Marmette kept her word, he didn't get a minute of sleep last night. They didn't even make it down to breakfast. A grin formed as he thought about her. Oh Marmette, I hate seeing our slice of life come to an end. But, that's what must happen. It was borrowed time. Geez, I'd like to be able to take a nap. He took a deep breath. He adjusted the pillow and read Alice's letters:

Dear Hal, I'm sorry I upset you, but only cats have nine lives. You seem so eager to do things that will get you killed . . .

Dear Hal, I wish you were here to talk to your son. I caught him on the back porch necking with the new neighbor's daughter last night. He's only fourteen. I'm afraid he's going to get into trouble. He won't listen to me. . .

Hal shook his head. What the hell could I tell him? Dear Joe, let me tell you about the foolish stuff me and my girl next door did for six years. He smiled.

Dear Hal, you should have been here to see Susan's ballet debut. The auditorium was packed. She was terrific . . .

He rolled over and looked at the 8x10 family portrait on the bulkhead. Each face generated memorable experiences. There's my real world. He closed his eyes and relaxed. A startled awakening had his heart beating fast; he turned quickly to see what time it was. Damn, I've been asleep half an hour. Geez, that was close. I've only got twenty minutes before the Admiral's meeting. He went to the small desk in his stateroom and reorganized the information he learned about Garr's sojourns to Japan. Sorting through the notes he'd made from various sources, he felt like he was on the verge of recalling or deducing something relevant to the puzzle. Despite his best efforts, he was unable to make sense out of it. When the clock showed 2125, he folded the notes, put them into his trouser pocket and left his quarters.

"Good evening Admiral."

Hawkins looked up from a thick publication he was studying, "Good evening Hal, take the load off. Help yourself," he said pointing at coffee and snacks.

Hal picked one of each of the three different sandwich halves the stewards had stacked artistically on the platter and poured a cup of coffee.

"Mine Warfare Tactics," Hal read aloud from the cover of the tome the Admiral was reading, "Anything that don't involve wings isn't worth knowing about," he joked.

The Admiral read on for several moments, then returned a volley with a straight face, "Well Captain Kirby, for your information, some mine sweeping devices do in fact have wings. If you were a highly competent Naval Officer worthy of selection to Rear Admiral you'd know that." He put the book down on a side table. "If the commies mine the approaches to

Inchon, it will sure complicate things. That's not why I asked you to come up here. What did you learn about Mr. Garr?" Hawkins lit a cigar and sat back.

"I have some notes of facts I gleaned from the records about these trips he's taken." He pulled the papers from his pocket, unfolded them and handed them to Hawkins.

After looking through the information, the Admiral said, "Interesting at best."

"Yes sir, I understand, standing alone there doesn't seem to be much there."

"Correction Hal, there's absolutely nothing there. You have something else?"

"No sir. I think there may be some pieces to a puzzle there, but for now, they're not evident."

Hawkins scanned the notes again and then handed them back, "Hang onto this stuff." He looked at Hal with a serious look, "I think it's time you told me what happened between you two. I read his service record; I know he lost his wings in a General Court-martial. It didn't mention the specific circumstances."

Hal took a sip of coffee, then began, "Since I've known him, he has tried to hide his own incompetence by scheming to make everyone around him look bad. He had no real friends. My personal conflict with him climaxed one day when he was my wingman on a carrier air patrol mission. We got bounced by Zeros. The moment he spotted them, he immediately broke off and hauled ass for the carrier, leaving me with four planes to defend against. I reported the incident to the squadron CO. Garr told the skipper some cockamamie story. That was the last straw for the skipper. Garr had been at best a mediocre pilot up to that point and he seemed to have a lot of mechanical problems just before takeoff for a hairy mission, or shortly after takeoff. Of course, the mechanics never found anything. The skipper and the Admiral saw to it that he lost his wings and shipped him to a tin can. Somehow, while on Seventh Fleet Staff, he managed to wangle his way into the intelligence staff. Basically Admiral, Garr has a yellow stripe down his back that's a mile wide, the personality of a rattlesnake, he is bitter with the Navy and he threatened to have my ass one day. I think that pretty much sums it up."

Hawkins was massaging the muscle of his leg above the prosthesis while he pondered the story. "What happened with you and the Zeros?"

Hal smiled, "I guess I could tolerate more Gs than they could. They ran out of ammo trying to nail me and went home."

Hawkins cracked a faint, rare smile, "Reminds me of my days as a wide receiver for Navy. The only thing that made me so damn fast and gave me such evasive footwork was my profound fear of getting tackled." His face took on a serious look again, "Why didn't you tell me about him when I told you he was coming aboard?"

"Well sir, I told no one—didn't think it was fair. I didn't have—"

Hawkins interrupted, "Never mind, I don't give a rat's ass. None of that crap matters now."

Hal's face flushed; he refilled his coffee cup and sipped cautiously at the steaming brew to cover his lack of something brilliant to say.

"I'm going to deny him permission to depart the ship," said Hawkins.

"Admiral, I wonder if keeping him aboard is a good idea? We'll never find out what he's up to—and I have a feeling we should try. May I suggest we let him go so he could be followed?"

"Followed? By whom? Kirby, if you think you're going to get me to sign a message to the counter-intelligence people about your loosely based suspicions, you're nuts. They'll come with straight-jackets and take both of us off this bird farm."

"Oh, no Admiral, I wasn't suggesting that. Actually, I was thinking about myself—about me riding his six."

Hawkins glared at Hal for a moment, "I find it difficult to find logic in a Carrier Division Commander sending his Air Group Commander on a gumshoe mission based on zip point shit."

"Well sir, think of it as a reconnaissance mission." The humor was lost on the Admiral. "Sir, I want to follow his conniving ass. I really feel deep inside that there's something fishy in Denmark and we need to know what it is. If you prefer, I'll just do it, uh, without your knowledge."

"What the hell is it you think he's up to?" asked Hawkins.

"I've just got a hunch about him, that's all. Something is lurking in the background as sure as God made little green apples." Their eyes sparred a few seconds.

Hawkins got up, "Let's go to the rail and get some air." Hal followed the Admiral to the starboard side of the U–shaped catwalk around the Flag Bridge. They stood quietly, searching for answers in the dark sea and the brilliant celestial display. Red running lights of the destroyers in the starboard half of the defensive screen around the carrier dotted the black velvet. A dull drone emanated from the ship's stack above.

"Admiral," said Hal, "The gym bag – I think it could be black market."

"You have to do better than that. Making a few bucks off booze or cigarettes isn't justification for—Hal, damn it, you have better things to do!"

Hal nodded, "Uh huh, but suppose it's not penny ante stuff. Suppose that damn bag is full of U.S. currency? If he's trading military payment certificates with the Japanese, that would be a federal offense. Scuttlebutt has it that they are getting ready to change the MPC; those bar owners know that. They start selling off their MPC holdings at a big discount when that happens. Garr could be making a huge profit."

Hawkins interrupted, "He couldn't deal Military Payment Certificates on the ship Hal, the word would be out on him and he's too smart to risk that."

Hal continued, with measured words, "Maybe so sir, but I know him all too well. I don't know what he's up to, but I know he's involved in some slimy scheme. He's not getting anything useful from the Intell Center."

Admiral Hawkins banged his hand on the railing, "Kirby, these are serious accusations and you have no basis."

"I just this moment realized what was out of joint about this Admiral. Taxis. Why always taxis between Haneda and Yokosuka? It's a piece of cake to get an official vehicle and driver."

"All you have is gut feelings and hunches," scolded the Admiral.

"Sir, my experience with the gummies is that they're used to dealing with tidbits and circumstantial evidence. What about this: send Admiral Joy an IMMEDIATE—EYES ONLY message with the details behind our suspicions, asking him to give us an independent assessment and, if he agrees, to contact the gumshoes. Hopefully, he can get the gummies on it fast enough to meet me at Haneda before Garr arrives on the COD. If they can't react that fast, at least I'll be able to tail him and see for myself."

Hawkins probed the darkness. A clacking noise began a deck above them. A Signalman was sending a flashing light message to a destroyer. "Admiral," said Hal, "I don't think we can wait until we have solid evidence. He's already made three trips."

The Admiral was quiet for a minute, then turned. Even in the darkness, the Admiral's barely visible eyes were boring into him. "And if you're wrong Kirby, we'll both look like flaming assholes." Hawkins paused, "C'mon." Hawkins hurried back to his cabin, picked up the phone and dialed, "Lewis, I need to talk to you in my cabin."

Hawkins skipped the formality of a return greeting when his aide arrived, "Lewis, I'm giving you a task which I want you to hold close to the chest. Get hold of the Disbursing Officer and find out the details of how the ship handles MPC sales and exchanges. And find out if he keeps track of anyone who buys or sells large amounts of it."

"Admiral, shall I talk to Captain Rice first? Disbursing may be hesitant."

"I'll call Captain Rice and let him know we're investigating something. If the Disbursing Officer is concerned, invite him to call Captain Rice."

"Aye, aye, sir."

"Do it now Rip and come back here when you're finished."

Hawkins motioned Hal to his desk when Ripley Lewis departed, "Go write the message to Admiral Joy. When Lewis comes back, I'll have him encrypt it in my personal key list and take it to the radio shack."

Lewis returned in half an hour with the list of MPC activity. The names that made large exchanges did not include Garr. Hal looked up from the list, gave a shrug of his shoulders and said, "Looks like we're still missing some pieces in this puzzle."

"Thank you Lewis," Hawkins said, "Now get this message encrypted ASAP and get it to Radio—immediate precedence—to Admiral Joy—eyes only." He put his signature under the text.

The Admiral opened his safe and handed Lewis his personal coffee-can shaped 'basket' of cryptographic rotors and the current month's crypto setup sheet. Rip departed for the Flag Office where the portable crypto machine was stowed.

Hal said, "I'll have Joe Kramer make one of his F9s available. We can have it readied and sitting by the elevator to bring up onto the flight deck the moment the COD leaves the ship. I'll have plenty time to arrive ahead of them and hopefully chat with the gumshoes."

Hawkins nodded and grumbled, "No guts, no glory."

Will Crandall's Office, SurvTech, Inc.
Falls Church, VA

Will greeted Tim Yardley with a handshake and closed the office door, "Have a seat Tim, you sounded excited, what happened?"

Tim made himself comfortable and began, "Something popped up this morning. I think I found a new project for SurvTech to work on. The electronic intelligence R&D shop wants to hang a broadband receiver and recorder on the AQUABALL aircraft. I volunteered to handle the project. Can you build one?"

"Hell yes! Are we talking about a pod, or what? And how many?"

"The specs are wide open, all they have is a top-level concept in their heads. They will commit to one unit, then after it flies, they'll decide whether to build more, change the design, or whatever."

Will smiled, "Well, we can build it. What time frame?"

"Oh, hell, they're ready to go now. They said they'd transfer money to me when I found a contractor and provided a proposal."

"Good show, Tim, we could sure use the cash flow. Any competition?"

"No, I can do a sole source contract. It's perfect. Here are some notes on the center frequency, bandwidth and sensitivity they want. The project name is AQUACRYSTAL. It will be a three-phase project. Phase one is the design, two is construction of a breadboard model and demonstration, and phase three is production of the first unit. Get started on the proposal and I'll let them know I found a contractor and get the money wheels turning. Can you make a presentation in two weeks?"

"Of course," said Will grinning from ear to ear. "Uh, HL and Logan?"

"They don't know yet. I wanted to be sure you could do it before I went any further with it."

"Do you think they'll go for it?" asked Will.

"Are you kidding? It's an AQUA project and it's near term money in the front door. We won't have to lay anyone off."

CHAPTER 12

Airborne, Near Yokosuka, Japan

Air traffic control at Haneda Airport vectored Hal to Yokosuka, then turned him to the northeast, giving him a ten-mile tour of Tokyo Bay. A left turn to the northwest put him on a five–mile straight-in final approach to Haneda. The airport sat on the bay's shoreline, south of Tokyo.

Hal taxied the Panther at a quick pace toward the Air Force hangar at the far end of the ramp. The hangar doors were open; he taxied up to the entrance of the hangar and shut the engine down. Several Air Force mechanics scrambled out from under a C47 cargo plane.

"Sorry we didn't flag you in sir, we weren't expecting you," said a Technical Sergeant as he climbed up the side of the Panther.

"I'm sure you weren't," Hal said as he completed the shutdown checklist. He climbed down the side of the Panther and shook hands with the Sergeant, "I need to take you into confidence Ballentine," he said, reading the name stenciled on the man's jumper. "I need this airplane pulled into the hangar ASAP, out of sight of taxiing aircraft. I'll depart late this afternoon. I'm on a classified mission."

"Like I said sir, we weren't expecting you. Since you're Navy, I'll need to talk with Master Sergeant Huxter. Got a copy of your orders, sir?"

Hal shrugged his shoulders, "There wasn't time to cut orders and I don't have time to work this out right now. I need you to make this happen. There's a case of Kirin beer in it for you."

"You got it sir, we'll pull her inside and close the doors."

A master Sergeant and two civilians came out of the hangar office and were walking toward the Panther. "You Captain Kirby?" yelled the master Sergeant.

"Affirmative," Hal replied. The master Sergeant turned and went back into the office; the two men in civilian clothes kept coming. Hal expected suits—they were in casual clothes.

"Commander Jim Carson," one said, offering a handshake.

"Lieutenant Walt Farrington," said the other.

"Captain Hal Kirby." Hal inspected their badges, "I've got some civvies. We have some time before the TBF lands." Hal opened a panel in the nose of the aircraft and extracted a GI laundry bag. He went into the men's room and changed into civilian clothes. "Ready," Hal announced when he returned and stuffed his flight suit into the plane's nose compartment. "Thanks, Ballentine, see you later this afternoon."

"Give us a description of him and the plane," said Jim as they walked toward the small USAF terminal building.

"Easy," said Hal, "it's a Grumman TBF, low-wing, single prop, fore and aft cockpit arrangement—he's the lard ass in the back. He's a Lieutenant Commander, five foot eight, 220 pounds or so, summer khaki's and wearing a piss cutter."

"OK, give me a fast rundown on what this is all about," asked Jim.

Hal briefed Jim on Garr's personality, the circumstances surrounding the court martial, Garr's behavior on the Valley Forge and his suspicions.

"OK," said Jim, "we'll get a chance to fill in the details while we're driving. There's several taxis out front—get in the one that has the word S–H–O–Y–O painted on the side. Start writing down everything you just told me and anything else you think of that's pertinent. The driver is expecting you. He's got paper and a pen."

Hal walked off the apron and through the terminal building. A shiny black taxi waited fifty feet from where the other taxis waited. It had "SHOYO" painted in white letters on the trunk and side. Hal opened the rear door.

"Are you Captain Kirby?" asked the Japanese driver in perfect English.

"Yes I am."

"You can call me Aku. I'm a sand crab in Jim's division." They shook hands. "Here's a pad. Jim wants you to make a deposition. When they come out, just slump over back there and keep your face out of sight."

"OK Mr. Tuna, you're the boss."

"Pulled some duty in Hawaii, huh?" asked the driver, acknowledging Hal's understanding of his Hawaiian namesake.

"Loved it. Best weather in the world," replied Hal.

"I sure miss it—was born and raised there. I'm trying to get transferred to Pearl. Looks like I have a pretty good chance too. My folks are still there and I haven't seen them in several years."

Hal finished his deposition and was chatting about Hawaii when Aku interrupted, "Get down Captain!"

Hal leaned over in the seat; Aku started the taxi. The rear door opened abruptly, "Scoot over," said Jim Carson, "but stay low. Walt's in the head with the subject, probably taking a leak right next to the guy. He's carrying the blue gym bag you mentioned." Jim pulled up his right pants leg, leaned over and checked the snub-nose pistol he had in a shin holster. "Hal, F–Y–I, in that leather bag on the floor under the front seat there is a couple of loaded thirty–eight specials, some boxes of ammo, cuffs and a few other goodies." Jim noticed Hal's surprised look and chuckled, "We don't plan to get into anything wild, but if things get hot and heavy for some reason, just help yourself."

"Rajah dajah," said Hal.

A few minutes later, Hal heard a car door slam, an engine start and then pass by. Aku put the taxi into gear but kept the clutch disengaged, ready to leap.

"There he goes," said Jim. Walt came running up to the car, opened the right front door and jumped inside. Aku took off before the door shut. "You can sit up now Captain. What do you think Walt?"

"He's nervous and wary," Walt said while he readied a camera with a long telephoto lens.

"Uh huh! I thought so too. He's definitely nervous," said Jim. Walt took several pictures of Garr's taxi as the situation allowed. "Thanks for the deposition," said Jim, while he selected a map from several in the leather pouch.

They followed the taxi onto the main highway that paralleled the coast south toward Yokosuka. "I hope I'm not being paranoid," Hal said.

"You did the right thing in any case. Don't worry about it; sometimes these things turn up positive, sometimes negative. Nobody gets ridiculed when the results are negative. The best tips we get come from people who become suspicious of their coworkers. You mentioned the Seventh Fleet Flagship—the USS Rochester. We're working a case on her. Garr's name came up in that mess too."

"I'm not surprised," said Hal. "I can imagine him doing most anything."

"They're turning off," Aku hollered.

Jim scanned his map quickly, "Captain, do you know any reason why he'd be going into downtown Yokohama?"

Aku said, "We're now on Osanbashi-dori—maybe headed for the docks."

Walt offered his theory, "Maybe he's got a Geisha waiting!" They laughed.

Garr's taxi continued to the waterfront and turned left at the T onto a busy street filled with bicycles, cars, trucks and carts. After proceeding a block, Garr's taxi made a kamikaze U-turn and pulled up to the curb in front of a corner building.

Aku drove on a bit further before turning around to avoid being obvious. "It's a shipping company, he won't find any Geishas in there," said Aku, reading the words painted on the side of the building. Aku double-parked beside an empty truck in front of a warehouse about ten car lengths away from Garr's cab.

Jim began a string of rapid fire orders, "Get pictures Walt, the ships in port, the building, get Garr going in, the bag, you know what I need. I'm going to find a phone and arrange a raid on this place ASAP, just in case. If he drops something off, I don't want it to get away from us. Aku, if Garr gets in that cab, you follow it—don't wait for me." Jim got out and went into the warehouse.

Walt handed Hal a pair of 7X50 binoculars, "Make a sketch. Write down the relative location, flag and name of every merchant vessel you see."

"Rajah dajah," Hal said enthusiastically. Aku was taking notes on a clipboard.

Walt said, "Aku, I don't have a good angle for the details on the front of the building. If you take off, try and keep it somewhat slow until we're past."

Time dragged. Aku picked up the running log he was keeping on a clipboard, "The subject has been in there for nine minutes. Jim's now at seven minutes."

"Roger," Walt answered, "guess he found a phone. Hey Captain, you've been very quiet back there. You awake?"

"I'm awake all right. I'm a pilot, not a gumshoe, so I'm just keeping my mouth shut, taking in the scenery. You guys are having almost as much fun as I do flying."

"Yeah this is panning out good," said Walt. "This little maneuver your shipmate's pulling certainly makes it interesting. I think we got lucky. We don't know anything about this place, though. If something is going on here, it's news to us."

"Jim's coming," announced Aku.

Jim got back into the cab, "They were kind enough to let me use the phone. No privacy, so I had to take what I could get. I got Dan on the phone and spoke Russian. If anybody in the office understood Russian, they just got an earful. The Japanese cops will have this place sealed off within half an hour or so; our people will be here too. They have Garr's description and will have a team at the Naval Base who will track him while he's on the base. We'll wait outside the gate."

"Subject!" announced Walt. Hal looked up to see Garr coming out and focused the binoculars on him. Walt was taking pictures in rapid succession. Garr looked around with caution and got into his cab.

"Look at the swing on that bag, light as a feather," said Walt.

"That son of a bitch dropped a load!" said Jim, "My estimate was five to seven pounds in that bag coming off the airplane."

"That's affirmative," said Walt, "he's been a bad boy. Still think you were paranoid Captain?" Aku started the engine; the cab leaped away from the curb. "Aku, don't forget to keep it slow until I get my frontal shots," reminded Walt.

The agents followed Garr's cab from a safe distance. They trailed it out of Yokohama and south to the gate at Yokosuka Naval Base.

"Looks like something's going on here at the gate," said Hal.

Jim replied, "Yeah, this is a pacifist demonstration by an anti-A-bomb group; we closed the base to all but official vehicles. I can't imagine that it has anything to do with Garr." A man with a banzai bandana wrapped around his head was standing atop a large rusty three–wheeled flatbed mini-truck parked fifty yards from the Naval Base gate. He was shouting into a megaphone with great animation. The vertical wooden slats on the side of the truck were wrapped with a grungy white banner on which large black Japanese characters were painted. There were a hundred shouting demonstrators being held away from the gate by Japanese police. Inside the gate were many armed Marines, ready to defend against any attempt by the demonstrators to breach the gate.

Garr spoke briefly to the cabby, walked through the gate and stood impatiently at the base shuttle bus stop.

"Captain," said Walt, "See the Chief Petty Officer standing twelve feet off Garr's left side—he's one of the on-base tails." The camera clicked. "See the Wave Ensign, she is too. She'll try and sit right next to him and strike up a conversation. By the time he gets to where he's going on the base, she'll know if the bag has something in it, what kind of watch he's wearing, his hat size, heart rate, blood pressure, the works. She's terrific."

Hal chuckled, "By any chance, is that your steady?"

"Yeah, how'd you know?"

Jim laughed, "Maybe Walt exaggerated a little, but she's unbelievably good at that stuff right there. Look, she's already talking to him." Walt took a couple more shots. Jim continued, "She was a theater and drama major in college—sure comes in handy."

Hal asked, "What's the Chief for?"

"The Chief will stay nearby as a backup, well out of Garr's span of attention. Garr won't even notice the Chief with her distracting him. She'll try and stay with him if it's not suspicious. When he goes into the building, she'll be coincidentally going to the intelligence center too, same floor and wing but a different office. Then the Chief will pick up the subject as he leaves the center and tail him back to the gate."

"Interesting way to earn a living," said Hal. "When Garr gets on the shuttle bus, I'll go over to the gate to call the friend I mentioned earlier, the one in the intelligence center."

Jim nodded, "OK. See what you can find out. That's a half hour shuttle route. You have plenty time." Walt began rewinding the film in his camera to reload with a fresh roll.

The shuttle bus departed on its route with Garr aboard. Hal walked to the Shore Patrol Office at the gate. "May I use your phone?" he asked the Shore Patrolman at the desk.

"Yes sir," said the Petty Officer and pointed to a phone at the end of the counter. Hal looked up the number for the center in a tattered phone listing sitting under the base of the phone and dialed the number listed for the XO.

"Commander Hargrove speaking."

"Hi Fred, it's Hal Kirby. How've you been?"

"Just fine. My God! Long time no see. You're on the Valley Forge, right? You in town for a while?"

"Yep, good old happy Valley. I'm only in town briefly Fred, but I need a favor. Know anything about Lieutenant Commander Garr?"

"Sure Hal. He's on the Forge too, right? What's up?"

"Yes, he transferred to us recently from Seventh Fleet. He's been visiting you guys lately. I don't know if anything is wrong with all that, but please keep all this under your hat podner."

"Sure Hal, what can I do?"

"Well, I've been chatting with the CI people here, and they asked me if he's been picking up classified info from the center to take back to the ship. It's the one thing I didn't think to check on the ship, the classified material receipt log. Could you check yours? Oh, by the way, he's on the shuttle, probably headed for the center right now."

"Sure Hal, I can do that real fast. Thanks for the heads up. Standby while I go check the files." After a few minutes passed, Fred returned to the phone, "Hal, I have some date/time groups of secret intell reports and unclassified short-titles of secret documents he picked up each time he visited."

"I don't need all the details right now Fred, just tell me how many pieces each trip."

"Nine, eight and thirteen, respectively. That all you need?"

"A–firm," said Hal, "He'll be there probably within the next ten or fifteen minutes. Make a report of all info on the receipts to and from this guy and keep it all handy. You're going to get a visitor today who will ask for it."

"OK my friend, glad to do it," replied Hargrove. "I get the drift. You sure you want me to let him get more stuff?"

"I think we better let him have whatever he would normally be given, Fred. Don't set off any alarms. Besides, we don't really know that he's doing anything wrong yet. He's been under a lot of pressure to give us good targets. This all could be on the level. If he tries anything stupid today though, they'll nab him."

Hal returned to the cab. "Hargrove just told me that Garr was issued thirty pieces of classified material on the last three visits. He's making a detailed list for you guys."

"Uh oh," said Jim and began thinking out loud, "I wonder if he's going to drop that stuff on the way back? He'll either try to make another drop today or save it for the next trip. Damn! If he tries to drop this stuff off at that place in Yokohama today, that's a problem! Our people will still be there, field stripping the place when he arrives. I need to make a phone call. We can at least lock the place up, clear out the cops and make the place look like it's closed. I don't want him to get there, sense a trap and make a run for it. He could lose us in a heartbeat and disappear forever. I want him back on the Valley Forge where we can get our hands on him if we need to. It will give us time to sort out the evidence we're developing and get this mess coordinated through Japanese and Navy channels." Jim hurried to the Shore Patrol Office.

Hal shook his head, "If that piece of whale shit is selling secrets, Geez, I don't even want to think about what he might have given away." Another thought struck Hal. He knows all there is to know about Chromite.

"Too bad this incident is destroying such a strong friendship," Walt kidded.

"Here comes Jim," said Aku. "You know, I wish they'd just let me have roaches like that for a few days all by myself."

Jim got into the cab, "All set—he'll never know anything is wrong, except that the place is closed."

"Let's hope that doesn't cause him to panic," said Walt.

They waited. Finally, Walt sat up abruptly, "Here comes the shuttle bus. Wonder if the fat boy i's on it?" They watched as the bus stopped and disgorged its load of sailors, Marines and sand crabs. Garr wasn't on it. A half hour later, the shuttle delivered another load.

"Tally Ho," said Hal, "that's him."

"That's our Chief right on his tail, too!" said Walt, "and look at the bag—it's damn sure not empty. I can see the corner of a package bulging out the side of it near the bottom." Walt's camera clicked several times as Garr walked toward the gate.

"Hey, he's going into the Shore Patrol Office," Jim said and leaped out of the cab. He walked briskly to the gate; when he went inside the office, Garr was dialing—Jim didn't have the angle he needed to see the numbers. Jim talked a Petty Officer into letting him use a phone on one of the desks. He dialed a bogus number and concentrated on what Garr was saying.

"This is Morgan," said Garr, "I have the shoes. OK, but don't forget the chocolates, and I need five pounds this time. It's five pounds or no deal," Garr said sternly and slammed the receiver down.

Jim maintained a fictitious discussion while listening intently to Garr with one ear and ignoring a busy tone in the other. Jim continued his imaginary conversation until Garr walked out the door.

The men in the cab watched anxiously for several minutes. The door opened and Garr came out, followed shortly thereafter by Jim. Garr walked to his waiting taxi and woke the driver. Jim walked nonchalantly until Garr's taxi pulled away, then trotted toward them. Aku started the cab, picked up the clipboard and scribbled a log entry. Hal ducked down as Garr's cab passed by; Aku pulled up toward Jim.

"And they're off," hollered Walt as Jim jumped into the moving cab; the wheels squealed under the strain of a fully depressed accelerator pedal and the torque of first gear.

"Listen to this, guys," said Jim, and related the one-sided conversation he overheard.

Walt shook his head, "Tsk, tsk, sounds like the fat boy is going to be bad again. He's greedy too," he said sarcastically.

"Curiouser and curiouser, as my son would say," said Hal. "Geez, I feel as useless as tits on a bull."

"Not at all, Captain," said Jim, "We needed you for positive ID and for the background on him, including the deposition. We couldn't have moved this fast on the case otherwise. The day ain't over yet. We may find something for you to do."

"Don't get me wrong, I'm not looking for a job," Hal said jokingly. "I'm perfectly happy just watching you guys."

As they approached Yokohama, Jim got out the detailed map of the city and began tracking their progress.

"It would have been logical for him to turn back there," said Aku, "It doesn't look like this guy's going back to the waterfront."

"Now that's interesting," said Jim, "either the driver is milking the meter or Garr is taking a little detour. Be careful Aku, he may be checking for tails."

"What do you want me to do if he starts doing alleys?" asked Aku.

Jim ran his finger along the map, keeping tabs on their location, "Stay on him Aku."

"Good. I haven't had any real fun for a while," said Aku. Hal could see a smile on the driver's face in the rear-view mirror.

After several miles, Aku broke the silence, "They're taking the Y to Haneda."

Walt turned to look at Jim with a quizzical look, "That doesn't make sense. What do you make of it?"

Jim looked puzzled, "It sure as hell sounded to me like he was going to meet someone today. Well, he can trade the 'shoes' for 'chocolates' at the airport, now can't he? Time will tell. Five miles to the airport now. When's his plane leave Captain?"

Hal looked at his watch, "ETA is in a little over two hours."

They continued north on the highway that ran along the Tokyo Bay waterfront.

"Boss, he ain't going to make the airport turn from that lane. Looks like we're going to Tokyo." said Aku.

"Maybe he's a ladies man after all," joked Walt.

Garr's taxi exited the highway and navigated the maze through the Ginza area.

Aku made a right turn that jogged Hal's memory, "I recognize this, it's Hibiya-dori Avenue, which goes past Hibiya Park and General MacArthur's HQ. That's the Imperial Hotel coming up on the right." I didn't think I'd see this again—not this soon, at least. As they passed by the hotel, Hal's mind drifted off to the land of Oz. Visions of Marmette drifted through his consciousness. Garr's cab turned left at the corner of the Imperial Palace moat and pulled to the curb.

"Uh oh! Fat boy's going for a walk in the park," said Jim. "Walt, you've got him. He got too good of a look at me at the Yokosuka gate."

"Roger," said Walt, and handed his camera to Aku. "I hope he doesn't remember me from the head at the airport."

Garr got out of the cab, gestured to the cab driver to circle the park and started across the street to the park, gym bag in hand. Aku turned the corner and pulled to the curb.

Hal looked out the side window at the Dai–ichi Building. So near and yet so far! Geez, how weird this is. She'd turn flips if she knew I was sitting here. I'd love to stroll in there. The look on her face would be priceless.

Jim slapped Walt on the shoulder, "I won't be too far behind you." Walt nodded as he watched Garr cross the street and start across the park grass and over a knoll. Walt got out and followed him.

Jim said, "Aku, wait here for us. If Garr comes out and we're not in sight, follow him. I want to be sure he doesn't drop that stuff somewhere else, although I'm sure he'll be headed for the airport." Aku nodded. Jim got out and crossed the street.

Hal watched as they all disappeared over the top of a small grassy hill. He turned his attention again to the Dai–ichi Building.

Walt followed Garr toward a pond surrounded by a narrow cement path. There were wooden benches spaced every 20 feet along the path. Garr sat on the end of a bench opposite a stout man in a dark blue business suit. There were three empty benches on one side and two on the other. It was clear to Walt that Garr was sitting with his contact. Walt walked to the water's edge, about thirty yards away from Garr. While befriending several ducks, Walt observed the two unlikely bench companions out of the corner of his eye. He noted they both had identical blue gym bags. Jim arrived on the periphery of the scene; he was sitting on the grass, propped against a small tree seventy feet or so directly behind the bench. Although Garr and the contact were admiring different parts of the pond, Walt could see their jaws moving slightly as they spoke quietly to each other. Garr nonchalantly reached over his bag and grabbed the handles of the bag next to the other man, picked it up and walked briskly back toward the moat and his cab. Walt acknowledged Jim's subtle hand signal. When the contact was looking the other way, Walt took his pistol from his shin holster and slid it into his pocket. He strolled leisurely back across the grass toward the sidewalk, in the general direction of the contact's bench. The man studied Walt suspiciously. Walt avoided eye contact and used his peripheral vision to keep track of the man's actions. The contact grasped the handles of Garr's bag and began walking down the path, away from Walt. When Garr disappeared over the knoll, Walt began jogging to catch up with the contact.

"Excuse me," Walt called out. There was no response—the man continued walking but sped up. Walt was now thirty feet from the man, "Halt, U.S. federal agent," he hollered, bringing the pistol from his pocket; Jim was also running, gun in hand, toward the contact. The man dropped the bag and began running. Walt yelled, "Halt, or I will shoot!" The man looked over his shoulder and saw Walt's gun drawn and stopped. He raised both hands and turned around. Walt ordered, "Do not move! You are under arrest for suspicion of espionage against the United States of America." A thousand Japanese eyes were watching in surprise at the interruption of the tranquility of the park.

"I have done nothing! I have done nothing!" the man said in a very heavy Slavic accent. His chubby pockmarked face showed panic. His eyes were darting back and forth between Walt and Jim. "Not to shoot, I have done nothing."

Jim stood to the side of the man with his weapon pointed at the man's chest, "Well Igor, what then is this little bag all about?"

"Is not my bag. Never see before," the overwrought man said.

"That won't work comrade," said Walt. "Lie face down on the ground with your hands out as far as you can reach."

Aboard the USS Valley Forge

Hal returned to the ship twenty–eight minutes before the COD brought Garr back aboard.

"Make yourself comfortable Hal," said the Admiral, lighting one of his gargantuan and piquant cigars. "What kind of a day did you have? I saw Garr deplane safe and sound. Must have behaved himself."

Hal relaxed into the chair opposite Hawkins in the Admiral's sea cabin after pouring a cup of coffee.

"In summary, Garr committed espionage today. Probably twice!"

Hawkins face was sullen, "Are you certain?" he asked with deep furrows above his eyes and inflated forehead veins. "Is there any chance you're mistaken?"

"There's no question. Let me start from the beginning . . ." Hawkins listened intently, puffing and chewing on his cigar while Hal related the day's activities.

"Sunnavabitch!" Hawkins said when Hal finished. "I hate the thought of him running around this ship loose. Do they know what the hell they're doing?"

"Makes you wonder Admiral. Listen to this, he's also a suspect in a case involving the USS Rochester. A burn-bag of classified information from the Seventh Fleet commander's staff was found when they busted up a spy ring in Yokosuka. They didn't have any evidence on him being the source; there were several other suspects too. Wheels of justice turn slowly—too damn slowly! Anyway sir, there's some technicalities they must work through on this thing. Stupid as it sounds, the fact that they didn't catch Garr himself with the material is somewhat of a problem. There also is liaison and coordination with the Japanese police and so on, but they assured me it would be taken care of in a few days. Meanwhile, they want us to keep him on the ship from now on, and somehow not arouse any suspicion. When they have the authority, they'll ask us to put him in the brig and he'll be promptly transferred off the ship."

Hawkins thought briefly, "Put Ted back into the mode of intelligence backup, but don't let Garr know it. Do not act on any intell info that Garr provides unless you or Ted verify it. We're coming down the home stretch to D–Day for Inchon and I don't want any problems."

CHAPTER 13

0355, Thursday, September 15, 1950
D–Day, Operation Chromite
Aboard USS Valley Forge

The wardroom was overflowing with five squadrons of pilots assembled for a consolidated mission briefing. Their energy and morale were high; their chatter was tumultuous. They were raring to get airborne and clear the way for the landing forces at Inchon.

"Morning CAG," a pilot hollered into Hal's ear. "I'm glad to see this day. I'm sick of this war."

Hal laughed, "Mornin' Sammy. Hell, it's only been two and a half months. You would have loved the last war." Hal watched Sammy push through the crowd toward his squadron. I hate to tell these guys, but this isn't the end. The beginning of the end, maybe—I hope.

"Attention on deck!" shouted the Admiral's aide as he entered the wardroom just ahead of Hawkins. Instantly, the room became quiet. The Admiral navigated through the tables to the end of the wardroom where Hal had set up an easel.

"Good morning Admiral," said Hal.

"Good morning gentlemen, at ease," said the Admiral and carefully scanned the mass of tan flight suits before him. He began his pep talk for today's landmark mission. "Chromite will be a long remembered and well-studied moment in military history. The fates of many of our soldiers, indeed South Korea and its people, call upon you today. As I speak, the landing force is an hour and fifteen minutes from Flying Fish Channel. As you know, you will be over the target before the ships run the gauntlet. Your job is to make damn sure there is no gauntlet by the time they reach the channel. Since the ceiling and visibility are forecasted to be relatively low, you must use great care. I don't want to lose anyone to a midair collision." He paused to let that thought have its effect. "I've heard scuttlebutt that some of you don't understand why this operation isn't being postponed for better weather. That would be disastrous. The next acceptable tides won't occur for another month. We'll lose our lease in South Korea by then. I can't count the number of times I launched in the South Pacific under far more ridiculous circumstances and odds. Captain Kirby has done it. Your COs have done it. Today you'll do it. You must use your skill, ingenuity and perseverance to provide the air support that Tenth Corps needs. We'll have massive casualties if you don't take out the enemy's defensive positions. But I have total confidence in your ability to accomplish your missions. You've proved yourselves in these past weeks." Thrusting a thumb high above his head, he yelled, "God speed! Good hunting!" His pumped-up aviators began shouting every gruesome and profane wish for the North Koreans ever conceived. Hawkins took a seat at the front table with Hal's XO, Lieutenant Commander Ted Spence and the squadron COs.

Hal quieted the men down, "Gentlemen, listen up," he hollered. He glanced to the back of the room where Garr stood, leaning against the bulkhead, staring. "I have an update to last night's intell briefing. It appears that the NKPA took the bait offered by the convincing feint of shore bombardment and extensive air strikes at Kunsan yesterday at dusk. They have sent reinforcements from Seoul and the southeast to the port of Kunsan. OK guys, back to Inchon. I can't overemphasize the potential hazards created by the reduced visibility. Once we start creating secondary fires in the port and the jarheads start dropping napalm on Wolmi-do, it's going to get thick, especially with little wind to dissipate it." As he looked around the room he saw a mass of fidgeting legs and arms. Anything else he said was sure to go in one ear and out the other. These pilots wanted to get in their airplanes. "Keep your stuff together. Zero mid-airs—zero fratricides. Watch your asses! Don't get careless! Good hunting!" Hal nodded to the Admiral's aide.

The aide called out, "Attention on deck!"

When the Admiral was clear of the room, Hal dismissed the pilots. They erupted into howls, yells, whistles and other noises common to aboriginal man as they streamed from the wardroom. The taste of imminent victory was sweet.

Hal went to his stateroom for a final pit stop. He paused by the little desk mounted on the wall and picked up the family portrait that he kept there. He focused momentarily on each of them. Alice looked so happy in this picture. The letter from his son and daughter, Joseph and Susan, was lying on the desk. When he read it last night, he felt an empty spot in his stomach. It returned as he looked at the letter. I sure hope Joe and Susie are wrong. Alice can't be that sick and miserable. It's unlike her. One thing's for sure though, she hasn't been her old self. Hell, she volunteers at Bethesda, surely she'd get herself checked out if she didn't think things were right. How do I ask her without compromising the kids? I need to be home. I need to be here. He focused on Alice's face. I love you. Hold on honey, this won't last forever.

He grabbed his helmet, rushed to the escalator and trotted up the moving treads. He stepped off the escalator and charged through the hatch onto the flight deck. It was still wet and glossy from a passing shower. Cool damp air sent a chill through him. The sky was a murky, very dark gray. The sun was just beginning to lift the veil of night. Floodlights on the upper levels of the island lit the busy deck. Aircraft were being brought up on the elevators and spotted on the crowded afterdeck in takeoff sequence.

A voice called from behind him, "Kirby!"

Hal halted and turned, "What the hell do you want Garr?"

Garr's face had an evil expression, "Think you'll make it back Captain?"

"I'll be back Mr. Garr, I'll be back."

"Maybe. Maybe not. Anyway, just thought you'd like to know something before you go," Garr's expression changed to a hideous grin, "Alice is going to receive some anonymous mail soon. Pictures of you and that broad in Tokyo. You can kiss your cozy little family life good-bye."

"Are you crazy? There's no broad in Tokyo. You're a sick son of a bitch Garr."

"Unfortunately for you Kirby, I'm not as sick as you think. I have a friend in Tokyo who has lots of details about you and that whore. He tells me you spent lots of time in the quarters of, what's her name? Marmette? Now, Captain Kirby oh great and wonderful leader, am I making all this shit up?"

"In the first place, I didn't know you had any friends," Hal said. "You've really gone off the deep end. Things are not always what they appear to be. Enjoy your fantasy world Mister Garr, you're living on borrowed time. I thought you'd be smart enough to leave me alone." Hal spun and quick-paced toward the bow of the ship; his Panther was waiting at the number one catapult. As he walked at a quick pace, his mind was reeling. Damn Garr! I don't think he is bluffing about the mail to Alice. He'd enjoy doing something like that. Geez, Dusty said Tullis was a photography nut. When I get back, I've got to see if I can talk the Admin Officer into rummaging through the outgoing mail for mail to Alice, just in case it hasn't left the ship yet. Just how am I going to justify that? Oh God, if that letter already left the ship - I don't even want to think about that. I'll have to write a letter to Alice and warn her that he'll try to slander me as part of his plan to get even. Hal saw the Admiral was just ahead, chatting with the ship's XO and the aircraft maintenance officer. Hawkins motioned for him to come over.

Hal greeted them, "Mornin' Admiral, gentlemen."

"Mornin' CAG," said the XO, "give 'em hell."

"Rajah dajah! said Hal."

Admiral Hawkins put his hand on Hal's shoulder, nodded toward Hal's plane and said, "Let's walk and talk." After several paces, Hawkins said, "I just wanted to say a few words in private. Don't take any undue risks. You've been very aggressive in the air lately."

Hal interrupted, "Admiral…"

Hawkins raised his palm at Hal, "Don't Admiral me, I know what it's like to be in your shoes and I know you. Just find that damn column of mechanized reinforcements intell reported being on its way to Seoul. They will be real damn trouble for the landing forces if they get through.

"Aye, aye sir. I'll get their reinforcements and I'll bring all your planes back too."

Hawkins walked back to the island and Hal hurried to his plane. There was a peculiar feel and smell to the 100% humidity. His flight suit already felt like a damp dishrag. The environment and the moment combined to create an ominous feeling - a strange mix of danger, adventure and challenge, all rolled into one sensation.

Hal's Panther was waiting obediently for her preflight check. The plane Captain saluted Hal and reported, "Good morning sir, she's ready for bear."

Hal returned the salute and replied, "Good job Krebs." Hal performed his usual thorough preflight walk-around, shining his flashlight over the skin, control surfaces, tires and wheel assemblies, speed brakes, tail hook, air intake, bombs and rockets. The plane Captain climbed up and sat astride the canopy, just behind the ejection seat rails. Hal completed the check, climbed up and slipped carefully into the cramped cockpit. "Seat's dry Krebs, thanks. When I saw the water beads on the airframe, I was sure my ass was going to splash when I got in."

"You have no faith Captain. I shut the canopy before the shower hit."

"You're a good man Krebs" Petty Officer Krebs helped Hal get strapped in and hooked up. Hal took a deep breath and adjusted his helmet. It'll be a sad day when I can't fly anymore. I feel sorry for Admiral Hawkins—he has to do all his flying vicariously now. I hope we can put Garr in the brig soon, before he does some real damage. For God's sake, he's already done plenty damage! I hope his mail hasn't left the ship.

"Anything wrong?" asked Krebs.

"Nope, just going over some things in my mind," said Hal. He pressed the master electrical switch; the red panel lights illuminated the instruments; needles whipped into position; gyros spun up. He completed the pre-start checklist and, satisfied, toggled the master switch to OFF. He and Krebs chatted while waiting for the word to start engines.

"We gonna be home for Thanksgiving Captain?"

"I sure hope so. It'll all depend on how successful this landing goes."

"What ya up to this mornin'?"

"We're going to squash some reinforcements coming down from the north to Inchon. How about you?"

"Nothin' that much fun."

"STAND-BY TO START JET ENGINES," announced the Air Boss over the flight deck PA system. Krebs shook Hal's hand and climbed down onto the flight deck. The carrier changed its heading, came around to the launch heading and began accelerating. He toggled the master electrical switch and looked over the instruments again. He looked due east. Although the horizon was barely visible, Hal could see the scant evidence that the sun was just below it. The sky would be getting lighter by the minute.

"START JET ENGINES," blared from the PA horns above the flight deck. Hal's Panther came screaming to life. He lowered the wings from their nearly vertical folded position. Beads of perspiration rolled down his face, teased his forehead and upper lip, lit tiny flares in his eyes and salted the corners of his mouth. His feet involuntarily tapped rapidly in counterpoint on the rudder pedals, draining off excess energy. Several dark spots on his tan flight suit thighs marked the places where he wiped his hands after clearing his profusely sweating brow. The shrill whine and penetrating vibration of raw jet power pleading to be unleashed commanded his soul. "C'mon, c'mon, let's get this damn show on the road, this son of a bitch is gulping kerosene I'll need to get back," he hollered into the din. He motioned at the Flight Deck Director to hurry up the process and grumbled to himself, "I don't have this Panther strapped to my ass for shits and giggles, let's go!" Green-shirted crewmen scooted underneath to attach the catapult bridle to the attach-point on the plane's belly while others pulled the starting cart away. Kirby scanned the dim horizon; only the destroyers in the defensive screen around the carrier broke the line separating the sea and the dim sky. Even with sunrise slowly progressing, it was obvious it was going to be as forecasted—gloomy, hot and humid with an ominous low level haze layer. The calm, silt-laden sea had a dull brownish-green color. Heavy black diesel exhaust gushed from the ship's funnel. Four powerful engines strained against the huge brass screws that propelled the ship at a brisk 30 knots, creating headwind for launching planes. Shortly, the powerful catapult will throw this six–foot Texan and his eight–ton plane from the flight deck. Hal's wingman will be launched seconds behind him, then the other Panthers of Fighter Squadron Fifty–one will also launch rapidly in pairs. Hal glanced at his wingman on the parallel catapult. He appeared to be sitting on an ant hill. No part of his body was still. They exchanged smiles and thumbs-up. It was only his wingman's second week of live combat. Kirby, on the other hand, was bringing seventeen years of Naval aviation training and experience to this mission, including carrier combat operations during WW II—he could not keep still either. Thoughts streaked through Hal's mind. They were rambling snippets that streamed uncontrollably through his senses. He thought about Alice and the kids. He thought of his fire red MG, up on blocks in the garage of his home in Great Falls, VA. There was a flash back to his graduation ceremony at the Naval Academy—hats filled the sky. Then, he was instantly transported to the Pacific, defending a carrier task force against Kamikazes. The face of Lieutenant Luther Garr flashed up. Hal relived the fear that came over him when he realized Luther had broken off and dove for the deck leaving him alone with a bunch of Zero pilots looking for glory.

A loud good luck slap on the side of the cockpit by a deck crewman jolted Hal out of his trance. The Flight Deck Director was whirling two fingers over his head—prepare for launch. "Time to go kick some North Korean asses," yelled Hal as he pulled his goggles down off his helmet and adjusted them. He lowered the flaps to the take-off position and pushed the throttle lever fully forward. The angry Panther shrieked and strained against the catapult bridle, demanding freedom. After rechecking his instruments and gauges one last time, Hal gave a nod to the Flight Deck Director, then gave the Launch Officer a snappy left-handed salute. The Launch Officer dropped to one knee and pointed toward the bow of the ship—the launch command. Hal pressed his helmet firmly back into the headrest. His heart was pumping hard and fast. The tremendous instantaneous energy delivered by the hydraulic catapult gave the soul jarring slam and swift acceleration that Hal found utterly exhilarating. In two seconds, he accelerated to one hundred fifteen knots across the deck in just under two hundred feet. Hal screamed a loud "YaaaaaHooooo"—the frivolous ritual he adopted in primary flight training at Pensacola. He promptly entered a climbing right turn, raised the landing gear and began retracting the flaps. Safely airborne and with the risk of an immediate ditching gone by, he pushed the canopy lever forward which hydraulically slammed the Plexiglas cockpit bubble shut. A quick scan to the wheels and flaps position indicator in the instrument panel confirmed that the nose wheel and main gear had tucked themselves neatly into their wells. Airspeed was building quickly; he climbed steeply through the low ceiling to 10,000 feet on a northerly heading and leveled off in a slow cruise. The sky was clear at this altitude and getting bright rapidly.

Shortly, all his Panthers were snuggled up in tight formation off each of his wings. They were flying a heading of 020 degrees toward Inchon. Anxiously, he awaited the beautiful rays and colors typical of the moment when the sun's blinding white fire nicks the horizon. He wasn't disappointed with nature's breakfast light show. It was no less a humbling experience this morning than any other morning. The edge of the warm front over Inchon was particularly well defined. He could see breaks in the cloud deck to the east.

Hal tuned his radio to channel six, which was assigned to the Marine Corsairs. They were just beginning to attack their targets at Blue Beach south of Inchon and Wolmi-do Island. Listening to channel seven, Hal heard Skyraiders commencing their first strafing pass at Red Beach and the emplacements to the rear of the Inchon sea wall.

Intense yet translucent rays of pink and orange were fanning out from the very tip of the sun's blazing aurora.

"Tally Ho, Kimpo," Hal radioed. He could see that there were no enemy aircraft in the traffic pattern at Kimpo Airfield and no planes were moving on the ground. Closer in, he could see three widely spaced massive bomb craters in the concrete runway. Men working on refilling the holes with fill dirt heard the approaching Panthers and ran for their lives. He noted that all the antiaircraft batteries defending the airfield were destroyed. So were the hangars and most of the buildings. All aircraft on the field were destroyed or damaged beyond use. There was nothing worth his cannon rounds or rockets. Last evening's massive air strike on Kimpo had been flawless. "Keep your eyes open for tanks and towed artillery," he said, rolling level over the Han River, which ran close by the airfield.

Hal refolded the area map on his kneeboard to display the Seoul area. He flew southeast, along the river's gently winding path. It was about a nine–mile route from the airfield to a point south of Seoul where the Han River angled to the northeast for four miles then meandered easterly away from the city. Recent heavy rains discolored the Han River. It looked like swirled light and dark milk chocolate. Black puffs of flak were popping up in front of him; he climbed to 15,000 feet to avoid it.

Someone radioed, "Can't we take out the triple A?"

"Negatory," replied Hal, "we're saving the good stuff for the reinforcements." As the few remaining air defense sites revealed themselves, he marked their locations on his map. Last night's attacks on those installations around the city had been effective. When the river turned away from the city, Hal turned northbound to fly along the highway that ran toward Uijongbu to search for reinforcements from the north.

"DRAGON flight, say fuel states," Hal radioed. Each responded in turn. All were consistent except Sharky's report.

"DRAGON–8, 3.5"

"DRAGON–8, this is DRAGON–1, confirm 3.5," Hal radioed.

"DRAGON–8, confirming 3.5 sir," said the young Ensign with excitement in his voice.

"DRAGON–7 check him out," said Hal.

"7 Rog. Hold 'er steady Sharky, I'm going to look up yer skirt to see if you took some flak back there."

Sharky said, "Roger Pete, you can look but ya can't touch!"

DRAGON–7 maneuvered a mere six feet under the Ensign's port tip tank, moved slowly to the right, paused for a minute under the belly and eased over further to inspect the starboard tip tank. "You can close yer legs honey, I've seen enough 'til I get you home." Pete dropped away and slipped back into formation.

"I'm so embarrassed," said Sharky. You could hear the smile on his face. The humor took the edge off the situation.

"DRAGON–1 from 7, he's clean, no holes and no visible fuel streaming."

"Rajah, dajah. Keep track of his fuel burn rate and let me know if it's different from yours. For now, I'll assume it's a gauge problem. I'd send you guys back now but I need you until the last minute."

Hal's DRAGONs were soon to be rewarded. A long line of dark-painted vehicles came into view. He couldn't discern the tail end of it from the city clutter in the distance. "You bastards are too late for the morning matinee. And you're going to miss the evening show too," Hal whispered into his oxygen mask. Hal quickly radioed another flight of Panthers for backup. He maneuvered to pass abeam the line of doomed machinery below. As he looked down, he noticed that the trucks were stopping at the side of the road. They were packed with soldiers that were piling out in panic. It looked like a hill of disturbed ants as the troops sought refuge from the high crown of the highway. There was nothing but wide open farmland with cabbage rows on either Tanks picked up their pace as best they could, continuing southbound on the highway. Jeeps—many pulling artillery pieces—were weaving through the tanks, trying to escape at high speed. Hal continued past the end of the long column. When the rearmost tank was off his port quarter, he rolled and pulled into a dive. He estimated twenty–five to thirty tanks, about the same number of large troop trucks and roughly twenty jeeps pulling howitzers. "Tanks first, make every rocket count," directed Hal. For an instant, he flashed back to his fateful attack on the troop trucks in the valley by the Naktong River. His mouth was already dry from adrenaline being pumped through his body by a pounding heart. Realizing that his grip on the stick had gotten as hard as granite, he relaxed and took a deep breath. Jeeps with wildly bouncing artillery pieces in tow were passing the tanks, hoping to escape the deadly blue Panthers. He kept the last tank in the column in the gunsight. Passing through 3,000 feet, he fired a rocket. It roared off the wing's outer starboard pylon and raced down to the tank, trailing a white exhaust plume. Quickly, he lined up the next tank, squeezed off another rocket and repeated that a third time before hauling back hard on the stick. Hal grunted hard in a high–G climbing left turn. As the nose came around, he looked down and saw that he and his wingman had hit three tanks.

"I got three that run, Marv. 'How about you?" Hal asked his wingman.

"Dreamer!" exclaimed Marv in contorted speech from G–force grunting, "Those three were all mine." The high G turns exaggerated their grins.

The Panthers headed back to Inchon, fully expended. There were many tanks, trucks and artillery pieces left in shambles on the road behind them. Hal conjured up the vision of that conference table full of stars in Tokyo, fretting over Inchon. Then the specter of Luther Garr came into focus. First thing I'm going to do when I get back aboard the ship is find that Admin Officer. Geez, this is a bitch of a situation.

As he approached Inchon, he found the visibility significantly improved. The dense overcast of the warm front had drifted off to the west, but some haze remained. He enjoyed the Inchon scenery, as best one could from two miles up. Burning trees, tanks and gun emplacements on Wolmi-do Island and burning structures in the port area provided a bluish-gray haze of varying density. There appeared to be no wind—the sea was calm and the haze just sat on the port. Hal counted nineteen ships in Flying Fish Channel. Two things were obvious, the landing had taken place on Wolmi-do and none of the ships had taken any hits. Marine aircraft were still working over the eastern side of Wolmi-do Island and the adjacent shoreline. Shore bombardment of the port was underway by rocket launchers, destroyers and cruisers in Flying Fish Channel. Craters and secondary fires were visible in the areas along and behind the dreaded twelve–foot sea walls that the landing force would have to scale on the next tide. He could see orange flashes spewing from the tips of the cruiser and destroyer gun barrels, then the grayish black puffs of the projectile explosions on the target. Sheets of parallel white exhaust trails rose from the rocket ships as salvos arced toward the ground targets in the port. No Valley Forge birds were visible. They were already back aboard the ship being refueled and armed for an immediate turnaround.

As he passed over Flying Fish Channel, he tuned his radio to the Valley Forge Combat Information Center, "COATHANGER this is DRAGON–1, DANCER flight feet wet, over."

"Radar contact," replied the Valley Forge air coordinator, "Everybody OK?"

"Gang's all here! DRAGON–8 has a low fuel indication. It's probably the gauge, but we need him aboard without delay," said Hal.

"Roger that DRAGON–1, I'll pass that along. Fly heading two zero zero degrees. Altimeter two niner eight niner, ceiling three oh double oh, winds light from two eight zero, visibility three to five miles with widely scattered light showers over."

"DRAGON–1 copy." Hal reset his directional gyro, made the heading adjustment, reset his altimeter and took a deep breath. It was always thrilling to depart on a mission, but it was one hell of a great feeling to be heading back without any losses.

"DRAGON–1 this is COATHANGER, talk to the Air Boss," advised the Valley Forge.

"DRAGON–1 rajah dajah," replied Hal. "DRAGON flight from 1, drop your hooks." His left hand found the tail hook cable release handle; his wingman gave him a thumbs-up. He looked back at his wingman's hook and gave him a thumbs-up too. "Down we go. Change frequency," Hal advised the others and pushed gently forward on the stick. Slipstream noise built up rapidly as the air speed increased in the descent. He adjusted the angle of attack to maintain .75 mach.

"Air Boss from DRAGON–1."

"Roger CAG, bring 'em aboard. Understand you want DRAGON–8 to trap first."

"Affirm Tom, low fuel or bad gauge."

"OK CAG, put number eight in front and we'll take the rest of you in normal order."

"Rajah dajah." They plummeted down into the tops of the gray overcast layer and quickly penetrated through the ceiling at 3,000 feet. Hal pulled back to slow the rate of descent. Valley Forge was just to his left about five miles away. She was steaming hard at 30 knots. As the carrier's bow cut into the sea it created a foamy inverted 'V' which created the proverbial 'bone in her teeth.'

They leveled off at 300 feet, in a single line, set up for the downwind leg off the ship's port side; Valley Forge was three miles ahead. DRAGON–8 slipped into the lead. Hal pushed the gear lever. There was a strange grinding noise. It sounded like it came from the starboard main gear. When the gear motors shut down, he did not have a down-and-locked indication for the starboard main gear. Slightly unequal drag required compensation on the stick and rudder that foretold trouble. He looked over at his wingman and pointed down.

"Standby CAG," said Marv, who slid underneath to take a look. As he came back alongside, he gave Hal a thumbs-down. Damn! Just what I need. What else can happen to me today? Hal was just passing down the side of the ship; number 8 was just turning onto his base leg. "Air Boss from 1, I'm breaking off with Marv to check out a gear problem on my bird," said Hal. Marv nodded. Hal banked right, turned forty–five degrees and climbed to 2,000 feet.

"Looks like an actuator arm on the starboard main snapped. In a peculiar place, too. The gear's not down. Let me swing under again and eyeball it real good."

"See if you think it might lock in with some high Gs maneuvers," said Hal, watching Marv move slowly underneath him. Marv was looking up, inching forward to a position directly under Hal's wheel assembly—only six feet between the wheel and his canopy.

"Don't think so CAG. I don't think it will retract either. If you actuate the gear, I think it'll just hang there," said Marv.

"OK, move away, I'll cycle 'em." When Marv was clear, Hal tried to retract the gear.

"Port's up but starboard's still hanging," said Marv.

Damn! Well, that means it'll collapse when it comes in contact with the deck. Belly landing! I'll be damned if I'm writing off this bird. We'll at least have a bunch of parts. Geez, I wonder if Garr had a hand in this. "Air Boss from CAG, Marv's ready to come aboard now. I'll orbit for a while. My starboard main is disabled. It's hanging free. It'll collapse on impact. I'd like to come aboard on my belly."

"CAG would you rather eject?" asked the Air Boss. Hal realized the Air Boss wanted badly to avoid a deck fire from a plane crash. That would curtail flight operations for too long. Butterflies fluttered in Hal's stomach. It's my ass, not his. I can manage the fuel dump to put me over the fantail with little more than fumes. Shouldn't be any fire. Besides, I hate to throw away a quarter of a million dollars.

"CAG, you still with me?" asked the Air Boss.

"Yeah Tom, was just weighing the options. I'd prefer to belly her aboard with minimal fuel," said Hal.

"Standby Hal," Tom replied. Hal was flying a three-mile radius orbit around the carrier at 2,000 feet at full power to burn off fuel. Several minutes passed. Damn, this means they are talking about making me eject. I do not want to eject.

"Hal, we'd like you to make an approach so we can look at the starboard main," said Tom, "How's fuel?"

"Rajah, dajah, coming at you, I've got plenty," said Hal.

"Roger, fly standard final, automatic wave off close aboard."

"Rajah, dajah," said Hal. As he passed a mile in front of the ship, he lowered more flaps, descended to 300 feet and turned to fly down the port side of the ship on the downwind leg. At the key position, he turned onto base leg, then onto final with full flaps; he began his descent to 70 feet above the frothy off-white wake. A pull on the canopy lever threw the canopy back and flushed the cockpit with humid air. Hal was noting the power, bank and rudder combinations necessary to compensate for the asymmetric drag presented by the crippled landing gear. The fantail of the carrier looked inviting; it was a perfect approach—speed, alignment and altitude were right on the money. He kept his attention on the Landing

Signal Officer.

"Wave-off," said the LSO's assistant on the radio simultaneously with the LSO's paddle signal. Hal applied full power, banked left, slowly retracted the flaps, closed the canopy and returned to 2,000 feet.

"Very nice Hal," said Tom, "gave us a good look. Carl had the big eyes on you. What's your fuel state?"

"Fuel one point one."

"Roger," said Tom, "take some laps while I ready the deck."

"Rajah, dajah," Hal replied, sighing in relief that Tom didn't make him to eject.

Several minutes passed. Flying the circling pattern around the carrier was the ultimate contrast of boredom compared to the potential danger that awaited him when his Panther slammed onto the deck. His mind occupied itself with the development of a table of minimum necessary fuel levels for different locations around the Happy Valley. Self-discipline restricted his repeated visualizations of the landing to successful outcomes. He jumped when the radio crackled to life.

"OK CAG, advise when fuel is point five and ensure tip tanks are purged."

"Confirm tips empty," he acknowledged and applied full power to hasten the fuel consumption. The fuel quantity gauge crept downward; the low fuel light in the panel blinked incessantly. Finally, he had burned off excess fuel and he radioed, "Point five Tom."

"Bring her aboard Hal, good luck. We're all set. If waved off, you must set yourself up for ejection alongside."

"Rajah dajah, here we go." He smiled. You can bet your ass I'm going to fly a perfect approach rather than risk an ejection.

As he passed down the port side of the ship Tom radioed, "Lookin' good CAG, good luck." A heat flash slammed into him as a mass of adrenaline released and surged through his body. He pulled the canopy lever and completed the landing checklist; the cockpit was flushed again with air, making his soaked flight suit feel cool. Turns onto base and final and configuration changes were made by his unconscious mind while his conscious mind focused on controlling the damaged plane. He jerked his safety belts to make them very tight. When he leveled out on final, fuel was alarmingly low but his position was good, directly astern the ship at seventy feet. His mind reconfirmed his decision to land aboard rather than eject. He could taste his teeth; the pungent smell of stack gas trailing behind the ship was particularly intense; powerful heartbeats boomed in his ears; the seat pad felt rock hard and very wet. An involuntary tremor in his knees was annoying. The LSO's paddles held firmly in the 'OK' position as he rapidly approached the flight deck. They had hosed down the deck with salt water; it looked like a peaceful glistening bass pond. Emergency crews on the port edge of the flight deck energized fire hoses with pole-like extended fog nozzles. Fog from the nozzles created clouds of water that painted faint rainbows. 'Tilly'—the mobile deck crane—was centered behind the barricade straps. That mass of iron would protect the planes and equipment parked behind it on the forward flight deck, if Hal's tail hook didn't catch a wire and the other obstacles didn't do the job of stopping him. Just the thought of slamming into that steel monstrosity sent a chill through him. The LSO signaled 'cut power.' "Perfect," he hollered at the top of his voice. He braced, recalling his spectacular 11–wire trap as a benchmark for what to expect. It was worse—much worse. The belly slammed onto the hardwood deck with a terrible impact. The starboard landing gear collapsed immediately on contact, as he predicted. The aircraft slid down the deck, screeching and groaning, slowly turning askew. One after another, arresting wires zipped by as the Panther skidded toward the Davis barriers. Without the benefit of the main gear shock absorbers, the tremendous impact transferred directly into the airframe. Some of that energy found its way to Hal's spine, stunning him into semi-consciousness. Somehow, the tail hook found the 12–wire, jerked the Panther straight and to an abrupt stop; the safety catch just forward of the windshield was straining a cable in the first barrier. Hal was not aware that the plane was at a standstill or that men in silver asbestos fire suits where releasing him from his straps. Suddenly he realized that he was being hauled bodily out of the plane and cold water was spraying all over him. He tried to stand when they got him to the deck but his legs were too rubbery. Two 'silver-suits' put his arms over their shoulders and hauled him to the island.

Glancing back at the Panther, he grinned—there was no fire. "That deck is as slippery as cat spit on linoleum," said Hal, flight boots barely touching as the silver-suits lugged him across the flight deck.

"Don't try and walk, we got ya," hollered an asbestos hood.

A flight surgeon and an emergency medical team were waiting at the edge of the flight deck.

CHAPTER 14

0715, Thursday, September 15, 1950
D–Day, Operation Chromite
Aboard USS Valley Forge

"I'm OK Doc, I'm OK," hollered Hal as the silver-suits delivered him to the medical crew at the island.

"Get on the stretcher, Hal," ordered Captain 'Doc' Bristol, the Flight Surgeon.

"Geez Doc, I'm OK, I was just hazy for a minute."

"Don't give me a bad time. You took a nasty jolt. We need to check you out," said Doc, as he looked analytically at Hal's eyes and flicked a penlight back and forth across his pupils.

The Hospital Corpsmen helped Kirby onto the stretcher and hurried him—griping all the way—to Sick Bay.

"Down to the shorts," said Doc.

After being checked from stem to stern, they wheeled him to X–ray and took plates of his spine and neck. When he returned to the treatment room, Doc checked his pupil reactions with the penlight again and asked him more silly questions.

"Dammit Doc, I'm telling you I'm OK. Let me out of here, I've got stuff I need to do."

"How do you feel, exactly? Any pain anywhere?" asked Doc, ignoring Hal's impatience.

"Great! My back and neck are a little sore, that's all, like I told you."

Doc pushed back on Hal's shoulder, "Lie down flat on this table and relax. Don't get up until I come back. Just take it easy." Doc stationed a corpsman by him with orders to continually monitor his pupils, keep him awake and monitor his vitals every ten minutes.

Later, Hal heard Doc's voice approaching the examining room. "Where you been Doc? When can I get out of here?"

"I just finished reading your x–rays. I don't see any fractures, but believe me, you're going to be one sore son of a bitch in the morning. I'm keeping you here for a while where I can keep an eye on you. Take these. I don't want any muscle spasms to set in."

"Geez, these are horse pills," Hal said and downed two large bitter tasting white pills with a paper cup of cold water. Doc gave him a bottle with more of them and instructions for taking them. "Doc, I've got to get out of here and get ready for-"

Doc cut him off mid-sentence, "Hal, I know what's going on today, but you're not safe to fly right now. You just suffered a mild concussion. Twenty minutes ago, you couldn't even stand on your own two feet. I'm watching for cerebral edema and it doesn't manifest itself right away." Doc looked over Hal's shoulder at the sound of someone entering, "Come in and help me wrestle this steer to the ground."

Hal strained a sore neck; Ted Spence was coming through the hatch. "How's it going at Inchon Ted?"

"Terrific. The Marines took Wolmi-do easily and have gone on to the mainland under very light small arms opposition. Our guys and the Marine pilots flattened the port defenses. General MacArthur has already sent a 'well done' from the Mount McKinley. It's short but sweet." Ted took a folded copy of the General's message from his pocket and handed it to Hal. Hal read:

"THE NAVY AND MARINES HAVE NEVER SHONE MORE BRIGHTLY THAN THIS MORNING X MACARTHUR."

Hal smiled, "I know what this operation meant to him. He put his career and reputation on the line for this, not to mention a lot of men's lives."

"Attention on deck," announced the Admiral's aide from behind Hal.

"He'll live Admiral," Doc said, peering into an otoscope in Hal's ear. "But, he's grounded for a while."

Hal's face instantly turned red, "Doc, come on, I'm fine. I've been more sore after a basketball game."

Doc shrugged his shoulders, "Admiral, he looks fine at the moment, but he's going to keep me company for a while. If he remains conscious and coherent and if his pupils continue to respond normally, I'll put him on restricted duty."

"Well Captain Kirby, you managed to prang a bird," grumbled Admiral Hawkins. He cracked a tiny smile, "At least you didn't burn yourself, my plane or my ship. Good job on neutralizing the enemy column. You earned your grits today."

"Thank you, sir."

"Gentlemen, would you please leave us alone for a few minutes?" asked

Hawkins.

When the hatch shut, Hawkins said, "I received a message twenty minutes ago directing me to place Garr under arrest. I know you would like to be part of that. I'll wait an hour—if you're not out of here by then, I'll have to go ahead though."

"I can't tell you how much I appreciate that. I'll work on Doc."

"Glad you're OK," said Hawkins. He shook Hal's hand, then departed; the others returned.

"Lay back and relax Hal," said Doc, "Since the pressure is off on the beach and things are going so well, you can let Ted have some fun for a change."

Hal looked at Ted and turned back to Doc, "How much did he pay you Doc? When can I get out of here?"

"Listen you mule, you're going to stay here with me for a while. There's a snowball's chance in hell that you'll fly tomorrow, so get that through your thick skull. In fact, just let me say you're down for 48 hours, pending reevaluation at that time. Without that medication, you'd be stiffer than a bridegroom on his wedding night."

"Doc, I need to fly the 1600 mission this afternoon!"

Doc laughed. "You're one stubborn son of a gun. You know you can't fly while you're on muscle relaxers."

Hal glared at Doc for a moment, "You—"

Doc laughed, "Relax and enjoy yourself. You're too wound up. Those muscle relaxers will kick in soon and take care of that though," Doc said as he walked away laughing.

Ted laughed through his hand, mocking an attempt to be kind. It was all Hal could do to keep a straight face. He took a deep breath and reread the message from MacArthur.

Kirby bellyached for an hour. Doc took a final check of Hal's vitals and pupil reactivity, "Well, the Admiral said he needed to see you in his stateroom right about now. You're released on restricted duty. No flying, no lifting, no exercising. Take it easy for the rest of today and I mean easy. Now listen to me, come back here every four hours so we can check you out. Come back anytime you feel anything other than what you feel right now"

"I feel fine," said Hal.

"I find that hard to believe, Hal. You're lucky, in any case. Shove off. Admiral Hawkins asked me to tell you to go directly to his quarters."

"Rajah dajah, thanks Doc."

As he weaved through the maze of passageways and ladders to the Admiral's cabin, Hal's excitement and hatred for Garr was being stoked with each step. Damn it, he should have been kicked out of the Navy a long time ago. *I need to think of the most cutting, despicable, vicious things I can say to that yellow bellied, traitorous piece of whale shit. Damn! In all this confusion, I forgot about the letter. Geez, I have to find time to talk to the Admin Officer. Damn letter's probably on its way. Kirby, you stepped on your weasel this time.*

As soon as he entered the Admiral's stateroom, Hawkins looked up, "Good! How do you feel? Meet Lieutenant Commander Mike Jefferson. Mike, this is Captain Hal Kirby, my Air Group Commander."

"Pleased to meet you Captain," said Mike, "I can finally put a face to the name."

Puzzled, Hal replied, "Pleasure's mine Mike. I think I've seen you around the ship lately—what division?"

Mike produced his credentials as a Navy counter-intelligence agent. "I've been aboard since the day after you went on your little tour with Jim and Walt," he explained with a grin.

Hal got over his surprise and chuckled, "That was an interesting ride. So, Mike, what the hell's been going on?"

"Well, we suffered from a nasty case of bad luck compounded by technicalities and politics. Mainly, the delay came about by not finding anything at the Yokohama drop site. We finally got one of the employees there to sing on the guy who departed with the material right after the drop. It took us quite a while to track him down; luckily, we succeeded in nabbing him before he could get rid of the stuff. If that wasn't enough, the security people at the intelligence center got two similar sized packages mixed up. They put Valley Forge labels on the outer and inner wrappers of another ship's package and vice versa. This broke the linkage with Garr, according to the lawyers anyway. That introduced some problems that we eventually ironed out. Anyway, Captain, we're ready to get down and dirty with Garr."

"I wondered what in hell was going on. Geez, he's had time to pull all sorts of shenanigans and has to be suspicious about not being able to leave the ship anymore," said Hal.

"You can imagine how upset Jim and Walt were," said Mike. "Uh, before we call the Marines, I want to give you something." He opened the zipper of a leather attaché case, pulled out an envelope and handed it to Hal.

"Geez," Hal exclaimed when he saw somebody else's writing on front, addressed to his wife, without a return address. "You have no idea—" he paused. "Thanks a million Mike."

"You know about this?" asked Mike, surprised.

Hal blushed and glanced toward the Admiral, who was busy with his paperwork, "I, uh, yes."

Mike whispered, "It's OK Hal, the Admiral knows. Sorry. I had to keep him informed."

Hal took a deep breath, "I understand. Yes, Garr stopped me on the flight deck this morning just before I launched and told me that he was going to send a letter to Alice," said Hal, "He also mentioned that a friend in Tokyo was going to mail pictures to her. I think he was talking about Lieutenant Commander Tyler Tullis, just for the record." He folded the envelope in half and stuffed it in his pants pocket without opening it. There couldn't have been more than a single, thin page inside of it.

"Garr is callous," said Mike, shaking his head from side to side in disbelief. "I've been censoring the mail and this one just seemed suspicious. I apologize for opening it, but it was done with official sanction. Only you, the Admiral and I know the contents. It matches Garr's handwriting, by the way. Dispose of it as you see fit. We'll deny ever seeing or knowing about it."

Hal shook Mike's hand, "An apology isn't necessary. I appreciate your consideration, Mike."

Mike interrupted, "Consider it a favor returned, for services rendered. Say no more. I regret that the Admiral was unable to share my presence with you. He had his orders too. Tell me more about these photos from Tokyo."

Hal explained in detail what Garr told him this morning, and all he knew about Tullis. Mike took notes. "OK Hal, thanks. Having Tullis involved with this scheme of Garr's is pretty damn interesting. We appreciate this information. OK Admiral," said Mike, "at your pleasure sir."

Hawkins promptly picked up his phone and dialed the Marine detachment OIC.

Within minutes, Admiral Hawkins, Hal, Mike, a Marine First Lieutenant and five armed Marines were proceeding to the Flag Intelligence Office. The Marine officer ordered the office's passageway sealed off at both ends by two muscle-bound Marines. The rest of the Marine party went to the office door, drew their .45 caliber pistols and cycled the actions, loading rounds into the chambers. Two Marines threw open the door, dashed inside and shouted for everyone to freeze. Two dazed enlisted personnel in the room were ordered to depart.

When the Marine officer called all clear, the Admiral, Hal and Mike came down the passageway and entered the Intelligence Office. The Marines had Garr sitting on the floor, cuffed hand and foot, and immobilized by Marines on each side of him. Mike read Garr the formal charges on which his arrest was based. Garr continuously shifted a crazed stare between the Admiral and Hal while Mike was speaking. He struggled intensely several times to no avail. Mike finished reading and nodded to Admiral Hawkins.

"Garr, you are a disgrace to the uniform," said the Admiral, "It is my distinct pleasure to have been part of your ensnarement and downfall. May your soul blaze in a hell of hells. I pray that you will remain sufficiently sane to suffer your consequences."

Garr's body was trembling, his face was kiln red and his teeth chattered audibly. "It's too late for you and the fuckin' Navy, Hawkins. Your career only has a few hours left. By then, the Chromite ships will be sunk and the main force will be annihilated when it attempts to go ashore." He spat toward the Admiral. Hawkins scowled, "Mr. Garr, you are an utter idiot. I can't stand to look at you another minute." The Admiral turned and departed.

"The joke's on you, scumbag," shouted Hal. "Surely you know we blew them away on the first tide. There's nothing left to defend against the main landing on the next tide. Nothing. The only thing the enemy is doing is running for the 38th parallel as fast as they can. I want you to know a few things before you retire to your luxurious quarters. I personally saw you make your last visit to the shipping company in Yokohama and take your last stroll in Hibiya Park. And I'll be there to testify at your last court-martial too. Whatever your sentence will be, it will be too good for the treasonous piece of shit that you are."

Garr's eyes widened; his mouth moved but no words came out. The Marines dampened his fits of violent struggling. They cranked hard on his arms; Garr grimaced and yelled out in pain.

Hal continued, "I suppose you realize what that means, you yellow, commie-loving, bastard. We not only shut your God forsaken ass down, but the rest of their operation too. You're no hero to the North Korean communists, the Russians, or the Chinese Communists."

"What do you know about heroes Kirby?" screamed Garr.

"I know this, if the reds could get their hands on you, they'd probably do worse than we will. My compliments to you on another job done incompetently—as usual."

"Kirby, you and the Navy haven't heard the last from me."

Hal shook his head, "You're a hateful, vindictive, misguided piece of dog shit on the Navy's shoe. Today we are scraping you off our sole for good. Sayonara asshole!"

"You didn't win this one Kirby. You're no match for me," Garr hollered at the top of his lungs, scuffling with the Marines again. He spat twice at Hal; a Marine slammed his fist into Garr's mouth.

Hal smiled widely and reached into his pocket. He pulled out the envelope Mike had given him, unfolded it and held it so Garr could see the face of it. Garr's rage level seemed to skyrocket. Blood was flowing from his mouth and nose onto the floor. He thrashed against the grip of the Marines, glowered at Hal with glassy, frenzied eyes and screamed, "You don't think that was the only letter, do you? I got you, Kirby, I got you fucking good!"

Later that evening, Hal retired to his quarters, sat at his desk and began to write a letter to Alice. This letter was one he wished he never had to write. He got as far as 'Dear Alice,' then thought through his approach. Do I lay it all out? No, she's in no frame of mind to deal with that, it would hit like a ton of bricks. She'd never understand that it was a mistake, over and done with. By the time she got to the part where I explain that I love her no less and that it's all over, well, she'd already be over the edge. I just can't drop this on her. Maybe I could if I was there and could do it in person, but I'm on the other side of the world. I'm trapped. I have no choice. Just explain that it was an opportunity for Garr to get even for his misfortunes and explain the innocent circumstances under which I could have been photographed with Marmette.

It took several attempts before he could finish the letter. He licked and sealed the envelope then flopped onto his bunk, emotionally drained. Even a mild stretch brought pain from his neck and back muscles. Damn, I hope Doc's muscle relaxers are working. There's a lot of work to do tomorrow. Can't believe my luck. It's been years since I've had a serious mechanical like that. Why now? His wife and kids smiled at him from the family portrait. He took a long, deep breath. I wonder if she's smiling right now. Geez, I hope my letter gets there before Tullis' package arrives. Wonder if she got checked out at Bethesda like I asked her to do. Man, if that stuff from Japan arrives before my letter gets there, she'll go nuts. God, there's not one damn thing I can do about this. Garr! I should have just shot him out of the sky. The phone rang. He sat up on the bunk and answered it, "Captain Kirby."

"This is Rip sir, the Admiral wants to see you ASAP, in his sea cabin."

"Rajah dajah." Hal got up from the bunk and did a couple slow, mild trunk twisters to limber up. He rinsed his face, ran wet hands over his crew cut, dried off, then gave his uniform a quick inspection before going topside.

"General MacArthur's coming aboard," said the Admiral, getting right to business as Hal entered Hawkins' cabin. "I just got the word. A helo from the USS Rochester is en route to us right now. They said he's by himself. That's as much as I know. I thought you'd like to be with me to greet him. Come on, Captain Rice will meet us plane-side."

When they stepped through the hatch in the island onto the flight deck, a thick night air enveloped them. The humid air reflected a dull glow from the flight deck floodlights. Shortly, the landing and running lights of the cruiser's helo approached. As the helo came to a hover above the center of the flight deck and began to settle, the Admiral began walking toward the landing spot; Hal and Captain Rice followed. When the wheels kissed the hardwood, the passenger door flew open. General MacArthur, bounded out right behind the helo crew chief with an expression that showed good spirits. He was sporting a brown leather Navy flight jacket. MacArthur smiled and nodded while foiling the attempt by the helo's rotor downwash to claim his hat. Hawkins and the General exchanged salutes and handshakes. MacArthur avoided attempts to talk above the blare of the engines. He spotted Hal, grabbed his hand and shook it vigorously. Hawkins introduced Captain Rice, the ship's commanding officer, then motioned toward the island. The welcoming party led the General to the Flag Mess, where the senior officers aboard the ship were waiting. The Admiral introduced each of the officers on his staff, Captain Rice introduced the ship's department heads and Hal introduced his squadron commanding officers. MacArthur graciously shook hands with each of them.

Introductions completed, MacArthur asked the Admiral, "May I say a few words to these gentlemen?"

"We'd be honored, General," replied Hawkins.

MacArthur collected his thoughts as his eyes toured the faces in the room. "Gentlemen, I am here to honor Naval aviators, whose skill, intrepidity and bravery this operation so surely relied upon for its success. The USS Valley Forge has, from the very inception, performed with distinction under sterling and courageous leadership. I salute you gentlemen!" He raised his arm in a rigid salute. Everyone promptly and proudly returned it. "Thank you!" he said and turned to the Admiral and Hal, "Now, I wish to meet with you and Captain Kirby before I depart for the other carriers."

"Dismissed, gentlemen," Hawkins called out. He gave his aide a nod and the room emptied.

"Coffee General?" offered Hawkins.

"No, thank you," replied MacArthur and took the Admiral's seat at the end of the green cloth covered table. He pulled a leather tobacco pouch from his coat pocket and began filling his pipe. Hal and the Admiral refrained from their beloved coffee and took seats on either side of the General. "First, I sincerely congratulate both of you on a job very well done. I shall report that to your chain of command. Second, as you know, I've been ashore and toured Inchon and beyond. The taste of victory is in the air. The enemy is in a rout. There has never been a more opportune time to drive the Communists across the Yalu River and reunite the Korean Peninsula." He produced a box of matches and a pipe, lit up and puffed with determination until satisfied he had a red bowl. "I have developed a contingency plan to accomplish that," said MacArthur, "However, despite this successful landing and the full retreat the enemy is in, pushing them across the Yalu and simultaneously policing the south will be no small task. Our forces will be stretched thin and logistics will be a tremendous challenge. I have stated in no small terms my dissatisfaction with the quantity, quality and timeliness of operational intelligence on the enemy's location in the North. My point is that air reconnaissance of the north will be critical if I am to employ my relatively meager ground forces effectively above the 38th parallel. My plan is to use the Air Force mainly for reconnaissance near and below the 38th. But, I want to use Navy armed air reconnaissance and a new airplane that is being made available for operations in the China-Korea border area. You need to know that Admiral Joy and I have conferred extensively on this." He paused, showed annoyance with his pipe that appeared to have extinguished itself.

Admiral Hawkins interjected, "General, we'll certainly support you fully as long as we are deployed, but our relieving carrier is already en route and we've been ordered to sail back to the states upon her arrival. I will receive orders to a new assignment very shortly and Captain Kirby may also, owing to his early selection to Captain."

MacArthur relit his pipe and continued, undaunted, "Details remain to be solved, of course, and Admiral Joy will be communicating with you shortly. But, Admiral, what I'm asking for is your consent to immediately release Captain Kirby for a special assignment. One that has been discussed with, and has the blessing of, Admiral Joy and your Chief of Naval Operations, Admiral Sherman." Hawkins and the General held eye contact a moment.

"Of course, General," said Hawkins. They both turned to Hal.

Hal nodded, "I am at your service sir. What is the assignment and when do I leave?"

MacArthur nodded approvingly, "Depart tomorrow morning. You will receive information about the details of the orders shortly."

Two pairs of intense eyes probed Hal's mind, which began wandering. Tokyo. Land of Oz. There's no way in hell I'm going to sit here and say no, but God help me. "I'll be ready; Ted can handle the duties of CAG." Hal bit his tongue a moment, choosing his words carefully, "But, wouldn't it be more effective for the Navy recon planning and coordination to be done by the relieving Carrier Division Commander and the Air Group Commanders on the carriers as opposed to me in Tokyo?"

Hal watched old poker face slowly render a rare grin, "Captain, we don't need you in Tokyo. We need you in Washington. You specifically because you have a unique combination of traits. You are the man we need on a highly-classified project in Washington. It involves a controversial Air Force asset that is militarily and politically sensitive. Admirals Sherman and Joy want a Naval aviator—you—to protect the Navy's interest in Korea and I want you to protect my command's interests. I am just not at liberty to explain more fully." Hal looked at Hawkins and back at the General. MacArthur sensed the many questions on Hal's mind. "Captain, you will be briefed thoroughly when you report to the Pentagon."

CHAPTER 15

Great Falls, Virginia

Furrows formed deep into Kirby's perspiring brow as the taxi neared the end of the cul de sac. *I should have called her when we stopped for fuel in Hawaii and California. It's just not possible that she has my last letter.* His mental meanderings ended when the taxi came to a stop. He paid the driver, retrieved his luggage from the trunk and banged on it. The taxi took off leaving a cloud of pungent pale blue smoke from the departing taxi. Hal's eyes soaked up the view of his stately old two-story red brick colonial for the first time in nine months. It looked magnificent, contrasted against blue sky and puffy cotton cumulus clouds. Bags in hand, he headed up the walk to the front porch steps. Hal could see through the front screen door, down the central hallway and out the rear screen door. He maneuvered his duffel and B–4 bags through the door.

"What are you doing home from school so early?" Alice called from the living room. "Which one of you is it?"

Hal put his hat and jacket on the oak coat rack in the foyer and inhaled deeply. His palms dampened as he walked the few paces along the oriental runner to the living room doorway. Alice was stretched out on the couch. She was facing away from him, propped on a pillow. Drawn curtains gave an eerie gloom to the room he loved so much for its warmth. Her long slender legs ran from jean shorts to her bare feet. Untidy light brown hair settled onto the shoulders of a white cotton blouse. A bottle of gin and a white opaque plastic ice bucket sat on the coffee table. Her arm swung out and thumped a heavy square-bottomed glass of naked cubes onto a magazine.

"Answer me! What's the matter? Why are you home?" Alice hollered. She sat up and craned her neck to see which of her kids came home. Color drained from her face. She might well have seen a ghost. She swung her feet to the rug and leaped to unsteady feet. "Well, well. Captain Kirby, the great war hero, has graced our hearth with his presence. Why didn't you go to Tokyo? Girlfriend kick you out of bed?"

"Alice, get hold of yourself," said Hal, walking toward her. "Damn it honey, you're drunk as a skunk."

"You bet your boots I am."

"There was no time to let you know I was coming. I received emergency transfer orders to the Pentagon. That should make you happy." Her bloodshot blue eyes bore into him like razor edged daggers. She stood frozen in place, wavering, with her hand on her chest. He put his arms around her.

She pulled away, "Don't touch me."

"Alice, knock it off!" He shook her shoulders, "You don't know what the hell you're doing or saying. We've got to get some coffee into you. Geez, the kids will be home soon. You don't want them to see you like this, do you?"

"I don't give a damn what they see. They're not babies anymore."

"C'mon, let's go into the kitchen. Calm down and let me talk to you." Hal put his arm around her. She opened her mouth to form a word. He interrupted, "Before you say anything, let me tell you what's in a letter that you haven't gotten yet. It will bring some sense to all this."

Alice burst into sobs, turned away from him and leaned against the fireplace mantel, knocking over a picture frame. "There's nothing to talk about. How could you?"

"Stop it Alice. I know how you must feel."

"You don't know how I feel at all."

"Just listen." He gripped her shoulders and turned her around. She turned her head away from him. "Look at me dammit!" She refused. "Look Alice, they're snapshots which have been exaggerated into something sinister. Garr had a friend on Admiral Joy's staff who's a camera nut. Garr took advantage of that as an opportunity to get even with me. Marmette was a friend of Dusty and LouAnn. The four of us did a lot of things together. Dinner, sightseeing, stuff like that. I told you about that. This guy was pissed at Marmette for not having anything to do with him. Then when his buddy Garr got into the act, they saw a chance for both to get some satisfaction."

"Horse hockey Hal, horse hockey, horse hockey!" she hollered, beating on his chest.

Hal pulled her shivering body in tightly and rubbed her back tenderly. "Garr went off the deep end when he got passed over for Commander. And being on the same ship with me just fueled his fire to make me pay. The pictures are just part of his sinister scheme to make me and the whole

Navy pay. Remember what I told you about catching him doing some things he'll be court martialed for? Well, he's in the brig now on charges of espionage. That's how crazy he got."

She twisted out of his arms and ran to the hallway and up the staircase. "I don't want to hear any more," Alice hollered back at him. He watched her navigate poorly up the normally unchallenging course of the spiral staircase. His heart was pounding. The slam of the bedroom door struck him like a 2x4. Tears welled in his eyes. Better let her calm down. Geez, this is a mess. I've never seen her look so bad. No makeup, stringy hair, sunken eyes with purple bags. She must have lost twenty pounds. She didn't have it to lose. Last time I saw her drunk was my first Christmas leave from Annapolis. Some welcome home. Damn, I'm tired. I've got to stay up until the kids come home.

It was nearly impossible to truly sleep on a droning C–121 Super Constellation, hop-scotching from Japan to Washington, DC. His ears still buzzed. The thirteen–hour time difference was taking its toll too. He found the can of ground coffee and got a full pot started. He splashed cool water on his face and dried off with a dishtowel. He hauled his bags up the stairs.

Alice was out cold, lying across the bed, face buried in a pillow. He rolled her over and sat next to her. Stupor gave her a dazed expression. Hal smoothed hair from her face and mouth and rubbed her hand. Sleep it off honey. You'll be more rational when you sober up. Geez, you look like you've been through hell. Hal bent down, kissed her gently and hugged her. "I'm so very sorry," he whispered, "I'll make it up to you. I love you." A brown envelope caught his eye on the dresser. Inside were ten pictures of Hal and Marmette. There were pictures of them walking in Hibiya Park, walking down the street, walking down the hallway of the Imperial Hotel, eating in the Imperial Hotel restaurant. Only one showed Dusty and LouAnn, the others were cropped to show just the two of them. The most damning shot was the two of them walking through Hibiya Park with Marmette's arm tucked under his.

Hal put the photos back into the envelope. He sat on the edge of the bed and stared out of the window. Well, all in all, not as bad as it could have been. Tullis is clever—we never even saw him.

A newspaper and a half-pot of coffee later, the heavy feet of his son on the porch steps brought Hal to his feet. He put his coffee cup down and hurried toward the foyer. Joe started up the staircase before the image of Hal's hat and jacket in the foyer sunk in. He stopped and looked down as Hal came through the doorway into the foyer.

"Dad!" hollered Joe. He rushed down the steps and slammed himself into Hal, hugging hard. "Mom didn't tell us you were, you know, coming home. You on leave? Let me see your ear. You're growing a beard?"

"Beard? No, I've just spent the last two days on an airplane. It happened too fast to let anyone know I was coming."

Joe let go to look at his dad's ear, "Shot half of it off. Hurt?"

Hal laughed, "No."

"So, dad, are you here for uh permanent duty?" asked Joe, "Do you have to go back to the ship?"

"No son, I'm here for a year or so I guess," said Hal, hugging Joe again. "Where's your sister?"

"She stopped at, you know, Sheila's house for a few minutes. I'll call her."

"Nah, let her be surprised. It'll give us a chance to talk. How are you doing? How do you like high school?"

"Too much homework dad. The teachers are, you know, too tough on us, but it's a lot of fun too. Where's Mom? I need a glass of milk."

"She's taking a nap. Come on, let's go to the kitchen."

"Was she glad to see you dad?" Joe asked. His searching eyes told Hal that it was a loaded question. "Was she, you know?"

"What son?"

"You know dad—drunk."

"Yes," said Hal and took a long breath. He gave his cup a warm-up refill while Joe poured a tall glass of milk.

Joe took a big gulp of milk then said, "I'm glad you're home. She's been really weird lately. Always fightin' with me and Sue. She started drinking a whole lot, you know, after you got shot down."

"Hey Mom," Susan hollered as she opened the front door, "I'm going to be at Sheila's house studying for a couple hours, OK?"

"Susie, come here," yelled Joe.

"How many times do I have to tell you not to call me Susie? Are you retarded or something? You're such a brat." When she rounded the corner into the kitchen she stopped short, burst into tears and flew to her father.

"I'm glad to see you honey," he said and kissed her forehead. "I think you've grown two inches since I left."

Susan looked up at Hal, still hugging tight, "What are you doing home? How long will you be home?"

"Let me look at you. Oh Sue, you're getting so pretty. I like your hair short like that. I've got good news. I was ordered back to the Pentagon." Sue started jumping up and down, clapping her hands nearly uncontrollably.

"Super cool daddy. Why didn't you tell us you were coming home?" she asked, still animated. "Where's Mom?"

"Upstairs, sleeping it off," said Joe.

"Oh daddy, I've been praying for you to come home. Mom's gotten weird and nasty." She put her arms around Hal, hugged him vigorously and began crying hard. He held her close.

"It's true dad," said Joe, "She's not the Mom she used to be."

"It's going to be OK kids."

"What's going on dad?" asked Susan.

"Look, why don't you both go get settled and wash up while I scrounge up a little snack. We'll talk about it all then."

"Why not now?" asked Joe.

Sue nodded, "I'll help you daddy. I know where everything's at." She opened the refrigerator and started handing things to Hal.

Where do you start in a mess like this? At the beginning. Which beginning? "When did your mother first start drinking?" asked Hal while relaying things to the table.

"She got a little drunk when she heard the Valley Forge made the first attack on North Korea," Sue recalled.

"Yeah. She was real worried, you know," added Joe. "When the news said there were no pilots lost, she calmed down. Wow, the time you got shot down, you know, and went to the hospital. That really upset her."

"After that daddy, she began drinking more and more. Now, the only time she's sober is in the morning," added Sue as she hurried the assembly of cream cheese finger sandwiches, trying to get ahead of Joe's ravaging.

"Geez. I had no idea it was so bad," said Hal. "Her letters started getting mean and testy about that time."

"It was the same here too dad," Joe said.

Susan shut down the sandwich factory, sat down and struggled for words. Hal could see the trouble in her eyes. "Mom has really changed an awful lot Daddy. Sometimes she's, I don't know, strange. She don't make sense sometimes, you know?"

Joe took a big slug of milk and looked at Hal. "She really went nuts yesterday when the pictures of you and that lady in Japan arrived."

"What's that all about daddy?" asked Sue. "Mom threw them down on the table and said, 'Here's some pictures of your wonderful father in the heat of battle.'"

"Yeah, then she went into the living room and got drunk," said Joe. "She doesn't talk about you anymore."

"Oh daddy, I'm so happy you're home." Sue grabbed Hal's arm and began to cry.

Hal fought against the knot in his throat. He told them about Luther Garr and how Garr used a friend in Japan to get revenge. "You've often heard me talk of my Marine classmate, Dusty Rhodes?" The kids nodded. "Well, he's assigned to the staff in Tokyo where I worked on the plans for the Inchon invasion. Marmette also works on the staff. She is a good friend of Dusty and his fiancé. The four of us went to dinner a lot and they showed me around Tokyo on the weekends. That's how Garr's friend got the pictures. Simple as that." Joe and Sue showed their relief. Hal sighed. *Oh God, how I wish it was just that simple.*

By 9pm, Hal's exhausted body begged for rest. Alice had slept the entire afternoon and evening. A fast shave and shower and clean skivvies felt good. He opened both bedroom windows; a light cross-breeze furled the sheer curtains and freshened the air that reeked of a drunk's breath. She slept through the removal of her shorts and blouse; he maneuvered her body under the sheets. He got in next to her and put his arms around her. *Good night honey. Let's hope tomorrow morning brings a better day. I love you.*

Hal awoke with a start and searched for the clock. 0822—*damn, I wanted to have breakfast with the kids.* He sat up in the empty bed and listened—dead silence. *God, I really want to just tell her everything, but she's in no condition to hear it. There is no reason for me to risk that. No, I'll leave it like it is. The important thing is that I love her. It was a mistake and it's behind me.* He found Alice leaning glumly on her elbows over a cup of coffee in the kitchen. She didn't look up as he came in and sat across from her. "Honey, let's straighten out this mess and get our lives back," Hal said softly, reaching across the table for her hand.

She put her hands in her lap. "What did I ever do to make you hate me so much Hal?"

"Geez Alice, I don't hate you-"

"Don't lie to me. You've hated me for a long time. I can't take it anymore." She unscrewed the cap on a large bottle of aspirins and washed four of them down with a gulp of coffee.

"Honey, stop saying such stuff. You're sober and you have no excuse for talking craziness."

"Crazy? You think I'm crazy huh?" She lowered her head. "So do I. So do I."

"What do you mean? Talk to me. You didn't think I hated you when I left for the Valley Forge. What's happened to you?" She sat quietly, gazing into her lap, rubbing her forehead and temples. Hal came around behind her and began massaging her shoulders.

She leaned her head back and looked up at him, "I'm not young and pretty anymore; I'm sorry. You want a divorce?"

"My God Alice, don't say such things. Don't even think crap like that. Hell no I don't want a divorce. I want you to stop drinking though. I want the Alice I knew nine months ago." Her head dropped back down.

"Why'd you leave me Hal?" she asked bitterly.

"I didn't leave you Alice. I received orders to the Valley Forge for God's sake. You're trying my patience."

"Admiral Karns thought you were sliced bread." Her words were flowing out of her in rapid fire. "You could have stayed on his staff in the Pentagon for one or two more years. But no. You knew there was a storm brewing in Korea. You got yourself orders back on a carrier, over there. You couldn't wait to get away from me. Back to those damn carriers and airplanes, where you can get killed on a good day. Let alone in a war."

"Alice, I used a lot of paper arguing this stuff weeks ago. I'm a Naval Aviator. I fly warplanes—off carriers. That's my career. That's how I made it to Captain. That's how I provided this cozy little life for you and the kids. That's how it's going to be tomorrow, next week, next month and next year. Geez Alice, after sixteen years, why are you so pessimistic all of a sudden?"

She shook her head, "What about your girlfriend?"

He gripped her shoulders and shook them hard, "Damn it Alice, you're not listening to me. Do you remember what I told you yesterday? Garr wanted to destroy me somehow and that was one possible way. He tried several other things on the ship too. Look, I'm here with you. I'm telling you that I love you. I'm telling you that there is no girlfriend. I don't want a divorce. I don't want to leave you."

She looked up, "Promise?"

He bent down and kissed her forehead, "Promise, honey, promise." He felt a barely perceptible tremor in her shoulders.

"I feel sick to my stomach," she said.

"Well honey, as long as you are boozing it up like you've been, you're going to feel like this every morning. I want you to stop drinking. Did you quit volunteering at the Medical Center?"

"No. Matter of fact, I need to start getting ready. I've got to be there by nine thirty."

"Alice, you are really too ill to be working today. Call in sick. It's not too late for dependent's sick call, let me take you over to see a doctor. You're run down physically and mentally. Even the kids are hurting about you." She began to cry.

"Do you really love me Hal?" she whimpered.

"Stand up honey, I want to hold you," Hal said, lifting her arms. She clung to him tenaciously and broke into unbridled sobbing; he cried with her. "I love you tons and tons honey. It's going to be OK. Let it out, it's got to come out."

They returned from the hospital armed with antacid tablets, a bottle of APCs, and tranquilizers. The latter made her drowsy. Between the pills and the exhausted state of her body, she slept away the afternoon while Hal got his red MG down off concrete blocks then washed and polished it.

That evening, after returning from dinner at one of their favorite restaurants, the Kirby family filled the couch in front of the TV and watched "What's My Line?" When it was over, Sue and Joe headed up the stairs for bed. "I'm tired Alice, I'm going up too, honey," Hal said.

Alice nodded, "What time did you say you have to report?"

"Oh, seven thirty. I'm setting the alarm for six."

"I'm going to take my pills and do a couple things before I come up." She turned off the TV and left the living room. He watched her disappear around the doorway; the hallway boards creaked softly under her bare feet as she walked along the runner toward the kitchen. He went upstairs and got ready for bed. Alice dawdled through her bedtime routine then slid carefully into bed with her back to him.

Hal rolled onto his side, moved close to her, put his arm around her shoulder and held her hand. She squeezed his hand tightly. "I love you honey. I've always loved you," he said.

She turned and whispered, "I love you too, Hal."

Hal detected a familiar odor. Geez, I smell booze. Damn. "Alice, do I smell gin?"

She threw his hand away from her, "Yes, so what? My nerves are shot. It calms me down. Helps my headache."

"I swear Alice, I'm going to empty every bottle down the drain."

"Look who's talking, you've done your share."

"Not in the last five years and never like this. When's the last time you saw me drunk?"

"You're never around."

"Oh get off it, Alice. What's the sense of going to the doctor if you aren't going to listen to him? Booze is the last thing you need right now." He rolled away from her. A million thoughts sped through his mind. In a short while, she began to snore lightly; the tranquilizers had taken her to a peaceful place. He explored the myriad things he might say and do. No answers came to him, only concern for her state of mind. It was no longer easy to merely attribute her behavior to her worry about the dangers of Naval Aviation and the complication of the pictures. Exhaustion soon claimed his consciousness.

CHAPTER 16

The Pentagon

Hal quick stepped the long hike from the visitor's parking area to the Pentagon's 'River Entrance.' He was anxious to get checked in and, hopefully, get a week of leave to spend some time with Alice. He suffered through the administrative formalities in the Personnel Office and headed for his new office in the C–ring, second floor. There was a small sign on the door: Office of the Joint Chiefs of Staff/J–2–9X—Ring for entry—Authorized Personnel Only. He pushed a button mounted on the door jamb; a faint buzz could be heard inside.

The door opened, "You found us easy enough, Captain," greeted a perky, attractive redhead with a slight Bostonian accent. "Personnel only called a few moments ago. I'm Patty Mindell sir, pleased to meet you. I'm the unit secretary and Jill of all trades."

"Mornin' Patty, my pleasure. I'm no stranger to this five–sided puzzle palace. I know all the nooks and crannies."

She laughed, "Colonel Bennett, our unit commander, left for a short meeting; he should be back in half an hour. Meantime I'll get you settled in. We have some clearance papers for you to take care of. By then, the Colonel will be back and wants to meet with you."

Hal quickly put two and two together and didn't like the answer, "It's a big Air Force Patty, but is that by any chance Colonel Logan Bennett, USAF?" More than anything right now, he wanted her to say the words that would ensure this would be a good assignment.

"Why yes Captain, it is. I didn't know you two knew each other. He never mentioned it." Hal's heart skipped a beat. Those weren't the words he wanted to hear.

Hal couldn't believe the irony in this. "We don't really know each other. We met briefly at General MacArthur's headquarters while coordinating the Inchon invasion." It wasn't necessary that Patty know the whole story. With any luck, Bennett left his hard feelings about Wonsan back in Japan.

He looked around. The pungent smell of fresh paint still lingered in the air. There was no office noise. Three doors lead off the sterile white outer reception area where Patty's desk, a coffee mess and three bulky file safes were located.

Patty picked up on the unspoken questions in Hal's mind, "It's just the Colonel, you and me right now." She pointed toward the door opposite the Colonel's, "This is your new home, Captain. That one over there is classified material storage, supplies and the like. I cleaned your desk inside and out last Friday and stocked it with some office supplies. If you need anything sir, just holler. We have a high priority and I can get stuff fast and without any questions."

"Well, then get me some windows, this place stinks," he said partly joking as he walked into his office.

"I guess I should have kept the door open to air the room out. The paint smell hasn't had a chance to thin out. I'll get a floor fan from maintenance, open the hall door and get some fresh air in here."

"Good idea Patty, a couple hours of breathing this and I'll have a headache." There were undisturbed circular swirls of buffed desktop polish glistening on the gray top of his metal desk. It was a typical Pentagon O6's office—private but small and Spartan. "Not bad Patty, ya done good, kiddo." Her high cheekbones graciously augmented her smile, turning an average face into a very pleasing one.

"Worked my butt off trying to put this place together in such a rush." She leaned back against the doorframe. "The guys who had these spaces before us left one hell of a mess. And the Colonel had his own idea of where the walls ought to be. I managed to get through it though."

"This organization was just created?"

"Yes and no, we've only been in these spaces for a couple weeks. The office was formerly part of another JCS J–2 code, but split off on its own. I worked in another part of J–2 and needed a change, so when this opening came up, I jumped. I hope I won't be sorry."

"Did you know Colonel Bennett before, Patty?"

"No, and it's Colonel Logan Bennett the third, if you please," she rolled her eyes. "No, I didn't. He came from General Stratemeyer's staff in Japan, well, I guess you know that."

"You said the organization existed before, what happened to the other people?" asked Hal.

"Everyone," she said, "consisted of Colonel Yardley, period. He retired and was relieved by Colonel Bennett. Yardley went to work for the CIA as the Project Manager for AQUAMARINE. You don't know anything about AQUAMARINE, right?"

Hal shrugged his shoulders, "Patty, I have no idea what the hell I'm doing here."

She laughed, "Well, this is going to be a lot different than most Pentagon jobs. Since you've been flying combat missions off an aircraft carrier in Korea, you're probably going to find this real boring. I should keep my mouth shut," she said with a grin.

Hal laughed, "Patty, every time in my career that somebody told me something was going to be easy, it wasn't. So, tell me what's going on."

"Colonel left specific orders that he'd do all the explaining. Let me go get the security clearance paperwork. They have to be signed before he gets back. They'll give you a top-level summary of AQUAMARINE. Oh, I also have to get your measurements."

Hal blushed, "Measurements? For what, the J–2 typist pool?"

She laughed, "No, for Lockheed, silly."

"Please be seated Captain," said Colonel Bennett. "Thank you, Miss Mindell, please close the door." Bennett tapped his fingers on the desk until Patty left and closed the door behind her. The moment the door closed, Bennett began, "I wish to proceed directly to business. I shall also be candid. I had someone else in mind for your position. However, your clout was bigger than his somehow. You've been forced down my throat and it's especially galling because you caused me great professional embarrassment with General Stratemeyer."

Hal could feel his ears getting red, "I'm sorry Colonel, but we had no choice with Wonsan; the Russians forced our hand."

Bennett's eyes wandered through his vanity gallery that filled one entire wall of his office. There were many pictures showing Bennett and important military and congressional dignitaries, letters of commendation and other memorabilia. "Captain, we cannot make any progress on that subject. Now, we do not have the luxury of the abundant time common to most Pentagon staff functions. You are formally my Deputy, as I said, under duress. Only the two of us will be assigned to this organization for the foreseeable future. We are a discrete element of the Joint Chiefs of Staff. As you know from the clearance documents, everything else I tell you about our organization is Top Secret Codeword AQUAMARINE and may not be divulged to anyone not specifically cleared for this project. In fact, you must have my explicit concurrence in each instance before divulging anything to anyone. No exceptions. Do you understand those restrictions, Captain?"

"Yes Colonel, I understand perfectly." Oh brother, this is damn sure not going to be fun.

"Superb. Such being the case, I shall continue. I'll be as brief as possible. We are the executive agent for the military portion of Project AQUAMARINE; the Central Intelligence Agency controls all other aspects of the project. Allow me to provide a brief history. When the North Koreans came across the 38th Parallel last June, the surprise embarrassed the intelligence community. None the least of which was the CIA. The President demanded better performance from the Director. CIA consulted with Lockheed about a program to provide better quick reaction strategic reconnaissance. Their 'Skunkworks' was already test flying an experimental airframe that would fly at extremely high altitudes. In fact, well above the range of any known anti-aircraft systems, fighters or interceptors. Representative Bradbury, Chairman of the Defense Appropriations Committee, facilitated the emergency funding of Project AQUAMARINE to accelerate its development as a reconnaissance platform. In deference to the Joint Chiefs, General Marshall specified that it be jointly managed by the Air Force and Langley, due to the military situation in Korea. At this moment in time, AQUAMARINE enjoys the highest priority funding and action codes. Langley controls the manpower allowances; they are keeping it lean and mean. That means we, you and I, will qualify in the airplane. This is your last chance to de-volunteer from this assignment, Captain. Do you wish to be reassigned?"

"Hell no Colonel. Beats flying a damn desk."

Bennett flipped his eyebrows, "You will, as you say, do some desk flying here. Your responsibilities include the operational mission planning and coordination of the technical aspects of the military missions. There will be two CIA recon pilots qualified as well, so neither of us shall be unduly burdened." Bennett leaned back in his chair, nursed his coffee mug and raised his right eyebrow. This accentuated an old scar that ran from his right eye, across his forehead to the left and into the scalp. His looks were no more pleasant than his personality.

I suppose his majesty is signaling that I may ask questions. "When will our airplane be ready, Logan?"

"There are four aircraft in the project. Two experimental reconnaissance aircraft, nicknamed AQUABALL ONE and TWO and two modified B-29s, nicknamed AQUABOX ONE and TWO. The latter are modified to be mobile communications and ground support facilities. They are all completed and going through final factory trials and acceptance. Air Force pilots and technicians will man the BOXes. I expect that CIA acceptance tests will be complete on the BOXes and BALLs within days. We depart Friday morning for training at Edwards Air Force Base, California. We'll get accelerated ground and flight training on the BALL aircraft for seven to ten days then we'll return here. It's not firm yet, but JCS wants to deploy us to Korea very shortly thereafter."

Hal's optimism for a week's leave to mend his family was dashed on the rocks. So were the thoughts of a duty tour that would allow him to be home every night. This news left a hole in his stomach. On the other hand, AQUAMARINE had an air of excitement and challenge to it. Perhaps to a fault, he was a pilot first and husband and father second. His mind focused on the unique opportunity this project represented. Also, General MacArthur and Admiral Sherman wanted him here for a good reason, albeit not evident at this point. "I'm looking forward to being part of the project, Logan." A phone call interrupted their conversation. Colonel Bennett exchanged cryptic phrases intermingled with yes and no responses.

Bennett hung up and turned to Hal, "Captain Kirby, I want to make one thing perfectly clear. I, and I alone, will act as the single point of contact with Lockheed, Langley, Congress, JCS or any other government agency. Unless I specifically authorize otherwise, of course." Bennett's stare and testy smirk reamed into Hal's composure.

Hal nodded, "Understood." It's not going to be easy to keep from rapping this guy between the eyes. I hope he loosens up.

"Superb. Have Miss Mindell provide you with all the project documentation. After digesting that, I don't expect that you will have further questions. Also, one more important thing. I prefer that you address me as Colonel Bennett. As they say, familiarity breeds contempt."

Hal laughed to himself. Logan old boy, I have nothing but contempt for you at this moment.

"Captain, your first message," said Patty as Hal exited the Colonel's office.

He read the note, "Who's Captain Castle, Patty? Name sounds familiar."

"He's in the Office of the Chief of Naval Operations. He and the Colonel have had some meetings recently."

"Yep, that's it Patty, thanks, I remember now, he's CNO's Aide. Call his office and tell his secretary that 0900 is fine with me."

Captain James Castle was coming out of Admiral Sherman's private office as Hal came into the reception area of the CNO's suite. "Nice to see you again Captain. Sorry I didn't have a chance to talk with you in Tokyo. That was quite a meeting."

"That it was, sir," said Hal.

"Please, call me Jim." He motioned for Hal to sit. "There are some things about this assignment that Admiral Sherman wanted you to know as soon as you checked in. You see, so far, AQUAMARINE has been a big rice bowl and glory battle. The Air Force, I should say Colonel Bennett, objected to you getting the assignment. He didn't want the Navy to have any part in this at all. Being Congressman Bradbury's son-in-law, he packs a heavy wallop, but Admiral Sherman had some political ace cards of his own."

"Bradbury, I've heard the name but can't place him. Bennett mentioned he was the Chairman of the House Armed Services Committee though."

Jim nodded, "Yes, he just took over that job. I emphasize that Bennett's connection with Bradbury makes him a force to be reckoned with. As an aside, I don't know if it's important to your situation, but Bradbury has an inside track to the President. Add to that, an Air Force friend of mine told me that Bennett would step on his mother to get to Brigadier General. It

143

looks to us that Bradbury got Bennett this hot little high visibility program to help him get his star."

Hal nodded, "Not a pretty picture. Bennett sure as hell has delusions of grandeur. I appreciate the heads up on the politics. By any chance is Bradbury's daughter ugly?"

Castle laughed, "She'd stop an eight–day clock with a full windup. But, she is Bradbury's daughter."

They laughed together heartily. "Figures! Geez, he is mercenary. Wait a minute Jim, what the hell am I laughing at? My butt is in jeopardy here!" Castle grinned. Hal continued, "My indoctrination so far has only dealt with the generalities of the platform and mission and I take it that JCS wants us in Korea. Bennett indicated that Korea might not happen. Are there wolves hiding behind the trees on that aspect of the project?"

"Well, probably so. Admiral Sherman might have more to share on that, but from what I know, the CIA doesn't want the platform to go to Korea. They paid for the development of the high altitude recon birds so they could fly them over Russia and take pictures at will of their military facilities. They know they probably won't get any Russian pictures for the period they are under Air Force control and are located in Korea. However, the Admiral said that the President signed off on the deployment so you are indeed going to Korea. That's being kept close to the chest for now and I doubt even Bennett knows that. So, act surprised when it's formally announced."

"OK, but why is it so important to have a Navy pilot, me specifically, on the project?" asked Hal.

"Frankly we didn't think that the CIA or Colonel Bennett had the foggiest sensitivity to the extent and nature of photo recon support the Navy carriers will need to fly safe and productive missions up north."

Hal nodded, "I've got the picture, thanks."

"Good, then you'll understand Admiral Sherman's request. He wants you to let us know immediately if anything comes up which is not in the best interest of the Navy or seems otherwise unusual. You have an open door to this office any time Hal. We'll protect you of course."

"Aye, aye Jim, I'll keep my eyes and ears open. Speaking of protection, the thought of Bennett writing my fitness reports doesn't make me the slightest bit comfortable. I've known him one day and I already know he'll crucify me. He knows about my role in the Wonsan flap, which apparently got him fired by General Stratemeyer. Do you think you can arrange for Admiral Sherman to write them?"

Castle replied immediately, "Consider it done."

It was 1820 when Hal drove his candy apple red MG into the driveway. As he came through the front door the aroma of spaghetti sauce and garlic bread put his salivary glands into overdrive. "Hi daddy," Susan yelled from the dining room. She was putting tall glasses of ice water by each place.

Hal found Alice in the kitchen, stirring stiff spaghetti strands into boiling water. She turned and smiled at him. He put his arm on her shoulder and kissed her cheek. "How was your day, honey?" he asked.

"OK," she replied.

"Where's Joe," asked Hal.

Alice shrugged her shoulders, "Next door. We called him. Go get changed. We can eat in five minutes."

Hal lifted the lid on a simmering pot and inhaled the vapors rising from crimson meat sauce. "Ummm, smells great. Lots of garlic."

Susan said grace when everyone was seated. Hal watched Alice pick at a small pile of spaghetti. "Honey, that's not enough food for a starling. Feeling OK?"

"Terrible headache, that's all," she said softly.

"I don't mean to hound you, but have you told the doctor about the headaches."

"I don't have them all the time."

Joe was eating like there was no tomorrow. He finally took his head out of the feed bag long enough to ask a question, "So, dad, did you find out what your job is all about?"

"Of course, son. Not much I can say about it though."

"Wow, you mean like real secret stuff?"

His son's innocence and curiosity made Hal chuckle, "Yeah man, you know, real cloak and dagger stuff, you know?" Hal imitated. Susan laughed loudly.

"What are you laughing at, Susie?" asked Joe.

"You, Joey, you're such a jerk sometimes."

"Knock it off kids. The supper table is no place for arguments," Hal scolded.

"Will you have to travel a lot daddy?" asked Susan.

Hal paused. Damn. I was hoping they'd leave this subject alone until later. "Yes, I will." His eyes switched quickly to Alice to gauge her reaction. She abruptly stopped chewing a bite of garlic bread. Her eyes remained on her plate.

"Will you get to fly?" asked Joe. Alice slowly lifted her head and looked intently at Hal.

"Yes, I will son." A barely perceptible grimace formed on Alice's face. Hal could see the fear building in her eyes. "Not fighters. Not combat flying. Experimental aircraft," he said, begging her with his eyes to find solace in his words.

"Will you be home every night?" asked Alice.

"No honey, there's going to be periods of TAD. But that's better than me being on a carrier for six to nine months at a time."

Susan asked, "How long will it be before you have to go on a trip?"

Hal felt his body stiffen, "I leave Friday for a couple weeks of school in California."

Alice pushed her chair back, "I don't feel well. Excuse me. I'm going to go to bed." She went into the kitchen. Hal heard her open a pill bottle, pour a glass of water and go upstairs. He went up to check on her. She was in a fetal position, crying quietly into her pillow. He sat beside her and wrapped his arms around her.

"You lied about the Pentagon," she said. "Experimental airplanes at the Pentagon? You're at Patuxent River Air Station, not the Pentagon. Don't you care about us? Are you trying to kill yourself? I can't do this by myself."

"No Alice, I didn't lie. Everything I've told you about this assignment is the truth. I'm sorry that I can't give you a lot of details, but I did not lie. What's happening to you? You've been a solid, supportive Navy wife for all these years. Now, you're full of fear." She began to cry harder.

"Me. Blame it on me. Why does it have to be me? Maybe it's you. If you loved me and the kids, you would give up flying and be uh, uh, I don't know, something else."

"Alice, Alice," he said, running his fingers through her hair, "I'm a pilot. I've always been a pilot. It's in my blood and I simply can't just do something else. Why, at this point in our lives, is it so terrible?" She didn't answer, just continued to weep. "I'm so worried about you honey," he said.

"Why can't you find an airdale job in the Pentagon that doesn't involve flying?"

"Oh Alice, you know it doesn't work like that. I've got orders to this outfit and I'm stuck with them. I don't want to be away from you right now, but I'll have to be away from time to time and we're going to have to get through it."

"Just hold me Hal," she whispered and rolled into his arms. He held her tightly.

CHAPTER 17

Over the Mojave Desert, California

Hal looked out the window of the C–47 Gooney Bird that served as a VIP shuttle plane. Tan and brown desert terrain intermingled with rugged gray mountain ranges in the background. In the distance he could see an oasis known as Edwards Air Force Base. He rested his head and daydreamed. *God, I sure hate to leave Alice like that. I never had to worry about leaving her before. I hope she stays away from the booze.*

The copilot leaned into view of his two passengers and waved at them. When he got Hal's attention, the copilot pointed downward, off the left side of the aircraft. The aircraft banked into a left turn. Hal could see nearly straight down. There were two white fighters flying as chase planes alongside a strange looking solid black unmarked aircraft. He smiled. *Well, I'll be damned, there's the AQUABALL. That's going be a real kick in the ass to fly.* The AQUABALL had a relatively small diameter single-place fighter-like body with extremely long wings. The C–47 pilot leveled off on the upwind leg of the airport traffic pattern. The wing blocked Hal's view of the airport. When the C–47 banked on the crosswind leg, the BALL was passing over the runway threshold. Hal noticed another curiosity. A pickup truck was waiting on the threshold end of the runway, as though waiting its turn for takeoff. When the BALL passed over the threshold, it turned onto the runway and began chasing the BALL down the centerline of the runway. A puff of pale blue smoke spewed from under the fuselage when the main gear touched the runway. The chase jets peeled off to come around for their landing. The pickup truck followed the BALL onto a taxiway toward a hangar. Idling of the noisy C–47's engines followed by commencement of a turning descent implied that the C–47 was given clearance to land.

The temperature in the C–47's cabin soared on touchdown. The hundred–degree heat of the Mojave Desert turned the passenger compartment into a broiler. The images of the mountains in the distance danced and shimmered in the distortions created by the heat radiation from the ground. It also made the runways and taxiways appear to be covered with gently rippling water.

Colonel Bennett and two civilians climbed out of a blue Air Force sedan waiting at the parking pad. The Project's personnel risk reduction policy demanded that Hal and the Colonel, as well as the two CIA pilots, not fly together on the same airplane at any time. Bennett arrived the previous day.

Hal was first to deplane. There was quite a breeze that was a welcome relief, despite its temperature. The lack of humidity in the air evaporated the sweat from his forehead instantly. It momentarily flashed him back to the stifling heat in the valley near the Naktong River. "Welcome to Edwards, I'm Kelly Johnson," said a bulky built man with a full and smiling face.

"Real pleased to meet you sir, I'm Hal Kirby. I've read about some of the fun stuff you've been up to at the Skunkworks." They shook hands. Kelly introduced himself to the other passenger.

Colonel Bennett exchanged a limp obligatory handshake with Hal and then quickly introduced the civilian in the greeting party. "Captain Kirby, this is Mr. Frank Conyers, one of the two civilian pilots on the project." After Hal and Frank exchanged a few words, Bennett interrupted, "And this gentleman is our other civilian pilot, Mr. Reed Forbes. Reed, this is Captain Kirby."

Hal shook hands with Reed, the man who had boarded at LA with him, but had avoided conversation for the entire trip. "I had no idea you were on the project, pleased to meet you," said Hal. Forbes gave a powerful but brief handshake, nodded and turned his attention to the scenic beauty of the distant mountains.

Kelly motioned toward the sedan, "Come on, let's get to the office where it's cool. It'll be a little tight, but no worse than a fighter cockpit. They'll take your bags over to the BOQ for you. Meanwhile, we'll take care of ID badges, then turn you loose to get settled in."

Johnson drove to a hangar that was foot patrolled by Air Police with submachine guns and German Shepherds. The large hangar doors were closed. A sentry at the gate in the fence around the hangar checked their ID badges against a list, saluted sharply and opened the door for them. They walked to a side door in the hangar, then down a windowless hallway. Kelly stopped at a door to the hangar interior, "Colonel, let's give them a sneak peek." They went into the hangar area. Two black aircraft filled Hal's eyes. Armed APs posted at the nose and tail of each plane came to attention as they approached. Several men in green jumpsuits with Lockheed logos were busy with the aircraft. Just looking at those planes brought excitement into Hal's thoughts. He tapped his hat against his leg several times. Hot damn. I can't wait 'til I get my ass into one of those things. He turned to Johnson, "Sinister looking Kelly, just flaming sinister."

Kelly nodded with a grin, "Tech crews are going over them. They both just flew in from Palmdale. Come on, let's take a closer look. Langley contracts guys signed off on them this morning. They belong to Uncle Sam now," he said with a smile.

"When do we fly?" Frank Conyers asked anxiously, smoothing his hand along the leading edge of an unusually long and downward curving black wing.

Before Johnson could get a word from his mouth, Colonel Bennett responded with his normal condescending tone, "Lockheed and Fairchild will conduct ground school on the aircraft and cameras all day tomorrow, starting at 0600 continuing until 2200, or however long it takes. You will be given sufficient breaks for meals and calls to nature, of course." Frank Conyers looked at Hal and shook his head. Reed Forbes left the group and walked to the tail of the aircraft. The Colonel cast a disapproving eye at Reed and continued, "Practical flight instruction will be conducted from 0600 to sunset on Sunday and every day thereafter for two weeks. I'll assign flight schedules tomorrow afternoon."

Hal also strayed from the group and walked around his new toy in awe. Oh man, I can't imagine what the view is like at such high altitudes. He knelt on one knee near the wing root at the fuselage. From this vantage point, the extreme length of the wing and its natural droop toward the spotless hangar deck was accentuated. 'Pogo sticks' with wheels on the end of them were attached two thirds of the length from the wing roots. The wheels came within about a foot of the ground. They were obviously designed to keep the wing tips from coming into contact with the ground. Hal turned his attention to the unique main gear assembly and tail wheel. There were just two narrowly spaced main gear tires and a tail wheel that kept the aircraft in what seemed to be a very precarious balance.

Kelly Johnson and the others came to where Hal was hunkered down. "Damn Kelly, what keeps this thing from tipping over?" asked Hal, jokingly.

"Gentlemen," announced Bennett, "You'll get your fill of these aircraft in due time. Follow me to the office now. It is a requirement that you get ID badges immediately. Having accomplished that task, you will be taken to PSD, the Physiological Support Division, for final pressure suit and helmet fittings. After that, you are free until this evening, when you will attend a command performance dinner at the Officer's Club, at 1900 hours. Uniform is business suits for civilians, dress uniforms for military personnel. We have a private dining room reserved. Attending will be Mr. Johnson, his project engineer, his two project test pilots who will be your flight instructors and a representative from Fairchild who will teach the camera systems and myself, of course. Are there any questions?"

Frank Conyers leaned over and whispered in Hal's ear, "Where did they find this asshole?" Hal skillfully restrained his need to burst out in laughter.

As Hal approached the BOQ reception desk, someone hollered, "Hal, I already called for a ride." Frank Conyers was waving at him.

"Evenin', Frank and Reed," Hal greeted the two CIA pilots.

"Gee, you look real pretty in your dress blues," teased Frank. "Say, is that guy Bennett for real?"

"Yeah, he's real alright, a real pain in—oops, I can't talk about my boss like that."

Frank laughed, "They don't make Air Force Colonels like they used to. Here's the base taxi. Let's go get it over with." They recapped their backgrounds during the ride to the O'Club. Reed only got energized when he bragged of being a Marine pilot in Pappy Boyington's Black Sheep Squadron during the war. Aside from that, the only other details of his life that leaked out were that he was single and that he used to fly for TWA. Frank was a retired Air Force Colonel, with a career in bombers. He flew 25 missions over Germany in B–17s and was married.

They found the private dining room marked "Colonel Bennett Party". Holding court at the door was, of course, Colonel Bennett. Next to him was a very short and overweight civilian, 50–something, bald down the center, gray and bushy around the sides. Hal examined the man carefully. Good grief, who's this stumpy porker with the loud mouth. I don't think you could jam him into a cockpit with a steam shovel.

"Captain, please meet Representative Horace Bradbury," said Bennett. "Horace, this is Captain Kirby."

Hal maintained a poker face, hiding his surprise. This is Bradbury? What the hell is he doing here? Hal gripped the Congressman's hand and squeezed as hard as he could. Bradbury winced as his palm collapsed. Hal grinned internally and relaxed his hold. "Pleased to meet you sir."

"Good evening Captain," he said with a slight Virginia drawl. Bradbury immediately turned back to his conversation with Kelly Johnson. As Hal moved on inside, he noted that Bradbury held animated and relatively long conversations with the other arrivals. Hal was not disappointed about being left off Bradbury's list of people to know. Being snubbed did peak Hal's curiosity though. Bennett obviously had told Bradbury something. While walking to the portable bar in the corner, Hal wondered what it might have been.

Frank joined him shortly at the bar, "Hal, is it my imagination, or is the good Colonel kissing the good congressman's ass?"

"Well Frank, the good congressman happens to be the good Colonel's daddy in law, but yes he is." Frank grinned and ordered a beer.

Reed finally found a gentlemanly way out of his trivial conversation with Bradbury. He came to the bar, ordered Jack Daniels on the rocks and asked the big-busted barmaid for a date.

"Reed doesn't let any grass grow under his feet," Frank whispered.

"I noticed," said Hal. "I also notice that despite a cute smile, her head is shaking from side to side." They laughed.

Reed came over to them and whispered with a big grin, "I heard that Frank. There are some old warrior's rules that apply here. Hesitate, and you are lost, and no guts, no glory."

Hal laughed and asked, "Turned you down?"

Reed grinned, "This time. But I'm not going to give up. She's an angel."

Hal chuckled, "Remember Reed, some great man, whose identity escapes me at the moment, said that without persistence, we are nothing."

Reed nodded with a grin, "I already knew that." They all laughed. "Not to change the subject, Kelly Johnson is a familiar name, but I don't know a lot about him."

Hal had done his homework, "Kelly designed the P–80 Shooting Star. In fact, they produced the prototype in some ridiculous amount of time. Back in '43 this is. They did it in five months or something like that. His outfit does their R&D."

Colonel Bennett interrupted the conversation with a call to the dining table. They dined on broiled filet mignon, French style green beans, creamed corn and wild rice. Following desert of apple pie alamode, everyone mixed, mingled and got to know each other better. Bennett and Bradbury spent most of the evening huddled in private conversation. Reed spent his time after dinner at the portable bar charming the barmaid.

At 2100, Colonel Bennett announced that the party was over.

"Let's retire to the Stag Bar," suggested Frank.

"Good idea," said Hal.

"I'm going to call it a night," said Reed.

Hal laughed, "Aha! Persistence pays!" They all had a hearty laugh. Reed nodded with an evil grin and departed.

Promptly at 0600 the next morning, Kelly Johnson came into the Top Secret lecture room in the hangar with Colonel Bennett on his heels. "Good morning gents," greeted Kelly. "Reveille came quickly this morning didn't it? Everyone seems bright eyed and bushy tailed though." He glanced at Reed Forbes, who had just swallowed a burp, nearly inconspicuously. "Well, most of you anyway." There was muffled laughter. Reed's eyes looked like road maps. He smelled heavily of metabolized Jack Daniels. "OK gentlemen, I'm going to kick this off and depart for Burbank. I just wanted to give you a few words, then turn it over to Tim and Hank for the nitty gritty. Gentlemen, these airplanes are little more than developmental models outfitted for field testing under live operational conditions. We built the airframes to merely explore high altitude flight designs and gather some performance data. So, you'll find the cockpits and systems austere and the flying challenging. But, they are the highest flying piloted aircraft in the world. The MIG ceiling is estimated at 35,000 feet—40,000 tops. You won't find it in writing, but AQUABALL can reliably climb to and maintain

50,000 feet. The absolute ceiling is about 55,000 feet. Stability starts falling off rapidly above 50K, however. With the data gained from experiments with this project to date, I have begun a project nicknamed "U–2" for the preliminary paper design of a plane that will be able to fly much higher. That presents some special problems, but they can be overcome given time and money. That's about it gents. Remember, this is an unfamiliar flight regime, plus there are physiological factors you've never had to contend with. So, be careful with yourselves and my two babies. Good luck."

With that prelude, the four pilots began their intensive ground training on the AQUABALL engine and flight systems operations and procedures. The two engineers and two test pilots from Lockheed lectured on those subjects until 2000. Another two hours and 45 minutes was spent on learning how to operate the top secret reconnaissance camera.

"Gentlemen," announced Bennett, I think we have accomplished all the ground school objectives for today. We'll be assigning independent study over the next two weeks. Dismissed."

"Colonel, there's something no one has told us yet," said Reed. "It's obvious that we're not in this big rush to fly test missions over California. What is our mission?"

Bennett wrestled with that question a moment, "Operational orders have not been received yet. I expect them to be received within two weeks. Captain Kirby will be responsible for coordinating the arrangements, tasking and scheduling necessary to accomplish those orders."

"Korea, right?" asked Reed.

"No," said Bennett, "Presently, there are several potential missions being proposed from different elements of the government, but the Agency has selected a top priority target. Although there is a war going on in Korea, I feel there are sufficient Air Force and Navy assets to support Korean operations. CIA has some things it would like to accomplish elsewhere in the world which they consider more urgent than mopping up Korea."

Reed outwardly showed two things: disgust with politics and exhaustion. Given what Captain Castle told Hal, Bennett's outright dismissal of Korea was surprising.

"OK, that is all. Captain Kirby and Conyers, I'll see you at PSD at 0600 tomorrow morning. Dismissed."

Hal decided to take the 15–minute walk back to the BOQ in the refreshing crisp night air of the desert. The solitude gave him peace and quiet although his mind was awash with divergent thoughts—Alice, AQUABALL, Bennett, Bradbury, Korea, to name a few.

0500 came all too quickly the next morning. After a fast shave, shower and breakfast, the base taxi delivered Hal and Frank to the Physiological Support Division building. They received physicals and EKGs and were now getting into their tailor-made high altitude suits for the first time.

"Damn, this helmet is heavy," said Hal. The PSD Sergeant grinned and finished securing the seal clamps between it and the suit collar.

The Sergeant finished securing their helmets and said, "OK, they look like good fits, now you need to lie on the table and relax for an hour. We're going to feed you pure O2 and pump you up for a while. As I mentioned in class yesterday, this is to check the suit seals and purge the nitrogen from your tissues."

"Rajah dajah," said Hal, projecting a large glove thumb. A brief hissing sound accompanied inflation of the suit. Geez, this is like wearing a football. Six feet away, Frank was stretched out suffering the same sensations. Hal noted that the rigid inflated suit was very uncomfortable, at least when flat on your back. Innumerable details about flying the airplane swarmed his mind. The tech studied gauges on small panels next to the pilots. Hal tried to relax and catnap.

Thumping noises and vibration on Hal's suit shoulder broke the tranquility. "Good morning Captain, ready for the ride?" asked Ryan Hall, the Lockheed test pilot who was going to be Hal's check pilot.

"Damn right!" said Hal, "Can't wait." Kevin Garcia, the other Lockheed test pilot, was chatting with Frank.

"Good," said Ryan, slapping Hal's helmet gently. "Just wanted to give you a few memory jogs and outline the plan before we get on the tarmac. We're going to do a couple takeoffs and landings with the pogo legs fastened. On takeoff, reduce to 95% power and hold 30–degrees pitch; level off at 5,000 feet. I'll be chasing off your port wing. I'll handle communications with the tower. Watch the airspeed, it's going to be difficult to maintain a slow taxi or traffic pattern airspeed, even with full bypass. Use the wheel brakes, air brakes, spoilers, flaps, whatever you need."

"Rajah dajah."

"Then we'll let them pull the retainer pins on the pogos for the second takeoff. Same drill, 95% and 30 degrees, but when the airspeed comes down to 115 knots, adjust the pitch to hold that, then level out at 20,000 feet and pull back to flight idle. I'll talk you through some maneuvers and emergency procedures to get you acquainted with the feel of the airplane. For the next phase, I'll remain at 20,000 and talk you up to 50,000 in 10K steps. Remember now, at 50K, you've only got a 20-knot margin between stall and airspeed at level flight. That's your only major threat aside from cabin decompression. Use the autopilot. Also, remember now, the pogos have dropped off at takeoff, so be real careful on the landing. Keep those wings level. If a wingtip touches the ground, you're going to spin out and destroy the aircraft."

"Got it!" said Hal.

"And let me know if you feel any manifestation of bends, or any other physiologic sensation which may develop during the flight."

When Hal and Frank completed their hour of breathing pure oxygen, the technicians disconnected their suits from the testing system. They reconnected them to umbilical hoses from portable yellow aluminum boxes that air-conditioned the suits. The pilots grabbed the top handles on the boxes and went directly into a van waiting at the PSD loading ramp. They were taken into the AQUABALL hangar; main doors at both ends were open. The BALL aircraft were parked side by side, just inside the hangar, engines running. They were already preflight inspected and were started when the pilots arrived at the hangar. Reed climbed out of the cockpit onto the ladder platform positioned alongside the aircraft. A Lockheed tech was also standing on the platform, where he coached Reed on cockpit startup checklist procedures.

PSD techs helped the pilots from the vans and up the maintenance platform to the cockpit. The weight of the suit, mass of the helmet, and the so-called portable air conditioner added a little challenge to normally second nature tasks, such as walking and climbing ladders.

"Morning guys, how's she look?" Hal asked, when he had scaled Mount Everest. He looked at Reed carefully. Geez, I don't like the idea of getting into an aircraft I don't personally preflight. Man, this takes trust. Why did Bennett pair me up with Reed? I hope he's sober.

"Four point oh," Reed replied matter-of-factly.

"Get in there before you heat up and suffocate," the tech said. They disconnected Hal from the portable air conditioner, guided him into the cockpit and assisted in reconnecting the plane's suit support system umbilical. A rush of very cool air sent a shudder through Hal. Radio microphone connections and seat harnesses followed. Hal reached into a side pouch for the checklists and ran through the pre-taxi checks.

"OK, let's go!" Hal said, pointing the thumb of his suit glove up.

Reed and the tech reached across and pulled the side-hinged canopy down; Hal operated the lever which pressure sealed the canopy frame into its gaskets. A stroke from a stiff index finger on a paddle switch actuated the cabin pressurization system. Hal watched as the needle in the gauge moved rapidly at first, then slowed gradually until it stood in the center of the green segment of an arc. He nodded to Reed; they climbed down and pulled the platform away. When Reed signaled chock removal, Hal released the parking break. A brief advancement of the throttle got the long-winged bird rolling. When the main gear ran over the hangar door tracks, Hal scanned from one long 35 foot bouncing wing to the other. Whoa! Good grief, look at those babies flap. Compared to the 38–foot wingspan on my Panther, 70 feet looks like it goes forever. Everything is big and clunky. Where'd they get this damn yoke, from a B–29? Bright desert sun bathed the cockpit when the aircraft crept out of the hangar. He rotated the dark green reflective filter down over the clear Plexiglas of his helmet face. A shiny white Lockheed F–94 Starfire chase plane was waiting for him on the ramp. Ryan was in the front seat of the F–94 and Colonel Bennett was in the rear.

Hal's radio came alive, "Red Fox this is Gun Slinger, you are first out of the gate. You anxious?" asked Ryan.

"A–firm Gun Slinger, let's go flying," answered Hal; his heart was racing.

"Edwards tower this is Gun Slinger Flight, Red Fox in company, request permission taxi to the active."

Office of Congressman Horace Bradbury,
Washington, DC

Bradbury's concentration on a document was broken by his secretary's voice on the intercom, "Sir, President Truman on your private line."

Bradbury picked up the phone and waited for the President.

"Horace?"

"Yes Mr. President."

"Horace, General Marshall was just in here. He says you're tying his hands with all the restrictions you placed on the AQUA project money. What's that all about?"

"Just precautionary Mr. President, it's routine language to prevent unauthorized redirection of funds."

"You're trying my patience Horace. He's my goddam Secretary of Defense and you're not going to play games with him. He says you are keeping him from using the system to support the effort in Korea and says it is imperative that he be able to do so."

"Mr. President, all due respect to the General, AQUABALL is a research platform sir; it's not equipped for use in combat. What they really want to get their hands on is the five million that is fenced for an AQUAMARINE pod contract. There are—"

"Pods, what the hell are pods?" asked Truman.

"Uh, an aluminum cylinder full of equipment that attaches to the aircraft wing. The R&D payload in this pod is the radar signal collection system we briefed you on."

"Look Horace, Marshall says CIA admitted that the aircraft can be used in Korea and that's exactly what I want to happen. We're trying to figure out what the Chinese and Russians are up to. We can't do that without those planes. I'm going to let General MacArthur sweep north. We need to know what's going on up there. I have no patience for games while this war is going on. Understand?"

"Yes, Mr. President. I'll correct the language. I didn't intend to tie his hands in that manner." The line went dead. Bradbury slammed the phone into the hook.

He pressed the intercom button for his secretary, "Sheila, get Colonel Yardley on the line." He got up and paced until Yardley was on the phone. "Tim, General Marshall says someone confirmed that AQUAMARINE can be used in Korea. What do you know about that?"

"I know that General Marshall and the Director had a discussion about it an hour ago. They called me up to the Director's office. When Marshall asked me if it could be done, I couldn't lie."

"You couldn't huh?" asked Bradbury sarcastically.

"Horace I'm sorry, but I got the word that they had already talked to Lockheed. Trying to lie would have made me look like an ass. That wouldn't be good either."

"They can't court martial you now, you're retired. Dammit, I can't believe this.

"I had no choice and you know it," said Tim.

"You know what JCS is trying to do! You should have stalled so we could come up with a game plan. We can all kiss our money good-bye now."

"HL, maybe we should discuss this somewhere tonight."

"I need to know now. Tell me more about this meeting with Marshall."

"All I know HL, is that I had the Deputy Director, CIA, Dulles and General Marshall standing three feet away from me and they weren't looking for an answer tomorrow or next week."

"Maybe so. All right, JCS said the Chinese are up to something. What are they talking about?" asked Bradbury.

"This morning, reports went out saying we have evidence that the Chicoms have begun massing along the Manchurian side of the Yalu. What that's all about is not yet clear. Every time the Air Force sends a recon bird up there near the Yalu, Mig–15s come up, harass them and prevent them from taking pictures. So, the playing field is changing."

"That would get everybody stirred up. OK. I'll talk to you later. If you hear anything, call me. First, dammit!" The telephone and hook got another beating.

"Sheila, get me Will Crandall." Bradbury paced some more.

"Crandall on your private line sir," Sheila advised.

"Bad news Will," said Bradbury.

"How bad and what about?"

"I think the AQUACRYSTAL money might be disappearing. Put together some information on the impact to the company. Keep it to yourself though. I just need it for contingency to minimize the losses. I may have a way to save it, or at least some of it."

"God HL, that's real bad."

"How about dinner tonight at 8, La Dolce Vita, bring that information with you. Uh, let's leave the ladies at home Will," said Bradbury. The telephone received yet another impact test.

"Sheila, try and track down Colonel Bennett at Edwards Air Force Base."

AQUAMARINE Hangar

Edwards AFB, CA

"Where the hell have you been, Logan, the shit is hitting the fan back here," said Bradbury.

"I just got back from flying, got your note and called immediately. What's the trouble?"

"Marshall did an end-run on me and got approval to take AQUAMARINE to Korea. You hear anything about that?" asked Bradbury.

"Nothing HL. I'd much prefer to remain out of the combat zone and out of Stratemeyer's way," said Bennett. "I cannot risk more problems with him. Remember, I've got to neutralize the letter of reprimand he gave me. The Brigadier General selection board convenes in November you know. There's not much time. You've got to stop them. At least fix it so I remain behind in the Pentagon to manage the program."

"Logan, you don't know what problems are! JCS wants to abscond with all the CRYSTAL money to support the Korean operations overruns."

It took a moment for Bennett to collect his thoughts, "You have to pull some strings, HL."

"I know what I have to do. If you hear anything, call me."

"Good God HL, this is terrible," Bennett said emphatically, "Surely you can do something. Korea is the worst place I could possibly go right now."

"Stop bellyaching Logan!" said Bradbury and slammed the phone down. He whispered, "I don't know what she ever saw in that guy."

"Colonel Gayonne, Program Manager in the Air Force Chief of Staff's office, is here to see you Mr. Bradbury," Sheila announced over the intercom.

"Send him in and hold all calls please." Sheila showed the Colonel into Bradbury's office. "Come in," greeted Bradbury, rising to offer a handshake, "Glad you could come over on such short notice. Nice to see you again. Please have a seat."

The Colonel gave Bradbury a polite handshake and took a seat. "How can I be of assistance?" asked Gayonne.

"I won't beat around the bush. They tell me you are watching the purse strings on AQUAMARINE," said Bradbury.

"Yes sir."

"Well, I need a favor. I need to know, just between you and me, if they are planning to redline the AQUACRYSTAL line item and transfer the money to a Korea operations item," said Bradbury.

"You put me in a difficult position sir," said Gayonne.

"This is off the record, of course, and I will not compromise my source. You have my word," urged Bradbury.

Gayonne studied the blue and green swirls in the plush carpet at his feet; he clasped his hands.

"It's OK Colonel, I'm sure they told you to keep your mouth shut." Gayonne gave an uncomfortable nod. "Well," Bradbury continued, "they don't realize what you and I have in common. Armory International put on one hell of a weekend bash last month, didn't they? It must have cost them a mint to rent the whole inn," Bradbury gave an evil chuckle. "Not to mention bringing in all those sweet things from California." Gayonne's face turned red. Bradbury continued, "I thought I had the prettiest one until I saw that redhead you went riding with Saturday morning." Bradbury gave a hearty laugh, "If our wives ever found out about that little soiree we'd be in big trouble, wouldn't we?"

Colonel Gayonne looked up at the Congressman and took a deep breath, "We've sorta got each other by the balls, don't we?"

Bradbury tilted back in his dark leather judge's chair and laughed so hard his eyes teared, "Colonel, I think we understand each other real well."

"The pod line item will be red-lined," said Gayonne, "We need the money for deploying AQUAMARINE to Korea. There's no other way to pay for the emergency logistics without external fund sources and that would compromise the classified nature of the program. JCS is meeting now to approve General MacArthur's Operation Plan for sweeping north all the way to the Yalu River. Of course, that's a hairy situation, because it appears that the Chinese will soon be coming down into North Korea and we don't know what the Soviets are going to do. They called for comprehensive intelligence and surveillance to sort it all out. That included ordering us to get the AQUAMARINE system to Korea ASAP!"

Bradbury thought for a moment, "Suppose I get $5 million more into the project account. Could you see to it that the pod item doesn't get red-lined?"

"No Mr. Bradbury, I don't have that kind of discretionary authority."

"How about your boss? Does General Killian have a pet project he can't get funded?" asked Bradbury.

"General Killian, this is Horace Bradbury. How are you this afternoon?"

"Just fine sir, thank you. How about yourself?"

"I'm good, thank you. The reason I am calling, now, I can't give the justification over the phone, but the sponsor of the AQUACRYSTAL line item has an urgent need for that equipment. The sponsor is upset because they heard a rumor that JCS was not going to fund it. Any truth to that General?"

"Yes sir, there is. When you removed the fence on that money, it became the only source of funds to support the emergency deployment of the AQUAMARINE equipment. The reasoning was that the BALLs aren't going to deploy to the original location, so the sponsor won't be able to use the pods anyway. We can work out the budgetary stuff later sir, but there's no other AQUA money we can get our hands on right quick."

"That's not acceptable General. The sponsor now intends to use the pods in the new deployment area, on a not to interfere basis of course. That research could save lives of pilots, General."

"With all due respect sir, I see that as the sponsor's problem, not yours or mine. At the moment, my problem is getting AQUAMARINE deployed to Korea."

"I have a plan General. If you will initiate the contract action for the pods immediately, I'll get another $5 million added to the project within two weeks. No funds you commit will clear in that time frame and there will technically be no violation."

"You are stretching the regulations on that. You are still suggesting that I spend money I don't have," said the General.

"Semantics, General. I can make it worth the Air Force's while," said Bradbury.

Killian paused, "I'm listening."

"General, I'm sorry I couldn't get funds for that communications modernization line item you submitted the last two years. I know how strongly the Air Force felt about that and I tried hard. But, if you do this favor, I'll call in a marker and get that project added to this fiscal year's apportionment. Deal?"

"I'll have to think about it. I'll get back to you. I'll have to discuss it with the Chief of Staff of the Air Force."

"There's nothing to think about or discuss with General Vandenberg. We're at war. The CRYSTAL systems are now necessary to the sponsor's war effort. Cases like this, well, you just have to use your imagination and initiative."

"I'm sorry sir, but I'll have to get back to you," said Killian.

"When can I expect a reply?" asked Bradbury, irritated to the bone.

"Tomorrow afternoon, or the following morning at the latest. My plate is very full right now and so is General Vandenberg's."

Telephone Booth, Bachelor Officer's Quarters
Edwards Air Force Base

"Collect call from Hal Kirby, will you accept the charges?" asked the operator.

"Yes I will. Glad to hear from you darlin'," said Alice, "Did you get to fly today?"

"Sure did. You sound so good. How are you feeling?"

"I had my follow-up with Doc Mahoney this morning. He thinks the headaches are now a side effect and changed my tranquilizer prescription. I feel so strange taking these things. I can't live the rest of my life on those."

"Yes, but you are on the mend dear. Your body's been so out of sorts, it's going to take a while. Be patient and don't worry. Everything's going to be OK. How are the kids?"

"Fine. They're both asleep or I'd put them on."

"That's OK. Listen honey, our training has been shortened. I'll be leaving here early next Saturday morning. I'm looking forward to seeing you."

"Then what?" asked Alice, "I've been following the news. Something happening huh?"

"The orders are classified, so I can't do much explaining."

"How long will you be gone?" she asked.

"My guess is two or three months. A lot shorter than a carrier deployment to WestPac or the Med."

"I guess," she said softly.

"Easy now honey, I'm not flying off a carrier, I'm not dropping bombs or dog fighting. I'll be perfectly safe. Just relax. We'll talk more about all that when I get home. I love you."

"I love you too," she said. "Hal?"

"I'm still here."

"Call me as often as you can, would you?" she asked.

"Sure sweetheart!" A very wide grin formed on his face.

CHAPTER 18

Great Falls, Virginia

Hal tipped the taxi driver, picked up his bags and started up the sidewalk. A cold front had come through the previous day. The light breeze had a frosty bite and was carrying the pungent smell of burning oak from fireplaces in the neighborhood. His breath vapors furled out of his nostrils and mouth, glowing white from the backlighting of the porch light. Alice came to the door and looked through the lace curtains. Her silhouette was comforting to him and invoked a warm feeling from head to toe. He had missed her badly and was glad to be home. When he stepped onto the porch, she opened the door and flashed the smile that won his heart the first day he saw her. The newest addition to the family, a black and white long-haired cat stood by her bare feet. He dropped his bags on the foyer floor, pushed the door shut and took her into his arms. They hugged, kissed and swayed silently for several minutes. No words exchanged, but the strength of their hugs, the emotion of their kisses and their eyes said many things. "You look and feel good honey," said Hal, "How you been feeling?"

"Some days are better than others, but not bad darlin'."

"I see you decided to take the Strickland's cat. What is its name?" he asked as the cat threaded herself repeatedly through their legs.

"It, Mr. Kirby, is our new daughter Fuzzy. Fuzzy, this is your new daddy. Tell your daddy how much you appreciate him letting you stay here instead of going to the pound." The cat looked back and forth at them, meowing. They laughed.

Hal bent down to stroke his new dependent, "Fuzzy, I've heard about you. You're as pretty as they said you were."

"Look at that face, Hal," said Alice, "White cheeks, black eyes, one white ear, she's precious."

He looked up at Alice, "You never did get around to telling me exactly why Jeanne had to give her away."

"Admiral Strickland got short fused orders to Naples and they just couldn't make arrangements for her."

"She's a pretty cat all right, but she's not my cat and I don't want to be stuck with the responsibility of taking care of her."

"Don't worry darlin', Susan and I are taking good care of her. She's very good, no trouble at all." Fuzzy dashed up the staircase, stood at the turn of the spiral with a playful look on her face, fluttering her thick black tail, eyes glowing with the color of green neon.

"Look at her tail honey, it looks crooked at the end," he said.

"Uh huh, caught it in the door last Sunday, first day with us, poor dear," Alice said, laughing.

Hal took Alice's hands and smiled into her velvet brown eyes. Alice sighed deeply; her eyes filled. She grinned through blushing cheeks, gave him a noisy smooch and pulled him by the hand toward the staircase, "Come on, get squared away, I'm sure you're hungry. There's a pot of vegetable beef soup waiting.

"Mmm, perfect, it's really gotten chilly; soup is just what the doctor ordered," he said. "Where are the kids?"

"Kids are out, of course—school dance. I drove them there and Ashley's mother is bringing them back. Go get washed up and comfortable. I'll get things started."

"Thanks for laying the jeans and shirt out on the bed for me," he said as he came into the kitchen. Her tall, lean frame was a pleasing sight in stovepipe jeans. A fitted western shirt of mixed reds and blues accentuated it.

"You've still got the cutest butt I've ever seen," he said and kissed her on the back of the neck as she ladled soup into bowls.

"Careful, this stuff is hot," she said.

"Good. I'm counting on it," he said and patted her on the buns. She giggled like a schoolgirl. It warmed his heart to see her returning to good health and a playful frame of mind.

Alice had the small round kitchen table set for two on a gray and white checkered table cloth. Hal lit the tall blue candle standing as the mast in a ceramic Spanish galleon centerpiece.

"Even repatriated my favorite candle holder," he said.

"Uh huh, I was thinking about that going away party the squadron gave us and dug it out. Thought you'd enjoy the memories of that tour. I loved Jacksonville."

"Me too. There were some really fine people there." He opened the cloth flaps of the breadbasket, tore off two healthy pieces of still warm whole wheat bread and put them on plates. "Home baked bread—smells wonderful."

She poured steaming coffee into large mugs. The aromas from coffee, soup and bread intermingled and set his mouth to watering.

"I didn't realize how damn hungry I was," he said.

"I didn't have much of an appetite earlier today," she said. "I had a dizzy spell this morning, but now I'm really ravenous. Oh, I saw the doctor yesterday. He said he's going to reduce my tranquilizer dosage at the end of the month and see how that goes. But, he says I'll just have to live with the migraine headaches for now. The medicine he gave me for them always works, so that's a blessing. The pain used to be so bad that it made me nauseous and dizzy."

"Does the doctor have any idea why are you have started getting these things?" asked Hal.

"Doc said it's fairly common for women to begin getting them at my age. But he's got me scheduled for some other tests in a couple weeks. I'm seeing an ophthalmologist next week."

"Well good. Sounds like he's covering all the bases." She put the full bowls at their places. As she leaned across the table, her deeply unbuttoned blouse fell open; she was not wearing a bra. "Whoa! Don't do that to me before chow," he kidded, bringing a perky grin and a blush to her face. He attacked the soup and bread with a vengeance. When their eyes met, he put his spoon down, smiled and patted her hand, "You know honey, there is nothing, absolutely nothing, like your home cooking."

"Uh huh, and there's nothing like having you home to cook for," she said as she squeezed his hand.

"You look so much better honey. I'm glad."

"I got rid of all the booze in the house. It's been hard, sometimes I really crave it. So, don't buy any beer. I don't want anything in the house at all."

"I can do without beer," he said, "I'm so proud of you."

Alice grinned, "I'm glad you were patient Hal. I was embarrassed and confused. The drinking and the pictures were hard things to face up to. There was so much happening in our lives."

"I know honey, I made my share of mistakes. Let's not look back. It's today and tomorrow that are important. I love you and always will."

Alice's eyes filled, "We've been through a lot of ups and downs over the years. I love you so very much. I don't want to lose you. I can't imagine life without you."

"Don't worry honey." He raised her hand and kissed the back of it tenderly." He got up and walked behind her. He held her face, tilted her head up gently and kissed her forehead lovingly.

She reached up and put her hands around his neck and kissed him passionately. His hands slid off her cheeks, down her neck and over her breasts.

"Race ya," she hollered. She sprang out of the chair and darted out of the kitchen into the hallway leading to the foyer. He took the other route, through the dining room to the staircase and tackled her part way up. They fell onto the stairs, laughing wildly. Her normally tight jeans were fitting a little loose these days; when he pulled hard on the pants legs they came right off.

"You've lost weight," he said and tackled her again as she attempted to escape. He straddled her waist and held her wrists over her head.

"This isn't very comfortable," she said through struggles and laughs. Hal bent down and kissed her repeatedly. Their mouths explored each other's faces. He let go of her hands and unbuttoned the remaining buttons of her blouse. She raised up to reach the top button of his shirt and worked her way down. He threw his shirt over his shoulder and bent down to munch on her belly. She pulled up her legs, placed her feet at the waist of his jeans, and pushed hard. It thrust him backward causing him to lose his balance; he grabbed the banister to keep from falling. She took advantage of the moment of freedom, yelled and bolted up the stairs and into the bedroom. She tried to close the door, but he was too close behind and blocked it from shutting. With a yelp, she let go of the door and ran for the walk-in closet.

Hal grabbed her around the waist, "I've got you now," he growled.

"Oh no you don't," she shrieked. He chuckled as he tightened his arms around her wriggling body, picked her up and carried her into the bathroom; he tried to put her into their doublewide shower enclosure. She struggled vigorously and managed to pull him into it with her. Her hands found the spigots and she turned them both on full. They began hollering when the freezing sensation of autumn cold water hit their bodies. He pressed her against the wall of the shower and began kissing her ardently. She threw her arms around his neck and melted into him. As the water rapidly became too hot, they frantically competed for the hot water spigot. They managed to get the temperature regulated and fell back into a strong embrace.

"Mmmmm, we haven't showered together for a long time," she said softly between kisses.

She unbuttoned and unzipped his jeans and pulled them down his legs. He kicked them out onto the tile floor. She gripped the waistband of his boxers and pulled them to his ankles. "I see you missed me! I sure missed your skinny little butt darlin'," she said while he struggled out of his wet t-shirt. He held the sleeves of her blouse while she squirmed out of it. He nibbled her belly and thighs while removing her panties. Hal caressed his way up her legs and belly until his mouth found her breasts. Sounds of delight began coming from her throat; her hands stroked his head and face. His arousal deepened; his mouth and lips progressed from caressing her breasts to devouring them. Their passion skyrocketed.

"Oh darlin', I've missed you so much," she murmured. She leaned back against the wall, gripped his buttocks firmly and pulled him to her. He kissed her slowly and deeply while his hands roamed between her bottom and shoulders. She wrapped a leg around him and hastily guided him. Their emotions exploded as he pushed forward. They lost all voluntary control of themselves and screamed into each other's mouths. Hearts pounding savagely, they tried to pull each other into their bodies until they collapsed into each other's arms.

The next morning, Hal was awakened by the sun shining through the bedroom window. His stirring awakened Alice.

"Good morning Fuzzy, reveille kitty," she said. Hal opened his eyes; his face was only inches from the cat's nose. Fuzzy was stretched out, upside down, in a semi-circle between the pillows. Alice was rubbing the cat's belly.

"Geez, the cat sleeps with us?" asked Hal.

Alice laughed, "Uh huh, she thinks she's a person. She liked your pillow a lot. I'm surprised she wasn't fighting you for it." Alice rolled over and turned on the radio.

The announcer's voice had sense of urgency to it, "Before we begin this segment of Sunday country music, we have a bulletin just received on the news wire. General MacArthur has sent a message to the North Korean Premier, Kim Il Sung, urging him to surrender and enter into discussions to reunite the north and south under democratic rule. No mention was made of actions that would be taken in the event that the Premier did not surrender. No additional information has been released by the White House, Pentagon or the military commands in the Pacific. We'll keep you posted as more information is available."

"Shit's going to hit the fan, isn't it?" she asked rolling over to snuggle with him.

"I can't picture the commies surrendering. It's a tough situation honey."

"Are you going over there?"

He gave her a hug, "I can't say where we are going. I'll have a Pacific APO address though. But it's a low risk project. Please don't worry."

"Uh huh!" she said sarcastically, "Have you heard the scuttlebutt that General LeMay's staff is making plans for A-bomb attacks on the North Koreans, Chinese and Russians? Scares the hell out me, Hal. Are you involved in that?"

"No Alice, I'm not, I promise. But the Pentagon must always have plans for all eventualities. Anyway, I think it will all be over by Christmas. Just relax honey. Don't stress yourself over it."

"The kids are up," she said. "I need to get breakfast going." Alice got out of bed, slipped on a pink velour robe and came around to Hal's side, "Reveille Captain, come on." A strong pull on his arms and he was up as well. They walked to the bathroom arm in arm. Fuzzy ran ahead, leaped up onto the sink counter, less concerned with the developments in Korea than she was with getting a drink. Alice twisted the spigot to provide a small stream of water. Fuzzy carefully positioned herself in the slippery, round-sided sink and began lapping at the stream of cool well water.

Hal chuckled, "Ahem, Fuzzy! Do you mind if I shave?"

"Get the papers off the table honey, I need to set it," said Alice, "kids will be down very shortly—coffee's ready too, get us a couple mugs. Alice hurried to set the table and poured a cup of milk into a small saucepan and put it over low heat. Hal poured their coffee. When Alice heard Joe's size 11–EEEs clattering down the stairs, she put two pieces of wheat bread into the toaster and pushed the lever down.

Joe counted loudly while he did twenty chin ups in the kitchen doorway, then plopped into his chair. "Mornin' Dad!" He looked up at his mother who was standing at the refrigerator waiting for his decision. "Mornin' Mom." He pondered a moment then said, "Strawberry!" Alice stood, waiting. "Oh. Strawberry, please," added Joe. She retrieved Joe's jelly 'flavor of the day' and chocolate milk from the fridge.

"Damn Joe, still only eating peanut butter and jelly on toast for breakfast?" asked Hal.

"Yeah dad, you know, nothing else tastes good in the morning." Hal laughed.

Alice kept Joe's favorites on hand: strawberry preserves, grape jelly, peach preserves and orange marmalade. Because she was unable to figure out his system for rotating the selection, she merely waited for his pronouncement.

"Hi Mom, hi Daddy," Susan said cheerfully as she came into the kitchen. Alice poured hot milk onto Susan's standard breakfast of raisin bran and brown sugar.

Having washed the first large chomp of peanut butter and jelly toast down with a gulp of chocolate milk, Joe asked, "Oooh, God Susie, how can you eat that stuff? So Dad, how long did you say you'd be home?"

"Joe, you're so stupid," said Susan, reaching down to pet Fuzzy who was begging for attention at her feet.

"Shut up, you're not as smart as I am," replied Joe.

"I'm a junior and you're a freshman."

"Knock it off!" Hal interrupted, "I'm not sure Joe, I'll find out tomorrow, but I think I will have to leave in a few days. I don't know for how long, but I doubt it will be more than a few months."

Fuzzy jumped into Hal's lap unsolicited, curled up and began purring loudly. Hal shook his head and smiled.

"Joey, don't you remember Daddy telling us that last night?" asked Susan.

"Susie you're such a pain," Joe said with a glare.

"If I smack you, you'll feel some pain Joey boy," Susan teased.

"I told you a million times, don't call me Joey boy."

"And I told you two million times not to call me Susie."

Hal gave the kids stern looks; the antagonism was over, at least for a while.

CHAPTER 19

Residence of Will Crandall
Falls Church, VA

"Shall we retire to the den?" asked Will Crandall, pushing away from the dinner table.

"That was one fine meal ladies," said Horace Bradbury.

"Quite outstanding indeed," added Colonel Logan Bennett.

"Think I'm gonna burst," said Tim Yardley, patting his stomach.

The ladies cleared the table for their biweekly Sunday bridge game while the men held a business meeting. Mrs. Crandall carried into the den a large tray containing mugs, a carafe of coffee, cookies, cream and sugar. She placed the tray onto a large hand carved claw footed mahogany coffee table in the center of the sitting area. The men got comfortable in the colored leather stuffed chairs. Coffee aroma soon filled the sitting area of the large red cedar paneled room. Will passed a box of Havana cigars around; Logan refused, as usual.

"Come on son, try one once, you'll get to love 'em," teased Horace. "You don't eat much, you don't swear, you don't drink, and you better not cheat on my daughter, so we have to find some vice for you."

"No thank you HL," said Logan, slightly perturbed.

"OK, let's get down to bees wax," said Horace. He struck a wooden match on the side of a matchbox with his stubby fingers and lit his cigar. Will and Tim followed his lead.

"We're out of the woods," said Bradbury. "I had to cash in a couple chits, but I got General Killian's JCS communications modernization project funded this fiscal year. He's happy as a pig in slop cause Vandenberg thinks he's a hero. So, he's playing ball with us. He promised he'd get the money and emergency procurement paperwork to contracts on Monday."

"That was a close one HL," said Crandall, running a hand over his bald head.

"How about Gayonne? Any chance that he could be a problem?" asked Logan. "He's a guy who plays by the book."

Bradbury shook his head, "Don't worry about Colonel Gayonne. He's no problem. Not at all."

Tim repeatedly ran his fingers through his gray hair; he wasn't convinced, "But HL, he knows the money game really well. When he gets General Killian's order to write that contract on money that's committed to mobilizing AQUAMARINE, he's going to get nervous. And Logan is right, when I slide that additional five mil into the JCS AQUA account next Thursday, he's going ask questions about how and where that came from."

"No, he won't, dammit. Look, take my word for it, he's handled. Handled! I'm not going to let some jackass rock my boat. I know what I'm doing. He's not the damn angel you think he is. Ya'll can just relax."

Logan looked at Will and Tim with a sinister grin. "Good enough for me."

Bradbury took a deep drag on his cigar, exhaled and continued, "Enough about that. We're getting the five mil we planned for and nobody is going to get hurt. Will, how's the fabrication coming?"

Crandall perked up, "Ah, pod number one is way ahead of schedule. I'm glad you guys talked me into ordering the parts on blind faith. We'll deliver it to Langley in less than two weeks."

"What's the status of the money on that?" asked Logan.

Will smiled, "We got paid the quarter mil for the design and brass-boarding phase. We also got one mil for the first increment of pod one; we'll get another 500K on delivery."

Bradbury leaned forward in his chair and pointed at Tim, "Your job now is to get the CIA operations people to authorize additional pods."

Tim nodded, "Yes, but they won't do that until they look at some live recordings and confirm that they are successful. They might be amenable to buying one more for the second BALL, but there's no guarantee. Hell, they are fighting it going to Korea as it is. Be patient, I'm working them."

"Patient! We're talking money here Tim," said Bradbury. "Three point five mil for four more of those sons of bitches. You just get those people hot for those pods."

Logan changed the subject to allow Bradbury a chance to cool off, "Tim, tell me again how you worked out the concealment of payments?"

"The covert ops people had several ideas for me. I settled on one that goes like this: after the ELINT shop runs acceptance tests, the contracts people present Will with cash, in hundred dollar bills, right on the spot. No paper, except for money of course. It's a verbal contract with cash on delivery. Simple and clean."

Logan shrugged his shoulders, "Excessively simple. I don't think—" Bradbury gave Logan a look that stopped whatever words were about to come out of Logan's mouth.

Bradbury's preoccupation with capturing new business reared its head again. He swallowed the last half of a chocolate chip cookie and turned to Tim, "Can you think of another black box project for Will to build?"

Tim thought a minute, "We have the CRIMSON BUGLE project to do yet. That's about 24 man months of effort and 600K of hardware. If that works out, they'll probably want to put the prototype on the AQUABALL too. But, scuttlebutt has it that if the CRYSTAL and BUGLE pods work as advertised they may eventually buy ten more of each over the next two years for use on other air recon platforms."

"That would be most extraordinary," said Logan. "We must hurry up and get those things into the air."

Bradbury looked over his reading glasses at Yardley, "Tim, get that thinking cap on and come up with some more ideas for hardware we can build. Things that will get funded fast."

Tim shook his head, "It doesn't work like that HL. The ops guys have to come up with a need. But, I have a few ideas. I'll brainstorm with them."

"And Logan," Bradbury said, "You make damn sure that Kirby don't get any information he ain't supposed to have. That goes for the rest of you too." They all nodded acknowledgment. "I smell a rat," Bradbury said, with a distant look, "It strikes me strange that somebody wanted a Navy guy on the project and had the power to make it happen. He's got to be somebody's inside man. I just haven't figured out exactly who or why."

"I'll try and work it out of him," said Logan.

"Yeah, get him drunk over there one night," said Tim.

"Hire some broad to get it out of him," said Will with a chuckle.

"Don't underestimate that son of a bitch," said Bradbury, "Leave him the hell alone or you'll wind up with the shitty end of a stick." He motioned to Will to push the box of cigars his way. "Another thing, keep a tight lid on this alleged Russian anti-air missile. I had breakfast with the President Friday and he's concerned that the word will leak out before the elections and complicate the issues. Not to mention that it will make it more difficult to keep General MacArthur and Senator McCarthy in check. Truman ordered Smith to keep it out of all intelligence reports until the last congressional election poll closes."

"I got the word already," said Tim. "By the way, the ELINT guys are highly irritated that the pods are going to be flying over Korea instead of Moscow and are making a lot of noise about it. They have info from a Human Intelligence source that the Russians have built a new missile guidance radar for that missile system. They want to collect that radar signal so bad they can taste it."

"Tell them to forget Moscow," said Bradbury, "You can tell them Marshall wants those planes in Korea and Truman is backing him up. Tell them to build more planes. We'd be happy to sell them pods for those too."

Tim was getting frustrated with Bradbury, "I wish it was that simple, HL. The fact is, it's not and I'm doing all I can."

Bradbury had enough of business for the evening, "Rack 'em Logan," he hollered and hauled himself out of the chair. "Time for a little 20–buck 8–ball. Put your money up gentlemen."

Office of Admiral Forrest Sherman, Chief of Naval Operations
The Pentagon

Admiral Sherman rose from behind a marvelous dark mahogany desk. It was a huge monster with intricate nautical carvings and gingerbread on the surfaces and corner posts. "Have a seat Captain, I'm sorry we haven't been able to have this private chat sooner."

"I'm sure you have been busy Admiral."

Sherman nodded. He noticed Hal eyeballing his ornate antique desk, "It's a beauty, isn't it? It's alleged that John Paul Jones once owned it."

"Wonder what he'd think of things today?" asked Hal.

The Admiral chuckled, "He's rolling in his grave. OK, first, Jim Castle suggested that it would be prudent that I write your fitness reports. The Navy Personnel office has been so directed."

"Thank you, sir. It's not going to be a picnic working for Colonel Bennett, if I may be so frank."

Admiral Sherman picked up a 3" X 5" card among several on his desk with notes jotted on them. "I have a few things to discuss with you in confidence."

"Of course, Admiral."

"Captain, let me recap where things are at. I realize you've been out of town for flight training. How was it, by the way?"

"An incredible experience Admiral. Aside from working for Colonel Bennett, I appreciate having the opportunity to work on this project," said Hal.

"You must tell me about the airplane one day. I'm envious. Back to the recap. I was told this morning that Chou En-lai, the Chinese Foreign Minister, informed the Indian Ambassador to Peking that China would not tolerate UN forces crossing the 38th parallel. General MacArthur plans to do exactly that in four days – we are sending the X–Corps up the western side of the peninsula. Admiral Struble's plan for an amphibious landing on the east side, at Wonsan, on October 20th is routing through JCS right now and I expect it to be approved promptly."

Hal's excitement was building quickly, "Geez, they are kicking off the northern operations sooner than I thought. Admiral, there's going to be hell to pay in North Korea if the Chinese or Russians get into it."

"That's my greatest concern," said the Admiral. "Especially since a lot of the northern air support operations are going to be Navy tasks. It's going to be damn tough going up there. The State Department pressured JCS to put General MacArthur on notice not to cross the Yalu River or any North Korean border with China or the Soviet Union, in the air or on the ground. SecState and the President are deathly afraid that irritating the Communists may cause them to come into the war directly. There's some intelligence that the Chinese may be in it already with ground troops, but that's not really been confirmed. In any case, the rules of engagement are so strict that the Air Force can't high-altitude bomb the bridges or the approaches close to the bridges at Antung without violating the border buffer zone JCS imposed."

"How about hot pursuit?" asked Hal.

"No hot pursuit provisions exist either," said the Admiral. "It's like fighting the war with one hand tied behind our back."

Hal shrugged his shoulders, "Well, as far as the bridges go, it won't matter much in a few weeks Admiral. Once the Yalu freezes solid, they can cross anywhere they please. Hell, they're already getting freezing weather up there; I checked. Maybe that's what they're waiting for. By the way, I've seen new reports of substantial troop and Mig–15 mobilization to the Antung area."

"Yes, I'm aware of that. The Mig–15 is big trouble for the carrier based aircraft."

Hal nodded, "Yes sir, intell says the Mig–15 has a top speed equal to the Panther, a service ceiling estimated at 33,000 and carries one 37mm and two 20mm cannons. That makes it a match for the Panthers."

Sherman replied, "They'll have a field day with our ADs and F–4s. That means the Carrier Division Commanders are going to need timely and accurate intell on where those damn things are based and how many there are."

"I'm beginning to see my role more clearly," said Hal smiling.

Sherman grinned, "The Air Force and CIA have other fish to fry and threats to Navy missions aren't high on their list. Worse yet, they don't want the AQUAMARINE aircraft to be there at all. They have fought tooth and nail to block deployment of those birds to Korea." Admiral Sherman stared off into the distance a moment, then leaned back in his chair, "It bothered me when they balked so hard about deploying it. And they sure didn't want a Navy man on the project either. I've played the game in this town long enough to know something questionable is going on with Bradbury and Bennett and this AQUAMARINE project. There are several of us who would like to see below the surface of it all."

Nervous energy caused Hal's left heel to begin bouncing into the thick carpet, "The old hidden agenda. Sounds like I've got my work cut out for me."

Sherman grinned, "Yes, but if you could handle the politics in Tokyo, you can handle AQUAMARINE. Keep your ear to the ground and watch your six though." The Admiral chased something through his mind for a moment, "I honestly don't know what to expect. Just a gut feeling of undercurrent."

"Speaking of undercurrents, what is Congressman Bradbury's connection with AQUAMARINE?" asked Hal.

"Why do you think he's connected?" asked Sherman.

"Because he attended the private dinner Colonel Bennett arranged on our first night at Edwards."

The Admiral digested Hal's words quietly. "That's interesting, real interesting."

Patty's smiling face greeted Hal when he returned to the office, "Captain, you don't know how nice it is to see people coming through that door again."

"What's the matter Patty, were you lonely?" asked Hal with a grin.

"It was like working in a morgue Captain," she said as she picked up the coffee pot, filled his mug and carried it into his office behind him. "I'm used to working in an area where there are a lot of people and a lot of stuff going on."

"Thanks Patty, I needed that."

She parked one cheek of her behind on the side of his desk and swung the free foot rhythmically off the end of the desk. He couldn't help glancing at her knee that had become exposed below the hem of a black and white plaid wool dress. She blushed and tugged downward on the hem. "Captain Castle wouldn't tell me what the subject matter was when he called for you this morning. Hope it wasn't trouble."

"No Patty, no trouble at all. So, what did you do with yourself while we were gone?"

"Solitaire, long lunches, read several books and lots of magazines," she said with a mock yawn. "What was it like to fly that plane?" Her eyes were sparkling with curiosity.

"It was absolutely thrilling Patty. I swear I could just barely detect the curvature of the earth. The Lockheed test pilots said I was imagining things. The panoramic view was so beautiful though."

"I should have been a man. I'd give anything to fly. I've always wanted to fly an airplane."

"Patty, you can learn to fly. Amelia Earhart proved that! All it takes is money to pay for the lessons. Tell you what. When I get back from deployment, we'll rent a light plane and go on a day trip somewhere. Alice and I haven't done that for quite a while."

Her face lit up, "Where would we go?"

"I don't know, anywhere we want to. Maybe down to Charleston. We really like it down there. You can bring a friend too."

"Would you let me fly it?" asked Patty.

"Of course I would. Well, if you can talk Alice out of the right seat." They laughed. "Where's the Colonel?" he asked.

"He came in right after you left, picked up some documents and went to a meeting. He rarely tells me where he's going. It's embarrassing for me to have to tell people I don't know where he is."

He shook his head sympathetically. "He's probably over in J–2. We're leaving for Korea very soon you know."

Her jaw dropped, "Korea? For how long? God, I'm going to go nuts around here."

"That's Top Secret Patty, it should be official today or tomorrow. My guess is for about a month or so. You better bring in a chess set, checkers and deck of cards-"

"That's not funny," she said. "It's awful here alone."

The buzz of the electric combo lock release broke the silence in the reception area. She hopped off the desk and hurried into the reception area.

Colonel Bennett stopped at Hal's doorway, "Captain Kirby, I need to speak with you."

"Coming right in," said Hal; he grabbed a pad and pencil.

"Close the door please," said Bennett, "and have a seat."

"When do we leave boss?" asked Hal.

"Captain, I've hated the word 'boss' ever since I heard a Master Sergeant telling an Airman that b–o–s–s was double s–o–b backwards." Hal laughed. "I'm serious, Captain," Bennett said sternly. Hal reacted with a curious look. Bennett looked away and continued, "There's no time for frivolity. We deploy to Kimpo Airfield, South Korea, in two days. I have a ton of paperwork to work on and many meetings to attend. Therefore, all aspects of the deployment coordination, planning and execution are your sole responsibility. In that regard, you have full authority. Yardley will be of assistance as it pertains to CIA personnel and assets. Coordinate closely with him on everything to ensure there are no misunderstandings. By the way, be sure that A and B teams fly in separate B–29s. The BOX aircraft are at Andrews Air Force Base now and will depart from there. The BALL aircraft and two chase trucks were loaded on Tank Landing Ships in Long Beach and are already sailing to Inchon. I will have Miss Mindell promptly make copies for you of the messages and notes I have collected relative to the deployment. Please excuse me now, I must go to a meeting."

"If I have full authority, Colonel, I'll be assigning some tasks to you if I deem it necessary in order to accomplish the deployment schedule. There's only one of me." Bennett gave Hal an icy stare. Hal responded in kind and said, "Remember Colonel, if something doesn't get done, you are going to look bad too."

"You wouldn't dare be insubordinate and fail to carry out my orders," said Bennett.

"Colonel, you can bet your entire ass I am going to be more concerned about the mission than keeping your calendar clear."

Bennett's face turned a shade of deep crimson. It contrasted the old scar across his forehead by contrasting its pale outline. "Don't push me, Captain."

"Colonel, you've been pushing me since I got here. Look, I'm sorry you got your ass in a sling with General Stratemeyer over Wonsan, but don't take it out on me. If the Air Force had hit that damn port, I wouldn't have had to do it."

"I didn't get my ass in a sling, as you so crassly put it. I am here because I was hand selected to head up this special project."

"I've got a lot of work to do," said Hal.

CHAPTER 20

Aboard the AQUABOX B–29; Noseart: 'Hot Blooded Redhead'
Andrews Air Force Base, Maryland

Hal listened over the sound powered intercom headphones as the pilot and crew went through the checklists. The B–29 sporting the noseart 'Gal of My Dreams' was just ahead of them on the taxiway, carrying Colonel Bennett and the other half of the AQUA personnel. Hal won the coin toss for the best seat in the house, the bombardier's seat in the Plexiglas nose. The bombsight and machine guns had been removed in the conversion. Communications, cryptographic, film processing and photo interpretation equipment were installed in the former bomb bay, waist and turret gunner sections. The tail gunner's section and every little nook and cranny were now storage areas. A 'Mobile High Altitude Reconnaissance Ground Support Laboratory' had been forged from a bomber that had distinguished herself in the Pacific during World War II.

The two newly assigned B–29 flight crews spent part of the previous week deciding what to name their aircraft and painting their distinctive nose art onto them. The "Gal of My Dreams" showed a beautiful woman with black hair, looking over her shoulder with a big smile as she hangs laundry on a clothes line. Her dress is being blown up by an apparent brisk breeze, revealing her panties and two long beautiful legs. "Hot Blooded Redhead" is a saucy looking lady all puckered up, leaning forward to kiss you, exposing herself innocently in a loosely wrapped towel.

Two C–54 cargo aircraft were holding short of the active runway, right behind the two B–29s, carrying additional AQUAMARINE equipment, spare parts and supplies. This was the first of several long flight legs that would ultimately end at Kimpo Air Base, Seoul, South Korea.

'Redhead' was sitting parallel to 'Gal,' angled across the taxiway, as both crews performed engine runups and completed their pre-takeoff checklists. Gal received her clearance for takeoff. Her engines revved up and she moved out onto the runway. Gal's engines went to full power. The vibration chattered Hal's teeth as she rumbled past.

"Prepare for take-off," the pilot announced over the intercom. It was a freezing cold morning. A cold front dumped rain on the area as it passed through and dragged a sharp tongue of frigid Canadian air behind it. Everyone was anxious to get airborne so the cabin heaters could be turned on. Hal wrapped his arms tight around his body with his gloved hands tucked into his armpits. Shortly, the tower gave Redhead clearance for takeoff. Redhead's engines responded to a modest throttle advance with a low roar. As the pilot turned onto the runway, he smoothly pushed the throttle levers all the way forward. Those four huge engines began wailing. 8,800 horsepower went to work on the propellers. Hal marveled at the noise and the feeling of brute power that resonated through his body. White runway centerline stripes and small shiny patches of ice were sliding ever more quickly under Hal's feet. Timing between tire 'ga-thumps' became progressively shorter as the nose and main gear rolled over concrete runway seams at increasingly faster speeds.

"48 inches and 2600 rpm," reported the copilot, who then began calling out each ten mile per hour increment reached by the indicated airspeed needle. At the call of 130 knots, the pilot pulled back on the yoke to rotate the nose of the Superfortress upward slightly. It was difficult for Hal to suppress his ritual 'yahoo' call. Redhead gently flew herself off the runway in trail of Gal. As the end of the runway slipped beneath the nose, the sound of the landing gear motors mingled in with the drone of the engines. Hal felt the telltale clunks of the big wheels being tucked into their wells and the well doors closing.

"Next stop, Travis Air Force Base, Cal–a–for–nye–yay," said the navigator. The base perimeter fence slipped underneath them. A thick expanse of pine trees stretched out far in the distance. A gentle bank to the west plus the increasing altitude changed the scenery and view perspective. A patchwork quilt of pine trees, gray farmland and country roads provided a peaceful, pleasing sight.

Hal's eyes began to droop from drowsiness induced by the droning monsters on the wings that clawed laboriously at the sky. He was also feeling the effects of a very early wakeup and little sleep before that. Alice and Hal kept each other awake most of the night, making up for lost time, past and future.

As they climbed to cruise altitude, the chatter on the intercom became more relaxed. Hearing his name woke Hal from a catnap, "Say Hal, don't forget, we swap every leg," said Reed Forbes with a tone of mock displeasure. Reed didn't do well in the coin toss for initial seats and wound up with a windowless seat in the aft compartment in front of the cryptographic unit.

"Rajah dajah. This view is terrific," Hal teased, picturing the scowl on Reed's pockmarked face. Reed didn't respond, which wasn't unusual. He had been somewhat distant from the beginning and difficult to humor. Reed was an excellent pilot, was highly professional and intelligent, but stayed mostly to himself. He was happy spending long hours lifting weights. This resulted, of course, in a build like the proverbial brick shit-house. The pilots gave up trying to get him to talk about his duty with Pappy Boyington's Black Sheep Squadron. Frank Conyers, the other CIA pilot wouldn't elaborate, but said Reed was absolutely fearless.

Hal crawled aft through the narrow cylindrical aluminum tunnel that connected the rear pressurized area with the cockpit area. The unpressurized bomb bay, which separated those two areas, made the tube the only pressurized access between them. When Hal got to the other end, he found Reed and three civilians sitting on the deck in the rear of the compartment. Reed was shuffling a deck of cards. "Deal me in," yelled Hal.

Nick, Ken and Luke made room for him. Nick was the team's photo interpreter—a CIA employee. Ken and Luke were Lockheed employees and were BALL aircraft maintenance personnel. They all came to know each other fairly well during the training at Edwards Air Force Base.

"Ante up ten bucks," said Reed, "Five card draw, nothing wild. No limit."

"My favorite game," said Hal.

"Pot's right, here they come," Reed announced and began dealing. "Hal, what are the areas of interest going to be over there?" This was the first time they had been together since the completion of training. The emergency nature of their deployment did not allow an opportunity to brief everyone on the details of their mission.

"The two ends of the northern border. Mainly the northwest, the bridges across the Yalu from Manchuria."

"Your bet Hal."

"Ten more bucks," said Hal. Everyone called him.

"Cards," said Reed.

"My lucky day," Hal said, looking at two pair: jacks and deuces. "Give me one." They all groaned and each took three cards.

"What exactly will we be looking for?" asked Nick, trying to roll his wide handlebar mustache with gloved fingers.

Hal drew a five of diamonds and slid it between his two pair. He made a subtle noise of joy as though he had drawn a valuable card. "Infantry, vehicles, tanks, triple-A sites and especially airplanes. Word is that the Chinese are massing forces near the border. Our job is to nail down the numbers. Twenty bucks for the full house."

"I heard the Russians are giving the Chinese a lot of Migs," said Reed.

"Yep, Mig–15s," said Hal, "There are reports that Chinese Migs are flying across the Yalu to harass the RB–26 recon missions. They fired across the nose of one yesterday."

"See your twenty and bump twenty," said Luke.

"Crap," said Reed and threw in his cards. Ken and Nick threw in also.

Hal studied Luke's face and put in another twenty dollars, "Call. Let's see what ya got."

Luke laid his cards down; there were two pair, aces and tens.

"Yours," said Hal, "He never bluffs, does he?" They laughed.

"I was worried about you this morning Reed," said Hal, shuffling the deck. "You played it pretty close. Same game guys."

Reed shrugged his shoulders, "Uh huh, but I made it."

Luke smiled and asked, "Did you see his driver? Open for ten bucks." Everyone called.

"Driver?" asked Hal. "Cards!" Everyone took three cards. "Your bet Luke."

"Ten bucks," said Luke, "Yeah man, I went into the hangar to make sure all the tool boxes got loaded. The front hangar door was opened partly and I saw him kissing a real pretty lady good-bye."

Nick piped up, "So, Reed, tell us about her."

Reed took a deep breath and reluctantly explained, "It was Shelley. I flew her in for the long weekend."

"Shelley?" Hal asked, "No kidding! Shelley? The barmaid from Edwards O'Club?" Everyone made call bets.

"Uh huh," grunted Reed.

Hal grinned, "Good for you Reed, I really liked her. You're right Luke, she's a knockout."

"No wonder you look so tired," said Nick. There was laughter.

"Damn," said Ken, throwing his cards down, "Hal, when will our birds show up?"

"Two pair, Kings over," Hal bragged, reaching for the pot, "They estimate 18 days en route—they sailed last Saturday. That puts them in port on the 19th. The chase cars are on the ships too. Pickup trucks actually."

"What the hell are we going to do for eleven days?" asked Ken, "I could have stayed home for another week or so and played with the baby's mother."

20,000 feet

Approaching South Korea

Memories began to flow through Hal's mind as the Korean peninsula came into view. Their flight from Japan to Kimpo Air Base passed near the location where he had been shot down at the Naktong River. From his vantage point topside in the turret gunner's bubble he located the area and recalled his ordeal.

The sprawling city of Seoul, surrounded by its muddy river, eventually came into view. Shortly, Kimpo came into view. Redhead and the C–54s circled the air base in the traffic pattern while Gal landed. This provided Hal an opportunity to survey air base K–14, as Kimpo was now known. Patchy dark clouds warned of rain and a nasty drop in temperature from the current 45 degrees. Construction was in progress all over the field. Bomb craters had been filled with concrete. They were obvious due to the color mismatches with the original runway. Bombing debris was bulldozed back to the rear area of the base, where it was pushed into large mounds of metal and wood. Quonsets were being hastily erected where buildings once stood. Only two buildings had been salvaged; tents were everywhere. There were two large fire-scorched concrete pads, cleaned of hangar debris. Three choppers were parked on the south end of the field. They had red crosses on white circular fields painted on their sides. Near them was a small community of tents marked with the same medical emblem. The opposite end of the field was apparently where the base commander decided AQUAMARINE would call home. There were two large three–sided sandbag revetments finished, waiting for the B–29s. The first layer of bags was in place where the two revetments for the BALLs were being made— alongside the B–29s. A hundred feet of steel matting laid over grass and dirt behind the revetments led to two adjoining concrete pads on which the half-round metal skeletons of Quonset huts were being erected. The intercom was alive with everyone's impressions.

"This ain't a purty sight," said Hal emphatically.

"Never in my whole damn career have I slept in a tent," said Tom, the pilot.

"Until now," someone quipped.

"I know what field rations and tents are like," said Reed. "This takes me back to the South Pacific."

"Let's go back to Japan for a couple weeks," said Gene.

"Those BALLs are used to being in hangars, not out in foul weather," said Ken, "We've got some challenges here."

"Just as long as there's an O'Club," said Luke.

"You mean O'Tent Luke," said Gene with a chuckle.

"It could always be worse," said Hal.

"I don't think so," said Tom, "OK, quiet down. Prepare for landing."

Gusty winds buffeted the Redhead all the way down the glide path until her four massive 29" diameter main gear tires slammed down with a simultaneous jolt and a loud screech of rubber.

Hal deplaned via the steep, narrow ladder from the tail section. One of the C–54s was taxiing to the revetment area; the other was just touching down. Hal saw a jeep coming toward them. The driver pulled between the two B–29s. Colonel Bennett walked to the jeep and exchanged salutes with a Colonel who jumped from the right front seat. Hal walked over to meet the welcoming committee.

Colonel Bennett had already exchanged pleasantries with the Base

Commander. "Colonel Driggerson, this is Captain Kirby; Captain, meet Colonel Driggerson, the Base Commander." Bennett was curt and was wearing the face of a miserable man.

"Pleased to meet you Colonel," said Hal with a snappy salute, followed by a handshake. Driggerson was gaunt, fully gray, and a good 6'3" tall. His face was that of a tired and overstressed man. His eyes were set deep and had purple bags under them.

"Morning Captain. I was just telling your boss how we've been busting our ass trying to create your little world up this end of the field."

Hal smiled, knowing what just registered in Bennett's mind when he heard the word boss. "Colonel, we really appreciate the head start you've made here. Are those our Quonsets over there?" asked Hal, pointing.

"Yes. Shouldn't take more than four days or so to finish them off. They go up real fast. All the furnishings are coming in from Japan tomorrow. Meanwhile, you'll have to camp out in an overflow tent. I only have one Quonset for officers' quarters, and it's full right now. Motor pool is rounding up some wheels to pick up the rest of the crews and take them to the mess tent. Why don't you two jump in and we'll go over and commandeer some tables. They're just beginning to serve now. Sauerkraut, pork chops and mashed potatoes."

In the short time it took to walk from the end of the mess line to his table, the cold aluminum tray and chilly air in the tent had made the food stone cold. Even the coffee had gone from finger burning hot to lukewarm in the aluminum mugs. The space heaters under the tables had just been lit so they hadn't warmed the tent yet. The heat billowing out from under the table felt good though. Hal opened his jacket to let the heat warm his body.

"It's going to be very rustic for a week or so," said Driggerson, "but we're making a lot of headway. The construction guys are miraculous. The Navy wiped this place slick as a whistle for the Inchon invasion." Hal blushed.

"Colonel, you might be interested to know that Captain Kirby commanded the squadrons that did the wiping, as you put it," said Bennett with a tone of disgust.

Driggerson looked at Hal and Logan, then went on. "I understand those C–54s are due to depart this evening. Can you hold them over until tomorrow?"

"Why?" asked Bennett.

Driggerson called over a mess cook with a pitcher of coffee spewing vapor; he motioned to refill everyone. "We have some foul weather due within a few hours as a cold front passes through. They expect it to rain like hell then drop into the 20s. We don't have a place to store the stuff in those C–54s, so we'd have to store it under tarps. Chance is, it will get wet tonight and freeze by morning. I'm guessing that would ruin a lot of it. We'll be able to get some tents erected and stow it by tomorrow afternoon though."

"They are under my command until I release them," said Bennett. "They will remain overnight." The two C–54 plane commanders nodded acknowledgment of the change in their plans.

Driggerson devoured the last piece of a pork chop and handed his tray to a passing mess cook. "Well, Colonel, you guys really have my curiosity up. What are you going to be doing?"

Bennett flushed, "Colonel, I regret to say that we cannot discuss our mission whatsoever." Driggerson shrugged his shoulders.

"Colonel Driggerson," asked Hal, "is there any place that we can use for an office until our Quonsets get finished?"

"Not until tomorrow," said Driggerson shaking his head, "I could get the grunts to put up a tent for you. I assumed you could wait for the Quonsets. I'm sorry, I just don't have the manpower today.

"Don't worry about it Colonel, you've got enough problems, we'll wait for the Quonsets," said Hal.

"Good, thanks. Gents, excuse me, I need to go."

"Colonel, may I get a lift to communications?" asked Bennett, "I need to send a message. I also need to make a phone call."

After the sumptuous feast, the AQUAMARINE personnel were taken to the two large tents that would serve as their temporary quarters. The C–54 flight crews took one look and decided to take blankets and sleep in their aircraft. Hal assigned himself and the seven civilians of Team A to one of the tents, and Bennett and the civilians of Team B to the other. The B–29 maintenance Sergeants talked the motor pool out of a beat up old jeep. They brought everyone's duffel bags from the B–29s to the tents and brought bed linens from Supply. The master Sergeant worked out temporary arrangements for himself and the six enlisted men.

Hal unzipped the outer entrance flap of his new home, rolled it up and tied it off; it was too dark inside to see anything. Reed and Gene circled the outside of the tent, rolling up and tying off the outer canvas flaps that covered the plastic windows.

"Home, sweet home," said Hal as light from the unflapped windows shown into the interior. He stepped in; the others followed behind him. Everyone was grumbling and cursing. It was in total disarray; it had never been inhabited. It smelled strongly of an unrecognizable odor, perhaps similar to a combination of bowel gas and diesel fuel.

"We better get started feathering this nest," said Hal. "Gordy, open the rear entrance and air this place out, then make sure the kerosene heaters are topped off and get them going. There aren't any bulbs in these light fixtures, take care of that too." Gordy, an Air Force second lieutenant, was the junior officer on the team. He was, by default, the SLJO [shitty little jobs officer].

Space heaters sat on loosely assembled brick bases in each of the four corners of the tent. Double-deck bunk parts, aluminum clothes lockers and a few other pieces of so-called furniture were strewn about the canvas floor. Four large black enamel lamp fixtures with white enamel reflectors hung from ropes that ran from the center pole to the corners. A thick black power cable ran down the center pole and terminated at the bottom with an eight–receptacle box.

They put their heads together and figured out a way to situate the lockers and other furniture items to afford some privacy and began the task of getting it done.

They were making their bunks when Colonel Bennett stuck his head into the tent and hollered, "Captain Kirby?"

"Over here, Colonel!"

"I need to talk to you outside," said Bennett.

Hal zipped his jacket and stepped outside. Bennett was waiting out of earshot of the tent. "I don't have much time before I catch a round-robin courier flight."

"Where you going?" asked Hal.

"I, uh, must confer with General MacArthur's staff and the CIA Tokyo station chief."

"How long will you be gone?"

"As long as is required, Captain. I spoke with Yardley and General Watson on the phone. There are many project messages queued up in Washington, so get those B–29s configured and establish back channel communications within six hours."

"I'll give it a college try. We're supposed to get some nasty weather in a few hours, and from the looks of those clouds, it's definitely going to happen and maybe sooner than that."

"Captain, I told General Watson we'd have the back channel established in less than six hours. So, weather or not, the back channel will be operational in less than six hours, is that clear?"

Hal bit his tongue, "I understand what you promised."

Bennett gave a quizzical look and continued, "Some of those messages are urgent and require answers. You have my authorization to answer them as you deem appropriate. If you feel any of them require my personal attention, forward them to CIA Tokyo. Ensure that you communicate with me via the back channel only. Advise me when the Quonsets will be habitable." Hal nodded. "That is all Captain," Bennett turned and walked away.

Hal's blood began to boil. Well, I'll be damned. That son of a bitch is going to Tokyo to keep from sleeping in a tent. That's what he's doing. He's not bullshitting me.

Hal returned to the tent. Gordy was just approaching with a wheelbarrow carrying two kerosene space heaters and a box of light bulbs. "Where did you get this stuff?" asked Hal.

"Ask me no questions, I tell you no lies," said Gordy with a wide smile.

Hal laughed, "OK, as far as I know, they were in here all the time. Let there be light. And heat!"

Setting up the long-wire HF-band communications antennas and checking out the communications systems in each B–29 proved easier and quicker than expected. Hal sent his arrival and status reports and replied to several messages. He then ordered the communications links shut down before the storm arrived and they retired to the tents for the evening. Everyone was exhausted from the rigors of constant travel, the time zone changes and the day's tasks. The cold wind began blowing hard and gusting, driving a heavy rain from changing directions, creating bone-chilling drafts and leaks in the tents. Space heaters, despite being set wide open, were incapable of providing meaningful warmth beyond a few feet. Squall winds beat against the sides of the tents, making the lights swing. Everyone felt miserable, huddled in their racks under four blankets, wishing they had more. Hal attempted to write a letter to Alice, but gave up so that he could get all his body parts under cover.

"Say Hal, I forgot to tell you," said Tom from under the covers in the bunk across from Hal, "I took the jeep this afternoon and drove around the debris piles, out of pure curiosity. I found a lot of interesting souvenirs, but off to one corner there are several YAK–9 carcasses. One of them was in fairly good shape and was right side up. The rest were dismembered and crushed. You ought to go over and check it out—interesting cockpit."

"I'll definitely do that Tom. It would be very interesting to see what they are flying."

"It's a very basic panel. Hell, I could fly one of those things even though I can't read Korean, just from instinct."

"If it's not too friggin' cold tomorrow, show me where it's at. I'd love to take a gander at it. I think you are right. There's bound to be something you couldn't figure out, but in daylight and a clear day, you could probably jump in and get from point A to point B with no trouble at all."

CHAPTER 21

AQUAMARINE Operations Hut
Kimpo Air Base, Seoul, Korea

A knock on the doorjamb of Hal's austere office broke his concentration on the operating manual for the BALL aircraft reconnaissance cameras. "Come in, Reed."

"Morning Hal. When's his majesty due in?" asked Reed."

"ETA 1030."

Reed sneered, "Damn sweet vacation huh?"

"Yep, real damn sweet," said Hal, shaking his head. "He didn't have to do any sleeping and eating in cold tents, didn't have to make any sacrifices or do any of the hard work it took to put this operation together."

"I didn't like that son of a bitch the first day at Edwards," said Reed. "I like him less every day."

Hal nodded, "You aren't alone. So, now that we got that off our chest, anything else on your mind? Heard from Shelley?"

Reed showed a rare smile, "Got the first letter yesterday. Say, I just came from the, uh, what are we going to call 'em, hangars?"

Hal laughed, "Revetment is too clumsy a word. Yeah, hell with it, let's call them hangars, just like this is a real airport," said Hal.

Reed grinned, OK, they're hangars. The maintenance guys said that both BALLs will be ready to fly by the end of the day."

"Good. JCS and CINCFE are anxious to get those birds in the air. Deep patrols up north are sporadically reporting Chinese soldiers on this side of the Yalu. CIA says informants are reporting a lot of Chinese among the North Korean soldiers. Everyone wants pictures, but the damn Migs are keeping the Air Force recon birds from getting any. That's not slowing our troops down though. Message traffic this morning says the 8th Army is going to take Pyongyang tomorrow. Things are coming to a head fast. God, it seems like yesterday that I flew the first strike of the war on Pyongyang airport."

"The ground war is going awful damn good. Taking their capitol from them should send them a message," said Reed.

"Good so far. But I can't imagine they'd just let us have Pyongyang."

Reed pulled a cigar from under his coat. He fished a chrome lighter out of his pants pocket and lit up. The lighter was emblazoned with a full color Marine Corps seal and was his lucky charm. Although well worn, he kept it brilliantly polished. "The North Koreans can't stop us Hal!"

"Not without the Chinese or the Russians," said Hal. "But that's what the folks in DC are really worried about. Apparently, General MacArthur's staff—despite reports to the contrary—is still sticking with the assessment that the Russians and Chinese will stay out of it."

Reed nodded, "Of course, they know we'll kick their asses good. They don't want any part of that. The Chinese that are coming across the Yalu are probably logistics people."

"I hope so. So, what's new with Shelley? I'm glad you two got together."

Reed sighed, "She's fine, same old stuff. You know, it's been a long time since I gave a damn about a woman."

"Serious huh?"

"I guess it could get that way."

Hal grinned, "She's good for you Reed, you used to be a miserable bastard. Now, you're just a bastard."

"I'm losing my image. That's not good. I take it we'll start flying tomorrow?"

"Rajah dajah. I will send missions to the Antung area to check on the Chinese and to Unggi in the northeast corner to check on the Soviets."

"I'd really like to fly one of those Hal."

"Oh, you will. There's a lot of pressure for photos in more places than we have time or airplanes, so I'll set up four missions every day that weather permits, two in the morning, two after lunch. We'll all get our feet wet tomorrow. I'll give you and Frank a shout shortly. We'll put our heads together and work out the flight plans and other mission details."

Reed started out of the office, "OK, I've got a couple things I need to do. You going to meet the Colonel planeside?"

"Hell no!" said Hal. The sound of the front door to the Quonset hut slamming shut got their attention. Heavy boots were making their way down the hallway toward Hal's office.

Reed, leaned out of the office doorway to see who was coming. "Well, well, the short, fat, hairy guy. What's the hot poop Gordy?"

Gordy came into the office and handed Hal an envelope, "Captain, I just got a priority double-encrypted Eyes Only message for the Colonel."

"DC knows he's returning from Japan today, so they stopped sending his stuff to CIA Tokyo. Thanks Gordy. I'll see that he gets it when he arrives."

Reed, Frank and Hal were working at the plot table, planning tomorrow's photo-recon missions. "Sounds like a C–47 just landed," said Frank Conyers. Hal nodded. Reed went to the front door and looked out.

"It's a C–47 alright," Reed reported.

"Damn shame to ruin a good day," Frank said.

"C–47? I didn't hear a C–47," said Hal. "But when I do, I'll send someone down to the terminal to pick up Colonel Bennett. In the meantime, let's keep our minds on tomorrow's mission plans."

Frank grinned, "I didn't hear a thing."

"Me either," said Reed.

Barely ten minutes had passed when the telephone rang. Frank picked up, "This is Conyers. No. Where are you Colonel? No sir. Yes. Hal, Reed and I are working on tomorrow's mission plans. No sir, none of us heard it." Frank took the phone away from his ear and looked into the receiver, "Son of a bitch hung up."

"Oh brother. We're in for it now. Look at these hands—shaking like hell," said Reed, holding up two sets of rock solid fingers. After exchanging grins, they got back to work on the missions.

A short time later, Colonel Bennett barged through the door of the operations hut.

"Is that you Colonel?" Hal called out. Bennett came to the doorway and paused.

"Welcome back Colonel," said Hal, "Sorry you missed all the fun. That's your office straight back at the end."

"I need to speak with you Captain," Bennett said coldly, turned and walked to his office. Hal followed him.

Bennett motioned for Hal to close the door, went to his desk and dropped a leather document case onto the floor next to his chair. Bennett's face was red. "I just came from our quarters. It is customary for the senior officer to get the biggest room Captain, not the smallest. Is that some kind of a joke?"

"Your room is no bigger or smaller than any of the others in there. They are all equal in size, all too damn small, but all better than those damn tents. I decided, for security reasons, to also bring the enlisted members of the project into the hut with us. That dictated that we all take minimum possible size rooms. I have the enlisteds doubled bunked though."

"That, Captain, was a mistake. You should have left the enlisteds out and used the space for showers and heads. Now we have to use the community facilities. Totally disgusting!"

"Colonel, the engineers advised that they couldn't' get running water in these Quonsets for another three months. Hell, by then, we could be long gone." Bennett slammed himself into a well-worn straight back chair that sat cramped against the wall behind a small, battered metal desk.

Bennett shook his head, "We have no business being in Korea. This is going to be nothing but trouble. Brief me Captain, what's the status?" He ran his hand across the top of his desk; his jaw dropped when he looked at his palm and saw it was black with dust and sediment. "This entire place is disgusting."

Hal held back a chuckle and retrieved a folded message from his shirt pocket, "First, here is a sealed Eyes Only message envelope which came in not too long ago. What are those about? Anything I need to be aware of?"

Bennett's eyes flashed as he opened the envelope, "Not in the very slightest, Captain." He seemed to study the message in the envelope, then put it back in the envelope. "You may begin your briefing of the AQUAMARINE project status."

"OK," said Hal, "the short version of status is that the BALLs will be airworthy by sunset today." He paused, hoping that was all Bennett was interested in hearing at the moment.

Bennett put the message envelope into his leather case and took out a pencil and pad. "Proceed Captain."

A deep breath allowed Hal to get over his disenchantment with the good Colonel, then he continued, "All supporting systems are ready to go. The BOX teams are on a 24–hour schedule, in shifts of eight on, eight off. The photo interpretation systems on the B–29s checked out OK and are operational. We have excellent direct communications with CIA Japan 24 hours a day, but Langley only comes in for a while in the middle of the day. Oh, there's one minor hitch with photography. It seems CIA didn't ship any infra-red film; plenty black and white and color though. They said they'd ship some IR to us ASAP. I have set up missions for tomorrow. As soon as you sign off on them, I'll send the details to Langley, CINCFE and the others. I thought we'd do two missions each on both ends of the northern border. I assume you want to fly the first mission; it's going to the Antung-Sinuiju area. I have Reed departing twenty minutes behind you going to Unggi in the northeast—JCS is anxious to find out if the Russians are moving anything to the border from Kraskino. In the afternoon, I have myself going to Antung and Frank going to Unggi. Oh, and to keep the B–29 flight crews busy and take advantage of the manpower, they are assigned to administrative support functions. Murph, your team's B–29 flight engineer, is our general admin guy; he's on a run to the base commcenter now. When he comes back, he'll break out your personal file of messages we sent and received since our arrival. That's about it. It's all coming together very nicely. How was Tokyo?"

Bennett pondered his notes for a few moments. "When was the latest Air Force recon flown to Sinuiju and what were the results?"

"An RB–26 made a run yesterday," said Hal. "They've flown fighter escorted recon missions up there every day for the last week, but they can't get near the Yalu because the Migs chase 'em the hell away. Mig–15s come up from the Chinese side of the Yalu and patrol deep into North Korean airspace."

Bennett interrupted, "Captain, I have an important meeting with Colonel Driggerson in the morning. Rearrange the schedule. You will fly the Antung mission in the morning; I shall fly the Unggi mission in the afternoon."

That evening, after another fine gastronomic experience at the mess tent, Hal stretched out on his bunk. He rolled a pillow up under his head, arranged the first set of letters received from Alice in the order of their postmarks and began reading them. All was well with her and the kids. She missed him badly. There was no evidence that she was having any problems coping with his absence. Her eye exam went fine, although she was now wearing glasses to read. She still experienced migraine headaches nearly every day, which sometimes were so painful that they made her sick to her stomach. The pills the doctor gave her usually provided relief within an hour. In her last letter, she mentioned that she didn't look forward to the next day when she would undergo the battery of tests a neurosurgeon prescribed.

Hal arose at the crack of dawn. Following a low residue breakfast, he began preparations for his first operational flight in the BALL aircraft. To say he was excited would be an understatement. Why Bennett would give up the opportunity to make reconnaissance history could only be explained with one word - cowardice. It seemed to take forever to complete the standard pre-flight physical, get suited up, then lie on the table breathing pure oxygen for an hour. From there, it went fast; he was grinning from ear to ear as he taxied the BALL to the runway.

"WINTER FOG this is Kimpo Tower, hold short of the active for arriving aircraft." Hal kept firm pressure on the brakes and waited impatiently at the end of the taxiway. A C–47 was on final approach, bringing food and other provisions for the weekend. As the C–47 passed over the runway threshold, Hal could see the copilot's head turning to keep his eyes locked on the very strange looking unmarked black bird on the taxiway. Hal tapped the heels of his gloves on the yoke to a nondescript tune in his head. When the C–47 began his turn off the runway, Hal's radio came alive, "WINTER FOG, Kimpo Tower, cleared for takeoff."

"Roger tower," Hal replied and released the brakes. He eased the BALL onto the runway, lined up on the centerline and braked to a stop. His eyes scanned the gauges as he pushed the throttle forward slowly with the brakes applied. EPR good, EGT good, RPM good, cabin pressure good, O2 good, fuel good. OK, take me to China honey. Hal released the brakes. "See you on the back side," he radioed over the special AQUA frequency to Reed in the chase pickup.

"Have a good mission," said Reed.

Speed built up rapidly. The cold, dense air was developing a lot of thrust and lift compared to the hot, thin air at Edwards. As the true airspeed indicator came through 50 knots, he could feel the plane getting light on her feet. At 70 knots, barely 700 feet down the runway, the plane lifted off. The pogo wheels dropped away from the wing tips. The men in the pickup rushed to recover them from the runway. He inched the nose up and allowed the airspeed to build up to 115 knots, then a firm pull on the control wheel brought the nose up to 30 degrees of pitch angle.

"Yaaaahoooooooooo, climb baby climb," he yelled, draining off excess energy. Those C–47 jocks are probably shittin' bricks watching this! Nothing I know climbs like this baby. Eat your hearts out, prop jockeys! Twenty minutes later, Hal was trimming the aircraft for level flight at 50,000 feet with a true airspeed equal to .7 mach. Thirty minutes into the flight, Pyongyang was passing underneath. No AQUA photos of Pyongyang were planned today; the Eighth Army was already in full assault on the city. Ten minutes later the Yalu River—the natural border between Manchuria and North Korea—was just minutes away. He could see it snaking its way from the mountainous horizon on the right, toward Korea Bay on the left. The target zone was unmistakable to the naked eye, even from that incredibly high altitude. A large metropolitan area was visible, which was composed of Antung, China, on the north side of the Yalu and Sinuiju, North Korea on the south side of the river. The mouth of the Yalu River was only about 30 nautical miles to the west of those cities. He adjusted the autopilot heading bug to facilitate the first pass over the Antung airfield. An hour of flying wide and overlapping cloverleaf shaped tracks above the two cities was planned after the first pass over the airfield. Photo emphasis was prescribed for the airport, anti-aircraft batteries along the river, the bridge and the approaches to it on both sides. Secondary photo recon targets were the military depots on the Manchurian side of the Yalu River.

While the autopilot flew the plane, Hal stared into the circular six–inch diameter ground glass screen at the top center of the instrument panel. He manipulated the zoom and lens turret controls until he located the airfield. Through a system of mirrors and prisms, the through-the-lens reflex system allowed the pilot to directly view the image that would be recorded by the reconnaissance camera. He analyzed the amazing scene provided by the camera. Not much snow left on the ground. It must have warmed up yesterday. Damn, too bad, I was hoping for lots of tracks. He zoomed on the airfield until the runways filled the ground glass screen. Good grief! Crawling with Migs—fifty or so. Cargo planes too. What a beehive. His thumb depressed the switch on the control wheel that controlled the camera. He took numerous photos at maximum zoom of various parts of the airfield. Just then, a blurred object obscured his view of the airfield. He reduced the zoom. Geez! There's three Migs under me. Oh baby, don't you dare flame out. Just keep purring honey. Smile pretty. Click. Ha! They'll have a hard time convincing their bosses that they couldn't climb up and engage me. Dang, this is fun. Now get the hell out of my way so I can take some pictures.

AQUAMARINE Operations Hut

EKG needles scratched their jagged traces of Hal's heartbeats while the physiology technician cleaned and stowed Hal's pressure suit. "Looking good Captain. Any dizziness or other symptoms?" asked the technician, going through his checklist.

"Nope. Feel fine," said Hal.

The technician shut the EKG machine down and removed the suction cups and wires from Hal's torso and legs. The technician tore off the paper strip, made some notations on it and stuffed it in a file folder where Hal's pre- and post-mission physiological data was recorded. "You're fine sir. You can get dressed now."

Hal rolled off the examination table and grabbed his trousers from a wall hook.

Reed came into the room, "Hal, I want to show you something in the storage tent when the Colonel takes off."

"What is it?" asked Hal.

"Beats the hell out of me and the Colonel won't talk about it. A C–54 arrived just after you departed this morning and offloaded a crate marked for us. It's a pod—standard size fuel pod—with an electronics payload. I didn't get a good look at it. Bennett had the maintenance guys uncrate it. Bennett grabbed most of the documents inside the crate and said he'd brief everyone tonight."

Hal shook his head, "Well, I don't know anything about it. Geez, this guy is full of surprises."

"He's full of something but surprise is not the word I had in mind."

Reed plugged in the cord to a hanging lamp in the storage tent. A cylinder painted flat black was sitting in the crotch of wooden V–cradles that were attached to a set of sawhorse-like supports. "Standard wing pylon mounts," Hal said, pointing to fittings attached to the top center of the cylinder.

"Look at this," said Reed, looking at the rear of the pod.

"That's an antenna sticking out the tail," said Hal. "So are these," he said, running his hand along antennas that resembled bath towel rods that ran along the sides of the pod.

Reed picked up a maintenance document lying on a nearby bench and read aloud, "AQUACRYSTAL broadband radar receiver."

Hal looked at Reed, "sunnavabitch, I have no idea what this is all about."

They looked at several pieces of electronic test equipment sitting on a bench. Reed showed Hal what was obviously an aircraft instrument panel control switch.

"That's easy enough, ON and OFF," said Hal.

"My kind of payload," Reed quipped.

Mission Planning Room
AQUAMARINE Operations Hut

Colonel Bennett convened his first meeting of all AQUAMARINE personnel. It was standing room only. They were packed in tight with overflow outside the doorway. Bennett sat on a stool in front of the plotting table. At his back, there were World Aeronautical Charts of North Korea on the wall. Colored string plots of the day's missions were pinned onto the chart. Bennett's notepad and a copy of the AQUACRYSTAL Operation Manual sat in front of him. The manual was marked with bright red Top Secret markings and, given a days' worth of rumor milling about the device in the tent, everyone's eyes were captured by it. Bennett began his briefing immediately upon taking his seat. "The purpose of this meeting is twofold: one, to discuss the failure of our first four operational missions of the BALL aircraft; and secondly, to brief you on the AQUACRYSTAL electronic intelligence system we'll be carrying on the missions from now on. First, relative to mission success, JCS finds it unbelievable that we could not report any evidence of troops or military mechanized equipment in the corridors to and from the bridges at Antung. I didn't fly any of the Antung missions, but I personally reviewed the films and there was no evidence of heavy military use of the bridge. But, CIA has reliable ground informant reports that Chinese soldiers are pouring across that bridge into North Korea. JCS has therefore ordered that we courier all film canisters to Japan after completing our analysis and reporting. They will then be sent to Washington via diplomatic channels. Captains Wallport and Cooper will jointly share all admin duties in order that they alternate as daily couriers to Japan." Wallport and Cooper, the two B–29 copilots, looked at each other; it was obviously the first time they had heard of their new job. Bennett continued, "This does not change our responsibility for prompt post-mission processing of the films and accurate interpretation and reporting of the results. I warn all of you, we are under close scrutiny by Washington. It is incumbent upon the BALL pilots to fly flawless missions and extensively photograph the targets. Likewise, the photo-interpreters must find and properly characterize all—I emphasize all—information of intelligence value. If you value your good names, don't let Washington find something that you missed. Now, relative to the AQUACRYSTAL system, there is little of direct importance or concern to us. CIA has developed a radar receiver and recorder system. It will collect radar signals for use in research of enemy radar capabilities. Pilot responsibilities are merely to turn the system on upon arriving at the target area, and to turn the system off when leaving it. The maintenance personnel will remove the wire recorder spools and install blank ones for the next mission. Recorded spools will be sent with the films to Washington." Bennett put his hand on the AQUACRYSTAL Operation Manual, "BALL pilots shall read and understand this manual before their next flight. Captain Kirby will keep this manual in his safe and will make it available to those with a need to know. That is all." Bennett promptly departed for his office.

Hal put his hand up to signal everyone to remain, "I have one thing to add, but the Sergeants are excused, thank you." When the enlisted personnel left the room, Hal closed the door. "Gentlemen, the Colonel who runs the MASH unit cornered me after supper. He was mighty hot under the collar about complaints that my officers were down there acting less than gentlemanly and were disrespectful toward his nurses last night. He didn't volunteer any specifics. Anyone care to tell me what happened?"

A long silence was broken by a voice in the back, "Tell him Nick." Everyone laughed.

Nick turned red, "It's taken care of. It was a misunderstanding. I went down and straightened it out already."

Hal looked around the room, "I don't want to hear any more noise from that Colonel about you people. Use your damn heads. I can't believe you'd risk screwing up your access to women in a combat zone. Now git. I have some missions to plan. Nick and Gordy, I need to talk to you." Hal paused for the room to empty then asked, "OK, spill it!"

"Well," Gordy explained, "Nothing really, Nick and I went over to the MASH unit to play poker with a couple ladies."

Nick added, "They had a booze stash and, well, we all got our snoots full and the game became strip poker. One of the gals caught Nick cheating. They got real pissed and threw us out. They decided to get even and told their CO a tall story, that's all."

"Don't take it so lightly. If Colonel Bennett finds out, your asses will be his."

"It won't happen again Captain," said Nick.

"I sure as hell hope not," said Hal. "So, how far did you get?" asked Hal.

Gordy smiled, "That's what made it so bad. We still had our coats on and they were freezing their little asses off in bras and panties."

"Geez, you guys didn't use your heads at all, did you?" Hal said, laughing. "What makes you guys think it's OK now?"

Nick said with an evil grin, "Cause they invited us to play cards again tonight."

"You guys better watch them like a hawk. I think it's going to be you two freezing your asses off tonight!"

CHAPTER 22

Office of Tim Yardley
CIA HQ, Langley, VA

Tim skimmed through today's CIA daily briefing script for the Joint Chiefs of Staff. A short paragraph under "New Developments" captured his attention:

. . . (TS) POSSIBLE SOVIET GUIDED MISSILE DEPLOYMENT TO KRASKINO. The Soviet Air Defense Command deployed to Kraskino what appears to be the first Soviet experimental anti-air guided missile weapon system. Kraskino is located 13 nm from the northeastern border of Korea. The system was reported to be installed and ready by the Kraskino Air Defense Sector Commander on 18 October. The significance of deploying such an early stage research prototype system to an operational commander is unclear. It is consistent with the heightened defense posture Moscow imposed on western Soviet areas on 16 October.

Background: The system was referred to by the short title quote G–267 unquote. A separate intelligence source links project G–267 with a research activity developing an anti-air guided missile system. Another source identifies project G–267 as a research program sponsored by the Air Defense Command being conducted by a military electronics design bureau in Moscow. The project was described by a human intelligence source as the conversion of existing air search and height finding radars and the development of a guidance system for a missile. . .

With a broad smile, he put the folder down and thought for a moment.

Tim glanced at his watch and calculated the time in Korea. Given a reasonably perfect world, there was time to get a message to Bennett before today's first mission.

That afternoon, Yardley and Bradbury met for lunch in their favorite bistro on K–Street in Washington, DC. "Glad you could meet me HL," said Yardley. He stood up and shook Bradbury's hand. "I ordered the special for you."

Bradbury pulled out a chair hurriedly, "Good, I don't have much time. This is a good place to talk at lunchtime. It's so damn noisy. I called the office before I left the White House and got your message. What's so hot?" Beads of sweat were forming on his forehead as he caught his breath.

"Looks like the bad guys deployed an early model of the guided missile system to a place near the Korean border," said Tim.

"You mean the one we were going to look for near Moscow?" asked Bradbury.

Tim nodded, "Yes, that one."

Bradbury's brow pinched, "What does that mean to us?"

"Look HL, the sooner we get an intercept on that new radar, the faster the R&D guys in Langley are going to write the contract for the additional pods. I sent a message to Bennett asking him to take the BALL aircraft with the CRYSTAL pod close enough to get radar line of sight with the air defense installation."

Bradbury choked on a drink of water, "He'll have to fly into Soviet territory to do that!"

"It's only about 13 miles from the Korean border," said Tim. "Why do you look so worried?"

Bradbury's face was on fire, "Rules of Engagement. They can't fly in there legally! Are you nuts?"

"Yeah, I know all that. That's why I told Bennett to fly it personally. They routinely fly into that corner of the Korean border area looking for Soviet infiltration anyway. He can just stretch one leg of the flight a little. Don't forget, Ivan can't do anything to that plane, and they can't bitch about it because that would just make them look bad. It's going to be all right HL. There's no way anyone will find out about it."

Bradbury sat in quiet shock for a moment then slammed his hand on the table. The noise startled the waitress just coming to the table with their sandwiches and iced tea. One of the sandwich plates jumped from its precarious balance on her arm onto the floor. "We aren't paying for that," Bradbury said angrily, "and don't bother bringing another. I don't have time to eat it anyway." He sat with his lips pursed, tapping his fingers on the table while she served the tea and Tim's sandwich. When she finished cleaning up the mess and was out of earshot, Bradbury leaned forward and scowled at Tim, "It would probably be all right if I knew for sure Logan would fly the goddam mission himself. But Tim, I think you screwed up!"

Kimpo Airfield

Hal sank into the seat of a BALL aircraft. It was already preflighted by Reed and was started as Hal drove up. Reed was helping Hal get hooked up for an immediate taxi to the runway when he spotted Bennett running over from one of the B–29s, waving his arms to get their attention. Reed tapped Hal's suit shoulder and pointed toward Bennett. They watched as Bennett climbed the roll-around maintenance platform next to the BALL. Bennett hollered over the jet noise into Reed's ear, "I need to speak to Captain Kirby, please excuse us Mr. Forbes." Reed handed Bennett the ground crew phone set, climbed down and stood at the base of the platform. Bennett put on the headset and pushed the talk switch, "Slight change of mission Captain. Give me your WAC chart."

Hal pulled the mission chart from his right pant leg pocket and handed it to Bennett, "Don't forget this baby is sucking fuel Colonel, we don't have a lot of time to waste here. Can't this wait until the afternoon mission?"

Bennett ignored Hal's suggestion and pulled a pencil from somewhere inside his wool lined bomber jacket. He drew a track extending from the Korean border to a small circle around Kraskino, USSR and back to the North Korean border. He wrote 'two orbits with CRYSTAL ON' by the circle around Kraskino, then handed the chart back to Hal.

"R–O–E!" said Hal, waving his glove finger, "We can't overfly Soviet territory!"

"Rules of engagement have exceptions Captain. I just received a Top Secret message which provided the authorization for this mission," said Bennett.

"Show me," said Hal.

"Captain, there's no time for trifles. It was an Eyes Only message and your name isn't on it. I am giving you a direct order. Make those orbits with the pod turned on and resume your normal mission."

"I am advising you, Colonel Bennett, that I am flying this mission with objection to violation of published R–O–E," said Hal.

"Just fly the mission Captain," said Bennett. He draped the headset over the edge of the cockpit, hurried down off the platform and quick-paced back to the B–29. Hal beat his fist into his leg. Damn. Do I fly this mission? This stinks!

Reed hurried back up the platform and put the headset on. "What was that all about Hal?"

"I want you to witness this Reed," Hal said, pointing to his WAC chart, "The Colonel drew these pencil tracks. He ordered me to make two orbits around Kraskino with the pod turned on and resume the primary mission."

Reed shrugged his shoulders, "Sounds like DC is onto something hot."

"I don't have time to discuss it, I have to get this baby out of here. Just take note of what I said. Now let's get the show on the road. Close the canopy."

Hal proceeded directly to Kraskino from Unggi, North Korea. A snow dusting made Kraskino difficult to recognize, but distinctive coastal geography made identification of the city possible. He flipped the panel switch that turned the pod system on. Manipulation of the lens turret and zoom controls brought the city into view on the ground glass screen in the panel in front of him. Tallyho. Geez, it looks like nothing more than a fishing village. Peaceful scene. Biggest outpost they got in this corner of their world and it's smaller than Inchon. Colonel didn't say anything about pictures, but there's an airport. Not much of one—grass with steel matting. Migs! About a dozen, a few transports and a cargo bird. That's a lot for this place. Well, well, triple-A sites near the airport too. That's interesting. Should I take some pictures or not? Nope. Bennett said two orbits with the box on. Period. Nothing about pictures. He can come back and get them if he wants them. No, hell with him, this is good poop and needs to be reported. Hal set up the camera and began taking photos of the western side of Kraskino, the airport and the air defense sites. At maximum zoom he watched two Mig–15s scramble. Oh brother, that must be rough riding on frozen grass and steel in a jet fighter. He smiled.

He proceeded on the orbital track around the northern periphery of Kraskino, keeping an eye on the Migs climbing up toward him. As he turned toward the southeast, he watched the Migs peel off sharply and move out of view. Hmm, they sure gave up fast. Where'd they go? Hal zoomed the lens out to relocate the airport and zoomed in on it. A rapidly blossoming dense gray smoke cloud caught his attention at one of the triple-A sites. Geez, the site is blowing up. Just what I need. I'll get accused of bombing the frigging thing. Damn, that's a missile launch. What the hell? They're not supposed to have those things operational. Kirby, you dumb ass, we're not supposed to have this airplane either. Look at this—it's following me along. Doubt it's more than 5,000 feet below me. He turned to the east to observe the reaction of the missile. After a slight lag, it turned and reestablished its position directly under him. It made several attempts to climb to him, but each time, it angled off and began to gyrate slowly. He was taking a series of max zoom shots of the missile structure when it ran out of fuel and the ground controllers detonated it. A fireball filled the ground glass camera screen; a shudder from the explosion shock wave followed quickly after the explosion. Dang! Get the hell out of here Kirby! Hal promptly turned toward the southwest and relocated the Kraskino airport with the camera. Butterflies accumulated in his stomach when he saw the second missile launch and watched another aluminum telephone pole begin its climb up toward him. His air-conditioned suit was making his perspiration soaked long johns feel like an ice blanket. This missile seemed to be climbing higher than the other, so he began evasive maneuvers. He was unable to track the missile with the camera while evading. A strong shock wave jolted the airframe. Geez! I heard metal. Took a hit; I felt it. His eyes scoured the instrument panel. Nothing was out of norm, fuel flow, temperatures, hydraulics were all fine. He tried to reacquire the airport with the camera. He was now too far away from Kraskino to get the camera gimbaled back far enough to see if there were any Migs or missiles coming after him. Calm down Kirby, get this baby back home ASAP. When his eyes glanced over at the gauges on the left side console, a nauseating feeling slammed into his solar plexus. The oxygen pressure had dropped notably. Oh, damn you red Russian sons of bitches. Geez, either the O2 system has a hole or the cockpit pressure wall does. I hope it lasts long enough for me to descend to 12,000 feet. Hal eased the nose over and pulled the throttle back to flight idle. Even at red-line airspeed, it was going to be a relatively long time before he would be at an altitude where the air was breathable. OK, emergency plan. Follow the coastline down to Wonsan and ditch near the Valley Forge. Pay a little call on Admiral Hawkins. Damn, ditching in this thing is probably either a serious injury or a fatality. They need to get ejection seats in these things. If I'm lucky, they'll have Wonsan wrapped up and I can land there. Look at that O2 pressure loss rate. This is going to be close.

Flying the airplane had become difficult only because Hal had to pry his eyes away from the O2 pressure gauge. It consumed his attention. Seeing the altimeter winding through 30,000 feet put a smile on Hal's face. A quick mental calculation told him he was about even in the race against oxygen depletion. The southernmost tip of the Soviet border with Korea was already underneath. The Sea of Japan stretched out forever ahead and to the left of him. A sun glint off the right caught his attention; the smile wiped from his face. An intense shiver sped through his body. Geez, three aircraft closing on a nearly constant bearing—an intercept. Where the hell'd they come from? Damn, not having guns is a hell of a disadvantage. An overwhelming feeling of helplessness was numbing Hal's mind. Come on Kirby, get your act together here. If you're lucky, they're props. Hell, they aren't props. OK, then they're either Yak–15s or those Russian Mig–15s I thumbed my nose at over Kraskino. I can outmaneuver the Yaks, but it's probably a tossup on the Migs. If I can outmaneuver them long enough, they'll expend their ammo taking potshots, get low on fuel and break off. It worked on the Japanese fighters that day Garr left me holding the bag. That no good bastard. He's getting his though. Geez, I can't get into maneuvers at this altitude—the O2 won't last. OK, I'm probably too fast for them to catch while descending—but when I level off at 12,000 feet, it'll be a different story.

Hal mentally rehearsed his evasive maneuver plan; he watched three dots hanging nearly suspended in the distance off his right wing. Heart pounding and trying to minimize his breathing, he continued on the southeast heading. He held the pitch attitude that gave him maximum allowed airspeed, racing for breathable air. His eyes spent most of their time on O2 pressure and altitude. Finally, the altimeter needles spun through 14,000 feet. Good God, there can't be more than five or ten minutes of oxygen left. That was close. He switched the cabin pressurization systems to outside air; then he switched the suit system over too. The change was dramatic; even at that altitude, the outside air had more humidity than the bottled O2. It also had a taste that was peaking the taste buds in his cotton dry mouth. A minute later, he was level at 12,000 feet, turning due south. Mountain peaks on the Korean coastline were visible in the distance. The three dark spots in the sky off his right wing were now growing. The Migs blossomed from dots to airplanes. At that point, two of them broke off to take up positions behind him—the best kill position. The other Mig closed to fifty yards off his wing and flew a parallel heading. Hal couldn't see the other two anymore; his view to the rear was blocked. He was sweating profusely; his chest was heaving inside the bulky suit and his ears were ringing. I can't just sit here and let those two guys come around to my six and drill me. Now Kirby, NOW. He began his evasive maneuvering while trying to maintain some semblance of forward progress. The Mig off his right wing banked toward him and fired several bursts. Brilliant white tracer rounds flashed past Hal's nose. Lucky me! They don't want to kill me. Not now anyway. Damn, that's good news. I think. Yeah, they'll hold off killing me until I deliver this crate to their doorstep. Hal stopped the evasion and steadied up a southerly heading to parallel the coastline. His mind was sprinting from thought to thought. I need to stall them off somehow while I keep flying further south. Stretch their fuel endurance. They'll soon be unable to make it back to their base. Hal tuned his radio to the international distress frequency, "MAYDAY MAYDAY MAYDAY this is Air Force seven fiver eight, Air Force seven fiver eight being pursued by three Mig fifteens, altitude one two zero, position approximately two zero nautical southeast Unggi." He stopped and listened. There was no reply. He repeated the Mayday several more times with the same results. The Mig pulled in close—real close. He was only five feet off Hal's right wing. Even at that, the Mig was some forty feet from Hal's cockpit. Just the same, the Mig pilot's hand signals were quite understandable: follow me down. I'm screwed. No way out. Well, now the big decision. Activate the self-destruct system now or just before I leave the cockpit on the ground. Hell, that's no big decision. Pull it now and I have no chance at all. To hell with that. I'm taking every inch I can get. Hal nodded to the Russian. Son of a bitch, he thinks he's going to be a hero for bringing home some tasty bacon. Hal looked down on the lower right side of the cockpit. A red and silver striped D–ring sat waiting. It was attached to a narrow steel cable that entered a small box mounted on the deck. It was labeled: THERMITE SELF DESTRUCT. He reached down and unlocked the metal safety strap that protected the D–ring from an accidental pull. The words of the Lockheed aircraft systems instructor drifted through Hal's mind: "It'll take a good hard yank of about eight inches of cable travel. From that moment, you have five minutes. . ." I wonder why these guys are letting me fly due south? That's fine, in a little while, we'll be flying into the Valley Forge's task group at Wonsan; that ought to be interesting. Shortly, Hal received some hand signals from the pilot off his wing to follow him toward the shore. When Hal acknowledged, the Mig banked right—Hal followed. He checked his chart. Ah, it's Ch'ongjin.

"MAYDAY MAYDAY MAYDAY this is Air Force seven fiver eight, Air Force seven fiver eight being forced by three Mig fifteens to land at Ch'ongjin." There was no reply. He kept trying to make contact. His anxiety was peaking. His eyes were repeatedly drawn back to the chart in his lap. Ch'ongjin, North Korea sits on the coast about 50 nautical miles south of the border with Russia. It was the last place on earth Hal wanted to visit.

Hal followed the Mig into a gentle turn for a straight-in final approach. It was not a pretty sight. Dang, a grass strip. That's going to be bumpy as all hell. Man, this thing is going to dig a wing into the ground and loop as soon as I touch down.

There was a lot of excitement on the airfield. Jeeps and trucks were very active doing God knows what. Soldiers with rifles were being stationed around the entire runway. This time, Reed wouldn't be driving down the runway behind him, giving him height-above-runway callouts. But, it didn't matter. He didn't give a damn if he damaged the main gear or tore a wing completely off. As long as he could activate the thermite and get out of the cockpit, it would be a good landing. Barbed wire passed under the aircraft's belly; armed soldiers at the approach end taxiway were looking up at him, pointing. Geez, I can't believe what I'm doing. However it turns out Alice, I love you honey. Careful with the wings, don't let one dig in. You must survive this landing. Easy, easyyyyyyy. There was a hard jolt when the wheels slammed down onto the runway, such as it was. Vibration from the crude runway was severe and made his teeth chatter. Hal managed to keep the wings off the ground for nearly 500 feet of ground roll. A mean dip in the field finally caused a wing to drop and make contact. At that point, Hal lost directional control and became a mere spectator on a wild circus ride.

After an eternity of ground looping rotations, the aircraft came to rest. Hal rapidly disconnected his suit hoses, wires and belts. He operated the lever to unseal the canopy and pushed it over to the side. His hand reached down and gripped the D–ring on the self-destruction mechanism; he yanked hard and checked his watch. There were two thermite grenade clusters, one on top of the camera system in the belly and one at the top of the instrument panel portion of the camera system. Several thousand degrees of heat would voraciously eat through the highly classified camera equipment, turning it into molten metal. Five minutes after that the timers on sixteen high explosive and phosphorous canisters spaced throughout the airframe would disintegrate the BALL aircraft. He stood on his seat and began figuring out how he was going to get out of the cockpit in the bulky suit and helmet without the maintenance ladder alongside. Geez, there's no push panel steps on the side of this bird. Long way to jump. He looked around; soldiers were running toward him from both sides of the field. A jeep was on the way as well. Hal managed to get a leg over the side of the cockpit, then with a few interesting contortions, he got his other leg over the side. He held onto the side of the canopy and lowered himself to full arm length before letting go. When his feet hit the ground, the inertia of the heavy helmet and high altitude suit immediately threw him to the ground.

A sea of foot soldiers with disbelieving faces quickly surrounded Hal. Everywhere he looked there were rifles pointed at him. He just laid back and tried to catch his breath. The suit's air was rapidly being depleted of oxygen. He was beginning to get the feeling of suffocation. In order to inhale and exhale, he had to force air in and out of the umbilical connection near his waste. He tried to hand signal for the soldiers to help him unscrew the wing nuts on the helmet base; they merely stood and gaped with their rifles pointed at him. Finally, he managed to unscrew the last wing nut and lifted the helmet off. Deep gulps of delicious air calmed his burning lungs. The appearance of white stars let him know he was hyperventilating. Suddenly, he remembered the thermite. A check of his watch showed he had one minute before the first set of thermite clusters were going to ignite, and six minutes before the high explosive and phosphorus blast.

A jeep arrived; an officer in the front seat began hollering and waving his arms at the soldiers. The soldiers motioned for Hal to put his hands over top of his head. They grabbed his helmet and threw him and the helmet into the rear seat of the jeep. Two soldiers got in and held handguns on him. The jeep took off and traveled about fifty yards when a commotion erupted. Dense white smoke was pouring out of the nose and cockpit of the aircraft. Soldiers were yelling and running. The officer began hollering but it was a free for all and nobody paid attention to him. He ordered the jeep to resume and pointed to the building where there was a fire truck. As they approached the firehouse, the shock wave of a tremendous explosion slammed into them. Where just moments ago there was an aircraft, the likes of which the soldiers had never seen, there was now an incendiary display. Smoldering parts were strewn about, there was a huge red and yellow ball of burning fuel and white rays of phosphorous spewed for a hundred feet in all directions. A solid column of black smoke was boiling upward into the sky. Infuriated, the NKPA officer began screaming at Hal. Amidst the long tirade, the officer grabbed the driver's rifle and slammed the butt into the side of Hal's head.

CHAPTER 23

Korean Army Jail
Ch'ongjin Airfield, North Korea

Hal was sprawled on the dark brown hardened soil in a tiny prison cell when he regained consciousness. He began shivering uncontrollably. They had taken his flight boots and socks and had also stripped him down to his long johns. A frigid 30 something degree draft poured into the cell from the open barred window above. Stench from the smoldering BALL aircraft was still in the air. A thin, foul smelling and moth eaten wool blanket sat rumpled in the corner of the cell; he wrapped it around himself and hunkered down in a corner. His fingers explored the source of pain on the side of his head; there was a large lump behind his right ear. Dried blood ran down to his neck from the middle of the lump.

The little jail had four cells, all side by side. Each cell was about five feet by eight feet. The walls were made of grayish-black volcanic rock and a mud mortar. Steel bar doors were set into the front wall of the cells. Furnishings consisted of a small foxhole shovel—nothing else. Two sentries were posted in the long narrow hall outside the cells. They were having a grand time drinking rice wine and telling stories. Their conversation changed when they saw Hal beginning to stir. One came over, grabbed the bars of the cell door, shook them hard and launched into a harangue. During the welcoming speech, the other sentry came over and unlocked the cell door. Hal watched them cautiously. Uh oh, you're going to get a little more North Korean hospitality. I'm so cold, I don't know if I have the strength to take on these two goons. If I can't take both of them, I don't stand a chance. What am I talking about, I can't be aggressive with these people. My life isn't worth two cents as it is. The guards pulled the door open and drew their side-arms. They exchanged several sentences then came into the cell. Their eyes were bloodshot and their faces looked haggard; both were bean pole thin and stood about five feet tall. Their uniforms were baggy, scroungy and tattered and their boots had deep cracks in the folds. Boot soles were gaping open to varying degrees. Geez, how in the world are these pitiful specimens of humanity kicking our asses? Expressions on their faces seemed a mix of fear and ire. One seemed unsteady, as though drunk, which answered for his mouth being in overdrive. He gave Hal a long paragraph of invectives, then kicked hard. When Hal ducked and scrambled to his feet, the alarmed guards jumped back. They were aiming their weapons directly at Hal's head. The one with the big mouth seemed anxious to do something. Hal raised his hands above his head and froze. Easy does it fellas. Don't get carried away here. Wonder what they're saying. The sober guard seemed to be urging a departure from the cell, but it was a tough sell. Then, without taking their eyes off Hal, they exited and locked the cell. 'Mouth' delivered another lecture of brimstone, repeatedly kicking the bars on the cell door. The other guard went back to his crude wooden table and chair and sipped wine. Hal huddled back into the corner. He pulled the wretched blanket over his head to preserve the heat of his breath and closed his eyes.

1010, Friday, October 21, 1950
2110, Thursday, EST
AQUAMARINE Operation Hut
Kimpo Air Base, South Korea

"Colonel Bennett, with all due respect, I think we should report the mission overdue," urged Reed.

"Not at this time," snapped Bennett. "You are not in the military chain of command Mr. Reed. Please don't concern yourself with military matters."

"Don't forget Colonel, I'm an ex-Marine pilot. I know how things work."

"Mr. Reed, I am the commander of this operation and I alone shall determine when the mission is overdue."

Reed looked at the Colonel and shook his head, "Well, as a CIA employee, I can go over to the B–29 and send a message to my project officer about any subject I so desire. And I don't have to go through you first to do it either."

"However, Mr. Reed, prudence would be in order here, would it not?"

"Prudence, Colonel Bennett, deems that I go over to the B–29 and fire off a message that tells CIA that Kirby is overdue on the mission to Kraskino." Reed's eyes held a constant stare into Bennett's shifting eyes.

Bennett blinked first, "Kraskino? What are you talking about?"

Reed stepped forward and leaned on the Colonel's desk, "Don't be stupid Colonel. I didn't just pull that name out of thin air. I know what you told Kirby and I saw the track you drew on the map. Now, don't you think it is time we reported Kirby overdue?"

Bennett squirmed in his chair, "I was waiting until the estimated time of fuel starvation had been reached," said Bennett, "which occurs in eight minutes."

"I'll walk over to the plane with you to send the overdue report to Langley and the Pentagon, Colonel."

"That won't be necessary Mr. Reed."

"No trouble, really, I've got to go over there anyway Colonel," said Reed with a stony glare.

0105, Friday, October 21, 1950
1405, Friday, Korean Time
Congressman Bradbury's Bedroom
Fairfax, Virginia

"Hello," Bradbury grumbled into the phone, awakened from a dead sleep. "Yardley? What in hell is so hot that it can't wait until a decent hour? What? Oh shit! Are you sure? Are you sure he didn't go down in Russia? This could be trouble Tim—big trouble. I have to hang up and think about this. God, I don't even know where to start. I'll call you back."

Several fingers of bourbon and a hand rolled cigar gave Bradbury time to think. He phoned Yardley back, "Tim, listen to me. You send a message to Logan and tell him to get rid of everything on paper about this—messages, maps, everything. And, you get down to your commcenter and get rid of any paper trail there. Make sure that damn encrypted message you sent doesn't exist, hear me? OK, good. Now, you mentioned a couple weeks ago that your pal Ben is handling a double agent? Tell Ben to get the word to the Russians that the pilot acted on his own behalf and has embarrassed the Soviet Union, the CIA and the United States. Have him tell the Russians that it is the CIA's preference that he not be returned or heard from again. Got it? That's your problem. I don't care Tim, do it! Just goddam do it.

0230, Friday, October 21, 1950
1530, Friday, Korean Time
Admiral Sherman's Residence, Naval Observatory Grounds,
Washington, DC

Captain Jim Castle hurried up the long winding sidewalk and rapped the shiny brass anchor knocker on the Admiral's door.

"Come in Jim. I'm glad you called me," greeted Admiral Sherman. "I just finished making us a fresh pot of coffee." The Admiral led the way to the den.

"Good, I need some bad. I called J–2 and got the latest poop before I left the house."

"Ah, good. Pour yourself some, have a seat and give it to me from the top."

Jim eased into a large chocolate brown velour chair by the fireplace and took a careful sip. Embers from the last log of the night were alternating between a deep reddish orange glow and dark gray. There was an occasional trace of the smell of creosote from the flue. Sherman took the auburn leather couch across from him. The Admiral grabbed a pad and pencil from an open attaché case on the middle cushion.

"OK. Here's what we can piece together as of ten minutes ago," said Jim. "Kirby flew the morning Unggi recon mission. We have no idea what the hell went wrong, but K–14 reported him overdue when he didn't return by estimated fuel exhaustion time. CIA Operations Center told J–2 that Migs appear to have escorted the BALL to the air base at Ch'ongjin. That's all we know."

"Where did the Migs come from?" asked Sherman.

"Admiral, I told you all J–2 knew about the incident. At the moment, there are no more details."

Sherman reached over to the phone sitting on the side table next to the couch. He took the receiver off the cradle and dialed. "Gen. Vandenberg please. Hello Hoyt, this is Forrest. Sorry to bother you, but I suspect you weren't asleep." Sherman sipped as he listened. "Sure did. Yes. Right. I agree. Assume that to be negative. Oh, no Hoyt, not for a minute. He just would not do that. But Hoyt, they aren't sure he overflew, right? Then that remains to be seen. No. I would have heard if any of the Navy ships picked up a Mayday. Good, that's why I called. I was going to suggest we do that. OK, see you at the briefing."

Jim refilled both cups. "New developments?" he asked when the Admiral hung up.

"Yes, he just got a call from his intell guys. They told him that the Russian air defense zone headquarters in Kraskino advised Moscow that it had put their zone on high alert due to an overflight by a high altitude aircraft. The time of this advisory is consistent with an overflight by Kirby, given the flight plan."

"I guess that's possible Admiral, but if he did overfly, it had to be a navigation error. Kirby is an aggressive pilot, but he's also by the book. He knows the rules of engagement. In any case, the question is, how did the Migs get him? Hell, if he strayed, he'd just get the hell out of there when he figured it out."

"That's what has all the Chiefs puzzled," said Sherman. "J–2 is concerned about the coincidence of this and that report of the Russians sending their new ground-to-air missile to Kraskino. That only confuses the issue, since it's pretty clear that he did in fact land at Ch'ongjin. OK. Let's figure out what our position is going to be and what we need to do."

Korean Army Jail
Ch'ongjin Airfield, North Korea

It snowed during the night as Hal slept. It blew in the window, onto the blanket and melted, waking him with a new form of misery—being both cold and wet. His body could no longer endure the pain from being badly chilled for so long. When numbness and the back side of shock crept in, he drifted off into an exhaustion-invoked sleep.

Hal awoke to the sound of a new voice outside the cell. A peek through a moth hole in the blanket revealed a bowl of 'breakfast' on the dirt just inside the cell door. The menu this morning included a cloudy white liquid with a pinch of rice and a few blades of grass floating around. It was not worth leaving his heat-conserving crouch in the corner. The new voice was a Korean Army officer in a clean uniform. After barking a string of orders to the sentries, the officer came over and looked into the cell. Hal stayed still as though asleep under the blanket. More orders from the officer brought both soldiers to the cell door. One unlocked it, entered and held a gun at Hal's head while the other pulled Hal up onto his feet. They hobbled his ankles and tied his hands behind him with a crude, bristly rope. All the while, the cold dark eyes of the officer studied Hal's face. They hauled Hal from the cell to a chair next to the rickety table where last night's wine tasting was hosted.

"My name is Major Pak, Kirby," said the officer in excellent English. He waited for Hal to reply. Hal merely stared at Pak; he didn't look like the other North Koreans. His features were that of perhaps the child of a mixed marriage. A well-trimmed goatee and thick mustache served well in hiding facial expressions. "You are too old to be a Captain in the Air Force, Mr. Kirby," said the officer as he sat down in the chair opposite Hal. "Are you a CIA pilot, Mr. Kirby?" Pak again waited for Hal to reply. "I know you are from the CIA, Mr. Kirby. You carried no wallet, no papers, and no dog tags. That and your incredible airplane tell me you are from the CIA. What was your mission?" Hal merely glared into Pak's eyes. This jackass thinks I'm just going to tell him everything he wants to know. If I could just stop this damn shivering. Geez, I've never been so damn cold.

"Do you smoke?" asked the major, holding out an opened pack of Lucky Strikes. Hal shook his head. Son of a bitch probably took those off a GI corpse.

"I noticed you didn't eat this morning. I don't blame you. These people don't know how to treat prisoners. If you cooperate with me, I'll see that you get much better treatment."

Hal didn't have the energy to laugh. He stared at Pak, trying to hide his disbelief. Uh huh, I bet you will. If I had any spit, I'd use it.

"Come now Mr. Kirby, say something, anything," said Pak. "Is that really your name or just a cover name?" Hal's eyes bored holes through the interrogator. After a long study of Hal's face Pak said, "I will show my good will. I will order these incompetents to bring you two blankets, a pair of heavy trousers, a jacket and a hat. Shoes I can't promise, your feet are large. And some hot soup and bread too. I will return in a few hours, after you are warm and have had a chance to eat. In the meantime, I will go search through the wreckage of your aircraft. When I return, I hope you will cooperate."

It felt wonderful to not be shivering anymore. Even though the NKPA uniform articles were woefully out of size and wearing them was a despicable thought, they were warm by any comparison. He had long passed the hunger threshold and wanted to pass up the thin bean soup with other questionable items languishing in the broth. But it was hot food and he knew his body needed the energy. He remembered reading about sailors of yore picking weevils out of their bread, but he never suspected he would be faced with a similar challenge. If those were insect parts in the soup, well, they were just a protein supplement as he saw it at this moment. If the opportunity to escape ever came, he wanted to have the strength and agility to take advantage of it. The empty ammo box they put in the cell was a nice touch too. Sitting on the cold packed dirt and leaning against a rock wall had cost him a lot of body heat. Life was good.

As promised, the kindly Major Pak returned to cash in on his good will. "My word is good, as you can see Mr. Kirby," he said as the sentry unlocked the cell door. The soldiers put a chair in the middle of the cell for Pak and stood on each side of him. Hal was sitting on the ammo box with his arms crossed and his legs stretched out. "OK Mr. Kirby, it's time for you to show your appreciation. Tell me your real name."

"Colonel Logan Bennett, U.S. Air Force. Could you let them know I'm OK?" asked Hal.

"Of course, if you continue to cooperate," Pak said. "Now, I am very interested in your airplane Colonel. I will withhold my anger at you for destroying it, if you cooperate. Tell me how high it could fly."

"You already know that," said Hal.

"Be careful about your manners Colonel. Tell me about the camera."

"Oh, I don't know much about that," Hal said with a poker face and shrug of the shoulders. "Everything was automatic. They told me where to fly and I flew there. I turned the camera on when I got over the target area, flew around for an hour, or however long they directed, and then returned home. I have no idea what the pictures look like. We sent the film to Washington. You are smart enough to know that the CIA wouldn't trust Air Force pilots with any information about cameras like that."

The interrogation officer watched Hal carefully, assessing his body language and facial expressions. "We recovered the camera from the wreckage Colonel, so don't lie to me."

Hal concentrated all his energy into not showing any response to anything Pak said. No facial expression changes, no muscles twitches, no blinks, nothing. That didn't stop his mind from wandering or making snide imaginary comments. Ha, who's the one telling lies here? There wasn't anything left of that thing. Nice try buddy. "Well, then you know what I'm telling you is true. All I had to do is turn it on. You saw the controls. There was nothing else I could do but turn it on and off."

"Colonel, how about the electronic equipment on the wing?"

"Oh, I have no idea what the hell that thing does. Well, I think it's a radar jammer because they have us turn it on when approaching the target and turn it off when we're clear."

"It's not a jammer Colonel! Don't lie. It was nearly intact."

"Maybe it's not," said Hal, "but I really wouldn't know, I just guessed that's what it was."

"Why wouldn't you know?" asked the interrogator.

"Look, just flying that thing is challenge enough. I didn't really give a damn what all that stuff was for. I had my hands full in the cockpit," Hal said.

"Why did you fly to Kraskino?"

"They told me to," said Hal, nonchalantly.

"You aren't telling me what you know Colonel."

Hal smiled deep within himself. You're damn right I'm not. I'm going to beat you at this game if it's the last thing I do. "There's nothing to tell. I thought it was strange, of course, but I do what I'm told."

Pak stood up; anger was building in his face. "Captain Kirby USN, you are a liar."

"I told you my name is Colonel Bennett. There is no Kirby, that's just a covername."

"Liar! The information we got from papers in a Skyraider that crashed near the Naktong River identified the pilot as a Captain Kirby, USN. So, Captain, did you retire and go to work for the CIA?"

Now Hal's heart was beating rapidly, "That's got to be a coincidence Major, I told you Captain Kirby is just a covername the CIA selected for the suit. I am Colonel Logan Bennett, U.S. Air Force, on loan to the CIA."

"Captain, I went to college in the United States; my degree in aeronautical engineering came from USC. Studying the Air Force and Naval Aviation has been my life for over five years. You are full of lies. You insult my intelligence. Now, are you going to cooperate or do I have to resort to more, uh, persuasive means?" They glared at each other a few moments. Pak stood and released the cover flap on his sidearm holster. Hal's eyes froze on the holster; the letters U.S. were imprinted on it. Pak gripped the handle of the sidearm and pulled it out; it was a U.S. military .45 caliber. When Pak cycled the action to send a round into the chamber, the clatter of the mechanism sent an icy chill channeling through Hal's core. Pak's face showed distinct pleasure at the trembling he created when he held the gun barrel a few inches from Hal's forehead. "Captain, do you think I wouldn't pull the trigger? I have done it easily many times before. This weapon once belonged to an Army lieutenant. He wouldn't cooperate. I killed him with his own gun—this gun. He had no further value. Which is what I think about you right now. Are you ready to cooperate?"

Despite the cold, Hal was now sweating profusely. The cold air turned the glistening droplets on his face to painfully cold points. He dared not raise a hand to wipe them for fear that it would alarm Pak or the sentries. Geez, that gun bore looks as wide as a tunnel. Don't weaken Kirby. Either way, they will probably kill me, but I have to buy some time—just in case a miracle happens. OK, keep your mouth shut. He knows that I have valuable info, so he will try some rough treatment over time to bring me around. "Major, I am Colonel Bennett and I really don't know anything more about the camera and the pod. I can't tell you what I don't know. Maybe I can help you out on something else. I don't want to die over something I don't know anything about."

Pak kept the gun at Hal's head while he thought, scowling intensely. In a quick move, he turned the gun to the side and fired a round into the wall. The involuntary reaction of Hal's mind to what it perceived had happened in that instant sent him crashing to the floor in a massive spasm. Pak roared with laughter as Hal regurgitated the soup and bread onto the dirt and

sorted through the confusion and the pain and the ringing in his ear.
"I don't have time to visit with you any more today Captain. I should
attend to other duties. When I return tomorrow, you'll have one last
chance. If you don't tell me about your airplane, I will not aim so poorly
and the bullet will go crashing into your brains. It is too much trouble to
hold uncooperative prisoners. Think about that Captain." Pak slapped the
holster several times, "Think about that Army lieutenant."

0720, Saturday, October 22, 1950
2020, Saturday, Korean Time
Joint Chiefs of Staff Conference Room
The Pentagon

The AQUABALL incident was a write-in item on today's agenda for
expanded discussion, just after the daily intelligence briefing.

"Gentlemen, I'd like now to take up the matter of the missing
AQUABALL aircraft," announced the Chairman of the Joint Chiefs of
Staff, General Omar Bradley. "J–2 has pertinent information on the
incident, please go ahead." He nodded to General Reynolds.

"Good morning gentlemen," said Reynolds. "The following recap is
Top Secret and is based on very sensitive sources of intelligence. All times
are Korean times. At approximately 0655 yesterday, there were indications
of a high defense condition declaration by the Soviet air defense zone
headquarters at Kraskino. That alert was canceled about 40 minutes later.
At approximately 0745 yesterday, the air base commander at Ch'ongjin
reported to Pyongyang that two Migs had escorted an unmarked black
aircraft of unrecognized type to the airfield. At 1435 yesterday, an
unidentified originator located in Sinuiju reported to Moscow and Peking
that Soviet Migs escorted an unmarked aircraft to the airfield at Ch'ongjin.
They stated that the aircraft was the one which had been conducting high
altitude recon along the North Korean border since the 20th of October
and that the aircraft belonged to the US. They reported that the pilot had
activated a self-destruction device that demolished the majority of the
aircraft. It stated that the pilot's name was Kirby due to that name being on
the captive's flight suit. The final item in the report was that the pilot was
being held pending disposition orders from Sinuiju. That is the sum total of
what we know."

General Bradley allowed no delay before picking up the discussion, "Gentlemen, the President and Secretaries Marshall and Acheson are all fuming over our agitation of the Soviets. I'm not sure they are convinced we had no foreknowledge, but that is certainly my understanding. Is there anyone here who had any inkling or knowledge that we were going to fly into Soviet territory?" He looked around the room—silence.

"What's the Soviet reaction?" asked General Collins.

"I talked with Acheson this morning; there has been none," said Bradley. "Nonetheless, General Marshall wants the AQUAMARINE project out of Korea immediately and out of the Defense Department. He also ordered that there are to be no unclassified references or releases relative to this incident. J–3 has the action item to draft Flash precedence recall orders ASAP. Also, J–3 will coordinate the withdrawal of the Defense Department from that program altogether and, last but not least, to initiate a board of inquiry."

Admiral Sherman interjected, "Since a Navy pilot is involved, I would like very much to head that inquiry, if there are no objections."

Bradley scanned the table quickly for comments, "Done. It's yours. Keep me and General Vandenberg informed and copy us on all reports. J–2, keep the Admiral updated on all pertinent intelligence as it becomes known and provide him any information you hold, without restriction." Reynolds nodded to both General Bradley and Admiral Sherman. "Is there any further discussion on this incident?"

While General Bradley was addressing the issue of the board of inquiry, a Colonel came into the room and delivered a note to General Vandenberg. When Bradley opened the table for further discussion, Vandenberg replied, "Yes sir. I've just been advised that General Stratemeyer has planned a bombing raid on the air base at Ch'ongjin. This mission was planned prior to this incident and he is unaware of the incident. Time on target is 0600 Korean, which is 1900 this evening."

Admiral Sherman felt like a mule kicked him in the stomach. He turned to General Reynolds, "What do you think the odds are that Captain Kirby is still there or will be moved before that?"

Reynolds' face showed dismay, "That's a tough question, I don't know."

Everyone looked at Bradley, who took a deep breath, "General Reynolds, we aren't going to hold you to a number. Just tell us what the enemy is likely to do with Kirby. Give us your gut feeling."

Reynolds squirmed in his seat, "It is very likely that they'll move him, but when is an entirely different question. I have no information on which to base an estimate. They have tended to promptly move high value prisoners to a headquarters location where they can be controlled and interrogated."

"Good point," said Vandenberg. "We don't really know that he's at the air base right now."

"Let's assume then that he is at the air base," said Bradley. "Let's make a decision. Comments?"

Vandenberg went first, "Ch'ongjin is a major staging base for logistic resupply and an air threat to ground forces. Our forces will be deep into the north very shortly. I say we must go ahead with the raid."

General Collins spoke up, "8th Army is two days north of Pyongyang, hell bent for the Yalu. Units of the ROK 6th Division are already at some points of the Yalu and they're getting battered. The enemy is getting progressively stronger up there and Ch'ongjin is a key player in their defense of the central north and northeast. I say we have no choice but to neutralize the air base."

General Cates, Commandant of the Marine Corps, offered his view, "The Marine 1st Division will be landing at Wonsan the moment the Navy clears the mines from the harbor, which will be in the next day or two. They'll immediately head north then arc across to join with the 8th Army. J–2 reported many YAK–9s in Ch'ongjin and they can make hamburger out of my troops. We have to take Ch'ongjin out."

Admiral Sherman was slow to make his contribution, "I think we should postpone the raid for one day. The Marines will be the most threatened and they are still aboard ship. Perhaps we'll get a better handle on Kirby's location in the meantime."

"I share your concern Forrest," said General Collins. "He's no doubt a very valuable man. But, delaying the raid jeopardizes the ROK forces in the near term. They are meeting stiff opposition and need all the help we can give them. We can't fail to do all we can. We need those Korean troops to supplement our forces up there."

General Bradley's face was grim. He took a deep breath, "Gentlemen, I must allow the raid to be executed as planned. Let's hope for the best. Next item."

Korean Army Jail
Ch'ongjin Airfield, North Korea

Hal sat on the ammo box, leaning against the rock wall in the pitch black, wondering. He could see stars through the cell window, twinkling in the clear, cold night. At this moment they were points of light at the end of a tunnel with a blocked entrance. He stared out of the cell window for long periods of time, thinking, at all times of the day and night. Falling asleep was difficult because he did it as often as he could. So much sleep upset his biological clock so that days and nights lost their significance. Now, his existence was relegated to either being asleep and at peace or being awake and deeply troubled. The feeling of helplessness was overwhelming at times.

The jailer's table lantern ran out of fuel early into the night. Snoring of the sentry was loud and disturbing. The clothes and blankets kept Hal reasonably warm, allowing his mind to wander and muse instead of fight death from hypothermia. He wrote mental letters to Alice, Joe and Susan. He began to think about the return of Major Pak the next day. I refuse to let that son of a bitch get anything out of me that's worth a damn. Can't play too many games though, he's smart. I'll wind up with a bullet between the eyes. Bastards will mutilate me and throw me in a ditch somewhere. Geez, I can't believe this is happening. I love you Alice. I love you Susan. I love you Joe. Tears flowed steadily down his cheek. He tried to blank everything out and just concentrate on the heavens. Time passed with agonizing slowness.

Eventually, the stars began to fade with the very first evidence of coming daylight. Intermittent chirping of birds and noises from a nearby sty of pigs broke the dead silence of the night. He was sensitive to every sound by Mother Nature's animals preparing for a new day. Distant voices became audible; then jeep and truck engines; then Korean aircraft engines. It struck him that there was unusual excitement outside. Someone opened the jail door, hollered something and ran off. The sentry awoke and ran from the building. The drone of B–26 bombers is unmistakable, even in the distance. Hal jumped up, moved the ammo box under the high window and stood on it and stretched to get a better look outside. YAK–9s were scrambling. The base was on alert. His view to the south soon yielded a sky full of contrails streaming from the microscopic dots he was certain were B–26s.

Geez, they're coming directly overhead. This is probably their target. Hell, there's nothing else around here worth all that. Damn, I'm only about a mile from the runway. That many bombers at high altitude, oh God, I'm going to get clobbered by my own bombers. Better than having that goddam Pak put me away. He crouched down with the blankets over his head in the corner of the cell. All he could think of doing was to recite the 23rd Psalm.

Intense rumbling and staccato concussions of large patches of exploding bombs beleaguered his senses. It seemed never ending. He could tell that the impacts were walking their way through the base—getting ever closer. Then the world became a nightmare; there was a surreal sensation of violent tumbling and ear-splitting noise. Then there was the contradiction of an eerie silence with loud ringing in his ears. Numbness and tingling sensations seemed to come from all parts of his body. Everything was dark. Movement was impossible; breathing was extremely difficult. Hal's mind slowly rejected the idea that he was having a nightmare and began to accept reality. There was a rubble pile on top of him. The blanket was still wrapped around his head and face, forming a delicate cocoon, but he was trapped under the rocks that once were the walls of the jail. A dreadful feeling of smothering forced him to try and inhale as deep as the weight and freedom of motion of the debris would allow. The fear of using up the oxygen in the air of his cocoon captured his senses and invoked desperation. He mustered all his might and pushed upward on his hands and knees. He felt some rubble movement. Another thrust upward with all his might brought more rubble movement. Again, he strained—this time he was free. His hand explored a swollen, painful spot on his face; it didn't feel wet. He hurt all over; pins and needles played havoc with his legs. Suddenly he was aware of total freedom. The rear half of the jail was shambles. He stepped through the rocks and boards and quickly surveyed the area. Most of the buildings were leveled or heavily damaged. Along the runway there were several fires raging that sent tongues of flame high into the sky that turned into dense black clouds that angled up into the morning sky. There were YAK–9s still sitting intact here and there, but most of those that had not gotten airborne were burning or demolished. He ran to a nearby jeep, found the starter and sped for a distant, solitary YAK–9. A slight detour yielded a hat from a dead soldier to help as a disguise. On the way, he recalled what he and Reed had figured out about the YAK–9 cockpit they found in the debris pile at

Kimpo. Bomb craters in the runway rendered it useless, but there was a grassy field, albeit not very level, which he chose as his best alternative for a runway. Hal arrived at the YAK–9, climbed up the side of it and jumped into the cockpit. His attempt to start the engine yielded nothing. The prop didn't even turn over. He decided the battery was dead or missing, scrambled out of the plane and got into the jeep. The next closest YAK–9 that appeared to be flyable was 100 yards away. As he approached the plane he saw a pilot running toward it. You unlucky son of a bitch. You may have survived the bombing, but you ain't going to survive this. Hal had the accelerator pedal to the floor. As he neared the plane, he angled directly for the pilot, now only 20 yards away. Shock from the realization that he was about to be run over caused the pilot to freeze momentarily. His attempt to jump aside was countered by a correct anticipation by Hal. The front of the jeep struck the pilot solidly in the abdomen causing his head to slam down violently onto the hood and crush his skull. Blood and matter splashed back across the hood and over the windshield. The front of Hal's jacket and lap were spattered with crimson gore. He hit the brakes, wheeled around and sped back to the YAK; the pilot slid off the hood. Nausea hit hard as Hal tried to wipe hot, salty blood from his face.

He climbed into the cockpit and hurried a startup attempt. The prop began turning. His heart was slamming against his chest. "Come on you son of a bitch, come on!" he screamed at the top of his lungs. Prop blades flopped endlessly in front of him, without the slightest cough until the battery became exhausted.

He climbed down the side of plane, leaving sickening streaks of blood on the side of the fuselage and once again set out in the jeep to find another flyable plane. One after another he bypassed damaged planes, getting ever closer to the beehive of activity at the center of the airfield. The first potentially flyable airplane he came to was an IL–10. It didn't appear that anything else survived further down the line. He hastily climbed into the cockpit and examined the panel and controls. Experimentation finally produced a rotating propeller. Some lucky guesses brought coughs, blue smoke and ignition.

"Yaaaa hooo," he yelled. He pushed the throttle forward but there was no movement. Much more throttle—still no movement. Full throttle—nothing. Damn! Where's the parking brake release? He slammed the toes of the rudder pedals, hoping that the parking brake release was the same as in

U.S. planes—no release. A search of the panel and cockpit for something that looked like a brake release produced nothing. Chocks! Damn! I forgot to look for chocks! Hal pulled the throttle back and climbed down. He no sooner pulled the chocks free when he heard yelling close behind him. When he turned around he saw rifle barrels. He put his hands up, then involuntarily bent over in convulsive vomiting. A soldier's boot smashed into his chest thrusting him over backwards. Boots and rifle butts came from all directions.

CHAPTER 24

On a road in North Korea

Hal came to his senses lying on his side in the back of a jeep that was speeding along a poorly maintained road. Each bounce brought renewed pain to many bruises and sore joints. His hands and bare feet were tied so tight that they burned and pulsated with his heartbeat. A rope was secured between the tethers on his hands and feet. It was sufficiently taught to pull him into a fetal position. The soldier sitting on the floor in the open back of the jeep noted Hal's awakening and told the driver and other soldier in the front seats. Both turned briefly to look at their prisoner, hollered something and laughed. The soldier in the back took his rifle from his lap and aimed it at Hal's head, barked something jokingly and made a loud pop sound. Hal closed his eyes to fight off nausea. His tongue found the source of a continuous flow of blood in his mouth—a split in a badly swollen lip. His right eye was throbbing and swollen shut. Intermittently he opened his good eye to take note of the sun direction and tried to keep track of time and direction.

They came to a large city after what felt to Hal like a couple hours. After navigating a maze of deeply rutted dirt roads, the jeep entered a military compound and pulled up to a decrepit looking building. The soldier in the shotgun seat went inside. Hal looked at the sun and recalled his navigation charts. Unggi. Gotta be. Geez, I've shot a lot of film of this area. Soldiers came from everywhere to gawk, holler, poke, punch and spit. Overwhelmed by pain, hopelessness and humiliation, he slipped into a trance-like state.

They drove to another building, removed the rope between his feet and hands, hauled him bodily inside and dropped him unmercifully onto the concrete floor of a crude room. The jeep driver gave Hal a good-bye present, a kick to the solar plexus that brought a black veil down over his mind.

When the wave of semi-consciousness passed, he opened an eye to look at his new digs. Ah! A decent cell. No dirt, no windows, a little heat and a bucket. Bamboo and rope cot too. This is more like it. You can bet your boots, if I ever get out of this mess, I'm going back to a carrier and bomb the frigging brains out of these people. Damn, I hurt bad all over. Totally exhausted and at his tolerance threshold he forced himself into sleep.

Hal awoke the moment he heard the keys in the cell's metal door lock. Two soldiers entered and cut his hands and feet free and stripped him from the bloodied and foul smelling North Korean uniform. They replaced the empty bucket in the cell with one half filled with water and departed. He managed to sit up, groaning as he did so, scooted to the bucket and rinsed the dried blood and Korean spit from his face and hands. Cool water soothed the cuts and swollen areas on his face. He sat quietly, collecting his thoughts, fighting against deep despair. It wasn't easy, but he managed to climb onto the cot to go to sleep to escape pain and despondency—it didn't work. Everything hurt—terribly. Lying motionless on the cot, eyes closed, inhaling only slightly so his ribs didn't have to move much was the best he could do to ease the compelling discomfort. His mind slipped slowly into neutral and gave him some peace.

Again, the clink of keys in the door lock brought back his consciousness. The two soldiers were back. When they bound his hands and feet he wondered if he could endure this much longer. They carried him outside, put him in the back of another jeep and tied him securely to a rear seat. Another scenic tour of the countryside was in progress. As they left the outskirts of the city, he noted the sun position. North again, maybe northeast. There's nothing much northeast of here. Where the hell are these guys taking me? A border checkpoint came into view in about half an hour. They pulled up to the barricade and shouted to two sentries as they came out of a ragged wooden shack on the side of the road next to the semaphore barricade. Hal's suspicions about the uniform differences were confirmed when he heard the sentries speak. The Koreans didn't speak Russian and the Soviet guards obviously didn't speak Korean. The Russian's were not happy with their unexpected visitors. The Russians were very nervous and argued with each other briefly. After they came to some agreement, they approached the jeep with their weapons ready. They inspected the identification papers of the two Koreans, gave a long puzzling look at Hal, directed the driver to park the jeep on Korean side of the road and returned to the guardhouse. During the course of an hour, the soldier riding shotgun walked to the gate several times, exchanged words and motions and returned in obvious disgust. Exposure to the 40–degree temperature—protected only by long johns—had taken its toll on Hal. He was shivering and chattering uncontrollably.

A black Soviet sedan arrived at the gate and parked. Its civilian driver got out and spoke with the Russian soldiers. The Korean jeep driver got out and walked to the gate. After hand motions were traded, he returned to the jeep and vented frustration on the steering wheel. Shortly, the Russian driver returned to the sedan and opened the rear passenger door. A portly man in a black fur hat and long black fur coat got out and had a brief conversation with the two border guards who then accompanied him to the jeep.

Gary's Cafe, K Street,
Washington, DC

"Sheila, there's going to be three of us, can you give me the booth in the back please?" asked Will Crandall.

"Sure hon, it's all set up. Can I get you something while you wait for them?"

"A double martini."

"OK, have a seat, I'll be back in a jiff."

Jingling of the bells that hung on the cafe door announced the arrival of Tim Yardley. Will waved to get Tim's attention. As Tim slid into the booth he shook Will's hand, "Did HL seem really upset when he called you?"

Will nodded, "Upset is an understatement. I thought I detected a quiver in his voice at one point."

"Good grief, I can't imagine what's happened," Tim said.

"When is Logan due back?" asked Will.

"ASAP. JCS ordered him back by commercial air," said Tim. "I tried to find out why they did that, but nobody seemed to know, or if they did, they weren't talking."

Bradbury plowed through the jingling door like a bull on a rampage. He dropped heavily into the booth, "Bad news gents, really bad news."

Sheila came over with Will's martini and menus, "Sorry for the delay hon, the bartender stepped out for a minute. Can I get you two anything to drink while you make up your mind on lunch?"

"Manhattan up," said Tim.

"Double bourbon and coke," said Bradbury.

"Back in a flash guys," said Sheila.

When Sheila was out of earshot, Will looked at Bradbury, "What is it?"

"Every time I picked up the goddam phone this morning, I got bad news. Haven't you heard anything Tim?" asked Bradbury.

"Nothing I haven't already told you," replied Tim, "Oh, one thing came in just before I left the office. Bomb damage assessment on Ch'ongjin showed all buildings sustained major damage and the runway is unusable. All planes reported dropping on target. If Kirby was still there, he's a goner. We can only hope. But, what's your news HL?"

"What about your buddy, did you contact him and give him the message for the Russians?" Bradbury asked Tim.

"No, his secretary said he's out of town, she couldn't say where. But she'll give him the message to call me if he checks in. Come on HL, tell us what's going on."

"Tim, you better find a way to get that goddam message to him fast. If Kirby lives to file a deposition, this whole damn thing is going to unravel," Bradbury whispered forcefully. "Even without him, I'm not sure we can hold it together."

"What the hell happened HL?" said Will.

Sheila arrived with the drinks, "Here you are guys; have you decided?"

"Hell no," barked Bradbury, "Nothing for me anyway. Uh, bring me another drink."

"Soup and sandwich special," said Will.

"Me too," said Tim. Sheila hurried off to the kitchen.

"HL, spill it," said Will.

Bradbury downed the bourbon and coke in one fell swoop. "Gents, I found out that Admiral Sherman is heading up a JCS investigation on the incident. There's not one single person in DC who wants to get a piece of my ass more than that son of a bitch. And that's not the worst of it. He has a connection with Hoover. That, Tim, is just a sampling of why Kirby better not make it back."

"Do you think the FBI could figure out who the investors are?" asked Will.

"Don't be so goddam stupid," Bradbury said banging his fist down on the table. "You two better make sure you don't do or say anything that will attract attention to SurvTech."

"Don't be so pessimistic HL, as long as Kirby is out of the picture, there's just going to be a routine military incident investigation that will close with the important questions unanswered. It's an obvious case of pure pilot error."

"I'm worried about other people too," said Bradbury, "people like Colonel Gayonne and General Killian. If the investigation expands to include questioning of them and they disclose the deals I worked on the pod funding, I think that would lead them to us."

"They aren't going to do that HL," said Tim, "for God's sake, that would put their careers in jeopardy. They aren't about to volunteer that info."

Bradbury was shaking his head, "It's not out of the question, especially if they were granted immunity."

Lubyanka Prison
Moscow

Cold potato soup in an earthen bowl and a handful of stale bread sated Hal's extreme hunger. He was sitting on a cot, gingerly chewing the last of his bread ration, favoring his swollen jaw. A cough brought tears to his eyes. Although blindfolded when they brought him in late last night, he knew his cell was located two floors below entry level, at the end of a long, narrow hallway, 52 paces from the stairs. Since he awoke, the only noise he heard was a guard's heavy boots patrolling the hallway. Hal's new arrangements were yet another step up in luxury. Upon arrival last night, the guards took his long johns from him escorted him to a shower and gave him a baggy gray cotton pullover with matching pants that string-tied at the waist. His cell was a cozy six feet wide by 10 feet long, with a coarse cement floor. The tan colored paint job on the walls and ceiling was probably the original. There were gouges and pockmarks in the wall plaster over the surface area that was reachable by a human. There was a wooden cot with a one–inch pad—one inch on the edges, that is. A flush toilet without a seat sat starkly in the corner. Next to that was a tiny single-faucet sink that was mounted on the wall. A heavy cell door made of solid wood had a thick glass viewing slit covered by a flap on the outside. A low wattage light bulb, coated with many years of dust, provided a dull yellow glow. It was hanging from a cord well out of reach from the center of the cell's 12-foot ceiling.

Hal's senses perked up when he heard multiple footsteps coming down the hall. Two were the bulky boots of the sentry, the other pair sounded like street shoes. They stopped at his door. The cover over the viewing slit moved aside; a pair of eyeballs peered through the glass. The lock rattled and the door swung open. A man in a black ill-fitting suit walked a few feet into the cell. A soldier moved into the doorway and stood stiffly with a rifle held snugly across his chest.

"Good morning Captain Kirby," greeted the man in quite broken English. "I am Alexei Yabokov. I am what you in CIA call handler." He paused for a response, but Hal merely mulled the final bits of bread in his mouth and sized up his new acquaintance. Alexei's dingy white shirt collar was slightly frayed and there were soup stains on the loosely tied green and black striped tie. He carried several sheets of coarse yellow paper and a short pencil in his left hand. "Captain, we both are professional officers and there is no use for us to beat the bushes. I see you need medical services and I will arrange the doctor this morning. In the meantime, you have information of very importance to us. If you give information, we will return you to America. If you do not, you go to trial for crimes of war against my country." Alexei came forward and put the paper and pencil on the corner of the cot, "While you wait the doctor, please make drawings of your airplane, and put measures. Since we have seen it, you don't worry of giving secrets." He again waited for a response from Hal. All he heard was the sound of Hal's closed mouth belch. Alexei left Hal alone to consider his generous offer.

1000, Tuesday, October 25, 1950
1700 Moscow Time
Office of the President
Blair House

"Good morning gentlemen, make yourself comfortable, we need to discuss new developments in the AQUABALL incident," said the President, motioning toward the couch. Truman called an urgent meeting with Generals George Marshall and Omar Bradley and the Deputy Director of the CIA, Allan Dulles.

Truman sat in a green stuffed chair in the sitting area of the office opposite the couch. "I warn you, I'm not happy," he said somewhat jokingly, "they told me this morning that it may be another year and a half before the White House construction will be finished. Damn people are slow as molasses. If I knew who to strangle, I'd do it. OK, enough of that. Allan, let's start with you. What's the latest information on this incident?"

"Mr. President, I have two things to report. First, we have evidence that they probably used their development model surface to air guided missile system, recently deployed to Kraskino, against the AQUABALL aircraft. The analysts figure it went like this: they damaged the aircraft with a missile and the pilot was forced to descend. The Soviet radars detected the descent and ordered the Migs to intercept and capture the aircraft. By the time the AQUABALL came within the altitude limits of the Migs, he had not only departed Soviet airspace but had gotten quite a way down the Korean coast. The Migs probably didn't have the fuel to escort the plane back the Soviet Union, so they took him to Ch'ongjin. Secondly, although we are unable to confirm it we feel strongly that the Koreans have surrendered Captain Kirby to the Soviets. We base this on fragmentary and circumstantial evidence, but our best analysts are convinced it is very likely."

Truman's face grimaced. He turned to his Secretary of State and nodded.

Marshall responded, "All of that information is borne out by the delivery of the letter from Stalin I briefed you on earlier. I'll read it for the benefit of Omar and Allan sir. Quote, I warn the overzealous President and leaders of the Armed Forces of the United States of America to make no further acts of war against the Union of the Soviet Socialist Republics. Further violations of our sovereign territory by land, sea or air will be met with lethal force. I have ordered my armed forces throughout the world to a high level of readiness. Unquote."

"Has he actually put his forces on alert Allan?" asked Truman.

"No sir, not that we can tell and we have good indicators for that."

"Posturing," said Bradley.

"Exactly," said Marshall, "and that is the reason I said the Stalin letter bears out Kirby's capture. He didn't complain immediately because he had no leverage at that point. He isn't making noise at the UN because he doesn't want the world to know that they can't defend himself against those airplanes."

Truman became animated, "Son of a bitch thinks he's going to rattle his saber, get us worried and then trade the pilot for something he wants. What's your guess on where is he going with this George?" asked Truman.

"I'd bet on a quiet repatriation. I just don't know what he wants in return. They need cash of course. They've also been raising hell about us holding one of their attachés that we caught spying in Japan. It would make sense for them to use Kirby to gain release of that guy."

"Too bad if they do, because he's been spilling his guts," said Dulles.

"If they want money, the pilot's in bad luck, because I won't give the communists one damn cent," said Truman.

"What about Korea?" asked Bradley, "Maybe they figure if we get out of there, or at least go back below the 38th, that they can work a deal with the Chinese for the north. Or just go in and take it. They've wanted it for years. The North Korean government is in shambles. When we took Pyongyang, the seat of government, such as it is, relocated to Sinuiju. This is a perfect time for the Russians to make a move."

"Interesting," said Truman.

"Yes, very interesting," said Marshall, "But I'm sure the Soviets know they won't get North Korea for a pilot." They all nodded in agreement.

"Gentlemen, we need to put together a reply to their letter," said Dulles.

"I agree," said Truman, looking at Marshall, "Do you have a draft prepared?"

"No sir, I didn't know what our approach might be. Omar, have you gotten everything completely out of Korea?" asked Marshall.

"Yes, the aircraft is aboard ship, the B–29s are airborne headed for Hawaii, and Colonel Bennett is coming back on PanAm. He should arrive in DC today."

Marshall nodded, "OK, then we should tell Stalin that it was purely pilot error, but to show our good faith, we have withdrawn those aircraft from Korea. Along with some syrup and apologies of course."

Truman nodded, "Draft it and get it to me right away."

1725, Tuesday, October 25, 1950
1025 Eastern
Lubyanka Prison, Moscow

"Captain, I cannot take my patience further," said Alexei Yabokov. "Comrade Beria has angered with me. All you tell me is name and rank." He leaned back against the wall and looked at Hal, who was sitting on the cot, intransigent. "OK Captain, foolish man, we are not Koreans. I don't beat and torture you." Yabokov turned to the guard in the doorway and gave some orders. The guard called down the hallway. Two large men returned with a straight jacket. "Don't make resistance Captain, this just for security purpose. We now go to the hospital for treatment of your wounds." The men put Hal into the straight jacket, hobbled his feet, tied a blindfold over his eyes and gagged him. One of the guards threw Hal over his shoulder. Yelling into the sock-like gag helped assuage Hal's pain from sore ribs and limbs. They lugged him down the hallway, up the stairs, down another long hallway and stopped. Cold drafts revealed the nearness of a door to the outside. After several minutes of waiting, Hal heard a car pull up. They carried him a few steps to the car and stuffed him inside.

It was a short ride—ten or fifteen minutes—before the sedan came to a stop. Hal got another painful shoulder ride into a building, up a flight of stairs, down a short hallway and through swinging doors. They laid him down onto a treatment table. Hal's mind ran wild. Well, I've heard and read about it, but now, I'm going to find out first hand. Geez, I can't believe this is happening. Attendants pulled leather straps across his chest and legs and cinched them tight. His eyes teared from pain. Biting the gag and trying to yell gave him some release for his anxiety. Someone pushed up his left sleeve, then he felt the unmistakable quick, sharp pain of an IV needle going into his arm.

"Captain Kirby, this is Alexei. You are taking a nap now while treating your wounds. Relax and rest well. Nothing will hurt you." Hal felt a burning sensation run up his arm. An unrecognizable taste developed in his mouth. It was a cross between lemon and something very bitter. A pleasant drowsiness evolved, then a feeling of great warmth flowed over his body. Unintelligible hollow voices filled his ears.

CHAPTER 25

Office of the Chairman, Joint Chiefs of Staff
The Pentagon

"Come in gentlemen, please have a seat," said General Bradley. General Vandenberg and Admiral Sherman took the two straight back chairs with leather-covered seats placed just to the right side of Bradley's desk. A large oil mural of a Gettysburg battle scene covered the wall behind Bradley's wide chestnut desk. A double lamp at the front center of the desk had two green cut glass shades and a gleaming brass base and uprights. A dark wood table with neat piles of files and documents sat immediately behind Bradley with matching bookcases on each end. Army and U.S. flags mounted on floor poles stood proudly beside the bookcases.

Bradley straightened up some papers while they took their seats and his secretary served them refreshments. "OK Forrest, it's your meeting, what do you have for us?"

Admiral Sherman's expression was somber. "General, my staff and I have conducted preliminary interviews and took depositions from the AQUAMARINE personnel. The CIA pilots provided the most significant information. Of particular note is the deposition of the CIA pilot, Reed Forbes. I spoke with him personally after reading his deposition. Forbes explained that immediately prior to Kirby's departure on the mission, Colonel Bennett came to the aircraft and modified Kirby's flight plan."

"How does Forbes know that?" asked Vandenberg.

"After Bennett departed the aircraft, Forbes climbed the service ladder to assist in the final cockpit preparations and to close the canopy. Kirby was apparently suspicious and wanted Forbes to witness the changes and explained that he had registered objection with Bennett relative to the rules of engagement. Kirby told Forbes that he was advised by Bennett that an Eyes Only message authorization had just been received and was ordered to fly the mission."

"Was there such a message, or one which might be construed as such?" asked Bradley.

"No message which even mentions Kraskino exists."

"Does that include the CIA?" asked Vandenberg.

"Affirmative. For the record though, I personally spoke with Colonel Yardley, the CIA AQUAMARINE Project Officer. I found his demeanor to be that of an unusually guarded and nervous man. At any rate, no copies of any back-channel communications exist. He explained that the direct link with the B–29s at Kimpo was merely a channel for coordination and liaison, not official messages and thus none of the Teletype chatter was ever saved."

"What about Bennett's side of the story?" asked Vandenberg.

"Bennett never mentioned the last-minute conversation with Captain Kirby. When confronted with Forbes' account of the events, he denied it, after recovering from a poorly disguised look of shock, I might add."

"Any other evidence?" asked Bradley.

"None, but based on that, I have a recommendation," said Sherman, "Sir, I respectfully recommend that a Court Martial be initiated for Colonel Bennett. Eyewitness testimony exists to show that he issued an unlawful order to Captain Kirby which resulted in the conduct of an act of war which precipitated an international incident."

Vandenberg came forward in his chair, "How do we know Forbes is telling the truth? Suppose he is covering for Kirby or has a vendetta against Bennett, or something or someone else. One thing that you haven't addressed is the motive."

"They were sworn depositions, Hoyt," said Sherman. "I spoke at length with both of them. I really believe Forbes. There's a ton of circumstantial information that I haven't mentioned. I'll just say that I'm hot on the trail of the motive."

"I think we should go cautiously here, before we ruin a man's career," said Vandenberg. "Your admissible evidence is purely that of one man's word against another. I can't even imagine a motive."

"Enough! I don't agree with either of you," said Bradley. "Hoyt, assign Colonel Bennett to your immediate staff. Forrest, keep the investigation moving. If you turn up an irrefutable motive for Bennett to give such an order, or other solid evidence, I'll convene a court. Keep us informed. Thank you gentlemen."

Office of the Chief of Naval Operations
The Pentagon

"Admiral, the Director's secretary has you on hold while he finishes another conversation. She said it shouldn't be more than five minutes," Sherman's secretary advised on the intercom.

Sherman picked up the phone and waited.

"Good afternoon Forrest, how are you? It's been a while since we talked," said J. Edgar Hoover.

"I'm just fine Edgar. Yes, it's been several months. I haven't had time for leisure since the war started. Edgar, I'm calling about the Soviet overflight incident. I am running the military investigation. When can I come over and meet with you?"

Office of the President,
Blair House

"Thank you for juggling your schedules gentlemen," President Truman said, nodding to General Bradley and Allen Dulles. "Go ahead George."

General George Marshall shuffled through a file of papers, "The Soviet Ambassador delivered this letter a short time ago," said Marshall. He handed copies of the letter to Bradley and Dulles and gave them a few moments to read it.

"Who the hell are these two people?" asked Bradley.

Marshall and Dulles began speaking at the same time. Marshall stopped and nodded to Allen.

"Nikolai Cheryakin is the guy I mentioned last Tuesday—arrested in Japan. We're holding him in a safe house out in Leesburg. Navy Intelligence people caught him receiving classified material from the other guy they want, Lieutenant Commander Garr. Garr was recently court-martialed and sent to Leavenworth. Interestingly, Captain Kirby was the guy who tipped off the counter-intelligence people about Garr."

"Strange coincidence, Allen. Or is it? Why do they want Garr?" asked Bradley.

"Garr has to be more than just a recent recruit. Perhaps they want him back before we get to all the facts surrounding his relationship with the Soviets," said Dulles.

"I have a decision to make here," said Truman, "I don't give a damn about these treasonous bastards. Can you think of a reason why we shouldn't trade them for Kirby?" The others shook their head. "OK, then we'll agree to that. I'm worried about this part of the letter that demands that we keep the incident and the exchange of personnel from the press. How the hell can we guarantee that? Once Captain Kirby gets back, sooner or later, his story is going to get out. We can't make a promise like that."

"I'll talk to the Ambassador about that. The Russians know we don't control our press. I'm sure he and I can come to an agreement on that issue," said Marshall.

"Gentlemen, I don't want any embarrassing leaks on this. I'm concerned about losing Captain Kirby from a snafu. I'll talk with Admiral Sherman. I mean it, keep this quiet. Make sure no one gets brought into this if it isn't absolutely necessary. And see that everyone who already knows signs sworn oaths of silence. I don't want anything to screw this up."

Office of the Director, Federal Bureau of Investigation

"Good afternoon Edgar, I hope you have good news," said Admiral Sherman.

"Depends on one's viewpoint," said Hoover, "but, I'm sure you'll be appreciative. Please come with me." Hoover led the way into a ten–foot square room off his private office. When Hoover shut the door, the thud and a feeling of compression in the ears made it obvious that the room was airtight. "Please have a seat. I use this soundproof room to discuss sensitive issues." The walls and ceiling were completely covered with material resembling egg cartons. The only furnishings in this room were a ceiling light, a brown wall-to-wall carpet, a round oak table and seven matching plain chairs. Sherman put his hat on the table and pulled out a chair.

"Forrest, I appreciate you giving me copies of your reports. They were very helpful. How's your investigation going?"

Sherman nodded, "Edgar, I know damn well that Bennett gave that order. I just can't prove it and haven't established a motive. I need something concrete before General Bradley will concur with a court-martial. I've hit a wall."

"What is Kirby's status?" asked Hoover.

"Marshall is negotiating with the Soviets for his repatriation. He's in Moscow. George thinks he may be ours within a week. You cannot repeat that. You never heard it from me."

"The President and I have discussed the spy trade. I was just curious to know if you were aware of that."

"I feel so damn sorry for Kirby. God knows what he's going through. There just isn't a finer man. I'm feeling somewhat remorseful because I personally put him into that job."

"Well, then perhaps my news will cheer you up. Your hunch was right, there is a lot behind the curtain here. Bradbury owns 51% of the stock in a company called Surveillance Technologies Incorporated. Bennett owns 20% and Yardley owns 10%. The company president, Willard Crandall, owns the rest. Crandall is Mrs. Bradbury's brother in law by the way and Bennett is Bradbury's son in law. Cozy relationship. Their company was given a top secret contract to build an electronic system for testing on the airplane Kirby was flying. Bradbury was using his influence to get contracts for his company, through the aid of Yardley, his inside man at CIA. They were very clever about all this, verbal contracts and so forth. But, the wiretaps and tails we put on them pulled it all together very nicely." He sat back and grinned slightly.

"My God Edgar. What balls! Just to think you could get away with something like that. But I don't get the motive in sending Kirby to Kraskino," said Sherman.

"I don't either, but a lot of their technical discussions escape me and the agents. However, I ordered the agents involved not to seek technical advice. We need to keep this quiet and bringing more people into this won't help. I have enough on all of them, without those technical details, to prosecute on federal violations, so motive doesn't really matter, at least not for the moment."

"Excellent," said Sherman, "I can get a court-martial for Bennett on conflict of interest and conduct unbecoming. When we get Kirby back, we'll get the remaining pieces of the puzzle."

A sinister look formed on Hoover's face, "Forrest, I have a fat file on Bradbury. He's clever but I knew his greed and immorality would eventually be his downfall. It was just a matter of time before I got him. I know a way to punish all of them without spending any public money—and fast. But I'll need your cooperation."

Sherman grinned broadly, "You know you have my support. What's your idea?"

"I can bring all four of them into this vault and offer them the choice of being charged with federal crimes, or, I can suspend the investigation if they all resign and forfeit all government retirement benefits for the rest of their lives."

"Excellent. He can't hide behind Truman on that. But, we need a little icing on this cake Edgar," said Sherman. "How about they also establish a trust fund for the Kirby kids, funded in the amount of all ill-gotten gains realized from the ownership and liquidation of the corporation."

CHAPTER 26

Lubyanka Prison
Moscow

Hal awakened to the familiar sound of boots coming down the hallway. Several pair of boots. His heart began beating fast and hard. Geez, another treatment at the hospital. God, I wish I knew what the hell they were doing to me with those things. They're really early today. I don't know if I like that.

"Good morning Captain," Alexei said when the soldiers opened the door. "Get up Captain. We are taking ride to country." The entire population of the world's butterflies descended into his stomach. His blood turned to ice water. Two soldiers jerked him to his feet, secured the straight jacket, a blindfold, a gag and handcuffed his ankles. They carried him out of the cell and down the hall. A rush of adrenaline set Hal's body on fire. Geez, I don't think I want to go on this trip. Today is a very different day. I think today is a very bad day. Oh god, I hope they give me just one chance to make a break for it, just one. I have nothing to lose. How the hell can I pull that off? I love you Alice; I hope you can feel it. I love you. Dammit, I don't want to die. Get hold of yourself Kirby.

There were few other cars on the snow-laden roads. The blindfold had slipped slightly off one eye, but no one noticed. The driver drove somewhat recklessly, sliding often, as they headed out of the city. About four inches of wet snow had fallen. Sun reflection from a white world was blinding. Evergreens, tree branches and structures were draped heavily with nature's bunting.

The driver seemed to be heading generally north. They slowed down after an eerily silent hour of sightseeing on a long, slippery country road. There was a black sedan parked on the side of the road ahead. Bright white exhaust plumes gushed from its tailpipe and furled lazily upward in crisp, dead calm air. Alexei waved to the soldiers in the sedan as they made a right turn just in front of it onto a narrow path. It was deeply rutted and covered with snow. A single set of tracks wound gently through pines and seasonal trees that were naked of all but their branches. All the adrenaline Hal's body could produce continuously discharged into his bloodstream. His heart was banging in his ears; a cold sweat broke out all over his body. Hal couldn't stand the silence any longer. He made noises and got Alexei's attention. A nod from Alexei resulted in the removal of his blindfold and gag. "Where are we going, Alexei?" asked Hal.

Alexei turned to look back at Hal in the rear of the sedan and spoke his first words since departing Hal's cell, "Snow is beautiful Captain, yes?" Hal nodded half-heartedly. He was too scared to carry a conversation. The two Russian goons on either side of him mumbled something to each other. The feeling of time running out was creating extreme anxiety.

The sedan passed by a frozen pond. A fieldstone dacha sat on a gentle slope in the distance. The slope ran down to the edge of a frozen pond. The snow adorned the shapes of a small dock and an upside-down rowboat that promised a good time in a pleasant summer. There was a four-foot rock wall surrounding the dacha. Dense gray smoke poured from the chimneys at each end of its roof. The sedan followed a gentle curve toward the dacha and up to an opening in the perimeter wall. Guards on each side of the entrance came to a snappy rifle salute. The sedan passed through unimpeded and struggled up the modest but slippery grade to the rear of the building. The driver parked near the rear door, alongside two other cars that were still burdened with last night's snow. Alexei spoke briefly with the guards, got out of the car and went inside. The driver raced the engine a bit while they waited so that the heater fan would turn faster giving more heat.

Hal listened to the chatter between the guards and the driver, hoping to hear an answer to the questions he had about today's adventure. He heard nothing he understood and could glean no answers from their attitudes and mannerisms.

Alexei came out of the dacha and approached the sedan. Hal noticed that Alexei was watching something while he walked gingerly over snow-covered ice toward the car. The sound of another car engine and tires crunching over frozen snow became audible. Alexei pointed to a spot somewhere on the other side of the parking area. Hal never got a good look at the other car; the view out the side window was restricted by one of the guards sitting forward to look out. Alexei came by the sedan, gave some orders without opening the door and walked off toward the area where he had directed the new arrival. Alexei's order quickly became clear—the guards in the back seat removed Hal's Russian shoes, straightjacket and cuffs. Shortly, Alexei and another man came to the car. Alexei opened the rear door, "This is Captain Kirby," he said to the man.

The man stepped closer, lowered his head and ducked just inside the door. He was wearing an obviously western made dress hat, long tan cashmere coat, brown leather gloves with a flash of squirrel and a white silk scarf—an American. "Captain Kirby? How do you feel?" the man asked in perfect English.

"Who are you?" asked Hal.

A broad smile formed on the man's face, "My name is Art Williams. I'm with the State Department. I've come to take you home. Are you OK?"

"Get me the hell out of here, Art," said Hal, beaming from ear to ear, "then I'll be OK!"

Williams stood up, "Are you ready?" he asked Alexei.

Alexei nodded sharply, ordered the guards to remove Hal's ankle cuffs and got out of the car. Alexi looked into the car at Hal, "Come out Captain."

Hal flinched when his bare feet hit the snow; he had to keep lifting them alternately, to relieve the pain that built quickly from the cold. He followed Williams across the parking area toward the big black Lincoln that was waiting, but the two guards stopped him at a point midway between the cars. Alexei and Williams went on to the Lincoln and began talking to someone inside. Rear doors of the Lincoln opened and four people got out. Hal's heart skipped a beat at the sight of Garr and the Russian that he saw Garr meet in Tokyo. Alexei pulled two photographs from inside his coat. He glanced back and forth between the photos, and the faces of Garr and the Russian. Alexei then nodded and motioned for the guards to escort them to the dacha. The moment they released Hal he hurried to the Lincoln. Garr's face showed shock when they passed just ten feet apart. Hal gave Garr a glare that could kill. The Russian looked dismal and kept his eyes down in the snow as he trudged by.

Williams ushered Hal into the rear seat of the Lincoln. He went to the trunk to get a small suitcase and got into the rear seat with Hal.

"Get that heater cranking Merv," Williams said to the driver. The other two men with Williams got into the front seat. "Go Merv," said Williams, "let's get moving."

"I can't believe this, Art," Hal said, looking out the side window at Alexei and others.

"I can just imagine, Captain," said Williams. He opened the suitcase; there was a white shirt, red and blue striped tie, dark gray suit and a pair of black shoes and socks. "Here you go, put this stuff on. It should all fit; your secretary gave us your sizes. How are you, really?" asked Williams. "Your face looks a little swollen here and there with a little bruising."

"OK now. Took a few lumps in Korea, but not too bad. I don't know exactly what the Russians did to me though," said Hal. As the driver backed out to turn around and head back out of the compound, Hal looked out the window; Alexei, Garr and the Russian were standing near the back door of the dacha having a very heated discussion. As the Lincoln got turned around and started back down the driveway, curiosity and intuition made Hal turn and kneel on the seat to look out the back window.

"What's going on?" asked Williams.

"Alexei just pulled a gun on them," said Hal. Williams turned around to look out. Alexei brought the gun up and in a very fast and fluid motion, he fired one shot each into their faces. Garr and Nikolai dropped to the ground like sacks of potatoes. The Lincoln passed by the Russian guards, exited the compound and sped back over their tracks through the woods toward the highway.

"Geez," said Hal, "What a great welcome home party." He turned around and sat down, shaken. "I just had this feeling something was going to happen."

"Things are done a little different in this country," said Williams sarcastically. "Come on, get changed, you'll be warmer."

Hal took a deep breath, still in awe of his fate and began changing clothes. "Why the hell did they bring me out here, Art?"

"They didn't want to take a chance of anyone seeing the exchange. They are paranoid this incident will get into the press for some reason. Part of the agreement on the exchange was that essentially, this never happened. You understand Captain? You are going to have to sign an oath saying you'll keep the Soviet portion of your imprisonment secret. Everyone involved is having to do the same thing. Well, except for those two guys back there."

Hal laughed for the first time in weeks, "Alexei just did the world a great service. Too bad he beat me to it." Williams looked at Hal strangely. Hal nodded, "It's a long story and I'm too tired to tell it."

Williams turned and quietly watched the trees going by the window.

Hal asked, "How's my wife and kids? Where are we going now?"

"We're going to the airport. There's an Air Force VIP aircraft waiting there for us. It has a small repatriation team aboard, including a CIA debriefer who wants to document your experience. We're flying to Andrews, with refueling and crew rest stops in England and Iceland. We will remain aboard the plane the entire time."

"Are my wife and kids on it?" asked Hal.

"No, they aren't. The repatriation team on the aircraft will discuss all those details. I don't have that information."

1155, Saturday, November 5, 1950
Moscow Airport

"This is just the miracle I've been looking for," said Hal as the Lincoln passed through a gate next to a hangar and moved out onto the concrete apron. Hal could see a bright white Lockheed Super Constellation with the words 'United States of America' painted in blue letters across the top of the fuselage. "There were times when I didn't think I'd make it. Oh God, this is a beautiful sight."

"Rough huh?" asked Williams.

"Let me ask you Art, have you ever been beaten and kicked so hard and so much that your whole body became numb and couldn't feel it?" Art just looked at Hal, speechless. "Have you ever had a crowd of people spit on you until your entire head and chest was covered with it?" Art looked away. "Have you ever looked down the muzzle of a loaded weapon with your life held in a balance that only a mere twitch of a finger could upset?"

"Captain, I cannot hope to appreciate how you must feel right now," said Art.

"I'm sorry Art," said Hal, "I don't mean to sound ungrateful or angry."

"It's OK Captain, I understand. We're all happy you are safe and sound."

As the Lincoln pulled up near the portable stairway of the aircraft, Art advised, "This won't take long, I hope. Everybody just sit tight in here until I clear all the documentation." KGB officials were posted at the base of the stairway alongside the Super Connie. Art opened his attaché case, pulled out two passports and got out. He presented the passports to one of the KGB officers, who studied Art's documents and then leaned over to look inside to compare Hal's face with his passport. When the KGB was satisfied that all was in order, Art opened the rear door and grinned, "OK Captain, time to board." Hal vaulted from the Lincoln and ran, two steps at a time, up the boarding staircase and into the hatchway. He nearly knocked over the military stewardess stationed at the door.

"I'm sorry, I'm just glad to be on U.S. property," said Hal, breathing heavily.

"Welcome aboard Captain Kirby, I'm Sergeant Kate Rydell. If you need anything just holler."

Hal shook her hand vigorously, "Can't tell you how happy I am to meet you."

She smiled, "My pleasure sir. There's three compartments back there," she said pointing toward the rear of the aircraft. "This one is the seating for takeoffs and landings. The next compartment is a conference and dining room. The rear one, which is the private VIP quarters, has a bed, lavatory and small office nook. You are the VIP on this mission, Captain Kirby, so you may use those facilities as you please. Please make yourself comfortable."

"That's just what I need right now, the lavatory," said Hal. He rushed through the conference area, past several people with just a nod.

By the time Hal relieved himself, washed his face and hands and shed his suit jacket, the hatch of Air Force 372 was sealed and the crew were in the process of completing their pre-taxi checklists. Hal reentered the center compartment, "Sorry for being so abrupt when I came through folks, but I had to see a man about a horse."

Art rose from his chair, "Let me make some introductions Captain." The others in the room came to their feet as well. Art introduced Dr. Lester

Boerman from Bethesda Navy Hospital, Bonnie Varelli from the State Department, Richard Torquey from CIA and Colonel James Nealson from Andrews Air Force Base.

Introductions had just been completed when Sergeant Rydell came to the door of the conference room, "Excuse me ladies and gentlemen, but I have to ask you to come forward and take seats. We are ready to taxi. I'll serve refreshments as soon as we get airborne."

There were five rows of oversized seat pairs on each side of the forward cabin, behind the forward lavatory and galley area. Art and Hal sat together in the first row. Hal claimed the window; he stared out in awe as they taxied to the runway.

"Snow is beautiful, isn't it?" asked Art, leaning forward to see out of the small port.

"Yes, when you are inside where it's warm," said Hal.

"Ever go skiing?" asked Art.

"No, never had a hankering to do that. I've gained a very strong appreciation for being warm. I doubt I will ever will try skiing or any other winter sports."

Air Force 372 turned onto the runway. The engines accelerated to a loud roar. When the brakes were released, the aircraft lurched forward and picked up speed rapidly. Patches of snow covered ice on the marginally cleaned runway created an increasingly noisy and bumpy ride. Art looked aside briefly and noted tears rolling slowly down Hal's cheek. Shortly after the nose lifted, the washboard ride became silk smooth; 372 was airborne. Hal had an overpowering urge to let loose with a 'yahoo' that would echo through the Kremlin. He watched the scenery change from a snow-covered city, to snow covered trees and quaint rural areas. There was an ironic beauty to this country. A country that once held his freedom, indeed his life, in the palm of its hand. His mind was freewheeling and tumbling. The nightmare is over. Really over. Geez, keep on humming baby; take me home! Wait 'til I get my hands on Bennett. That sunnavabitch is a dead man. I'm going to give Admiral Sherman an ear full.

Art tapped Hal's shoulder, "The seat belt light is out Captain, it's time to go to work. Here's the schedule, Colonel Nealson, the flight surgeon, is going to give you a physical, then Richard Torquey will debrief you. Captain Boerman will be next, then Bonnie, from Protocol, will give you the details on all the arrangements she's made for your reception at Andrews."

"What's Boerman's role?" asked Hal.

"He's from the Psychiatric Department at Bethesda." Art noted Hal's reaction and continued, "It's just a routine procedure on repatriations, to ensure you have a smooth transition back into the real world."

"I'm hungry. I'm not doing anything until I get breakfast," Hal said forcefully.

Art looked across the aisle at Colonel Nealson, who nodded affirmatively.

Art got up and stepped into the galley where Sergeant Rydell was already at work preparing coffee and juice.

Sergeant Rydell promptly came out to tend to her VIP. Hal's face brightened, "I'm starved Sergeant, I'd give a million bucks for steak, eggs, hash browns and black coffee."

"First, let's see the million bucks?" she teased.

He laughed for the first time since he left Kimpo, "Give me a napkin and a pen. I'll write an IOU."

She tilted her head and smirked, "Promises, promises. Tell you what Captain, I have a filet mignon in there with your name on it, and I have eggs and home fries. I'll get to work on them as soon as I get everyone juiced and coffeed." Kate returned to the galley feeling good about sacrificing the filet mignon from her dinner tray.

Colonel Nealson conducted the physical examination in the VIP quarters. Richard Torquey came into the suite when Hal got dressed.

"OK Richard, let's get this show on the road," Hal said as they took seats on either side of the small blue Formica topped table-desk.

"Please, call me Dick," he said as he opened his thick attaché case and retrieved a typed document, a lined pad and a portable recorder. He checked the tape reel and turned the machine on.

"Hal is fine for me Dick. Where do you want to start?"

"First, I must ask you to sign an oath to never reveal the Soviet overflight and that portion of your imprisonment. It was part of the deal we made to get you back. The cover story is that you had engine trouble and were forced to land in North Korea, were taken prisoner, escaped and then rescued by friendly ground forces."

"Fair enough. I'm just damn glad to be back," he said as he signed the oath.

"OK, now let's go back to when you began planning the mission, Hal. From that moment on, give me as detailed a description as you can of everything that transpired. It's important that you don't gloss over anything."

Several hours and recorder reels later, Hal completed his debriefing. Captain Boerman then discussed Hal's feelings, emotions and anxieties. Reliving the entire episode in the process of the debrief was a powerful, unnerving experience.

Boerman shook his head, "I have to tell you Hal, you are in an exceptional frame of mind, given your experience and I have treated a lot of men held prisoner by the Japanese. The brevity of your imprisonment is a large factor, of course." He reached into his bag, opened a bottle and tapped a small white pill into the cap. "I want you to take this, Hal, it's a very mild sedative. I want you to relax and catch up on sleep. You've been through a lot."

Hal was reluctant, "Is it really necessary doc? I hate the thoughts of taking medication."

Boerman smiled, "That's the pilot talking. Yes, I strongly recommend you take it."

Hal held out his hand. As he got up to get water from the sink, he asked, "My wife is a volunteer at Bethesda, have you ever met her?"

"No, I never had the pleasure. OK, listen, we're about an hour from London. I'd like to see you lie down and rest until we land in London. In the meantime, I'm at your disposal anytime on this flight, don't hesitate to ask. I will schedule some follow-up visits during the coming weeks."

Landing at London, refueling, galley replenishment and departure were all uneventful. Sergeant Rydell served a delicious lunch of fish and chips, in the finest British tradition. Hal tried Earl Gray tea for the first time. He found it interesting, but no replacement for his old Navy habit—strong, black coffee. After Kate removed the tray, he retired to the VIP quarters, stretched out on the bed and drifted into a deep sleep.

When Hal entered the conference compartment, everyone interrupted their crossword puzzles, newspapers and report writing to greet him.

Bonnie Varelli reached into her soft leather attaché case for some papers and asked, "Is it OK if we discuss the arrival arrangements, Captain."

"It's about time," he said and took the open seat next to her.

She put her hand on his arm, "I think we should do it in the back." Captain Boerman followed them into the private quarters and closed the door. Hal looked at Boerman and Bonnie quizzically. Boerman motioned for Hal to take the single soft chair opposite the table desk. Alarm built up quickly when Hal saw that they were sullen and seemed hesitant. "What is it?" asked Hal.

Boerman had the lead, "We have some bad news, Hal." He watched the color drain from Hal's face. "Alice suffered a fatal cerebral hemorrhage on Halloween—a burst aneurysm."

Hal's body stiffened, then he bent over double, with his head in his hands, "No. Oh God, No!" he said in a wavering voice.

Boerman and Bonnie came to his side; Bonnie held his clenched hands while Boerman rubbed his shoulders. Hal spoke muffled words, over and over, through sobbing and episodes of shaking.

Tears streaming, Bonnie said, "We're so very sorry Hal."

"My kids, Geez, my kids," he said.

"Your secretary Patty has been terrific, she took care of all that. Your mother and father arrived the next morning. Your wife's folks came in that afternoon," said Bonnie. "They are all still there, so don't worry about the kids."

"I have had Susan and Joseph on medication. They are holding up very well," said Boerman.

"Halloween, hell, I don't even know what day this is," said Hal.

"It's Saturday," said Boerman.

"Which Saturday, don't you understand?" Hal growled out of frustration and remorse. He leaned his elbows on his thighs and buried his face in his hands.

"November 5th," said Bonnie, rubbing his shoulders.

It took several minutes for the sobbing and waves of tremors to subside. He sat up, then slouched deep into the chair, eyes closed, still pale. Boerman soaked a washcloth and put it in Hal's hand.

"Thanks," Hal whispered and cleaned his face. "I feel nauseous."

Boerman patted his back, "Do you need to go to the head?"

"I think I'll be all right," said Hal, handing the washcloth back to Boerman. "When is the funeral?"

"Here, I put a trash can beside your feet," said Bonnie. She took a deep breath, "It was held last Wednesday. At that point, we didn't even know if we were going to get you back. I'm so terribly sorry. She's in Arlington."

The dam broke again for Hal. He wept and suffered more tremors and eventually regained his composure. Bonnie rinsed the washcloth with cool water in the sink and gave it back to him.

"I can't go back to Korea and leave those kids alone. Maybe my folks can stay with them," he thought aloud.

"You aren't going back, Hal. Admiral Sherman will discuss those things with you, but you are reassigned to his staff."

A thought flew into Hal's mind and he sat straight up, "Geez, you son of a bitches held this back until the CIA could drain my brain. Damn you! Damn you all!"

Boerman interrupted him, "That was my call Hal, it wasn't an easy one, but I take full responsibility for it. I thought that it was in the best interest of the United States to get all those details, which may have been overshadowed and lost, given the circumstances."

Hal leaned back, slouched down, folded the washcloth over his eyes and remained quiet.

Bonnie took his hand, "We had a Navy Chaplain lined up to come with us, but he got hung up in traffic. We waited as long as we could, but we had to depart without him. He'll be there at Andrews when we arrive. If you wish, we'll have him come aboard before you deplane. You can make that decision when we arrive."

Hal sighed, "Thank you. Will the kids be there?"

"Of course Hal," she said, "along with your mom, dad and in-laws. Also, Admiral Sherman has asked to come aboard briefly before you deplane."

2035, Sunday, November 6, 1950
Andrews Air Force Base, Maryland

A multitude of emotions began to tumble randomly through Hal's consciousness when the wheels of Air Force 372 hit the runway. He shaded his eyes to hide interior light reflections so he could see out into the black.

It seems like yesterday that I was sitting in the nose of the 'Hot Blooded Redhead,' rumbling down this very same runway. Oh man, how splendid ignorance can be. This war has really destroyed my life. Geez Kirby, think of the poor bastards that left Korea in body bags. And those pitiful souls those God forsaken red bastards destroyed and threw into ditches like animals. Damn it to hell if it wasn't for the kids, I'd get my ass on the next plane to a carrier on the line and give those sons of bitches some payback.

Air Force 372 came to a stop in front of a hangar. Clouds of smoky white breath spewed from the noses of the ground crew personnel and glowed from the backlighting of large floodlights beaming down from the edges of the hangar roof. Just inside the half open hangar door he could see a small group of people waiting in relative warmth, protected from the sharp night air. He quickly recognized those who were waving—Susan, Joe, his parents and Alice's folks. He wiped tears from his eyes as Admiral Sherman hurried to the plane and waited for the steps to be brought snug against the fuselage. Sherman was the first through the door when Kate broke the seal and pushed it open.

The Admiral strongly embraced Hal. "My prayers have been with you. I need a few moments with you in private."

"Certainly Admiral. Glad to see you." They retired to the rear compartment and closed the door.

"I know you want to be with your family. I'll just be a few minutes. First, I want you to know how terribly sorry I was to learn of your capture and then this personal tragedy. But I bring you some good news."

"I could use some, although just being back in the U.S. is hard to beat right now," said Hal.

"I will sit down and chat with you about what happened in Kimpo and so on after you have had a chance to spend some time with your family. I didn't want you to go another minute without knowing a few things though. I bring regards directly from President Truman. His exact words were that the United States of America is indebted to you. He promises you, and made me promise as well, that you shall have your choice of duty appropriate to your rank as long as he or I are in positions to exert our influence. In the meantime, you have received orders to my personal staff and you are hereby given leave until the 2nd of January."

"I'm overwhelmed, Admiral. Thank you," said Hal.

"Are you aware that you were traded for Lieutenant Commander Garr and his Russian handler in Japan?"

"Aware? I saw both of them get executed as we departed the trade site."

Sherman showed surprise, "Good riddance. We'll talk about that later. Have you been informed about Bennett and his cohorts?"

Hal shrugged his shoulders, "They didn't mention them, Admiral."

"Briefly, AQUAMARINE was recalled from Korea and stripped out of the Pentagon. The FBI conducted an investigation which revealed that Bennett, Bradbury, Yardley, and a guy named Crandall, wholly owned a company, secretly of course, which was manufacturing electronic systems for the AQUA program."

Hal interrupted, "Geez, AQUACRYSTAL, the pod Bennett ordered me to fly to Kraskino!"

Admiral Sherman was surprised again, "Aha! There's the motive we were looking for." He explained to Hal details of the plea bargain accepted by the conspirators. Hal smiled for the first time in several hours.

Hal came through the door of Air Force 372 with a cue ball lodged in his throat. He took a world record deep breath of American night air and regained control of his emotions. Near freezing tears burned his eyes. He grabbed the handrail and hurried down the stairs. When his feet hit concrete, he stooped down and slapped the ground hard. As he walked toward the welcoming party in the hangar, he strained to see who was doing the loud weeping—it was Patty Mindell. Reed Forbes and Captain Castle stood on either side of her.

Reed jogged out to meet Hal and gave him a long bear hug. "I should have convinced you not to go," he said with a faltering voice. Susan and Joe followed Reed's example and took off for their father.

"Don't ever think that again, Reed," said Hal, "It was my decision all the way." He grabbed Reed's shoulder and shook his hand vigorously.

His kids flew into his arms when Reed let go. They couldn't talk; they all cried together as they hugged. Patty Mindell got to Hal next and joined in the mass hug. She looked up at him and asked, "Remember that first day when you told me your easy jobs always turned out to be difficult?" She couldn't finish her thought. "I'm so, so sorry. Come on kids, let's get your father out of the cold."

* * *

ABOUT THE AUTHOR

Peter J. Azzole is a retired U.S. Navy Officer, a cryptology specialist, who served 20 years of active duty. During his Navy career, he served in several locations abroad, afloat and in the United States. After retirement from the Navy, he became a part-time Commercial Pilot and Flight Instructor. His Navy and flight experience provide authenticity in the texture of this story.

Pete's inspiration for this novel was the non-fiction book "The Sea War in Korea," by Malcolm W. Cagle and Frank A. Manson, 1957.

Pete recently published another historic fiction, ASSIGNMENT BLETCHLEY, which is a WW2 novel, set in the London area, involving intelligence, spies and intrigue. It is available via Amazon.com, Goodreads.com and other online bookstores in soft cover and Kindle/e-book formats.

Pete and his wife, Nancy, are enjoying their retirement in New Bern, NC.